Running Downhill Like Water

"This magnificently orchestrated novel, spanning three continents and four connected lives, made me laugh and cry and feel grateful for its profound truths about human suffering and the chance of redemption. Jane Woods's writing sings and soars, transporting us to a deeper knowledge of our own hearts."
~ Claire Holden Rothman, author of *Lear's Shadow*

Running Downhill Like Water

a novel

jane woods

CANADA

Copyright © 2021 by Jane Woods

All rights reserved. No part of this book may be used or reproduced in any manner whatsoever without the prior written permission of the publisher, except in the case of brief quotations embodied in reviews.

Publisher's note: This book is a work of fiction. Names, characters, places and incidents are either the product of the author's imagination or are used fictitiously, and any resemblance to actual persons living or dead is entirely coincidental.

"When in the Soul of the Serene Disciple," by Thomas Merton, from THE COLLECTED POEMS OF THOMAS MERTON, copyright © 1957 by The Abbey of Gethsemani. Reprinted by permission of New Directions Publishing Corp.

Library and Archives Canada Cataloguing in Publication

Title: Running downhill like water : a novel / Jane Woods.

Names: Woods, Jane, 1950- author.

Identifiers: Canadiana 20200384341 | ISBN 9781989689196 (softcover)

Classification: LCC PS8645.O6388 R86 2021 | DDC C813/.6—dc23

Printed and bound in Canada on 100% recycled paper.

Now Or Never Publishing
901, 163 Street
Surrey, British Columbia
Canada V4A 9T8

nonpublishing.com
Fighting Words.

We gratefully acknowledge the support of the Canada Council for the Arts and the British Columbia Arts Council for our publishing program.

For Tommasino

It was a lucky wind
That blew away his halo with his cares,
A lucky sea that drowned his reputation.

—Thomas Merton

Lucy

Lucy Brickwood hasn't looked full on into a mirror since she was twenty-four. She combs her slab-straight grey hair with three brisk downward slashes: side, back, other side. When she hacks it back to chin length every six months, she squints just enough to know where to aim the scissors. She hasn't touched makeup in these forty years either, her sagging face as pale and bumpy as unsanded plaster. She brushes her teeth with her eyes closed. Never turns on the bathroom light.

Which may explain her shock at the sight of that face, mauled by tears, caught in the mirror by accident after she knocks her ashtray off the edge of the bathroom sink while slapping cold water onto her inflamed cheeks. Her lit smoke has plummeted into the wastepaper basket, immediately igniting—she can smell it!—the mounds of used Kleenex in there, so that she's forced to turn on the overhead light to empty the wastebasket onto the floor and, wheezing and cursing, stamp out the smouldering mess. And then to her horrified dismay, she looks up, and . . . ta da! *Heeere's* Lucy! Red-nosed, ravaged, utterly wretched.

And she's been doing so well, damn it! So, *so* well!

So well, she's almost come to believe there's no pain, no shock, no sorrow she can't climb out of, hand over hand, like scaling a rock face. She buried her mother only a few years ago, got through that okay. Got used to living in the house alone, solitude the same fierce friend to her it's always been. She even got through the ratty package arriving from France, stray scraps from her father's estate that his elderly wife—Veronika still remembered her!—had thought she might like to have. Some fifty-year-old photos he'd kept of her, Jesus, who knew? Polaroids of a dour, combative-looking kid in pedal pushers and scuffed saddle shoes, sunk into an armchair with a book in her lap, crabbily ignoring the camera. Another one taken the Christmas she was nine, in front of the tree, holding up a new book in each hand, *Robinson Crusoe* and *The Magic Mountain*, crumpled wrapping paper mounded at her feet. And tucked underneath the photos, at the very bottom of the box—oh dear God, no—a fat spiral notebook. *A Girl called Lyudmilova*, scrawled across the cover, elegant lettering in purple Magic Marker. *A novel, by Agatha Crystal Ball*. With the same bright silver ribbon around it she'd tied so carefully when she'd mailed it to him at sixteen, her heart glutted with hope. The ribbon clearly never untied.

So she untied it. Pried open the notebook's pages, all glommed together with the glue she'd used for the illustrations, pictures galore of young, lovely models clipped from the pages of *Seventeen*. Beautiful girls in sweaters, bathing suits, skiwear. Young lovelies shilling shampoo, lipstick, Clearasil. These were the many and varied faces of Lyudmilova, the illustrations far outweighing the text. Lucy unstuck a few more pages. *"We are so dull here, Mavra," cried Lyudmilova passionately. "And how tormenting you are! Yes, it is true, as Prince Oleg decrees, I am more beautiful than you, more beautiful perhaps than the most gorgeous of courtesans of old! Still, I will always stand up for the forgotten and ugly people of the world!"*

Oh, thank God he never read it!

Well never you fuckin' mind, she told herself, pitching the box, notebook, photos and all, into the recycling bin. I fall down, I haul myself up again. Down, up, down, up, story of my life. Nothing can hurt me, as long as my boys are safe down there on Loony Street. As long as my sweet boy Neil's okay, I'll be just fine, fuck you very much.

Except now sweet Neil, her heart's darling, the closest thing to her own natural child, isn't okay. A reprieve rescinded, a spell broken, and more likely than not, all her fault. She's only just left him, an hour ago, back in the hospital, sick and getting sicker. Furiously mute. In serious trouble too, the little neighbour boy nearly drowned because of him. He won't talk to her, is all hopped up on new meds. Turns his face to the wall as if she were *nobody!* Made her bawl like a baby all the way home in the car, yelling, pounding the steering wheel, a hot day and her car window open, astonished heads swiveling in passing cars.

She snaps that overhead light off fast. Gets a fresh smoke going, her chest tight. Suddenly ferocious, snapping the light back on again to stare herself down. Pulls her glasses out of her shirt pocket to get a *really* good look. What the hell are you afraid of, Brickwood? Just a few weeks ago, you called up someone you were terrified of facing, met her for *drinks,* for fuck's sake! Remember how scared you were? But you did it . . . okay, you lost it a little there at the end, but still, you did it. You were doing so, *so* well! You'll be okay, my girl. Just give it time. Time is all it's ever taken.

She flinches from her reflection at last. Worthless, ugly loser bitch! She's only been doing well because she thought Neil was. Because she thought everything was okay down on Loony Street. But it's not, and maybe time's run out, and she's to blame, and she will not survive this, not this time. Without her Neil she's a goner.

For fuck's sake, pull yourself together, Brickwood! Where's your backbone, fool?

This at least produces a wan smile. Her mother had never stopped rubbing that in her face after she'd come skulking home from university, mortally flayed, thoroughly trashed. Her life, at twenty-four, a smouldering ruin. *"Where's your backbone, Lucy? You're tougher than this!"* It had made her rabid at the time; now, it almost feels as if Pauline's in the bathroom with her, perched on the edge of the tub, washing her grimy feet after a humid afternoon shoving the lawnmower around. And Neil? Still, a wiggly, chirpy little kid giggling with his brother in the living room, waiting for her to climb right out of her own skin and burrow into his.

Hard to remember when those two had been no more than irritants in her peripheral vision as she sat on her front porch in the enervating heat and screaming tedium of a Sainte-Clémence July afternoon. She wasn't supposed to be anywhere near that piddly town, that crap house. She was supposed to have been launched into a brilliant life, light-years away from her mother and her drab childhood home. But there she was, back again, hunkered squarely on the tail tucked between her legs. Beaten all hollow.

The sun was burning her scalp, making it feel like the parched yellow lawn looked. Two in the afternoon and she'd just rolled out of bed, breakfasting on Rothmans as she watched an ant on the lowest step making frantic attempts to bury a dead companion under a stray leaf. Every time it managed to lay its friend to rest, Lucy would nudge the leaf with her foot several inches across the hot step. The ant finally stopped in its tracks and reared on its back legs, feelers waving, as if crying out to heaven: As God is my witness, I swear, I tried!

Next door, two little boys were sitting quietly on their own porch, drawing on the concrete with stones. Whispering to one another. Staring at her. They hadn't been there when she'd left home the previous fall, though the single lady who lived there hadn't moved. The single lady who hated her and her mother like poison, who had gone gossiping to the whole town about how the Brickwood girl had gone off to university only to crash and burn, a severe breakdown, the sins of the mother so clearly visited on the child, the Lord, as always (bless his heart!) refusing to be mocked.

She lit up another smoke. It was too hot to breathe and the skin on her bare legs was reddening rapidly in irregular blotches. She could've gone inside except Pauline was home, had called in sick again to her only recently restored job, was probably still sitting at the kitchen table blubbering, pretending to read the paper, tears plopping onto her untouched cheese sandwich.

Pauline cried mostly at night, an awful thing to hear, snuffles and chokes and sharp, intermittent wails. As if Lucy didn't feel shitty enough. It would have been nice to think the tears were on her behalf, but she knew they weren't. They were for Pauline's hideous buttinski "friend," who, four months ago, had moved on to greener pastures, leaving her mother a sodden mess.

Lucy could have gone inside, barricaded herself in her room, but she was as bone-weary as a nonagenarian. There was nothing on the entire earth she wanted to do but sit iguana-still and burn medical emergency red on her front porch. Even the thought of getting up for a walk was disturbing. The minutest shift in the breathless hot shroud of dread draped over her just made her feel more suffocated, more sluggishly hopeless. She was long past the point of expecting this aching torpor to let up any time soon. There wasn't a damned thing she could do for herself, so how could she possibly help her mother? The two of them barely spoke at the best of times. Pauline was just going to have to tough out her busted heart on her own.

It was the boys' muffled giggling, their relentless eyes on her that finally forced her to her feet and down to the sidewalk, stopping in front of their house to shoot, "What's so funny?" at them. "Keep it up, you little shits. I'll give you something to laugh about." She picked up a fist-sized rock from the edge of the road and wound up for a pitch. "I've got a real good aim. Wanna see?" The boys fell immediately silent, dropping their eyes, feigning deep interest in their knees.

She'd set off then with a stiff gait, heading down to the end of Lunenberg Street, down to the edge of the lake that bordered Sainte-Clémence. She'd been there several times since she'd come back home, but the blinds were always drawn tight at the last house on the street, the home of the Loony Ladies, in whose company she'd spent so many hours pumping air back into her deflated heart when she was fourteen, after her father had flown the coop. It didn't even look like they lived there anymore; the colour of the blinds was unfamiliar, and the purple plastic hyacinths that used to march up the walkway to the front door were uprooted and gone. So much for bursting in on them to announce that she was now a university graduate, local gal makes good, how about they stuff that in their pipes? Flourishing her degree in library science, a career choice she'd lost interest in halfway through her first year and had just barely earned through sheer bloody-mindedness, snatching it from the grim jaws of death before ringing down the curtain and collapsing into the dust in a ragged heap.

Damn it, *somebody* ought to be impressed!

Across the water she could see Oka, which she'd always pretended was France back in the dark old days. Imagining that instead of standing flat on the weedy ground, she was on a high, blustery outcrop, gazing over the thrashing grey Atlantic at the French coastline. Willing her father to come back, come back! I'm going through an awkward phase, that's all! I'll bloom, Daddy! I'll blossom, I promise! Imagining him lazing around his new girlfriend Veronika's chichi family home in Paris, Veronika paying the bills while he read and typed, typed and read. Veronika, the glamourous visiting fellow lab assistant, The Spy Who Loved Me, From Russia With Love, who'd stolen his heart. She'd been everything Pauline would never be, an expat Russian, over here to oversee some stupid seed mutation project. *And* beautiful, *and* a PhD, *and* an accomplished pianist! Her daughter Milena, who was Lucy's age, had been a budding ballerina, beautiful beyond describing, every father's dream daughter. Radioactive Renaissance women, the pair of them!

Five decades later, the memory of her first meeting with Milena still brings a hot flush to her neck. A few months after he'd left the family home, her father had taken her to meet the sparkly new women in his life. Lunch at the Beaver Club in the city, Veronika and Milena all tarted up and swank. Milena, who spoke Russian and French, with her long, smooth, dark hair and blue doll's eyes and pink minidress, knocking all the air out of Lucy's lungs. Even sitting down, she'd been as graceful as a willow branch, whereas gimpy Lucy, in her school uniform skirt and poorly elasticized knee socks, had tripped on a carpet edge as she came into the restaurant, executing a spectacular face plant and having to be helped to her feet by supercilious waiters.

She'd sat through the entire meal in silence, fighting furious tears, so painfully clear was it that her father had traded *way* up, replacing both her and Pauline with dazzling new models right off the showroom floor. Refusing to look at him as he explained, like the father in some lame Hayley Mills movie, that he hadn't asked for this to happen, but now it had, and surely Lucy, so clever, so mature for her years, understood that at last, at *last,* he had found true happiness, true love. A rare second chance! And in a month, when Veronika's job ended, they'd all be moving back to France! All this while making cow eyes at Veronika and Milena, holding their hands on the table; in truth, he'd tried to hold Lucy's hand first, but she'd snatched it away and sat on it.

Veronika hadn't bothered her; she *was* a trade-up, in her shimmery blue shift and matching heels, her dark blonde hair in a French twist. Perfect nails painted pearly white. A Natasha Badenoff accent. But the stark contrast between Lucy and his new replacement daughter had been humiliating beyond bearing. Milena was a luscious rose just coming into bloom. Lucy was a dandelion crimped and flattened after a blast of weed killer.

But—and how could *anyone* not have picked up on this?—the girl was pulverizingly stupid! Even from the little French Lucy could understand, Milena's chitchat sounded vapid and childish. Couldn't Daddy *tell*? This girl knew nothing of the Life of the Mind, gabbing on about tutus and hairdos and how funny her new puppy was. And Daddy and Veronika had just smiled and smiled, charmed out of their senses.

From that day onward, Lucy had shut her father down. Sitting numbly through his falsely hearty phone calls from Paris, replying in monosyllables. Keeping her stormy thoughts to herself, seldom emerging from her room, where she beavered away at the novel she'd begun writing, her ace in the hole, a promise she would hold out to him as soon as it was finished and ready for his eyes: Savour this rich prose, Daddy! And see all these gorgeous girls? This is who *I'm* going to become one day, and when I do, you'll be so very, very sorry you chose mouth-breathing Milena over me.

And she had sent it to him, two years later, tied up in a gleaming ribbon it had taken her a sweaty half hour to tie into a perfect bow. Eight years on, she was still waiting for him to even acknowledge that he'd received it. And wondering how long she'd have to wait now for an answer to the breezy, detail-free postcard she'd sent to announce her graduation from university.

It had taken the whole of that July and August before Pauline had finally stopped weeping, throwing herself, between crying jags, into washing and simonizing her dented old Volkswagon Beetle, cleaning the gutters, banging a stepladder from one side of the house to the other. In the hot haze of that red-letter August morning when Neil and his brother had first come over to watch their TV, she'd been out mowing the patchy lawn with the old rotary mower, in grubby running shoes with no laces, sweat blooms under her arms, her hair chopped as short as a boy's. Turning at the bottom of the driveway to plow back toward the house, leaning in hard, her grim face flushed and dripping.

She'd drawn to a halt at the foot of the steps. Lucy was on the porch on a kitchen chair, an open book in her lap, glancing up at intervals to watch the little Labossière orphans next door play catch with a sorely mutilated stuffed rabbit, shrieking in a garbled mix of English and French.

Pauline had planted her foot on the bottom step, mopped her brow with her forearm and announced with no little vigour, "I've had just about enough of this!" When only silence ensued, she raised her voice. "Lucy! Look at me when I'm talking to you!"

Expelling a gust of exasperation, Lucy had squinted down the steps and snapped, "What? What is it *now?*"

Pauline didn't seem to care who heard her; the little boys in the driveway had stopped playing, were huddled close together, clearly eavesdropping. "You need to see someone," said Pauline, in a voice that Lucy thought must carry for blocks. "Talk to a doctor, maybe start on some kind of medication."

"There's nothing wrong with me. Would you mind keeping your voice down?"

"Nothing wrong, my ass! I've had it, Lucy! I've had all I can take of you lumping around the house all day, sleeping till three in the afternoon. You live on cookies, you're smoking up the place, and you don't lift one finger to help out."

"What, you want to kick me out now?"

Pauline breathed in and out several times. "Lucy, I know you had a rough go of it this past year—"

"A rough go? A *rough go?* Mother, if you put me out on the street, I'll be dead in a week."

"Why? *Why*, Lucy? I don't understand what the problem is. I never did. You don't *have* to spend your life in solitary confinement. What is so special about you that you can't make friends, you can't make your way in the world? Damn it, where's your backbone? If you could get a nice place, maybe find yourself a roommate, try living on your own again—"

"I can't be around people. You know that!"

"Then you need to see a doctor."

"The hell with that. I'm fine! This will pass. You need to get off my back."

"All right! Great! There's nothing wrong with you. In that case, you need to start looking for a job. If you want to live here, you need to pay room and board. I can't manage everything."

"Yes, the standard of living around here has certainly gone into steep decline."

Pauline ignored this. "There's a marvellous library at Macdonald College. They might very well need someone with your qualifications. Take the bus down to—"

"Where *daddy* worked? You've got to be kidding me! And you *know* I can't be on the bus. What's wrong with you?" She was half up out of her chair now, shrill and red-faced herself.

"Can't be on the bus, can't be in crowds, can't hold down a job. But you're fine. This is insane, Lucy."

"I'll get a paper route. How's that sound?"

"Goddamn it, Lucy, I need you to snap out of this! You're impossible to be around. You're like some giant spider that nobody can come near in case you spring and run right up their arm!"

The boys in the driveway howled in delight at this. From the edge of the porch, Lucy turned to shout, "I'm so glad you two goons are enjoying the show!" but they didn't seem to hear; the bigger one, Neil, waved happily back at her. "Hi, Lucy! Hi, Mrs. Brickwood!" The littler one, Evan, tried to pull his brother's arm down, whispering, "Shush! Don't!" But Neil was undeterred. "Can we come over and—" Little Evan tried to muffle his mouth with the stuffed rabbit, but he wasn't tall enough. "Can we come over and watch your TV?"

"No!" shrieked Evan in mortified despair.

"Your aunt will tan your little tushies." Lucy was taking full advantage of this distraction, as Pauline turned on her heel to attack another strip of grass. "Your aunt has a big mouth. I happen to know you guys aren't allowed TV."

"Just let us in fast! She's in the basement, ironing all the clothes."

"Neil, no!" Evan was nearly hysterical. "We're not s'p-p-posed to!"

"Well, that's good enough for me. Hustle your little asses over here. Come on, move it!" She yanked open the screen door. "Welcome to the Den of Brickwood Iniquity, kiddies! Abandon all hope, why dontcha."

Neil took the steps in two bounds. His brother poked up behind him, trailing his grubby rabbit by one much-chewed ear, casting worried looks back at his own front porch.

In the living room, Neil made a beeline for the TV, flicked it on, clicked the channel dial like a pro, shouting, "Yay! Tom and Jerry!" as he plopped backward onto the couch. His brother stood uncertainly in the doorway. "Evan, come on. It's Tom and Jerry!"

Evan plodded over to the sofa, wiggling himself with caution backward into the cushions. Lucy dropped down next to Neil. "Scootch over, sofa hogs," she said, cuffing Neil as if she were his age, her mood rising like a helium balloon. "So, what happened to your front teeth, Mister? You get in a fight?"

"No, they just falled out!" he replied with a screwball grin.

"So, who's got the best TV in town?"

"You do!"

"Who's waaaayyy nicer than your aunt?"

"You are!" said Neil, with only marginally less certainty.

Pauline had come inside through the back door, and now entered from the kitchen with two glasses of chocolate milk, each with a striped straw. She leaned over to ruffle little Evan's hair, standing for a moment to watch Jerry scuttle into his mouse hole in the nick of time. Neil began blowing into his straw, making milk volcano over the sides of the glass and onto his shirt. Evan giggled in spite of himself.

"When are you bucking broncos going to come out with me to see the horsies at the riding school?" Pauline asked. She executed a quick draw with an invisible six-shooter, blew into her pistol's smoking barrel, and tipped back her imaginary Stetson, a rootin-tootin' cowpoke. Both boys' heads swivelled, their faces lighting up, then falling. They shook their dejected heads in tandem.

"Aunt Louisa'll say no," sulked Neil.

"Oh, man! What's her problem, anyway?" Lucy felt a choke of indignation. "The nasty old tan lady doesn't come here anymore. The nasty tan lady doesn't want to have a *girlfriend* anymore, she's turned straight and gone off to Arizona with her chubby hubby. No more sinful carryings-on in this house, boys! Your aunt should be rejoicing."

Pauline, who had just sunk into a chair, emitted a brief strangled grunt, got up abruptly and bolted.

Lucy and the boys sat in silence, taking in a Sugar Pops commercial. The living room was baking hot and airless, the sun pulsing against the drawn drapes. A fly buzzed disconsolately from a corner of the window. The music hopped and scampered, Tom running poor Jerry into the ground. Lucy leaned chummily over Neil's head to ask Evan,

"What's your rabbit's name?"

"P-p-plooshy," he replied in the tiniest peep, not daring to raise his eyes to hers.

"It's short for Ploosh Botome," Neil explained with grave authority. "He got it from Maman before she went to be with the Lord. It says his name on him. Evan, *donne ton toutou à Lucy*." Evan, with a darting, wary look, placed the rabbit in her lap, still clutching one of its ears. "He doesn't talk English as good as me, *c'est pour ça qu'y parle c-c-c-comme ç-ç-ç-ça, c'est vrai, hein, Evan?* He has trouble saying his words, and he can't read yet, but I can, because I'm six, which, I'm practically a grandfather."

Lucy read the tag on the rabbit's mangled hindquarters: Made by - Plush Bottom®.

"I see. Ploosh Botome. Excellent reading skills there, Neil." She wedged the rabbit in between the boys; Evan snuggled up against it, and Neil pulled his brother closer, a protective arm around his little shoulders.

"School starts next week," Lucy said then, making cheerful small talk, feeling almost giddy. What was it about these kids? She couldn't remember the last time her spirits had been so high. "You must be going into grade one, Neil, right? You excited?"

"We're going to have school at home," said Neil, bouncing on the cushions, his face all lit up, his speech a train clickety-clacking down a greased track. "Evan too, but he's only four, but he can sit and colour or learn his ABC's and every day we're gonna get a new Bible story because we have our own Bibles with pictures Aunt Louisa got us, and we can't go at the big school because then we won't stay pure for Jesus, that's how come we're not supposed to watch TV." He declared this happily, his eyes never leaving the screen, one hand stroking Evan's head. Evan remained mute, his thumb and most of one rabbit ear in his mouth. "We used to could watch TV at our old house but Jesus doesn't have to be mad about it because there could be a mouse hole in Jesus's house too, in his house in heaven, and then he'd have to get a cat to catch it except a real cat, not like Tom, he's just a man in a cat costume, but it would have to be a cat that died and went to heaven, and not a runned over cat because it'd be too squashedy to run after a mouse." At which Lucy had erupted into a "What?" and a wet belch of hilarity that felt like the first laugh she'd ever laughed, so long had it been since she'd laughed at all.

They'd come again and again to watch cartoons, every chance they got. Their aunt Louisa never did find out. In fact, as time had gone on, she'd come to rely increasingly on Lucy—who had lurched through that autumn and winter in the slough of despond, with no job in the offing and every evening free—as her go-to babysitter, convenience overriding the woman's strong, principled aversion to Brickwood *mère et fille*.

On more evenings than not she'd be over there, sitting at Louisa's kitchen table, perked up for the first time that day, dealing out cards for poker. Neil, and to a lesser extent Evan, were the only friends she had. She'd have been mortified if anyone knew how easily, how shamelessly she came down to their level, how she gloried in their adoring company.

Louisa's house was even uglier than hers, spartan in the extreme, tatty brown plaid furniture in the living room, a wobbly dinette set in the kitchen. Mismatched skinny beds in the boys' room. Everything they owned looked to be thirdhand items picked up at church rummage sales. Colour and flair were provided by inspirational art: behind her head as she shuffled the cards hung a wooden wall plaque requesting the LORD JESUS to BE OUR HOLY GUEST. On the wall opposite, another, more ominous message: FOR I KNOW THE PLANS I HAVE FOR YOU. Over the sink there was LET YOUR FAITH BE BIGGER THAN YOUR FEARS.

Much as she resented the wall-to-wall propaganda, she had to begrudgingly admire Louisa's astonishing energy. A nurse already working regular double shifts at the hospital, she was always bounding out the door on some church business, organizing food drives, visiting shut-ins, witnessing door-to-door. This was in stark contrast to her pal Dorcas, the boys' homeschool teacher, whose path Lucy often crossed at the end of the day, shuffling up the walk as Dorcas shuffled down, tugging her own two weary little girls like sacks of wet cement.

Stacked on the dining room table, beneath a Footprints in the Sand poster, there'd be the boys' homeschool textbooks, rows of sharpened pencils and rulers, a smeary whiteboard on an easel. Neil and Evan were supposed to be sitting at that table doing their homework, but the minute the door would shut behind their aunt, off at a trot to her Missionary Society meeting, Neil would spring from his chair to begin pogoing around the room, careening into end tables, knocking plants off their stands.

Evan would sit quietly, studying the pictures in his kiddie Bible with deep concentration.

"Did you bring the cards, the cards, the cards, the bards, the fards, the shmards?" Neil would shout, sproinging into the kitchen, then doubling back to Evan's side to holler in his ear, "Evan! Stop reading! Lucy brought the cards!"

Evan would get up, stand timidly in his usual lurking place in the kitchen doorway, one leg wrapped around the other, his hand nervously cupping his crotch, a spooky little kid with big, scared eyes, getting ready to whimper a panicked, *"J'ai envie! P-p-p-p-pi-piiii, Neil!"* So many p's in that *pipi*, she was afraid he'd have a seizure, his little face convulsed in fear, teardrops trembling on his lashes as he danced from one leg to the other, a little puddle already forming on the floor, till Neil jumped off his chair and led him gently by the hand to the bathroom. He was five years old, for crying out loud, way too old for shenanigans like this, and in his own house, too! Just to see him so terrified—of *what?*—terrified *her*.

Over time he began to relax a little. One night, he even had a bold question for her, which he piped shyly all the way across the room.

"Are you a kid or a lady?"

She'd shuffled the cards with a grand flourish before Neil's delighted eyes, spattering them against the table, sifting them from hand to hand, before ordering Neil to "Cut." Then she'd shot over her shoulder, "What kind of a wacko question is that?"

"It's 'cause I think maybe you're old. You have to have children soon."

"What do I want with children when I have you two little freaks?"

"Shut up and deal," Neil ordered, making her splutter with loud, appreciative laughter.

"Neil, my fine lad, you are a fucking caution. If your aunt finds out you're gambling with the babysitter, she'll poke a spear up my ass and roast me over hellfire."

"Evan will tell her you swear," said Neil calmly, fanning his cards in his hand, studying them with a practiced eye. "Do I got aces, yes, no, you'll never know, yes I do, no I don't, aces and kings and queens, every single one I got."

"Swearing's wrong," Evan pouted. "Jesus w-w-wants you to stop."

"Well, he hasn't said a fuckin' thing about it to me." When Evan wasn't scaring her, he got on her nerves, so clearly aware was he of being the best and holiest little boy who ever lived. Politely refusing to learn the card games, while Neil shuffled and dealt and wagered his allowance, chattering nonstop, making her laugh so hard spit splattered the table.

"Don't bat those fuckin' daddy-long-leg eyelashes at me, Mister," she teased Evan. "Neil, your brother's gonna be a lady-killer when he grows up."

"I'm not going to kill ladies!"

"It doesn't mean that, dummy. It means girls will be chasing you through the streets, trying to tear your clothes off!"

"Evan, you're getting all red!" Neil shouted, bouncing in his chair. "Come on, come and play with us. It's okay, Jesus won't be mad. It's so fun! You'll get rich!"

Oh, she was enjoying herself, as happy as she could ever remember being. "Tonight, I'm gonna teach you greenhorns Five Card Stud. I learned it from two devil ladies who used to be my best pals. It's a *devil* game, Evan! Satan invented it."

"Don't scare him," said Neil, suddenly serious. "Evan, don't be scared. It's just a game for fun."

"I only want to p-p-play Go F-f-fish."

"Let him play Go Fish," Neil told her then, laying down his cards, gravely in command. Evan brightened, began inching toward the table.

How her heart had gushed with love! "Neil, you're so sweet I might just gobble you up like a cupcake."

"You should always be our babysitter, all our lives, till we're dead."

"Jesus, what else do I have to do? Sure. Why the hell not."

Oh, how she'd loved him. As her spirits slowly rose, as her darkness began to dissipate. As they crossed paths, she on her cautious way up, he on his helter-skelter way down. His fall so much steeper than hers.

That day in the church. The muffled but unmistakeable bell of dread ringing deep within her.

She who had never darkened the door of a religious institution in all her twenty-nine years, had been slouched low in the very last pew, as far away from the other cheery, upbeat attendees as she could get. Panting in the unbreathable, ecclesiastical heat, accordioning the church bulletin into a makeshift fan, but not before reading under "Statement of Faith" that the congregants subscribed wholeheartedly to *the sinfulness of all mankind, separated from God, subject to His eternal wrath and condemnation.*

Down in front, Vacation Bible School was winding up its programme with a concert, a jumble of kids of all sizes bunched up on the raised platform, the girls in preposterously flounced dresses, the boys in suits and ties. Evan stood in the front row, shoehorned in between two much bigger girls, arms jammed flat at his sides. Eleven-year-old Neil, who'd really shot up that year, was in the back row, grinning over everyone's head, his tie yanked askew. When he pushed, bright-faced, through the group to the front for his solo, his shirt was completely untucked on one side, and Lucy had to stifle a snort when she noticed that his socks, visible above the outgrown, too-short pants, didn't match.

He waited, cheeks pink with excitement, for the end of the slightly warped intro, issuing tinnily from a cassette player off to the side. Then he opened his mouth and released, to the slack-jawed wonder of the crowd, the purest, sweetest, most chilling soprano she'd ever heard. His phrasing was effortless, his natural vibrato stunning in its artlessness. Her heart had cramped with love augmented by an old, deep pain, recalling that time when . . . but no, gutted by the soaring beauty of her boy's voice, she'd refused to remember that other time, refused to go back there.

She'd had no idea he was this good. *His eye is on the sparrow, and I know He watches meeeeeee,* he sang, and she wondered, trembling, how long could this perfect joy she was feeling last without shattering?

Judging from experience, not long at all.

Evan's eyes were on his brother from behind, his solemn little face lit up as he kneaded his hands in pride and excitement. The whole congregation, in fact, was sitting up straighter, rapt, transported. Neil's solo ended to spirited, heartfelt applause.

He bowed ten or twelve times, to right and left, beaming. Clasped his hands over his head like a heavyweight champ, then yanked his tie skyward, making a strangled face, eyes crossed, tongue lolling. As the applause died, he turned to wedge his way through to the back row again, knocking against several girls, who tottered and shoved him back. And she had thought: Baby, don't wreck it now, as she watched him regain his place, bopping the boy next to him playfully on the head as the ragged chorus launched into *What a Friend We Have in Jesus*.

Out on the church lawn afterward, kids tumbling around her, she'd copped a furtive cigarette, tapping ashes into her palm, afraid to sully the pristine church lawn. Neil and Evan were on either side of her, bobbing up and down, Evan tugging on her shirt, crying, "Neil was good, w-w-wasn't he, Lucy, w-w-wasn't he?" She turned to tell Neil just how good he was, but he was already off chasing another kid. Evan kept on chattering, "Aren't you g-g-glad you came to our church? W-w-wasn't our show good?" Looking up, she spied Louisa just outside the church doors at the same moment that Louisa, spotting the cigarette, shot her the evil eye.

"Do you w-w-want to know the Lord now, Lucy?" Evan asked earnestly, still yanking on her shirt, as Louisa plowed down the steps, heading their way.

"So glad you could come, Lucy," she said, offering a stiff smile, extending a stiff hand. "I pray that you'll be touched by the experience, that you'll come back and visit us again. You're certainly welcome to fellowship with us this coming Wednesday evening."

"I work Wednesday evenings." She avoided Louisa's eyes, looking off over her shoulder.

"Oh, that's right. You're at the municipal library now. How do you like it?"

"It's not much of a library. I'm just a way overqualified assistant."

"But never too overqualified to ask the Lord Jesus into your heart," murmured Louisa sweetly. "We'd love to see you here any time, Lucy. Our Sunday morning services begin at—"

"My mother's teaching me to drive on Sundays."

This mention of Pauline effectively stifled Louisa. She gave the hand into which Lucy had deposited her ashes a vigourous pump and moved off briskly to chastise a group of beruffled girls running amok in the flower bed.

Neil, who'd tiptoed up behind her then, was bouncing little pebbles off the back of her head. Coming closer, he dropped a handful of them down her shirt. There was a group of boys behind him and he was plainly drunk with the pleasure of making them laugh. A pebble pinged her ear. "Bullseye!" Neil crowed. Then another stung her neck. Emboldened, all smiles, he crept up with a fat handful of grass and loamy dirt to drop down the front of her shirt.

She twisted herself away from him, pushed his hand down. Said, "Neil! Knock it off." He grinned at her, pelted her with his handful of dirt anyway. "I said, knock it off!" she repeated, brushing herself down, her voice rising in irritation. Neil stood still, his grin fading by slow degrees into uncertainty, colour rising in his face. The little wobble around his mouth threatened to break her heart.

"You're a loon," she told him softly, a shivering fear clutching at her heart as she looked down into his eyes, the only eyes on earth she was able to meet without fear. "Simmer down, okay?" She noticed Evan watching, worried, from a distance as Neil, flapping his arms, raced to the top of the church steps. Without looking, he propelled himself sideways from eight stairs up, landed in a heap on the grass, rolling and bouncing to his feet, laughing fit to split, his good pants grass-stained, his hair standing on end, his lunatic volatility releasing all kinds of pain within her, like black birds rising in a swoop from a wire.

By now, standing here at the bathroom window, she's chain-smoked five cigarettes. She lights up a sixth, moves her ashtray to a safer perch on the window ledge. She never looks out this window at the view of her neighbour's side door without remembering Neil, that day, the summer he was fourteen, when her heart had finally, irrevocably broken for him.

She'd been out on the front porch reading when she'd heard the squeal of rusty hinges, Louisa wrenching their side door open and hurling Neil's beloved collection of cassettes onto the cracked concrete of the driveway. His Cure, his Anthrax, his Jesus and Mary Chain, all that raging music he loved so much, that he had to listen to in secret in the Brickwood basement. Louisa, shrieking as if her hair were on fire, "No, Devil, no! Not in this house! You won't win, Devil!" Down the steps she barreled in that long, brown skirt she lived in when she wasn't in her pink nurse's uniform, kicking and stamping on the scattered cassettes, cracking the plastic, then bending to pick them up one by one, yanking out the ribbons of tape. Finally, flinging the whole smashed and tangled mess onto the Brickwood lawn. Neil had hurtled down the steps after her, trying to grab her by the sleeve, a donkey noise coming out of him, his just-changing voice the saddest thing, cracking and bleating. Louisa knew she had an audience all right, knew Lucy was watching, probably hoped her mother was watching too, as she drew herself up in all her towering righteousness and ordered her sobbing nephew to sing. Right there in the driveway. "You're the anointed singer," she yelled, her face an inch from his. "You're the one the Lord wasted the blessing of a golden voice on, so that you could praise Him mightily. Now you sing! Sing unto the Lord! Beg His forgiveness! Purge this vile filth from your ears and your heart!" Hands on her hips, her face a scarlet balloon, and when Neil just stood there, slapping him hard, his head knocked sideways. The poor kid attempted to squawk through the first two lines of *Amazing Grace,* quavering his way to *a wretch like me,* till Lucy, in tears herself, had leapt to her feet and shouted, "Leave him alone, you evil bitch!" But Louisa hadn't heard her, she was hustling Neil back inside, kneeing him from behind when he tripped on the steps, the door slamming with finality behind her.

No wonder, my sweet baby. No wonder you're such a mess, she whispers to him now. Poor Neil had come knocking on her back door that night—not for the first time, either, nor the last. They'd hunkered together on the stoop, sharing her smokes, his head on her shoulder, then dropping to her lap, her hand smoothing his unwashed hair, neither of them speaking. A closed circle of two, a perfect understanding, though she was into her thirties by then, and must have seemed ancient to his young eyes. Wanting him to know just how desperately she cared, how hard she knew his young life was becoming. Fearing the worst for him. Because they were so alike, weren't they? So fragile, so shockingly easy to smash beyond repair.

She stubs out her smoke. The ashtray's overflowing, the bathroom choked with foul air. She remembers him coming over more and more often, never being sure whether the things she, and sometimes Pauline, would say to comfort him sank in or not. Once, she recalls with a hot flush, he'd turned suddenly before ducking out the door and bent to kiss her hand. That had made her cry herself to sleep, remembering herself at university, crumbling into wreckage, unable to make a single friend, hiding in her room, tears coursing down, no one's hand to kiss, no one to whom she could unburden herself. Other times she'd see him out the window, slouching down his driveway, Sundays, Wednesday nights on his surly way to church. If she called out a hello, she might get no more than a glimpse of his face, sour, pimpled, clenched. Always in that same old sweater, no matter what the weather. Neil's broken life, and hers, collapsing together like blackened kindling into a dying fire.

She'd been fourteen too, that summer of '64, when her own downslide had begun. The summer before high school was to start. The summer her father's clothes had suddenly de-materialized from his closet, leaving only a lingering waft of Old Spice, the dust outline of his shoes. The suits in their dry cleaning bags, the tie collection, the shirts, his underwear from the top drawer, all spirited away to a new and far, far better life.

And not so much as a scribbled note of goodbye.

She'd always thought that if he ever left, it would be entirely her mother's fault. But standing there, staring into that musty vacant space, she couldn't keep that conviction alive. It couldn't be Pauline; it had to be *her!* Just a few days before, he'd opened the door to her room where she'd been sprawled on her bed reading, her transistor radio, tuned to CKGM's top forty, swarming with tiny British lads, all bangs and tan teeth, living and luvving and twisting so fine. In between songs, numbskull girls were calling in to request sappy dedications: "Can you play *Can't Buy Me Love* for Bomber and all the kids at Riverdale Pool? Riverdale, yay!" She knew he'd just polished off a vicious set-to with Pauline downstairs, and now there he was, looming in her doorway, looking daggers at her. As if he were trying not to gag. Finally shouting, "Turn that miserable crap off! You can do better than that!" Then he'd slammed the door so hard her radio toppled to the floor.

He was ashamed of her. She'd let him down. All it took was that music to convince him that despite his best efforts, she was her mother's child after all. Thick, plodding, dull. Undiscerning. A child who could only bring disgrace to a Literary Man, a Man of Culture, a dabbling linguist, an intellectual—unlike Pauline, who couldn't crack a book if she blammed it with an axe. Talk about having nothing in common; Lucy couldn't begin to fathom what had brought these two people together in the first place. They had no friends in common, no visitors, and no family either; Pauline's parents were dead, and Daddy's whole family was estranged. It was just the misbegotten three of them, thrown together, randomly assigned, a nuclear unit about to blow. Pauline had her own friends and a social life, but not Daddy: he was a Brain, a Loner Egghead, had the big black glasses to prove it, wore ascots tucked into his shirt collar on Saturdays. A genius wordsmith who wrote his own stories, holed up in his basement den, typing like a runaway train. Stories he wouldn't let her read, though she begged. Stories he sent off in stacks of manila envelopes to publishers. Stuffing his rejection notices into the bottom drawer of his desk; she'd found one, skimmed through it, come across the words, *so much, so badly wrong*. Hot with indignation, she'd crumpled it into a ball and slammed the drawer shut, never to be opened again.

They'd even written stories together, silly things, four or five pages long, the two of them in the kitchen, kicking each other's legs under the table for fun, the only touching they ever did. She knew his patience had severe limits, the beam of his attention fickle in its focus, but for the time it was turned on her, she was in heaven. A bowl of chips between them, plots that were all her idea, that made him laugh, the two of them throwing snatches of dialogue back and forth, cooking up haywire scenarios. *The Assassination of Queen Jeanne. Blue Murder in the Den of Crimson Blood.* Instant classics. He called her Agatha Crystal Ball. She called him Isotope Feeney because he had a scientific job and worked in a lab, a job he hated, studying seed mutations under microscopes. More than once she'd asked him, "How come you don't just write books if that's what you like? How come you have to be a scientist?"

"Because I'm good at it," had been his airy reply. "I'm what's known as a Renaissance man. It's a cruel twist of fate, because lab work is not where my heart is. But I have to make money, don't I, so you and your mother aren't forced to crawl down the street foraging used gum to stay alive."

"ABC gum," she'd corrected him smartly. "Already Been Chewed. It doesn't taste so bad. I tried some." And they'd immediately begun work on *The ABC Gum Caper.*

But he was moody, unpredictable, given to long bouts of cold silence. Sinking into himself, shutting both her and Pauline out. Lucy had never blamed him, instinctively grasping that he suffered some inner desolation reserved for the geniuses, the illuminated ones. She understood; she felt a junior version of that same desolation budding deep within her own self. A loner since kindergarten, she'd been paddling her own canoe socially for years, sustaining herself entirely with books. Haunting the town library, pursuing one passion after another: butterflies, space travel, magic and sorcery, books about horses, books about baseball, and devouring novels too, adult ones, *Exodus* and *The Sundowners,* her ever-expanding cache of knowledge her greatest source of pride. Her brief sparking friendships with other misfit girls never got off the ground. She'd been completely cut out of the preteen social scene of ballet classes and sleepovers and florid note-passing, of crushes and confidences. Butterflies and baseball were one thing, charm bracelets and giggling and pinky swearing were a whole alien other, with no book to explain how they worked nor how to worm one's clumsy way in.

Daddy was erratic, but she'd long ago learned how to wait him out, enduring till he emerged from his funk and she could go back to being his steadfast sidekick, the Tonto to his Lone Ranger. Sometimes she counted down the hours, recorded them in a notebook like crossed-off days scratched onto a prison wall, drawing a big happy star at the bottom of the page when he resurfaced, friendly once more.

If they weren't writing stories, they read together, in the living room, he sprawled on the sofa, she in the big armchair. Pauline—she'd called her mother by her first name since she was four, though Daddy had always been Daddy—would be banging things around in the kitchen while Lucy plowed through *Robinson Crusoe,* and her father worked his way through the complete works of Ian Fleming. If he and Pauline weren't on speaking terms—not a rare occurrence—the two of them would bring their books to the dinner table. Reading while they ate, reading while Pauline washed the dishes, shoveled the driveway, mowed the lawn.

But during the times when he and Pauline were getting along—nothing mushy, just him saying something neutral to her after a week of silence, drawing a weak smile out of her in return—the companionable table reading stopped. And the writing. Such an agony of jealousy she'd suffered then, sometimes purposely knocking over a glass of milk or breaking a plate just to pull the focus back to herself. The pain of being forced to share, of being shut out of exclusivity, was intolerable. The quiet hum of conversation leaking from behind closed doors filled her with dread: maybe he would only love Pauline now, Pauline, who didn't deserve or even need him. How could he have room for *two* people in his heart? That wasn't the way hearts worked!

When she'd come home that day to find him gone, she'd marched straight to her room, slammed the door, inked SO SAD, ONE DAY YOU'LL BE HAD, DAD, THEN I'LL BE GLAD, GLAD, GLAD!!!! with savage ferocity onto her desk blotter. Not, not, absolutely *not* crying! Stumping back down the hall again to shout into his empty closet, "You didn't hurt me a bit! I'm perfectly able to withstand shocks of this nature!"

But without him in it, their life in that house made no sense. They needed to pack up, clear out, board up the windows, now, this instant! If he was getting a brand-new life, then she deserved to have one too! First things first: get light-years away from hayseed, hickburg Sainte-Clémence; they only lived there so he could be close to his job at the agricultural college in Sainte-Anne-de-Bellevue. Why the hell stay now?

But her mother, possessed of no taste, no culture, no elegance, who, what's more, hadn't dropped a tear since Daddy left, refused to budge an inch.

And wasn't Pauline trying to "comfort" her a sorry picture! Sneaking up behind her in the bathroom while she was attempting to tease her hair, laying her dishpan hands with their ragged nails on her shoulders, not saying anything, trying to look all loving. Lucy biting her lip hard, opening her eyes as wide as they would stretch so that the rising water table would spread over the entire eyeball surface and not spill over. Pauline's face seen backward in the mirror looked as if it had been broken and clumsily reglued together, the wrong eyelid drooping, her crooked mouth all wonky. Sunny, sporty Pauline, lumping around in her sweatshirt and baggy bermudas, her body already going to male-pattern gut fat, making Lucy cringe on behalf of all womankind.

And what were the loving words that dribbled out of that zigzag mouth?

"Lucy, you look like a parsnip."

"Kindness forbids me from telling you what *you* look like."

"Would it kill you to get out in the sun? Get some exercise?"

She'd looked her mother square in the eyes over the tangled hair bulge she'd raised on top of her head. Spoke with a steely calm she didn't remotely feel. "I refute the sun, Mother. I renounce the day. I make my abode in realms of shadow and gloom. Please don't make me have to tell you this again."

No, no, *no*! It had to be Pauline who had wrecked everything. What man could put up with her beefy body, or endure her hooting and slapping her big, wide-spread knees while she watched Hockey Night in Canada? Not to mention the new, sporty "friend" she'd recently picked up at the horse-riding academy just outside of town where she worked in administration, ordering new saddles and bridles, keeping the horses stocked in oats, oh hell, Lucy hadn't the faintest idea what she did.

Daddy had only been gone a week when Pauline, in another sorry attempt at offering support and consolation, had twisted Lucy's arm to come out to the riding academy, saying she wanted to show her the new horses. Didn't Lucy love horses? Well, there was a new dappled grey that would take her breath away. But instead, she'd been treated to the sight of the She-Beast of the Underworld stepping out of her white Jaguar XKE in jodhpurs, tall, gleaming boots, and an impeccable platinum pageboy. The Beast striding right into the stable, where she boarded two chestnut mares. Spotting Pauline instantly. Her face lighting up like a Hollywood premiere as she came closer, held out her withered old paw. The two of them greeting each other with overacted surprise, distant acquaintances just bumping into each other, how do you like that, instantly putting Lucy on high alert.

Under tight scrutiny, the platinum vision, who introduced herself as Glynis Glover MacGregor, was mercilessly stripped of her glamour, her face far too tan, her flaxen hair far too unlikely on a head of her vintage. Lucy would forever afterward associate her with the smell of cracked leather and horse shit.

Then, only a week later, Pauline, who one would assume needed all the income she could get in her newly reduced circumstances, gave the horse people her notice and became a lady of leisure. In no time at all, Glynis, when she wasn't sunning on Corfu or shopping in Pretoria, took to dropping in during the long, bug-buzzy summer afternoons, slumming outside with Pauline on plastic chaise longues on the weedy Brickwood patio. In the blink of an eye, the two of them were joined at the hip, running off to play golf or tennis, or swim at the exclusive club Glynis belonged to. Or off to ride Glynis's sleek horses. Or they'd disappear for lunches that lasted all afternoon, from which the normally placid, levelheaded Pauline came home giddy and unsteady on her feet. Lucy thought of herself as a cool sophisticate—she'd read *The Children's Hour*—but as she slowly twigged to what was actually going on, she was appalled. She had long assumed that the only act of sexual congress indulged in by her parents had been the sacrificial one that had produced her. But *this*? Her own mother, with that wizened crone! Instead of playing tennis, were they sneaking off to Glynis's stately mansion, to snuggle up all day in Glynis's Marie Antoinette bed? Oh God! What . . . what did they *do?*

Other days, Glynis arrived, not in her Jag, but her "doggy" car, the ten-year-old Mercedes she drove when accompanied by Princeling, her unspeakable Doberman. Into the kitchen they'd barge, before Lucy, eating breakfast, could make her escape. Princeling's nails clicking on the linoleum in the kitchen, his horrible, stiff tail festively throbbing, dog smell poisoning the air. Woofing as he tore around or slurped water from a silver bowl Glynis brought just for him. Pauline would scratch him behind his ridiculously militant ears, while Glynis cooed, "Say hello to Pauline, sweetie pie. Say hello to Lucy. Are you my own darling little boy? Yes, you are, oh, yes you are."

"I certainly see the resemblance," remarked Lucy sourly, clattering her cereal bowl into the sink and banging out the side door. The sudden silence behind her, like a forty degree drop in temperature, assured her that her zinger had hit home.

Everything was upended, tilted sideways, all the old certainties destroyed. Lucy had always felt comfortably superior to Pauline, but this unheralded turn of events, not to mention Glynis herself, utterly unnerved her. The gruesome old reptile didn't have the slightest conception of how repugnant she was, always bending over backward, trying to make nicey-nice. Urging Lucy to join them on the patio, pull up a chaise, tell them all about herself. Lucy, shaken, had mumbled, "For your information, I am by inclination a solitary wanderer of windswept places, a haunter of lonely moors and the silent abodes of the dead." It was a line out of the novel she was writing, but it failed to impress Glynis, who only met her gaze for an excruciating length of time, clearly taking her sorry measure.

Crowded out of her own house, she'd walk, long strides, head down, toward the lake, furious tears choking her throat, fogging her eyes. Heading for Lunenberg Street, which sloped all the way down to the water's edge. Loony Street, she called it, because of the gauntlet she had to run before reaching the bottom. The two skinny Rottweilers who went berserk every time she passed their house, charging and snorfling, sniffing up her skirt, driven wild by Princeling's evil pheromones, their horrible probing noses wet against her knees. The fool who owned them running down his walk, thwacking them on their tight, quivering hindquarters with his rolled-up *Journal de Montréal*.

"*Heille! Crotte! Ti-Cul! C't'assez là! Aweille en-dedans!*"

Then, three houses down, the raggedy geezer who sat on his porch in all weathers, yelling at everyone. Half rising from his busted chair, shaking his fist at her. "*Si tu farmes pas ta yeule, câlisse m'a t'la farmer, moi!*"

And in the very last house, the Loony Ladies.

They were some kind of anian or arian—Roumanian, Ukrainian, Hungarian. They'd seen her back in the spring out on her windy outcrop staring down France; the windy outcrop was at the end of their bedraggled lawn. She'd heard them knocking on the window and was sure she was going to get chewed out for trespassing, but no! They'd invited her in, sat her at the kitchen table, brought her barky-smelling tea in a glass and a plate of gooey pastries. Sofia, who was about three thousand years old, wore a tattered paisley bathrobe thrown over a quilted pink housecoat and capri pants. Shiny alopecia patches on her head, mottled calves ropey with blue veins. Backless mules with green plush pompoms. A black cigarette riding to and from her face in a yellowed, ivory holder. Croaking, "I have tuberculosis," before Lucy had sunk her teeth into the first pastry.

Her sister Tamara lurked in the archway between the kitchen and the living room. Thin as a length of string, nose like a sharp wedge of cheese, a long, long body of rough terrain:

conical hillocks, knobby knolls, sharp outcroppings. Dressed in a shin-length black sack, her chest adorned with a six-inch bejewelled crucifix that appeared to weigh many pounds, doing her posture no favours. A skinny grey braid of hair hung to her knees, the bound end tapering to the width of a needle.

Now she was dropping in on them several times a week, sitting in their musty, low-ceilinged living room on a velvet sofa the colour of primate labia in estrus, its enormous ram's horn sides higher than her head. Next to the sofa, a floor lamp, a life-size shepherdess hoisting on her crook a lilac lampshade with four-inch black silk tassels. The dark drapes were drawn tight, making it impossible to tell if the chairs and gilded tables, the bloated vases and candelabra that crammed the room were genuine antiques or just painted plastic. On the walls were several gilded icons, and a large postcard of vacation life behind the Iron Curtain: two lovers lying on a hard, stone beach, catching up on sleep. In the dead centre, a gold-framed portrait of the Holy Family hard at their tasks: Joseph measuring two-by-fours, Mary making what appeared to be bagels at an electric stove, the curly-haired tyke Jesus, in a short judo robe, looking on hungrily. The march of art continued, a slew of velvet Elvises (Velvises? Velvi?) making their way up the wooden stairs leading from the kitchen to the creepily dark second floor.

Sofia kept her apprised of her health issues, letting it be known that she'd soon be visiting a faith healer for her tuberculosis, a wonder-worker who she once saw make a man puke out a whole cancer—"black, as big as my head, with hair growing out of it"—into a trash can. Tamara, for her part, was able to hear other people's thoughts and communicated regularly with angels. Inside her dress she wore an amulet, a blue oval the size of an Oreo cookie with a heavy-lidded green eye painted in the centre. Telling Lucy darkly, "This eye will reflect any curse which is put on you right back to the one who has cursed you."

"Can I borrow it?"

"Aha! You have some enemy, I see. Then you must buy my magic feathers." Tamara slid a long, flat box out from under the sofa, pried back the lid, and there were the feathers, tatty, grey, piled in heaps. "Seventy dollars apiece. Twelve of them will remove any curse and cast it back onto the enemy of your choosing. These feathers are smuggled into this country. If the government knew I had them, they would have me put to death." Then she set the box aside, gliding across the room as if on casters, returning with a black album under her arm, a scrapbook fat with yellowed clippings. She plunked it in Lucy's lap and turned the pages which to her were upside down. Pointed with an index finger half a foot long.

"My dear departed papa was the one who taught me about the feathers. This is his obituary. We wrote it for the *Gazette* when he died because we loved him so." Slithering onto the sofa next to Lucy. "R is for the Rosebushes in his cheeks. O is for the Overall good times Roger gave us. G is for the Good times Roger gave us. E is for the Empty heart Roger gave us. R is for we will always Remember Roger."

"His name was Roger," she explained, shutting the album.

When conversation flagged, Sofia would bring out an ancient deck of playing cards with strange symbols on the back, single eyes embedded in pyramids or multiarmed demons, and deal out a game of poker. Lucy, blessed with a natural poker face, learned it in no time; she began bringing her allowance, which she was soon doubling and tripling, wheezing and hacking as she gamely smoked Sofia's evil-smelling cigarettes. It was wonderful; unlike with the two witches at home, here she wielded tremendous power. These two crackpots were in *thrall* to her.

At some deep, deep level, she felt that this was her true home, that Sofia and Tamara somehow pointed the way to her own iconoclastic future, though she'd be better looking, of course, with a better wardrobe, and a flourishing, lauded career in some as yet undetermined discipline. Oh, how she'd hated having to drag herself home from the Loony Sisters' sprightly company, slogging through the village, past Sainte-Clémence church with its green copper steeple, past the ugly presbytery, the stupid *casse-croûte,* the dingy dep, the boring Rossy five-and-ten. Past the old wooden houses that came right down to the sidewalk. Turning down her own street where the houses were newer but nothing to get into an uproar about.

There was no estrus furniture at home, that was for damn sure. The Brickwood décor featured beige carpet and boxy beige furniture from Sears. Only the bookcase in the corner held any trace of Lucy's own dear departed papa, books he'd bought in his last six months at home but had never gotten to, their spines still uncracked. She'd lugged a pile of them into her room; it was easy enough to see where *his* head had been: Russian novels and plays, every single one. Many pages, miniscule print. And a weighty instructional book as well, *Teach Yourself Russian*, a project he'd certainly never once mentioned to her.

Russian, she soon discovered, looked hard, but wasn't really. Once you learned the alphabet, it was a snap to read; all the letters stood alone, making only one sound. No combinations, no diphthongs, no complications. And wouldn't Daddy be astonished, wouldn't he be *knocked flat,* if she wrote her next letter to him in Russian?

Consumed by this new passion, she'd abandoned her visits to the Loonies. As the midsummer sun beat against the closed blinds of her room, she plowed through those novels, becoming intimately acquainted with boyars and onion domes, burials on grey days under swirling snow. Regiments posted just outside the town of N———. Serfs huddled on the tops of stoves for warmth. Lavish sturgeon dinners at three in the morning, vodka and the singing samovar. Corseted women fainting dead away with monotonous regularity.

Pauline and Glynis would be sunning themselves in the yard, lying *side by each*, as Glynis liked to call it, slurping iced tea with just a *smidge* of sugar, as Glynis liked to say. Holding hands, flaunting themselves, trying to shock Louisa next door, whom they could see spying on them from behind her curtains. Pauline, who had become strangely, annoyingly, girlish, would blush and giggle as Glynis stroked her arm outrageously, or even kissed her cheek; Lucy, spying on *them* from behind her blinds, could tell Glynis was calling all the shots, forcing these public shows of affection on Pauline. If Princeling happened to be visiting for the day, he'd have to get into the act too, jamming his pointy head under their linked arms, whining piteously. For the briefest of moments, she felt sorry for her mother, her other friends no longer calling her, stuck in sordid bondage with a needy Doberman and Glynis in her old-lady bathing suit with its flouncy skirt, her wizened brown hands crinkling the cellophane off a fresh pack of Cameos every couple of hours. Looking like a potato you find two years after it rolled under the fridge.

And that voice! Like she was going hoarse shouting for the geriatric nurse.

Lucy made a point of keeping her distance, but sometimes got caught sneaking down to the kitchen for a snack when she thought they were outside but were really sitting at the kitchen table silently leafing through home décor magazines. Glynis looking up, squinting at her like something she'd just pulled out of her chin with tweezers.

"Lucy! What, no hello? Pauline, wouldn't you scurry if you saw a glower like Lucy's bearing down on you?"

Pauline, not looking up from the spread of patio furniture she was studying, murmured, "I defy you to get a smile out of that girl. It can't be done."

Lucy rallied smartly. "No, it can't. I come from a broken home. What could I possibly have to smile about? I have no father, you know."

Glynis, unmoved, rolled right on.

"My goodness, kids must be running for cover from that scowl of yours!" She lit a Cameo, exhaled like Ava Gardner on somebody's yacht. Lucy gave her ripply, mud-brown body a slow, contemptuous once-over. But Glynis just wheezed merrily, winking at Pauline. "And don't be ridiculous. Everybody has a father." The implications of this, issuing from her railroad-tracked anus of a mouth were so salacious that Lucy needed to take several deep, steadying breaths.

Under control again, she issued her riposte. "I'm quite familiar with the facts of life. And so are the two of you, *very* familiar, unless I'm reading everything wrong, which I doubt." When

Glynis reared like a cobra, she feigned baffled consternation. "What? Is something wrong?"

"I would watch my tone, young lady," Glynis snarled, drops of spit glistening on her chin.

"Don't, Glynis," sighed Pauline. "Don't encourage her."

Elated at her victory, Lucy executed a courtly bow, first to Pauline, then Glynis. "You will forgive me, ladies. I need to catch the four o'clock train to Smolensk. I have many versts to go before I sleep."

But before she could spin on her heel and make a graceful exit, Glynis made a cobra lunge and grabbed her wrist, Indian-burn hard.

"Ouch! Let me go, that hurts!"

"Why do you put up with this?" Glynis shot at Pauline, pounding her cigarette butt with her free hand into the ashtray with unnecessary force. Lucy looked to her mother for help; surely she wouldn't allow this vicious hag to maul her only child without *some* protest.

She saw a light flare in her mother's eyes, a light just as quickly extinguished, and she knew in that instant that Pauline, so capable, so unflappable and easygoing, had lost all her powers, that she'd chosen Glynis over her and that Glynis was inside her head, pulling all the levers, making all the decisions. And no wonder. Just over her shoulder, on the arm of the living room couch, lay the new winter coat Glynis had just bought for her, sealskin, its short, bristly pelt just like Princeling's. Odd gift choice for a woman who lived in denim and squalid old ski jackets. Even worse, there were expensive new boots in the hall closet, a camel hair coat and a white fur hat. The two of them were clearly planning to step out in style together come winter. Not only that: there were new golf clubs and a spanking new saddle parked in the hall.

Pauline refused to look at her.

"Glyn, I told you. We're oil and water. I threw in the towel with her a long time ago."

"I'm standing right here, Mother!"

Glynis still clutched her wrist, the raised veins blue in her mottled hands. "What I'd like to know is, where are your friends, young lady? Why are you always hanging around by yourself? Doesn't anyone like you?"

"She doesn't *have* any friends, Glyn." Pauline's voice sounded odd, alien, and perilously close to tears. "She'd rather mope in her room. She's never gotten along with other kids. In her entire childhood, she went to *one* birthday party, and then I found out she spent the afternoon in their kitchen reading a book, that she only pulled her nose out of to inform the child's mother that she needed her privacy since she was recovering from intestinal cancer."

"You're just jealous! You're so jealous because Daddy liked me more than you! And I did so have friends, lots. Debbie in grade four, and Jill that one summer—"

A sour laugh from Pauline.

"Yes, Jill. The one you tried to buy by giving her the camera you'd stolen from your father. And Debbie, who you bribed by giving her all your allowance. And that teacher you had a crush on, who you gave three of my sweaters to—she was actually *wearing* one, Glyn, on parent-teacher night. That same teacher who told me she'd caught you chewing gum you'd picked up from the sidewalk."

"Something of a pariah then, are we?" smirked Glynis, letting go of her wrist.

"Because she made me that way! Daddy thought I was fine, he never tried to force me to play sports or—and when Debbie and her friends beat me up that time, you didn't even take my side! Daddy did."

"Of course he did. He recognized a fellow liar, didn't he? Glyn, you wouldn't believe the stunts she pulled to get kids to like her. She told that girl Debbie that Hayley Mills was her cousin, that she spent summers on her yacht and that she'd be happy to introduce her any time. Strutting around like the big cheese until the other kids called her on it."

Glynis lit another cool cigarette, sat back in her chair, enjoying the show.

"Good old Daddy. He always let you do exactly what you wanted, sit inside reading for ten hours straight, on the most beautiful days of the year, all the other kids outside, running around, skipping rope, playing hopscotch. He thought that was just fine, he didn't care how weird you were getting. You *still* think the sun shines out of his ass." Pauline's face had gone blotchy, tears just barely held in check. "I guess you'll just have to find out about him the hard way. Selfish prick, skipping off into the sunset, here, *you* pay for the divorce, honey, I'm too much in love! He's moved on, and he's not looking back. I give him six months before he forgets all about you!" She sank into a chair, Glynis immediately leaping to her feet to wrap her in a bear hug. Lucy, sick with rage—no one was calling *Glynis* out for buying affection—screamed at the cozy hump they made.

"What're you doing here, anyway? It's because no man in the world can stand to look at you, that's why you have a stupid dog for a kid! You think you're fooling everybody that you're so young, like you dip your face in a barrel of makeup every day, but even a blind person can see that you're practically eighty and all spindly and your face is all shriveled up. Being rich isn't saving you from anything!"

Glynis raised her head from Pauline's neck, turning to meet Lucy's eyes. Languid as she was attempting to appear, Lucy could tell she'd hit her mark dead centre by the tightness of Glynis's lips, the smoky breath inhaled and expelled with just a little too much propulsion.

"You, my sad little child, are the last person in the world who will ever know anything about true friendship and love."

She burrowed her head again in Pauline's neck. They sat holding each other, breathing audibly in tandem for a few moments. Then, as if on cue, they rose, gathered up their suntan oil and magazines and headed outside to resume browning like stewing beef under the blazing sun.

Lucy thundered up the stairs to her room, her face burning. Who cared what they thought? Twisted old bitches! Crack-faced crones! Daddy and me, we laugh you to scorn!

She gave the door of her room a mighty slam. Caught sight of herself in her closet mirror, took note of the greasy lankness of her hair, the jamlike smear of pimples on her forehead and chin—even Glynis, that grisly abomination, was acne free. No wonder no one liked her. Nobody else came within miles of being this ugly. All the other kids were on joy rides to teen paradise, with no time to stop and offer a friendly hand, a kind word. Snot puddled on her upper lip as she spat, "Ugly, disgusting bitch freak!" at her reflection, slapping herself in the face several times, hard. Everyone in the world was paired off, had eyes to gaze into, a hand to hold, except her. Even Glynis, who was decrepit and ghastly, and who, she now knew, had *her* number. Because for all she pretended not to care, the epithet "friendless" was the one that always struck home with the keenest pain.

On the floor at her feet was a copy of *Seventeen,* open to a personality quiz she'd been filling out. She bent to pick it up. *"Developing a personality: How do YOU rate? A: Everyone likes me. B: I have a small group of loyal,* no. *C: I try to . . .* no. *D: People endure me but don't enjoy me.* She'd circled D. She crumpled the quiz, kicked it under her bed, High school about to begin in a matter of weeks. There'd be no friends there either. She should just kill herself now.

She sat on her bed, shoulders heaving, the muffled sounds of sapphic chitchat drifting through her open window from the backyard. To drown it out, she tuned her radio low to a classical music station, as if Daddy could hear, as if she could invoke his presence. Growing calmer, she turned the pages of the magazine, proceeded to cut out the image of the girl from the Summer Blonde ad to paste into her novel about a girl called Lyudmilova.

She'd already completed the book jacket blurb.

Maybe, just maybe, if you are dissatisfied with waiting and want your life and your dream NOW, well maybe you can follow in the adventurous, terrifying, sometimes ultimately joyous and sometimes unbearably sad but always beautiful footsteps of . . . that girl called Lyudmilova.

She was well into Chapter One, where *morning stole in on silent, padded paws.* And she'd filled eight whole pages with cutouts of *Seventeen* girls. Lyudmilova, her heroine, was a bewitching blonde, *made of hay and honeycomb, like sun-ripened wheat billowing over the Ukrainian steppes. Eyes of deepest jade, cheeks of palest rose. Luscious curves spilling from her taut bodices.* She could already hear Daddy crying, "Lucy! What a stupendous literary masterpiece! I always knew you had it in you!" over the crackling long-distance line from Paris. "As soon as you're eighteen, I'll set you up here in an apartment on the Left Bank, how's that sound? And you say you're learning Russian all by yourself? You're a marvel!" Her spirits revived, she put her cutting and pasting aside to read a few more pages of *The Collected Plays of Chekhov*, copy out a new Russian vocabulary list, and hand-letter a cardboard sign reading SMOLENSK in bold Cyrillic. She loved the sound of it so much, like a wet sneeze into a sopping handkerchief. Chin high, she taped it to the outside of her bedroom door and slammed herself inside again.

Coming downstairs the next morning to a safe, Glynis-free kitchen, she shook out a bowl of Trix, saw Pauline across the table pretending to read the *Montreal Star,* looking guilty and sad; she hadn't apologized last night at supper, but now Lucy could sense her drawing in her breath to speak.

She cut her mother off at the pass. "For tonight's supper, instead of number eight hundred and six in a series of Swanson's TV dinners, I would like to request the following items: snipe, beluga, borscht, pickled smelts and blini."

Pauline's mouth hung open, words failing her.

"Oh! Loosen her stays, Semyon Ivanovitch! She is quite overcome!"

"What in God's name are you talking about now?"

"I shall go on speaking as I please, my dear Nina Petrovna!" Cupping her hands round her mouth, she opened the back door to shout to the neighbourhood at large, "Yevgeny Fyodorovitch! Do tell Alyosha to fetch the sleigh round straight away!"

"Lucy, I need you to open the windows in your room, air it out. It smells like a mausoleum in there."

"Whatever can you mean, little Mother?"

Pauline sighed, lit a cigarette, a Cameo, a new habit. Turned back to her paper.

"Just do it. I also need you to vacuum the living room."

"Yes, of course! Dear me, but it is a hard business! And yet, is it not fitting that I should work for my kopeck of bread? Yes! I shall go to Moscow and I shall work, work, work!"

Glynis no longer even bothered ringing the doorbell. Just crashed in at eight on Saturday mornings, in her cheeky little tennis skirt and socks with tiny pink pompoms, her eyelids smeared cerulean blue, her hair petrified with Spray Net. She'd execute a balletic practice serve before rasping at Pauline, "How's my spring chickie this morning? Are we all bright-eyed and bushy-tailed?" She'd turn to Lucy then to inquire, "And how's Casper the Unfriendly Ghost?"

Witticisms this feeble deserved nothing but rolled eyes and a glacial shoulder.

After a quick coffee, the ladies would be off for a morning of mixed doubles, bouncing and squealing all over the country club court with girls Lucy's age, girls Glynis never failed to characterize as self-starters and Miss Personality Plusses.

Lurking on the stairs, she winced at their coffee chatter, hissed savage epithets, each one a shade louder, in Glynis's general direction. "Shut *up*, you hag, you old bag, you fright-wig scrag, you broken-down nag, you reeking little old RAG!" When Glynis failed to react, she was forced to head back down into the kitchen to inquire sweetly through her teeth, "Isn't your lumbago bothering you, Ma'am?"

"Lucy, why don't you come with us," suggested Pauline with a discernible lack of enthusiasm.

"Pardon me while I retch."

"Yes, well. Why do I even bother?" Pauline sighed yet again, bent to tie up her tennis shoes. Unlike Glynis, she was in shorts and an old white shirt with the sleeves cut off. Her hair slicked back under a paisley bandanna. She looked like Glynis's stocky son.

"If you get any scrawnier, you'll blow away," contributed Glynis in high cheer. "Tennis does wonders for building up the bust, you know."

"Neither busts nor sport hold the slightest attraction for me. And I would kindly ask you not to involve yourself in my developmental situation."

"Your mum's only trying to get you out into the world of *normal* people, honeybun. I shudder to think what a lonely, sad time you're going to have in high school. There was a girl at my school whom nobody liked, and she ended up, if I'm not mistaken, in a straitja—"

"I am not IN-ter-ested!"

"She's not *interested*," Glynis mimicked, winking at Pauline.

"Nyet!" The sight of the two of them, so completely recovered from her bitter, truth-to-power denunciation, and so *pleased* with each other filled her with a resentment so visceral she shuddered as if she'd just bitten down on a spoon.

From now on, she decided, she would speak only Russian to those two dazed heifers. But it was easier said than done; Glynis rattled her, making her forget the vocabulary words she had so diligently studied. So she made it up instead.

"Gladnooski vyet bogomyet kravonets!"

"What's that supposed to mean?" Glynis inquired archly, smoke rings issuing from her face like a calling-all-cars signal in the movies.

"Pa-russki."

"Rooski? You mean Russian? What is the *matter* with you? *Why?*"

"It doesn't sound much like Russian. You need to swallow your L's more," advised Pauline in a maddeningly neutral tone. "My high school basketball coach was Russian. You're not getting it right at all."

"Plasstynyet das vidasnya ponymayet da krakowski!" In a paralysis of rage, her throat had closed to a pinhole through which only garbled invective could splurt. "Fodor bledzni puskinimayet!" But Pauline, as she trailed Glynis out the front door, carrying both their tennis rackets, only threw her a smug, pitying smile over her shoulder.

High school, of course, went awry from the jump. Her nerve endings lit like fuses, her head full of Russian words and pictures, she was still, weeks into the school year, getting lost in the halls, running, breathless and sweaty, after the final bell had sounded. Turning up late for algebra, Mr. Ainsley already on the job in his dusty suit, the dull clack of chalk, x's and y's spreading like cholera across the blackboard. The rest of the class all in their seats as she wisped through the door, her chin absurdly high, the Romanoff princess visiting the mental hospital, eel thin and elegant in a tiara and a sequined dress no wider than a sock. All faces turned her way, the shining ones and the sleepy ones, the oily-haired boys with their loosened ties and grubby shirt collars, the daisy-fresh girls with pale lips, petal cheeks, chains round their necks weighted with going-steady rings. Every last one of them transfixed, profoundly humbled by her beauty.

Mr. Ainsley's chalk tap danced across the board, shelving squiggly letters in brackets above other letters in brackets.

"Who can tell me the value of ab in this equation?"

Not me, thought the svelte Russian émigré in her boxy blazer and drooping, pleated uniform skirt. Stare at me all you want, fools. You cannot harm me! Come what may, I *always* land on my feet, ha! Like an ant you flick off a table, I hit the floor on all six legs and run away laughing, ha ha HA!

Mr. Ainsley stopped his chalk-tapping to hand back the corrected quizzes from last Friday. Smirking as he flapped the last, unclaimed quiz in the air. "Who, may I ask, is Loodmyloova?"

She stepped, flaming face down, to the front of the class, snatching the paper out of his hand. Desperately pulling the flickering delusion of her beauty around herself like a protective cloak, she silently denounced her snickering peers: *Degeneratay!* You are all unsalvageable degenerates!

"May I humbly request that you sign your real name to papers in this class, Miss Brickwood?" requested Mr. Ainsley with a thin smile. A back-row wit underscored the name in question: "Juicy Shitgood!" The class convulsed as one, Mr. Ainsley shushing them mildly before turning back to the board, his arm arcing high, erasing in wide, smeary swaths.

She kept her mortified head down in the hall afterward, heading for her regular post at the last table in the farthest corner of the seething lunchroom. Unwrapping her flattened cheese sandwich, she silently addressed the fuzzy-haired girl also sitting alone at the end of the long table. This girl had jelly on her chin and her nose in a book. She looked just unprepossessing enough for Lucy to manage.

"You have to understand," she muttered under her breath, "my parents never had one iota in common. My father is an intellectual, a brilliant writer and also a language enthusiast, though I can't help but wonder if his skill level is as high as he claims. I recall him trying to speak Portuguese to Mr. Gracez at the hardware store. Mr. Gracez could never make out a word and kept telling him, 'Ask at cash, please, mister.' Anyway, it's no secret why he found a new love to replace my mother. She's the hale and hearty type, with prominent teeth and a predisposition to stomach blubber. She wears no makeup, ever, and has this big, booming voice . . . well, why beat around the bush? Are you familiar with the euphemism 'inclined to the ways of Sappho?' You look like you might be. Anyway, if there ever was a woman who does not have and never will have 'it,' Pauline is that woman. And now she's gotten all chummy with this antiquated hellcat who's as rich as creosote. She's a ghoul who's stolen my wayward mother's soul and turned her into a zombie. I suspect my poor deluded maternal parent is being kept; do you know what that means? I leave the whole sordid affair to your lively imagination."

The fuzzy-haired girl was eating an apple, still reading, oblivious. Someone across the room dropped a tray, soup splashing, girls screaming. When the din had died down, Lucy rolled right on: "I myself am a fluent Russian speaker." She was suddenly aware that she was moving her lips as she shot her silent story down the long table. Looking up, she saw that the fuzzy-haired girl was gone.

Day after day, she slogged home after school, banging into the kitchen only to be assaulted by Princeling, his paws on her chest, hot breath like a sewage pipe in her face. Pauline and the Beast stealing one last smooch. Pauline's fingers stroking Glynis's cement-hard hair, Glynis—she was sure of it—smirking at Lucy out of the crow-tracked corner of her evil eye.

September bled into October, but it was still hot as July, too hot for blazers. School letting out under a cornflower sky, girls with their glinting, swinging hair bulldozing three abreast down the sidewalk, sleeves rolled to the elbows, books held to their lovely, budding chests, binders full of homework assignments no one was taking seriously yet written out in neat, fall handwriting, hearts dotting all the i's. Red and yellow leaves, hot and musky, kicked through and crunched underfoot, boys pitching them in handfuls, wrestling, falling onto the hoods of parked cars, begging for hilarious accidents.

Crushed with loneliness, desperate, she began to tag along with Sheila O'Meara of the fuzz-ball hair, trying to keep up with her brisk stride. Shoving in beside her during lunch, making stabs at audible conversation. Anything not to have to sit alone, because alone, she had trouble chewing, convinced that she was under covert, amused observation by the entire cafeteria, her jaw continually seizing, drooly chunks of sandwich tumbling down her front. Though of course, as Glynis so enjoyed reminding her, "No one's looking at you, believe me!" Which, of course, was worse.

Sheila wore her uniform skirt at regulation length, an inch below the knee. She clearly didn't care how she looked, her dark hair unfashionably short, indifferently combed, her glasses black and severe. She chewed with calm impunity. Instinctively, Lucy had identified her as an equal in solitude, a fellow haunter of lonely moors, though perhaps not quite such bleak ones.

"Do you ever read Russian novels?" she blurted as they walked, pulling up close to Sheila's right ear before it moved out of range again.

Sheila glancing back, slowing down a jot, a faint smile playing around her rather pretty lips. "Nyet, comrade," she said.

"Nyet, *tovarich*," Lucy corrected her sternly, just as a wall of man-flesh bore down on them from the opposite direction, four large boys, blazers off, loose ties flapping, bangs flecked with orange leaf bits. Their eyes narrowed as they quickly appraised and stepped around both girls as if skirting steaming mounds of excrement. The word "scrag" floated after them on gusts of snorty laughter.

Sheila hadn't even noticed; she was stepping lively again because she had two hours of violin practice to get through before supper. This certainly commended her; the violin was a very Russian sort of thing to be involved with.

"You're a Renaissance girl," Lucy told Sheila warmly. "You're probably good at lots of stuff." Before she could stop them, the words, "I have an aunt, my aunt Zoshia, who lives in Moscow," leapt unbidden from her mouth. "I visited her two summers ago and took violin lessons from Grigory, that's her dear friend who plays in the Leningrad Symphony and also for the Bolshoi Ballet."

"Really? What book are you on?"

"Well, they don't use books in Moscow. The Soviet system is, you just play by ear. My aunt is going to send me a balalaika for my birthday. I learned to play that too. I also had my own dancing bear, you know, the kind with the muzzle on. His name was Boris."

"Wow. You've been a busy girl." With that, Sheila was off at a trot, leaving her in the leafy dust.

Sometimes Sheila disappeared before Lucy could find her, leaving her to walk home alone past red-kneed girls huddling in groups around the football field pretending to watch their bantam and junior boyfriends tackle dummies and run laps in their snug knee pants and gladiator shoulder pads. The girls passed around a hairbrush, bending to brush from the nape, flipping their heads back up, long, straight hair all whipped in the same direction, like sails at a regatta. Backs to the wind, they shared a communal smoke, as she watched, feeling as if she were on safari, hunched in the bushes with binoculars, shivering. The raw wind needled with raindrops finally sent the girls running like a herd of gazelle that's scented the cheetah upwind, running with their binders over their heads, while the boys soldiered on, grunting and sliding in the mud, whistles piercing the air.

Dusk dropped early with a delicious smell of fireplaces, hearths and homes, *normal* ones! She could keep moving, head down, maybe over to Loony Street to check in with the Sisters; it had been a long time, maybe they'd missed her. On the other hand, if she loitered a while, the boys would soon come her way, cleated shoes hanging from their shoulders, hair damp, cheeks pink from the shower. So she slumped on a bus stop bench to wait, willing herself into invisibility as they passed, scanning the horizon as disinterestedly as a lioness after lunch, though her peripheral vision greedily took in the real story: Did they look? Did they notice her? Did they laugh?

Lights began to wink on in houses. Behind picture windows, she imagined big guy feet in white socks resting on hassocks, smiling moms dishing up gargantuan portions of meat and potatoes. A boy, let's call him Toby, just home from football practice, cuffs his cute sister: Get off the phone, fink! But Kitten, because what else would she be called, was growing out her bangs, and had to discuss it with Amy and Kath! And now, hey ho, Dad's home! Jovial, capable, protective, hopelessly corny old Dad! Say! What're you kids up to this weekend? Toby's forthcoming but doesn't mention beer. Who's for poached eggs tomorrow, twinkles Mom, in her ruffled apron and pearls. Upstairs, Kitten cries, Mom! Make Timmy get out of my room! Aw gee, pouts freckle-faced Timmy, stumping down the stairs, cuddling a wiggly puppy. But Mom knows, she understands this is a delicate time for Kitten. She reprimands Timmy gently in soft, Greer Garson tones, as Dad looks on, beaming; Mom's still his old-fashioned girl, stymied by high school slang and the louche ways of the young. And now Kitten trips downstairs, dainty in a fluffy pink sweater, her perfect Summer Blonde hair falling to her shoulders, the very picture of youthful dignity and gentle grace. Dad, she begins softly, cuddling up to him on the sofa: Do you think the boys will ever like me? Well, back in the Bronze Age, Kitten, when I was a pup, he begins, pulling her onto his brown-trousered knee, I fell in love with a girl who looked almost exactly like you do now, the dearest girl in all the world—and Kitten sighs as she realizes that Daddy's right, as always: being self-assured and popular means nothing more nor less than being true to your own sweet self.

Oh! If she were only Kitten material, with the sweetest smile on earth, that crinkled her pretty eyes, dimpled her rosy cheeks, made the whole darn world glad to be alive! And if she were, then what if she . . . what if she *died?* Or were murdered! Got kidnapped by a sex fiend, who raped and strangled her! But would any sex fiend consider her worthy of raping and strangling? And, say he did—what would Daddy say? Would he forget all about Milena and slash his wrists on the spot in despair? Would Pauline collapse with grief, roll on the floor, wail her head off? Or, say she got disemboweled, how about that? Say someone tore out her guts from the outside, just reached in and yanked, everything ripping and coming out in chunks. Would *that* get people upset? Like Glynis, for instance? Or would she just laugh? Would she and Pauline just mop up the mess and forget her in a week, same as Pauline forgot Daddy, same as Daddy forgot her?

Her throat closed. Scorching tears welled, were stifled. Stupid, stupid shit, all of it! Toby and Kitten? Please! Good old understanding Daddy? Don't make me fuckin' *barf!*

Springing to her feet, she marched, head down, homeward, praying not to meet anyone she knew.

In time, though, Sheila seemed to have become resigned to her insistent company. This was a hopeful sign, though she couldn't rid herself of the suspicion that she'd been taken on as some kind of science project, Sheila drawing her out with cheery curiosity, as if watching unstable gases interacting. Saying, "Hmmm," nodding and pondering, sometimes laughing out loud.

On the walk home, they often covered nine blocks with Lucy speaking only Russian, asking things like, "How long will we be stopping at Sevastopol?" or declaring stoutly, "I am dizzy, my forehead is hot and I have chills." If she couldn't remember the real words, she made it up, but tried to keep the gibberish to a minimum; Sheila wasn't stupid, and she might catch on. In an attempt to affect the look of a young Soviet miss, she'd pinkened her chalky cheeks with circles of rouge filched from Glynis's purse back in the summer while the ladies were out grilling in the sun. Made two thin braids of her flat, brown hair, tied a babushka over it. Pulled her blouse out over her uniform skirt, belting it the way Tolstoy did, using the tie from her bathrobe. It was the best she could do without access to fur.

Sheila simply flicked the two sorry braids over her shoulders, saying, almost tenderly, "It would be funny if it weren't . . . tragic."

When she wasn't pontificating in Russian, she tried to worm her way into that mysterious inner place where the secret of her friend's unflappable calm and cheer resided. Needling, "When are you gonna let me hear you play that fiddle?" She thought Sheila must be amateur-hour terrible, because really, she was only fourteen, and the violin was *hard*. Besides, if anyone on earth *should* have been playing the violin, it was she herself, with her riotous Slavophile blood, and intimate acquaintance with the most remote and desolate reaches of the human soul. How could sedate, plodding Sheila have anything to do with that squalling, sobbing thing?

Every day they walked a little farther together, as the leaves blew down and the snows blew in, and every day Sheila quickened her pace, waved and escaped. Loath to go home so soon, she would trudge the beaten path to the bottom of Loony Street, to the edge of the lake, dusk falling fast, only a raw pink strip still visible at the horizon of a leaden sky, too proud finally to knock on the Loony Sisters' door, but not too proud to drop her books and spin in ecstatic circles at the lake's edge, in her childish plaid coat, arms outstretched, eyes shut, crying, "Oh Mother Russia, come and save your lost child, who has wandered so far from the steppes and the deep birch forests!" Imagining, against all sense, that her father could hear her from across the water, stopping dead in the middle of a tedious chat with his Milena, ears pricked, heeding the siren call of the girl he left behind.

One day, two weeks before the start of the Christmas holidays, she'd put her foot down. Refusing to be shooed away, she dogged Sheila all the way to her front door.

Sheila's house was in a better neighbourhood than hers. It looked like a big, tippy farmhouse, yellow with green shutters, lopsided additions tumouring out the sides. Barren oaks and maples surrounded it with a delicate filigree, like a Christmas tree ornament. It had no window without a coloured glass bauble, an artful drape of lace or a sleeping cat. The front door was on the side.

As Sheila approached the door and Lucy stood in the road kicking a lump of ice, Sheila's mother leaned out between the billowing white curtains of an upstairs window, shouting, "For goodness sake, Shee, it's freezing! Bring your friend inside!"

Her very heart had ceased to beat.

Yes! Inside! Inside her friend's house—my *friend's* house, ha *ha*, Glynis—where she took off her boots and walked in her socks on splintery hardwood floors that dipped in soft hollows. There was a warm, white kitchen with geraniums in the windows and two scowling grey tiger cats on top of the fridge. There was a hallway so long it felt like an underground burrow, winding round and round, descending straight into the embracing earth. She followed Sheila into a dim, low-ceilinged central room with a deep-red carpet woven with threadbare blue peacocks. Friendly little orange lamps winked in all the corners. Everywhere she looked, alcoves and window seats, and books; books lining the walls, piled on tables, spilling onto the floor. She was astounded: could plain, pedestrian Sheila really have sprung from such reckless, Bohemian disarray?

Sheila flung her coat onto a chair, kissed her mother. "This is Lucy," she said, adding after a beat, "The one I told you about."

Lucy turned in a full, bedazzled circle. All the furniture was draped in flowery throws, no two alike: hyacinths and roses, chrysanthemums and pansies. There was a grand piano with a fringed purple shawl that hung to the floor. A bass fiddle stood in one of the corners. Two guitars lay on a long coffee table like a companionable married couple at the beach. Even the knick-knacks were musical: dusty brass harps and carved wooden mandolins.

On top of the piano sat a photograph of a beautiful young woman with auburn hair, chin uplifted, eyes alight with confident hope. Mrs. O'Meara noticed her looking.

"That's our Colleen," she said, smiling and rubbing her hands together like Baba Yaga gloating over her treasures in a Russian folk tale. "Our budding concert pianist." There was a glamourous, deliciously soothing hint of New York in her soft, contralto voice. So unlike Pauline's uncouth hoot.

"My cousin Grushenka is a concert pianist," Lucy put in briskly. "She plays with the Bucharest Philharmonic." A crash of music filled the room, preventing her from elaborating further. Someone was sitting at the piano, slashing it to ribbons, making birds fly out of it.

"That's Hardee," shouted Sheila in her turn, waving toward the shadowy figure hunched over the keys. "My disreputable brother. Hardee har har." Hardee took no notice, pounding and banging, as if painfully aware of his hackneyed entrance into this amateurish play entitled, "Here Come the O'Mearas!"

"That's Scriabin," beamed Mrs. O'Meara. She was a tiny thing, barely up to Lucy's shoulder. Her heap of messy dark red hair with an inch of grey roots was held up with a thousand pins in a most becoming Slavic manner. She wore a black turtleneck sweater that fell to her knees. Lucy nodded knowingly at her remark, assuming she was describing Hardee's technique: scriabbing. It sounded about right.

Sheila leaned over Hardee's shoulder, turning a page of his music, reading along as he played. Lucy had never heard music like this before, certainly not on the classical music station she still dutifully listened to with half an ear. And snooty as her father had gotten about highbrow music, there had only ever been one classical record at home: *Mantovani Plays the Strauss Waltzes*, listened to only on Christmas day, she and Pauline and Daddy all sitting stiff as boards on their clunkety beige furniture. This stuff of

Hardee's was from a different universe. It sounded like trucks being driven over cliffs by weeping, cursing drivers.

The music unsettled her, but she had an immediate interest in Hardee, a lone boy, not part of a sneering, threatening group, possessed—she assumed—of a penis and wearing it in the same room she was in. It was an interest that needed some kick-starting; Hardee was chubby and wore a tight argyle vest that rode up. His whitish-blonde hair was fuzzy like Sheila's, but it did curl fashionably over his collar. There was also the shadow of—yikes!—a moustache forming an anchor under his festively reddened nose. Splotches of high colour in his cheeks made him seem impetuous, temperamental, a tortured artiste playing his heart out in a Saint Petersburg salon. His big black glasses reminded her of her father.

"Hardee's leaving for Europe in the spring," hollered Mrs. O'Meara over the din. "This is his sabbatical year; next September he's off to Juilliard." She smiled like the Good Witch Glinda as Hardee moved into a slower, quieter piece. Sheila had disappeared down a dark side burrow, and Mrs. O'Meara also melted away into the shadows, leaving Lucy alone with him and the slow, round rumble he was coaxing from the piano, bent low over the keys, almost licking them into this frightening, ominous music. But then he segued into Mozart, which she only knew was Mozart because Sheila materialized for an instant in the doorway and said, "Mozart." It tinkled like Christmas decorations in a high wind.

Reluctantly, she followed Sheila to her room, which she shared with yet another sister, Marjorie, a flame-haired junior version of herself, twelve years old and serious as the grave. She was hauling her cello, a reddish-brown monster violin, out of its coffin case and onto her narrow bed, where it took up the entire space.

"Did you work on that adagio passage?" Sheila asked her, flipping through the music on her stand. She'd forgotten Lucy entirely. Marjorie perched on the edge of her bed and mournfully addressed her plaid kiddie slippers.

"I still can't get it. Istvan keeps saying, 'Lighten, lighten, lighten,' but when I try to loosen up, I start to panic, and I lose the tempo." She pronounced the three "lightens" as if she were Bela Lugosi.

"Who's Istvan?" Lucy wanted to know. Sheila replied without looking at her, "Our music tutor."

Lucy sat down on Sheila's neat chenille bed. Rummaging in her bag, she extracted the half pack of cigarettes she'd found in the school washroom that morning.

"*Gday vahgon dla kuryashchikh?*" she asked, meaning, where is the smoking car, not precisely the phrase she wanted, but who was to know? Sheila ignored her.

"Can I smoke, tovaritch?"

"In the living room," snapped Sheila, eyes on her music.

"But I want to hear you play!" Lucy enthused, with a winning smile. Marjorie scowled at her from beneath nonexistent eyebrows. Sheila lifted her violin out of its plush, royal blue bed. Over her shoulder Lucy could see the page of music on its stand, festooned with garlands, trellises and curlicues, fairly choked with black ivy. She made out the name Tchaikovsky at the top. Russian stuff! This was going to be a treat!

Sheila raked her bow back and forth, adjusted some knobs. Lucy leaned back on her elbows, waiting for the screech, settling in for a chuckle. With a sudden, almost violent movement, Sheila slid the violin into position under her chin, wobbling a bit to find her stance. There was something scary about it all, like children in a concentration camp: far too much gravity and dignity for someone so young.

There followed two heartbeats of silence. Lucy jumped right in.

"Can I try?" If she could just get into that imposing, arty stance, she bet she could make that sucker sing.

"Not a chance." Sheila drew the bow back and forth a few more times, pushed her glasses up her nose, squinted at her music, and then, like a thunderclap, began to play. The trellises and garlands leapt like tongues of fire from the page.

Lucy's spine curled and shrivelled. Her stomach started to hurt.

Sheila was good.

Sheila was really, really good, and she, Lucy, was crushed, trampled flat with annihilating inadequacy and loneliness. No one had ever touched her the way Sheila touched that violin. And it got worse: Marjorie lifted her cello, set it between her white, freckled knees, and with that same sudden movement began sawing away, raising the underworld like black smoke from beneath the floorboards, turning the whole wide world as bleak and barren as Siberian midnight.

But a half hour after leaving the O'Meara house, she'd forgotten her humiliation, engulfed as she was with O'Mearaness, longing to be back in that house, burrowing inside all that warmth and coziness. Every day after school she stuck like a burr to Sheila all the way home, earning her keep by declaiming passages inexpertly memorized from Pushkin. When they arrived, she leapt in before the door had a chance to slam, tiptoeing down the hall after her friend like a feral cat, its face gashed, one ear askew. Mrs. O'Meara always smiled and clucked when she saw her, insisting, "Please, call me Anny, sweetie."

After a week or so, she no longer trailed Sheila to her room to sit and listen meekly to snatches of music played over and over, to ceaseless talk of *accelerandi* and *glissandi, cantabile* and *contrary motion*. Instead she stayed in the living room gazing at Hardee, who was invariably at the piano. Her staring finally threw him off; he stopped abruptly, his hands still splayed over the keys.

"So what kind of music do you like, Lucy?"

"Uhm. Uhm. I don't know. Whuh, like, most of, everything, sort of, but, oh but, you're gonna think I'm stupid, ha ha, uhm, but." She needed to employ brute force to bring her floundering, run-amok face back under stern, Soviet control. "I like anything Russian."

"Rimsky-Korsakov? Mussorgsky? Rachmaninoff?"

"My four all-time favourites!"

"Do you like Dillon?"

Who?

"Sure. Who doesn't?"

"You look like you would." He smiled at her. He sounded sincere!

"Oh yeah. Dillon is great!"

"Come on!" he cried, jumping up to lead the way down a brand-new tunnel, turning to make sure she was following, as if she hadn't scrambled to her feet in ecstatic terror, willing to follow him through the gates of hell. A boyfriend! A done deal! This was friendship master class: Glynis would choke on her own shrivelled heart! A sharp left, and she was standing in the doorway to his bedroom, blinking in the overhead light that cruelly revealed what an overheated complexion he had, how frowsy and old-womanish his hair was. But never mind! Where should she sit? His bed wasn't made! Aieeee! She couldn't look. But Hardee patted a pile of cushions near the door—wild!—and she sank down, hands folded primly in her lap, praying he wasn't noticing how bloodless and breastless she was in this pitiless light.

There was a hi-fi in the corner, albums all over the floor, frightening things featuring moody-looking men with patent-leather hair looming behind pianos and oboes, men with names containing many y's and z's, men threatening Sonaten and Kantatas and Klavier Konzerts. Hardee reached into the pile, pulled out a Dillon album—oh, *Dylan*—who turned out to be a glowering guy in a plain shirt who looked like he had a lot of things he needed to get off his chest.

"This'll blow your mind," Hardee grinned, extracting the record. Excitement had fogged his glasses, making her think, Ewww. But never mind! She wriggled down into her cushions as the record started. Hardee took up a battered guitar from the floor, began strumming along.

One track, two, three: not even a pistol-whipping could make her admit she was bored senseless. Dying sharecroppers in shacks lined with newspaper, tumbleweeds, cupboards full of dust. Yawn. Broken plows, spavined horses, hollow-eyed children under lowering skies. All the distress and mayhem of a Russian novel, but without the sleighs and the complicated patronymics, it was a monotonous drag. Hardee changed records. Bob seemed to be cracking jokes, and Hardee keeled over, clutching his sides. Lucy didn't get it, but pretended to, grinning like a chimp.

She walked home afterward, lank hair blowin' in the wind, a bilious grin etched on her face. By bedtime, the mild nausea of induced love had worn off. She was in love for real. Argyle would forever be sacred. Her heart felt as huge and cloud puffed as a Dakota sky. Unable to sleep, she sat on the cold floor by her bed writing a poem for Hardee cribbed from the back of an album he'd lent her.

I feel such a warmness
An who t'tell?
An I'm a burstin' with singin'
Out here an where
The crows . . .

The end. The crows cawed, wheeling away over the horizon. Who was she kidding? Hardee was just humouring her. And would continue to, unless she sharpened up her look but good. With grim purpose, she flipped open the latest issue of *Seventeen*. From every page, girls gaped up at her, raffish, ice cool, impeccably turned out. Appalled at the turnip face gazing hungrily down at *them,* they averted their lovely eyes, hugged their knees, tossed their sleek heads like the feisty little fillies they were.

Over the next week she and Hardee listened to the same albums, over and over. It was the price of admission into his inner sanctum.

"This is *protest* music," he explained with reverence, his face all rosy and bothered. She couldn't imagine what *he* could have to protest about, unless it was his hair, but the times they are a'changin', she was given to understand—take that, Pauline and your senile relic of a consort—and sure, she was with him so far, until they had to tromp back out to the desolate prairie and fret some more about hate and strife. She had developed a pimple on the side of her nose so huge it throbbed visibly along with the music; that's what bothered *her*, never mind Ban the Bomb and Masters of War. Hard rain and branches dripping blood just wore her out. Play me the one about Peggy-O with the yaller hair! Let's pump some *juice* into this corpse of a romance!

Instead, Hardee took up one of his several guitars and, sporting vampirish purple picks on all the fingers of his right hand, played her his own version of *The Lonesome Death of Hattie Carroll*. Steel strings buzzed like locusts as he rasped away in his Dylan voice, wheezing into a harmonica scaffolded to his face like a giant retainer. From down the hall she could hear Sheila and Marjorie scraping and groaning, an eerie accompaniment from another century.

Afterward, there was the usual sermon. The rich could kill the poor with impunity, Hardee informed her, as if she hadn't already had that message clobbered home in the fourteen hundred identical stanzas she'd just sat through. Hardee droned away about Ginsburg, the Merry Pranksters, the Berkeley Free Speech Movement, the threat of ground troops moving into Vietnam: he knew everything. She nodded away, her eyebrows climbing to painful heights. More albums lay stacked up for her listening pleasure: Theodore Bikel. Pete Seeger. Leadbelly. Hardee, grinning fit to split, asked her if she liked jazz, pointing to an entire cupboard of albums behind his head. Her spirits howled a silent NOOO even as she compelled her facial muscles to register delighted anticipation.

But he wasn't as finicky as Sheila: he let her try his guitar. The thing sat bulky as a child in her lap as he taught her a few simple chords, G major, E minor, A seventh, pressing her fingers one by one onto the strings, which cut like razor wire.

"It'll stop hurting once your fingers have gotten callused," he told her, letting her touch his fingertips, which were tough as cowhide. The touch felt like a kiss. It made her stomach heave.

Later, she wandered into Sheila's room. "What would you do if Hardee and I got married?" she asked.

Sheila didn't look up from her sheet music. "Have both of you committed."

The holidays imposed a ban on visits to the O'Mearas, where she sensed she'd be something of a fifth wheel. This left her with nothing to do but hulk in her room, dismally alone. The *Seventeen* girls were off to catch snowflakes on their tongues, off to skiing parties and Christmas toasts with their boyfriends' parents in front of the lavishly card-hung mantle. Kitten's first sip of sherry, she thought, as she cut out girl after girl, picturing herself as a coy dolly bird with Yardley eyes, a red velvet minidress, sparkly silver stockings. Holding a small glittery package containing some adorably girlish thing, tied up in a pink bow perfectly matched to her lipstick. Daddy just out of frame. "Look at you, Kitten! When did you become so grown-up, so beautiful?" Whoa! Was that a tear in his eye?

The *Seventeen* girls took rude exception to her staring. They threw their tawny arms wide for one another, crying out in luscious alto voices: "Oh my God! You look gorgeous!" "So do you! So do *you*!" "Let's *go* somewhere, okay? There's no *air* in here!"

Meanwhile, Glynis took Pauline to Mont-Tremblant for a weekend of skiing. Days later a Polaroid appeared, taped to the fridge door: her mother and the Abomination in matching pink parkas, exuberantly rubbing snow in each other's faces as if it were wedding cake.

Downstairs, Glynis littered the house with Yuletide gimcracks: candles with woodsy scents, gilded wreaths, crystal icicles and snowflakes dangling from the house plants. Shrieking, "We're just a couple of giddy gadabouts on the go," as she and Pauline charged off to Holt Renfrew to buy presents for Glynis's other friends. One night she dropped over with the very unfestive Mister MacGregor, a grumpy old sod in a crested blazer and tartan tie, who sat on the sofa jingling his car keys while Glynis and Pauline knocked back Screwdrivers and horsed around, singing in an inflamed way about sleighbells jingaling as they stumbled around the living room draping tinsel over the drab furniture.

Lucy ducked into the kitchen for a quick nip from the pitcher of booze, her bangs combed down to her nose for maximum privacy. But Glynis spotted her, squealing tipsily, "Look, Jerry. It's Cousin It!" Jerry just grunted, checked his watch. "Ha ha," murmured Lucy with a flush of glee. "Your husband hates you!"

She spotted Glynis's glamourous beaded Christmas purse thrown onto a kitchen chair, did a quick rifle-through for smokes and minor makeup items Glynis would never miss from her colossal stash. Upstairs in Smolensk, the door locked, she drew on cat's eyes, plumped up her thin, chapped lips with a thick topcoat of Where's the Fire red. Posing with an unlit cigarette, her meagre hair spindling over her shoulders like a spill of pins, she was forced to come to terms with the leaden death of all hope. She informed the fright in the mirror that she looked like Anna Karenina *after* her fated appointment with the train. A *week* after.

Falling onto her bed, she cracked open *Crime and Punishment* and read until she fell into a coma as sluggishly peaceful as freezing to death was reputed to be. Her dreams were complicated, long, and entertaining.

The holidays dragged like a barefoot trek from Moscow to Vladivostok. The door to Smolensk remained locked, while Glynis and Pauline sat outside in the driveway on their lawn chairs between the four-foot snowbanks. They wore their pink parkas, held sun reflectors before their faces like prayer books till they were both as crispy as burnt bacon. Glynis even exposed her chest to the sun, the skin cracked like a dry riverbed, blotched all over with dime-sized freckles.

On Christmas Eve, she would be leaving for Greece to spend the rest of the holiday with no-fun Jerry. She'd pulled every possible marital string to get Pauline invited along, but Jerry's kibosh was final, and there was no court of appeals.

On Christmas morning, after coolly receiving Lucy's gift of Rowntree chocolates, the small size, a very subdued Pauline, wearing a huge, fuzzy, snow-white turtleneck, another ill-advised gift from Glynis that made her look like a linebacker, presented Lucy with a pleated skirt and sweater set from Holt

Renfrew. Its subtle grey and lavender tones were terribly demure and refined. "Glyn thought the colours were lovely," she said, stroking the soft, expensive sweater with erotic intensity.

"I guess it's the thought that counts," Lucy said. "A good funeral outfit, should the occasion arise. You never know. Anyhow, if you'll excuse me, Mamushka, I have vocabulary to study." And with that, they'd headed off to their separate rooms to get the day over with as fast as possible.

The house was silent, save for wan carols emanating from the radio in Pauline's bedroom. They sat down at supper to a shriveled turkey and cranberry sauce still tube-shaped from the can. Lucy brought *Crime and Punishment* to the table. Pauline stared bleakly into space. In the evening, they silently took in some TV: the Queen's message, and a dispiriting holiday special featuring Andy Williams's giant bobbing head. If the entire holiday was going to be like this, there would be nothing for it but to drink a bottle of rubbing alcohol and cash in her chips for good.

After two more days of terminal ennui, she decided to throw caution to the winds and pay the O'Mearas an unannounced holiday call.

Neither Hardee nor Sheila was around. Anny opened the door with a breathless smile, crying, "Oh, my!" She had to hop backward as Lucy barged in, stamping her snowy boots on the mat, shrugging off her coat.

But what next? Lucy stood there awkwardly as Anny perched on a stool at the kitchen counter and resumed shelling peas. She didn't seem to mind having company, so Lucy pulled up another stool and watched her work, her small, quick hands, the curve of her neck, her elegant beige sweater. Her lovely russet hair looped and swirled onto her head with a tortoiseshell comb.

"My father should have married you," she offered, a little breathlessly, the notion of Anny as her mother warming her to the core. "He must have been undergoing a psychotic break when he chose my mother." Anny looked up, smiling uncertainly. "He ran off with this home-wrecker he met at work. But I wish him Godspeed, I truly do. It's a pity he couldn't meet you and Sheila and everybody. He would just adore you! You're his kind of people!"

She felt herself spinning, falling into the arms of a heavenly idea: what if Anny were to lead her down the burrowing hall to Colleen's empty room, throw open the door, kiss her cheek and say with a wistful smile, "We'd love for you to stay here, sweetie. It's so obvious you're meant to be one of us. We want you to make this your home from now on."

Yeah. Don't hold your breath, Lucy advised herself wryly.

She held her breath.

But Anny just nodded thoughtfully, hooked a fallen hank of hair behind one ear, began chopping carrots with a cleaver. Suddenly afraid that she might be bored, might just be putting up with her to be polite, Lucy decided to take a bold chance, turn on the klieg lights, step way out on a glamourous limb.

"My Aunt Zoshia wants me to come live with her in Leningrad."

That perked her up all right. "Why, Lucy, how exciting! You'll get a chance to visit the Hermitage." She pronounced it the French way. Lucy had no idea what she meant. She gave an emphatic nod.

"Yes, I expect we'll be going there first thing." After a moment adding, "I'm pretty sure it's on her street."

"Your last name is Brickwood, if I'm not mistaken. I'm guessing the Russian roots are on your mum's side?"

"Please. She couldn't be Russian if she were locked up in a gulag for all eternity. No, my father's real name was Bryknoodjinsky. He changed it when he came here. Nobody could spell it, so they made him."

"How interesting! What brought him all the way to Canada? It must be terribly difficult to leave the Soviet Union."

"He's not a Soviet spy, if that's what you're thinking. He came here when he was ten. His father had this raging quarrel with Stalin, and the family had to flee for their lives in the middle of the night. In a sleigh, wrapped in fur rugs, which they had to take the bells off of, the sleigh, I mean, so they could race across the frozen steppes in silence. Both their horses dropped dead in harness from the strain and they had to cross over into Finland on foot, with their feet wrapped in rags because they'd been forced to barter their shoes for grain. From there—"

"Excuse me a moment, while I get started on my bread." Anny took a bowl full of swollen dough from the fridge, slapped it onto a flour-dusted spot on the kitchen table, and rolled up her sleeves. "I started making my own bread three years ago, and it's a lot of work, but so healthy. No one will touch the store kind anymore."

"So, because I'm of Russian descent, I've made it my business to read all the famous Russian classics, in the original Russian, of course. It's not a literature that's widely known or appreciated. My math teacher caught me reading Dostoyevsky in class and he yelled, 'Put away that damned Dostakovsky!' That's the kind of ignorance I'm forced to deal with on a daily basis."

Anny plunged her fists into the dough, beads of sweat dampening her forehead, an unbudgeable smile playing around her lips.

"Hardee was reading French novels last year, in French," she said, concentrating hard on her kneading. "He tackled Proust, of all people. When I saw the size of that book, my heart went out to him, but he got through all three thousand—"

"Did you ever notice how in Dostoyevsky's novels, they have same-day mail service? Russia is so advanced! People write letters and then they get an answer back in a couple of hours. Also, husbands and wives live on separate floors in their houses, if they're rich. My father instituted that practice at our house, pretty much. He spent many nights sleeping in the lower quarters, because—"

Diablo, one of the three O'Meara cats, leapt from the floor straight onto Anny's kneading surface. Anny shrieked, then laughed. "Oh, my baby! Are you jealous of Lucy? Are you wanting some of Mama's snugglies?"

Lucy, outrageously upstaged, groped blindly for a new, more promising tack. "Where's Colleen? Doesn't she come home for Christmas? Is she gone for good?"

"How sweet of you to ask!" cried Anny. Her loving eyes strayed to the refrigerator where a newspaper photo of Colleen was taped. Lucy slid dutifully off her stool to go and peer at it.

Beneath Colleen's glowing face was the depressing caption: *Young activist looks forward to speeches, agendas, resolutions.*

"What's she an activist in?"

"Where do I start?" cried Anny, still kneading and punching, long, loose tendrils of hair dangling over her work. Colleen, it turned out, was a brilliant musician, but she'd decided to take a year off from her studies to go to Sierra Leone with the Peace Corps and whip Africa into some kind of shape. "She's extremely self-actualized. You'd love her; everyone who knows her just adores her to death. She's a regular Mother Courage. Now she writes us every week, and . . . wait, I got a letter just yesterday." She slid a blue airmail envelope out from under another cat on top of the fridge and opened it, perching the delicate gold reading glasses hanging from a chain around her neck onto the bridge of her nose. "Ah yes, here we are. You'll love this. *Oh Mum, this is my peak experience! And how beautiful the children are here, in the midst of so much want! Of course, there is sadness too. Yesterday, a tiny babe died in my arms, and oh, Mum, part of me died with it! And yet, life goes on, does it not?*"

From beneath an avalanching sludge heap of limitless personal shortcomings, Lucy mumbled in reply, "If that child were mine, I'd fry it in a frying pan and eat it."

Anny looked startled for the briefest of seconds before clearly deciding that she couldn't possibly have heard right. She read a few more lines of the letter silently, lovingly, to herself, then folded it back into its envelope.

"I quote Solyony, from *The Three Sisters*, a famous play by Anton Chekhov," Lucy bumbled on, a betraying edge of hysteria creeping into her voice. "Solyony is my all-time favourite play character. He had a highly critical attitude and he could see through everybody and all their pretensions and he wasn't afraid to say so. Nobody understood him. He's the man of my dreams."

"Ah, dreams," sighed Anny, picking out the one word she could relate to. "Dreams are special, aren't they? Our little life dramas, all jumbled up and out of sequence, like riddles we have to decipher. Sometimes at night I visit with people far, far away, and when I check with them later, they've dreamed about me too on the exact same night! Often, when you care deeply about someone—"

"Who would care deeply about me?" Lucy was perilously close to tears, to dropping to her knees to beg: Please let me stay! Let me be one of you!

But it went no further because the door banged open and Sheila, Anny's rightful owner, bustled in, her cheeks rosy from the cold, wearing a kid's tall, pompommed toque. She was carrying a portfolio of sheet music which she waved gleefully in Anny's face. New Year's Eve at the O'Meara house was traditionally Opera Night, and this year, the whole family would be singing *Turandot* right off the page for the amusement of relatives and friends. A night of wet-your-pants hilarity, with prizes in many categories. Last year they did *The Magic Flute*, Sheila bagging the awards for Worst Singer, Best Costume.

"This year I shall be gorgeously appareled in the Oriental manner," she crooned, swanning about the hall as Lucy stumped after her to her bedroom. Sheila yanked up her bedspread and wrapped it around her shoulders, launching into the first few lines of *Tu che di gel sei cinta*, her signature tune.

Lucy feigned disinterest, scoffing, "You don't even know what the words mean."

"You who are enclosed in ice."

"Why, because *you're* so warm and special?"

"It's what the words mean, bonehead."

She waited for an invitation to this opera extravaganza, but none was forthcoming. "What are you doing here anyway?" Sheila wanted to know. "I have practicing to do."

Offended, Lucy tossed her head and made her way to the dim, friendly living room where soft, swirly music floated, not from Hardee's red-knuckled hands but from the stereo, lacing the air with ornamental flourishes and startled, sudden turnings. There was a fire in the fireplace and shortbread cookies shaped like pine trees and poinsettias in a dish on the coffee table. Marjorie could be heard down a maze of tunnels playing slow and heavy, dragging down the eddying whirls from the stereo with chains and lead weights.

She sat forlornly at the piano, begging her heart to leap into her fingers and begin scriabbing professionally over the keys. There was so blisteringly much she needed to express! But the piano refused her, sat mute. She plinked out a few thin, sour notes of *She Loves You*.

"Could you please not?" requested Sheila, who appeared in the doorway looking as pissed off as Lucy had ever seen her. In a huff, she got up from the piano, threw on her coat and left without saying goodbye to anyone.

All the way till the middle of March, she trudged home alone, but the snub sailed right past Sheila, who was now picked up after school every day and whisked off somewhere. Bereft, Lucy had tried breaking the ice with another unprepossessing, unpopular girl. Crashing down beside her in the cafeteria, she grasped the table with white knuckles, and gasping for breath, channeled old Sofia, croaking, "I just found out I have tuberculosis. And leukemia!" The girl gaped at her as a wondrous fantasy spun itself with lightning speed in Lucy's head: the entire student body parting like the Red Sea, shouting, Make way! Make way! as she stumbled bravely down the hall. Teachers, their contorted faces awash with tears, leaning in to offer a kind word. Heartfelt applause greeting her gentle pronouncements of gratitude, her insistence that she was doing wonderfully well and that no one need worry. Love and admiration zooming her way from all directions like iron filings to a magnet.

Her new candidate friend gathered up her books and her lunch tray and bolted for her life.

And then it was spring. The snowbanks shrank to shit-garnished cinder heaps. Icicle spikes loosened from the eaves in clumps, crashing to the ground like stacks of dishes. Maniacal birds swooped from tree to bud-swelling tree. Plodding home from school, she cut across soggy lawns, sinking inches deep into mud, her coat flapping open, solitude and futility weighing on her like the stuffy winter coat it was high time she put away.

Her life, a sluggish river under a scorching sun, had baked down to mud. She was able to hold her own academically by virtue of a nearly photographic memory that enabled her to reproduce pages of text at will during exams, but she had long realized she was virtually invisible to her teachers and fellow students, too invisible even to bully, completely shut out from the ambient swirl of sports, dances, crushes, outfits. She came home to a house in which Glynis sucked the oxygen out of every room, except for the times when she wasn't there, which was almost worse; she disappeared regularly into her own sumptuous life, blew hot and cold with Pauline, was sometimes gone for weeks. There were testy, tearful phone calls, receivers slammed down, Pauline slumped in a chair in front of the chattering TV, her old spirit nowhere in evidence, turning down ever rarer invitations from her other friends. And crying, when she thought Lucy couldn't hear her. The crying was truly awful—this was not her mother, this was some broken-willed, pinwheel-eyed love slave! Feeling exactly the way Daddy had made *her* feel.

But then the Beast would reappear, grey roots re-blonded, in Gucci boots, her knobby knees poking out under an Yves Saint Laurent Mondrian shift dress, bearing yet another of her extravagant, inappropriate gifts. Pauline would allow herself to be kissed on her submissive neck, abashed and blushing, not an ounce of pride in her. Murmuring, in a state of shock, "It's beautiful, Glyn," as she stroked the glossy fur of the mink jacket she'd just lifted from the billowing tissue of a gift box.

Lucy, coming in from the kitchen, had burst out laughing.

"That is the stupidest present in the universe! She'll look like a grizzly bear in that. And I bet it's just some old thing you don't want anymore." At this, the colour drained from her mother's face, which only made Lucy angrier. "You don't even know her! Where's she gonna wear that piece of junk, to clean out the garage in?"

Glynis turned to her with overhyped heartiness. "And how are you, Lucy? Bearing up under the social whirl, are we?" She proffered an envelope which Lucy, after a moment of resistance, took and opened. It was a birthday card.

"My birthday isn't even for two weeks!" Still, cowed, she skimmed through the purchased poetic sentiments, skipping straight to the bottom where Glynis had offered some timeless wisdom in her chicken-scratch hand: *Happy thoughts make for prettier feces*. It took her a minute. Oh. Faces.

"A thank you would be nice," Glynis purred. She was blocking the stairs, so there was no way Lucy could edge around her to escape to Smolensk. "Do we have any party plans for our big day?"

"Maybe."

"You know, I was wondering about that girlfriend you were seeing so much of before Christmas. Why don't you bring her home one afternoon so we could meet her? Unless, of course," and here she stopped to filch a cigarette from the pack in her purse and light up, "unless, of course, she's imaginary."

Pauline lay her mink on the arm of the sofa. "Please, let's not fight, okay?"

"I'm just curious," wheezed Glynis.

"Yes, she is imaginary, if you must know. I spent all those weeks last fall just walking the streets, brokenhearted."

"What's this friend's name?"

"I don't have to tell you."

"Interesting. Your mother told me you've cooked up imaginary friends before. Some girl, Linda, in elementary school. That you actually *were* walking the streets when you said you were at her house. That is so sad. Couldn't you at least—"

"Svetlana Pushkinova! That's her name. And why would I bring her here, so she could laugh at us? Her mother is beautiful! She has a real father, and he's an actual man! And she plays the violin! She's a genius!"

"I'm sure she is. I'm sure you're just the kind of friend a genius would seek out."

"Please, Glyn. It isn't worth—"

"Yes! Yes, I am! Geniuses are dying to hang out with me! But you, you're just the kind of friend who goes around giving people coats made out of dead animals just so they won't notice that your face could stop a train. Just so they'll let you kiss on them with that smoke stink all over you. Just so they'll—"

Pauline slapped her. Hard. Stunned, Lucy slapped back blindly, but missed. Glynis, gone dead white under all the Maybelline, reached out for her mother's hand, and in an instant, Lucy understood that she was entirely, irrevocably alone.

Spinning on her heel, she banged out the back door. Ran-walked all the way to the O'Mearas' without raising her eyes from the sidewalk. Rang the doorbell under dripping eaves. Waited, rang again. And again.

It was Anny who answered, at last.

"Why, it's Lucy! I thought you might have left for Leningrad!" She stepped back as Lucy plowed her ferocious way into the kitchen. Sheila, sitting at the table reading and scarfing a doughnut, looked up with a bemused expression. The familiar, cinnamon warmth enveloped Lucy like a cashmere blanket. "Not yet. I'm waiting till after my birthday."

"Oh, when's that?"

"In two weeks."

"And it's your *quinceanera* too, I'll bet! Isn't that exciting? I love birthdays!" Anny threw exuberant arms around her, exclaiming, for some reason, "Yay, team!"

Lucy could hardly believe the sweetness of this reception. "I wouldn't get too excited. No one's making any fuss at my house. Children of divorce often get lost in the shuffle."

"Why, we'll throw a party for you right here!" cried Anny. "A special dinner! Two weeks from today, Saturday night, how's that? Wowee Zowie! What fun!"

"What fun indeed," echoed Sheila, with almost indiscernible sarcasm.

"Just ignore my personal aging process," she breezed to Pauline on the Big Morning before noticing the envelope propped against her cereal bowl. She took a long time pouring in the milk, thoughtfully stirring her Trix, adjusting her chair several times before deigning to open the card, skimming through the Hallmark poetry with a censorious frown.

"Very nice, Mother, but I don't *have* a heart, I don't *have* dreams, and I don't *have* any hopes, so it's no use blathering on about them." She scanned the table and the kitchen counter. "Is this the only card?"

"If you're entertaining hopes and dreams of a birthday card from your father, allow me to disabuse you of that notion." Pauline, seeing Lucy's face and realizing how on the mark she'd been, softened a little. "Would you like me to make you some oatmeal?"

"It's my birthday, Mamushka! How about a bowl of fresh puke?"

Pauline was mixing a Duncan Hines cake when Lucy sailed through the kitchen at five o'clock, eyes outlined in black, lips chalk white.

"I hope that's not for me. I believe I made it clear that I have an outside engagement tonight. The O'Mearas are throwing me a bash." The door shut behind her with a satisfying ke-bang as she imagined Pauline slowly licking the beaters clean before dumping the bowl of batter down the sink.

She arrived on the O'Meara doorstep with a smile she couldn't control, the deposed princess at long last reentering her rightful realm.

But nothing much was doing. She sat alone at the dining room table waiting for the party to get off to its piddling start. Anny had made Shake n' Bake chicken and mashed potatoes, just as if it were any old supper. The rest of the O'Mearas filed in one by one, looking preoccupied. At the head of the table sat the rarely glimpsed Mr. O'Meara, rudely reading, his rumpled grey head just visible over the *New York Times*. Mr. O'Meara, she knew, wrote books about music history, something she realized, shocked at the ferocity of her bitterness, that she would love to rub her own father's face in: See, Daddy? Here's what a *successful* writer looks like! Imagine all the things he can give his beloved daughters!

Apart from Mr. O'Meara and Anny, the attendees included Sheila, Marjorie, Istvan the music tutor, and Hardee. And Hardee's new girlfriend, Violet, who had waist-length, glossy brown hair parted down the middle like a real New York folkie. She was turned out in a chic black sweater displaying a healthy two inches of cleavage that Hardee could barely pry his eyes away from. Lucy could feel her own visible ribcage glowing like neon through her blouse.

Anny kept talking to Violet as if *she* were the honoured guest, calling her Pretty Vi, spilling intimate details about her new boyfriend, like, "Hardee's just an old scare bear in the morning!" Violet grinning, mussing Hardee's horrible hair.

Should she spring her leukemia diagnosis on them? She pictured Anny, her eyes brimming, voice cracking. "Oh, beautiful, blithe spirit! You just keep astounding us! How brave you are, facing down chemo and still keeping up with your brilliant novel and your studies, leaving us all in the dust! Lucy, our cherished treasure! We will not know a glad moment until you are healed and well!"

And she, speaking softly from deep reserves of calm, understated strength, "There's no healing, Anny. There's only . . . waiting." Sheila's glasses fogging over. Hardee crushed beyond—

The doorbell chimed in the nick of time. Everyone jumped and then shouted in unison, "Uncle James!" In breezed an undulating gentleman with bee-stung lips and long, limp hair that he had to keep shaking out of his eyes. He pulled up a chair, sat in it backward. He wasn't staying, had only dropped in for a drink and a schmoozette. Suddenly the party began to feel like something out of a Chekhov play: the elderly teacher, the bachelor uncle, the mother and sisters, the distracted patriarch, the unsuitable suitor. Lucy's spirits rose several notches as Uncle James turned his sleek head her way.

"Is this the birthday girl I've heard so much about? Are you one of Sheila's musical friends?" He had a pronounced lisp, which she knew could mean only one thing.

"No, she's the one with the relatives in Leningrad," interjected Sheila. Marjorie snorted.

"Leningrad *and* Saint Petersburg," Lucy corrected her, elated at being the centre of attention but nervous too, feeling like some fool on Ed Sullivan who had to keep fifty plates spinning on sticks to maintain their interest. "I have a great-uncle Alyosha in Saint Petersburg who—"

"Oh, my dear," sighed Uncle James, with a delicate curl of his rosy lip. "Leningrad, darling, *is*—" but Sheila shot him a signal-laden look and he dropped his eyes, curbing his smile. Lucy, realizing her mistake too late, stung by the quiet mockery, informed him darkly, pointedly, "Just so you know. My mother's one too."

"One . . . what?" asked Uncle James, raising his head, looking straight into her eyes.

"*You* know," she replied, squinting across the table at him. Someone—it had better not be Hardee—kicked her under the table.

Uncle James gave her a long, appraising look. Very long; she was the one to blink first. A burning blush climbed northward from her neck as raw panic set in: had she gone too far, completely blown it? Would they turn on her now as one and order her to get out? On her *birthday?*

But Uncle James rolled resolutely on. "The real reason I stopped by was to congratulate our lovely and supremely gifted young Sheila."

Anny took her daughter's hand, giving it a happy little squeeze. "Sheila's going to begin preparing for the Paganini Competition in Genoa, did she tell you, Lucy? She's taking extra classes at the Conservatoire every afternoon. Istvan thinks she'll be ready to compete within three years, if she really applies herself. We're hoping to have a champion sitting here at our table by the fall of 1968!" The whole family broke into spontaneous, sustained applause; even Mr. O'Meara putting down his paper, pounding the table like he was in the House of Lords, while Anny gushed, "And kudos to you, darling Istvan, for mentoring her so magnificently."

The geezer at the end of the table, whom Lucy had only registered as a freckled, bald head and a long nose with a bulb at the end, nodded and smiled.

Istvan was old, old, old, a grey man in a droopy grey cardigan, a bow tie pinned crookedly to his starchy collar, a cane hanging over the back of his chair. She dimly recalled Sheila telling her that he played piano, viola and cello, had performed with several major symphony orchestras, had toured Europe with his own string quartet, and had taught in Paris, Rome and Budapest. So she'd better be on her guard with any Eastern European references. If he caught her in a fib, who knew where that cane might land?

Catching her staring, he raised his head and winked at her, droll and slow, as if his eyelids were all gummed up.

"I didn't catch your name, dear," he said in his I-vant-to-bite-your-neck accent.

"It's Lyudmilova."

Sheila spluttered into her napkin. "Her name is Lucille. As in Ball." But Anny just patted her hand. "Well, if she wants to be called Lyudmilova, we'll indulge her," she said. Lucy raised her eyes to her in abject gratitude, but Anny was already up from the table, bustling toward the kitchen, wearing a sari, of all things, purple and gold, and silver earrings that grazed her shoulders.

"And vat do you like to do vit your free time, Lyudmilova?"

She cleared her throat. "Well. For starters, I'm a fluent Russian speaker." She almost launched into Russian right then and there but stopped herself in time; Istvan might not be the undiscerning audience she was accustomed to. "I also read widely, not just Russian classics in the original language, but also the classic works of many lands. I've finished every book I've ever started."

"And on that note," drawled Uncle James, rising languidly from his chair, "I'm off." He got up, raised a hand, waggled it like the Queen. "Toodles, darlings!"

"Love you bunches!" cried Anny, jumping up again to throw her arms around his neck.

"May I be excused?" asked Marjorie. Hardee and Violet had already left the table, disappearing down the burrow that led to Hardee's room.

"I am expecting to hear Shostakovich played to perfection," Istvan said mildly to his plate.

"I know," said Marjorie, a little crossly. "I'm going to work on it now."

"I vant to hear human voice in Shostakovich! Human voice vhen you play!"

"I know, I know. Human voice," repeated Marjorie before disappearing.

"I say nothing," said Istvan with the faintest of smiles. "Have I said a verd? I have not."

"Lucy studied violin in Leningrad," offered Sheila with a wicked smile. Istvan looked up with interest, opening his mouth to ask, "Vhere?" and "Vith whom?" But the dinner seemed to be officially over, Anny busy collecting plates, Sheila pushing her chair back, getting ready to make *her* escape. Once again, the leukemia story bubbled blackly to the surface: Don't trouble yourselves over me, all you happy O'Mearas. Personally, I *long* for the sweet release of death! She slumped, her eyes beginning to sting. "I mean, come *on*," she mumbled. "Not even dessert? Not even *cake*?"

Istvan looked inquiringly at her. She sucked back her tears, rallied grandly.

"Well. One thing I can't play too well is piano. It's because I've spent so much time with the violin and the balalaika. Maybe you could give me some pointers." After a moment, she added, "Sir."

Anny breezed by, plates in both hands. "Come, Lucy! Come Istvan! Into the living room, my loves!" So there *was* a cake after all, slices of which Anny brought to the alcoves and deep armchairs everyone had drifted to. Hardee poked logs in the fireplace as the general talk turned to music, with some extraneous Colleen-lore thrown in. Suddenly scalded with self-consciousness, her mouth gobbed up with cake and icing, Lucy realized she'd been cut cruelly adrift. If only, like Princeling, she could jam her head in beside people, force them to look down, pat her, scritch behind her ears.

She lay her plate on the floor, picked up a recorder from the little table next to her chair and sat for a long time, bleating into it. Nobody noticed.

Suddenly, Istvan was looming behind her.

"Shall ve sit at the piano and begin?" he asked, not unkindly, but neither taking no for an answer, hoisting her with surprising strength by one elbow. She dropped the recorder with a little yelp and followed him to the piano bench, slouching and sullen, as he lay his cane on the floor and eased himself down beside her.

"This, young lady, is octave. Beginning from middle C."

"I *know*," she said, but he wasn't listening. He played the scale once for her, very slowly. "Now you." He placed his veiny, spotted hand lightly over hers, directing the fingering, making her do it eight, nine times, to her exasperated sighs. This was only lesson one, and it was already hard and boring! Sheila must have learned all this when she was two, had moved ahead into realms of beauty, lightness and perfection that she, Lucy, would never attain if she practiced twenty-four hours a day for the next forty years.

Should she even be allowed to touch music with her grotesque skeleton fingers?

"I don't hear any human voice," she complained, while Istvan proceeded to demonstrate the G, D and A major scales, adding black keys one at a time, gabbling incomprehensibly about the function of sharps and flats, just making it *harder*.

"I don't get it! How come you can't just start at the right note and play them all the same? Just start higher up or lower down."

"No, no, my dear. That is not how the *clavier* verks. Every key is different, and every key is unique. D flat, for example, though played with the same notes, is not C sharp. D flat is *darker* key," he explained, darkly. "Surely you have learned this in Leningrad, my dear Lyudmil—"

"I really don't think I need any more lessons," she interrupted. "I already studied scriabbing *extensively* under an extremely diligent taskmaster in the Soviet Union." She swooped her hands up and down the keys, jabbing at random notes, banging, stomping on the pedal, muddying the noise, playing as ugly as she felt. Who knew, maybe this was how it was done; any minute now he'd cry out in astonishment: "Lyudmilova! You are touched vith genius!"

From the rose-covered armchair he was sharing with Violet Hardee sprang to his feet. "Lucy, if you don't cut that out, I'll come over there and break both your arms!"

Istvan, from behind, placed his splayed hands over hers, stilling them as if mercy-killing two wounded, twitching birds. She could feel his old-man breath on her neck, smell his old-man smell, tweedy and cologny, with distinct top and bottom notes of rot and decay, so used up and musty and sad, she almost screamed, so desperately did she need to shake him off.

He was bending close to whisper in her ear, an overheated puff of air, like sitting too close to a boiling hot radiator. The secondhand smell of his dinner crawled down her back, into her clothes. His hands on her shoulders were surely leaving radiation burns.

"I think you are good girl, Lyudmilova. Smart girl, brave girl. And very sad girl, yes?" She bit the inside of her top lip so hard she tasted blood. Her eyes stung as if they'd been socked.

"But banging, crashing is not useful, dear girl. Maybe you bang and crash so people vill see real Lyudmilova that is inside of you? But banging, crashing, this makes people vant to run avay. They see only sad, angry girl, telling tall tales, fighting vith everybody, vith everything. And only Lyudmilova suffers. People vant to be kind, but you make it hard for them. Do you understand me?"

"No," she spat back through a clog of snot and sobs that manifested in piggy snorts and horrid torsions of the face, the way boys in school used to crumple their features to mock crying girls. She sat rigid on the piano bench, then crashed down again onto the keys, using her elbows this time. But Istvan had let go and turned away, and nobody else was listening either.

She sat on her hands, head hanging, for twenty eternal minutes while the talk swirled around her, trying to get up the nerve to move. When it seemed at last that she had slipped through a crack in the floor and truly been forgotten, she slid off the bench and slunk into the empty kitchen.

Someone began playing the piano, properly, in the living room. She heard Violet laugh, then Sheila. She wiped her besnotted nose on a lace curtain, helped herself to a couple of chocolates from a box on the counter. Should she just leave? She badly wanted to go, but loathed the thought of the long walk home, the reentry. She loitered for five minutes, ten, waiting for Anny to perhaps appear, but Anny had forgotten her, she was disgusted with her, they were probably all laughing at her in there, having her birthday party without her.

She pulled on her coat, slipped out the door.

Pauline was alone on the couch in the living room, watching TV.

"How was it?" she asked in an uninflected tone. Her face looked overscrubbed, red and abraded, her eyes unusually small.

"It was wonderful, the peak of perfection. I'm so glad I've been given honourary membership in such an outstanding family. It's refreshing to be appreciated for a change, especially on milestone days such as this one."

Pauline sighed a sigh of uncharted depths, turned back to the giggling television as Lucy tripped up the stairs and slammed into her room.

She was certain she'd worn out her O'Meara welcome for all time, but on the following Monday, as she was coming out of Geometry, Sheila overtook her, wordlessly pressing an envelope into her hand before turning to walk away.

"What's this?"

Sheila, over her shoulder, called, "Open it and find out, dummy."

She waited till Sheila was out of sight to tear open the envelope. Inside was an invitation to the O'Meara Easter weekend spring concert, handwritten by Marjorie in an exotic script, six colours, three languages. The show was to begin at midnight on Saturday, would last till dawn of Easter Sunday. Scanning the programme, she read:

Vivaldi: Presto, Concerto no.2 in G minor, tempo impetuoso d'estate.

Bach: Ohne Satzbezeichnung. Concerto for two violins, strings and basso continuo, d-moll.

It went on and on. *Paganini.* Blabbity blah. *Massenet.* More blabbity blah. RSVP.

Easter weekend was five days away. She'd tell Pauline she'd been invited to a sleepover, her first ever. She felt simultaneously proud and deeply humiliated to be doing something so likely to meet with Glynis's grudging approval.

She arrived at the O'Meara house at nine that Saturday evening, far too early. She could hear rehearsing going on inside, whoops of laughter. She walked up and down the street in an intermittent drizzle till she saw cars begin to pull up, disgorging a startling number of people dressed, it seemed, for the Oscars. She walked away quickly, like any old passerby, returning twenty minutes later. Waiting till there was no one else in sight, she rang the bell.

Hardee answered, decked out in a thrift store tux and canary-yellow bow tie, his wispy hair greased back under a cocky beret.

"Lucy. Didn't know you were coming." He stood back so she could kick off her damp shoes, then walked away, leaving her to find her own way in.

The living room was set for an extravaganza. She stood in the entryway, her heart plump with excitement, thinking: Look at me, Daddy! Look at the wonderful artistic friends I have, the glamourous parties I'm invited to! The floral furniture had all been pushed to the walls, five rows of folding chairs fanning out to face four chairs and a harpsichord set in a semicircle next to the piano. Musical aunts and uncles and family friends, ladies in huge hats and ropes of beads swarmed the room, yammering and hugging. Uncle James, draped in a lime-green silk scarf, had one arm around Marjorie. Anny was working the room in a long, black satin skirt, her hair puffed up hugely and knotted in a Gibson Girl bun, passing around tall, thin glasses of something amber and alcoholic. And there was Sheila, also in a long skirt, clutching people's hands, double-cheek kissing like she was Maria Callas. Lucy tucked herself into one of the flowery armchairs, way at the back, hoping Sheila wouldn't see her. Nobody had told her she should "dress"; she was wearing brown corduroys and a grey, inside-out sweatshirt. She scrunched down, made herself small, relieved to be ignored, till Anny bustled over and whispered in her ear, "Lucy!"

She sat up, smiling sheepishly. But Anny only said, "I'm so sorry dear, but would you mind sitting on one of the folding chairs? We want to put Glenda here, for her back." A beaming old lady in a beaded cape and elbow gloves trailed behind her, clutching a gold purse. A real gardenia, beginning to droop brownly, was pinned precariously to the side of her head above a prominent hearing aid.

Mr. O'Meara, in white tails with a royal blue cummerbund, was glad-handing his way through the crowd, slapping backs, rocking with laughter. Just behind him, she spotted Istvan, smiling, leaning on his cane. She tried to catch his eye, almost succeeding; was he looking, was he, yes? She attempted a little wave, a lurch in her stomach, a desolate, formless hope, wanting to run to him, grab his sleeve, cry: I'm here too! You told me I was a good girl, a brave girl, remember? But he was bowing low to have a private word with some old biddy in bugle beads, raising her hand to his lips to kiss.

Mr. O'Meara began to make a great show of synchronizing his watch with Hardee's and Uncle James's. Someone flicked the lights on and off, drawing squeals from the crowd. Mr. O'Meara picked up a cornet from a window seat, blatted an inept fanfare. The guests made a huge production of bustling to their chairs, pretending to be intimidated by the Master of Ceremonies. Someone shouted, "You, sir, have been forbidden to touch brass and woodwinds!" This was a colossal knee-slapper, everyone hollering "Bravo!" amid stomps and applause.

Mr. O'Meara unscrolled a long imitation parchment, and as the tittering petered out, began to read.

"Here ye, here ye!" Someone cried, "Huzzah!" Mr. O'Meara looked fit to split. He held up one hand, waited for the din to die down. "Silence, please! Welcome one and all to the Easter of Sixty-Five edition of the O'Meara Mob's Madness! You may holler! You may shout! You may warble! But don't, I repeat, don't try and stop us!"

Sheila stood to one side, her violin against her black velvet hip, smiling at her father. Her hair had been pinned up somehow, she wore lipstick, and excitement had put colour into her cheeks. In no time at all, perhaps by tomorrow morning, bolstered by all this love, she would blossom into another lovely Colleen.

Lucy, on her hard chair, slid down on her spine as the last of the applause died away. Mr. O'Meara graciously took Istvan's arm and led him to the harpsichord. The old man squeezed in behind it, his legs jammed underneath like a grownup at a child's desk on parents' night. Mr. O'Meara fetched his viola from atop the piano, taking a seat in the semicircle of chairs. Hardee, Sheila and Marjorie followed.

He tucked a white handkerchief under his chin, raised his instrument. The crowd hushed, everyone's head inclining forward, a smile on every face. Sheila and Hardee lifted their chins, slotting in their violins. Marjorie hulked at attention over her cello. They raised their bows, waited motionless for an eternity of seconds, nobility harnessed in their uplifted arms. Absolute silence but for the flutter of curtains wafting inward on the night breeze.

The sound, when it came, punched her in the lungs. The O'Mearas moved like candle flames in a capricious draft of air, all banking to one side then the other, their eyebrows rising and falling in hesitancy, in insistence, their faces rapt with delicious pain. Only Marjorie held back, and when at last her cello joined in, lifting them from below, Lucy was destroyed. The audience swayed too, as forgetful as children with linked arms, seven abreast, careening through fields of daisies. Lucy looked at Sheila and was dazzled; she couldn't look, she was so proud of her! Watching her friend excel, she felt wholehearted, profoundly glad, deeply consoled. She thought she'd never known such cleanliness, such lightness of heart. It was as if she were letting out her breath for the first time in her life.

A thought she barely understood seized her heart: This, *this* is the real thing!

She began to cry, audibly. Heads turned, then turned discreetly away; this crowd was accustomed to helpless gaggings of emotion. The music shifted ground then, Mr. O'Meara taking Hardee's violin, zigzagging into a jazz solo while Hardee slid in behind the piano, thumping along. As they moved from one piece to another, they relaxed, smiled at each other, winked at audience members. Hardee did some solo scriabbing, then Sheila played a long, achingly sad piece, and suddenly people were jumping from their seats, pulling instruments out of cases under their chairs, joining in. Hardee took up the guitar and Uncle James manned the piano, hitting a showstopping clinker that broke up the room. With perfect precision, Sheila led them into a Cape Breton reel, flushed and grinning, stamping her foot while Hardee produced spoons from his pocket and played them on his knees. It was so joyful, it hurt so much! Everyone clapped along, even Glenda in her elbow gloves whooping and bouncing. Deep inside, Lucy's heart did a gimpy jig in its cramped closet, while on the outside, she sat on her hands, shoulders juddering, tears pelting her shoes. And tears or not, she felt ready to look up in perfect honesty, to meet anyone's eyes with no dark quip on her tongue, nothing shameful she needed to shovel dirt over, no lunatic whopper to tell. It felt marvelous, it felt awful; could it hold, could it really? And if it went on and on and never broke, then who might she possibly be for the rest of her life? One of them? Could she do it, could she be someone who *counted*, someone her father would be very, very sorry he'd missed knowing?

An errant thought slipped in sideways: If it were true that these people wholeheartedly accepted her, then just how discerning could they possibly be? But she stifled it, sitting up straighter as the music finally stopped, the instruments laid lovingly on chairs and tabletops, the happy chatter resuming. Anny approached wordlessly, offering her one of the amber drinks, just as Sheila escaped from the crowd to flop down in the chair next to hers. The warm drink moved like a river of smoke through her trembling limbs.

"How did you like it? Oh, your face!" Sheila laughed, not unkindly. She reached into her skirt pocket, handed her a hanky; who but Sheila would have such a thing?

Lucy's body felt fused to her chair. "I can't get up," she gasped. "I'm all stiff! I feel like Frankenstein."

"It's *alive!*" cried Sheila, reaching out for her, pulling her to her unsteady feet. "Come on, let's go get some air." Hand in hand they loped through the dining room, where the big table was spread with a buffet fit for a Czar, and into the kitchen. The coat tree by the door was piled high, and Sheila pulled someone's big, black fur off the top, draping it around both of them.

They didn't need it; the near dawn was balmy, rain washed, the backyard's flat, brown winter grass slowly getting to its feet. A handful of stars were still visible, puncture wounds in eternity. Sheila raised her arms over her head in a gesture of rapture, the fur coat dropping to the ground behind her, forgotten.

To her dying day Lucy will remember standing close behind her friend, the breeze cooling her swollen face. Sheila turning abruptly, grinning, close enough to kiss. Saying softly, "I'll walk you home!"

And she breathing back, "Then I'll walk you home."

"Then I'll walk *you* home," giggled Sheila. They found this crampingly funny. Sheila picked up the fur coat and they ran together to the end of the yard. She lay the coat over the boggy grass, fur side up, and lay down on it, pulling Lucy down beside her.

And Lucy thought: I'm not going to miss another thing as long as I live.

With deep reverence, she said, "That was a great concert."

Sheila laughed. "You're tellin' me. A memory lapse or two short of perfection, but nothing too disgraceful."

"I didn't notice anything. I thought it was perfect." A silence. "You never fail at anything, do you?" A stray wisp of disdain floated through her for all these coddled people who had it so easy in life, who didn't know what it was to feel lost or unloved. She shook it off.

"Please," Sheila said, grandly humble. "You just haven't been around to hear my outtakes."

Lucy drifted back in time with the still echoing music, then forward to going home, to Pauline's and Glynis's charbroiled faces turning to stare in dull tandem, like cows over a fence. Her old self, sensing peril, began inchworming back; she was never going to belong here, would never in eons possess Sheila's easy grace. She had nothing to offer these people. She had nothing to offer a living soul.

You had to *deserve* to be an O'Meara!

Sheila, next to her, was still lit up with ecstasy, proclaiming her fabulousness to the slowly lightening sky. "Three years! Three years till I get to play Paganini in Italy! I'm going to be magnificent! I'm going to have the greatest career ever!"

This wasn't what Lucy wanted to hear. She wanted to lay her head in Sheila's lap, feel her gentle hand on her head, like a benediction, a heart-stirring declaration of eternal friendship, of unrescindable welcome. This true friendship, she realized with a sinking heart, would naturally require her to be admiring and encouraging of Sheila's greatness. But what was there for Sheila to admire and encourage in *her?* Nothing. All the good stuff would always be going one way only. She would always be the nobody, the sad Pauline to Sheila's indulgent, Lady Bountiful Glynis. The supporter, the fan. The hanger-on. Everybody's second, fourth, everybody's tenth choice.

She looked up then, and as if to ram the point home, there were Hardee and Vi, arms around one another, heading across the lawn. But not before Hardee had shot her a look. Not before he'd called out over his jaunty, tuxedoed shoulder, "Go home, Loose Lips. It's past your bedtime."

All her life she'll remember. She'd only wanted to make it appear that she and Sheila were deep in animated conversation, that she was having too much fun to be bothered by a stupid remark from a paunchy, frizz-headed guy nobody in their right mind would want. So she'd jabbed Sheila playfully in the side, and blurted the first thing that came to mind: "But what if you get some terrible disease like leukemia, and you croak and everybody forgets all about you? It could happen. The world wouldn't even care, it would just roll on without you."

When Sheila didn't answer, she'd kept going, "You never know. Maybe I'll become famous instead of you. Your teacher told me I have an extremely fiery gift for music."

A long, long, yawning space of nothing.

"He said if I practice hard, I could be better than you in six months. He wants me to start right—"

"Okay, Lucy." Sheila's voice was a sliver of ice. "Here's something I don't think you realize. We're all, our whole family, absolutely sick of you and your stupid lies and pathetic grabs for attention. My mother *made* me invite you tonight, okay? I didn't want to. Even she thinks you're a loser. Nobody wants you here. Nobody can stand the sight of you."

All her life, remembering. How she'd flushed hot, then shivered.

"What?"

"What's *wrong* with you, anyway? Why don't you try actually *accomplishing* something, for once in your stupid life? How about for starters you just try being *normal?*" Sheila was sitting up straight now, turning as a gaggle of people stepped out the patio doors onto the lawn. Raising her arm, waving gaily as she scrambled to her feet, dragging the coat unceremoniously out from under Lucy.

How she'd tugged in vain at the hem of her friend's velvet skirt.

How she'd raised herself on her elbows in the muddy grass, watching Sheila join the happy huddle of ladies on the lawn. In the middle of them was Istvan. *He told me I was a good girl but I'm not, I'm not, I'm not. I'm useless and ugly and abnormal.* The ladies opening their arms as Sheila approached, enfolding her and the old man in a massive group hug.

How she'd sprung up to trot after them, reaching out to glom on, spreading her arms around the outermost lady, but the curve was way too wide, the joyful, chattering mass already rolling away like a giant Earthball. How she'd tripped after it with small steps, arms still open, till they began to ache, and she dropped them, and turned, and walked away.

Evan

For two hours Evan's been shivering on this hard bench, March wind snapping at his cheeks, clouds low and ominous. His stomach roiling, hands tucked up his sleeves.

Once again, he raises his eyes heavenward: *Please, Lord, please. Give me one more chance! Please let her come. Please! Please let her come at least before it starts to snow. Haven't I been humiliated enough without being forced to sit here waiting like a chump through a blinding blizzard?*

Then he thinks: Smarten up, numbnuts. If there's a blizzard, she definitely won't be coming. Snow starts, you can safely slink away home.

And then, to himself, irritably: Just who exactly are you asking to hold back the snow? You don't still think that's the way weather works, do you?

And finally, bleakly: *She's not coming, is she, Lord. She hates me, and it's over. I've lost her. I blew it, I never deserved her, I'm a weakling. I'm a worm. I'm never going to change. I must make you want to vomit.*

You're punishing me, aren't you?

Except, can't you, can't you please, Lord, do something to fix it? Come on! Please, please, please, please, PLEASE!

Seriously, what good are you anyway?

A deep breath, in, out.

I'm sorry. I didn't mean that last part.

A dry sob rolls in, jerking his shoulders inside his windbreaker. He may as well still be ten years old. He's crossed over into the shady side of his forties, but at desperate moments like these, he still feels like the sorry kid he once was, his neck permanently cricked from gazing heavenward, prayerful little hands clasped, crimped, worried little face so hoping for the best. Shrinking, scrupulous to a fault, terrified of incurring the Lord's so easily aroused wrath.

What the hell is wrong with him? It's been twenty years now since that day on the other side of the world when he'd held his broken brother in his arms and put all that miserable religiosity behind him. Twenty years since he'd turned his resolute back on the harsh teachings he'd grown up with, all that "total depravity of man, sinners in the hands of an angry God" bombast. Twenty years since he'd made the choice, the absolute *commitment,* to seek the face of God by his suffering brother's side. So how ridiculous is it to be regressing like this now? As if all the old knee-jerk beliefs about divine retribution and his own puling cowardice in the face of it have been lurking in his brain like multiple aneurisms, biding their time, maliciously waiting for the hour of his greatest vulnerability to rupture and spew poison over everything.

No, damn it, he'd stuck to his guns! It had cost him professionally, and now it was costing him the love of his life. That wasn't being weak, was it? And what if he *had* ditched Neil as soon as he realized that was what she wanted him to do? Would winning her love at that price have been worth it? Would it have made him surer, stronger, bolder, turned him into the winner-take-all man she pined for? Or would he have forfeited his very soul in the frantic race to keep up the pretense of being someone he had no business even imagining himself to be.

And what about Neil? Is it possible that, cared for somewhere else, by someone who actually knew what they were doing, his brother would have done perfectly well, would have thrived? Or even perhaps . . . been cured?

What the hell was I supposed to have done, Lord?

Uh huh. Dead silence, as usual.

Damn it, I know you're there! Would you mind speaking up for once, if it isn't too much fuc—sorry—trouble?

To distract himself, he begins spinning a resolutely secular fantasy, pretending he's waiting for his CIA contact. A shadowy individual in a grey fedora sliding in next to him, sitting for a spell, leaving. Forgetting, of course, one of his gloves, in which, stuffed into the thumb, are coded instructions for a mission that, if successful, will foil a massive terrorist attack on the city aproned out below him. He, Evan, may well lose his life. But millions will live on!

His last words: Don't worry. I got this. No, those are his second last words. His very last words would be: Tell Rivka to be happy, tell her to live on knowing I adored her, that in spite of everything, she was the undying love of my—wait!

That flash of orange over by the coin-operated binoculars . . . is that . . . could it be . . . ? He stands up, squints. Rivka's orange runners? Her car left at her parents' place on McTavish, a jog up the mountain like they'd done so many times together, in the old days? Rivka, sleek in spandex, her face bursting into light when she sees him, breathing hard, her glorious hair blowing parallel with the Saint Lawrence shimmering steel blue in the distance . . .

No. (Thud.) They're not her runners.

Oh, the stupid, *stupid* shame of it. Fantasizing like a teenager, waiting for a *girl*. Woman. *Young* woman. Whatever! Face it, you witless boob: she's not coming. She's not ever coming again! Don't pretend you didn't know the score. You've *always* known.

He'd cried, no, *bawled*, into his cereal that morning, salty bloblets splashing into the milk. And the night before too, curled fetally on the kitchen linoleum. Profoundly grateful he didn't have to appear on set with his smeary, swollen face for the next few days.

She's had it. She's done. Only a year and a half into a love story meant to last till the twelfth of never. And it's his fault, all of it. At the very first sign of her waning interest, instead of manning up, he'd panicked, spinning on a dime back to his old unhipsterish, unstudly, undudely self.

A blind man could have read the signs: for six months now she's been making him walk on eggshells, loving him one moment, freezing him out the next. Toying with him. Insisting everything was fine when he asked, then turning mean again. Just two weeks ago, indulging in some idle mockery—oh, she was a dab hand with the mockery—sitting on her couch, messing around with Tinder *right in front of him!* Then having a little meltdown after getting dissed by some nineteen-year-old. Holding up her phone in disbelief. "Little shit told me I looked crusty. *Crusty!* I don't turn thirty till September!" Looking up at Evan from the couch, unexpected tears splurting from her eyes, yes, but also, laughing. Twenty-five parts sobbing to seventy-five laughing.

"He wants a shot of me on all fours before he decides." Her flawlessly drawn eyeliner wings were smudged, parallel mascara trails wending their way to her chin. And still she weakened his knees.

"Well, it's his loss," was his inane reply, after which he gave some thought to walking over to the wall and knocking his head against it till it exploded.

It crushed him to see her so vulnerable. Though he could see the little shit's point: Rivka's wasn't a face or body that turned younger men's heads. Older men, though, and women of every age, were always walking smack into lampposts when she passed them in the street.

She was still studying the picture on her screen. Softly telling his little face, "You're really rockin' those sunnies." A text whooshing away.

No, Rivka, no! This is not you, this is not us!

But he didn't dare say this out loud, dreading one of her whiplash retorts. Instead he frantically conjured a treasured mental image: Rivka huge and ripe as a watermelon. Composed a brief, fervid playlet straight out of a Lifetime movie.

RIVKA

Darling . . . sit down. I have something to tell you. *(She smiles mischievously at him over the back of the sofa.)*

EVAN

Oh! *(He stands in the doorway, gazing across at her, sick with love.)* You look so beautiful right now! Like a blossom bursting on a peony bush!

RIVKA

I'm . . . *(she hesitates, blushing)* I'm pregnant, darling.

EVAN

No! Oh! Oh! That is the best news! The best! How far along are you? Oh, we're going to need a crib, and a—

RIVKA

Whoa, lover! Slow down! *(She sinks down into the sofa cushions, holds out her arms to him)* You're going to be the best daddy!

EVAN

And you're going to be—*(Words fail him. He reaches for her, his heart pounding.)* Rivka? Sweetheart—?

She was still scrolling through male faces. When once, his had been the only face she'd cared about. When she'd stood behind him, twisting the hair he'd let grow long just because she'd asked him to, into a dudely man bun. Murmuring, "You're so handsome! Tell me you know how handsome you are."

And he, grinning sheepishly: "I'm handsome."

"Say, I, Evan Labossière, am handsome as fuck!"

"I'm handsome."

"Handsome as fuck, I said."

"Handsome as fuck." He'd blushed like a girl, so happy it hurt.

And now, Tinder. Which, according to her, she was only on for the laughs, so he *really* needed to get over himself. She and her besties, scarfing mojitos, swiping their screens, shrieking, "Whoo hoo, l'appel du boot-ay! Dude wants to hook up in the next half hour, hit and quit, he's downtown, near the Guy metro. Got a dick pic here, and I must say—! Is a half hour enough time to get blind drunk?" Laughing themselves sick, but one of them maybe shrugging into her coat, pulling out a mirror, repairing her lipstick. Evan having the impression that whoever cared the least, guy or girl, came out some kind of winner.

Random boning, Rivka called it. As in: "No more random boning for me, now that I'm livin' the dream with you, Sugarnuts."

And then, when she saw what she called his "priss face," his "I want to marry you, darling, and have babies" face materializing, cutting him off at the pass with another installment of her "Babies make me feel all clammy" lecture series. Crying, "Where do the little fuckers even come from? Under rotting logs on the forest floor? Educate me, oh venerable Father Time!"

He's always known she has a cruel streak, not the least when it comes to his brother. She's never held back from making sniping remarks about him, causing Evan no end of pain on Neil's behalf. She's had it in for Neil ever since she first clapped eyes on him, that first and only visit she ever made to Sainte-Clémence, almost a year and a half ago. But never, till lately, has she unleashed her venom on Mr. Handsome AF himself.

Maybe it's just her fear of turning thirty that's bringing it out, he tells himself, fanning faint hope. She keeps up a brave front, but she's really feeling it, poor kid. To hear her talk, she's on the cusp of ninety-seven, toothless in a wheelchair, riddled with dry rot, unable to remember where her knees are. He's tried so hard to be patient, calm, praising her youthful beauty every chance he gets. Which, these days, only seems to stoke some underground, volcanic fury in her, which in turn is causing him to backslide into the timid fool he was when she first found him. A circle growing more vicious by the day.

Had he felt the same panic about encroaching decrepitude at twenty-seven, twenty-nine? He can't even *remember* being twenty-seven, twenty-nine, though the year he turned twenty-four—the Thailand year—certainly stands out in a blinding light.

But then, everything involving Neil stands out in a blinding light.

When they were kids, Neil, two years older, had been the soul of solicitude to his awkward little brother, who stuttered like a jackhammer, who spent the hours outside of homeschool sitting at the kitchen table illustrating Bible stories or reading quiet books from a more gracious time, *Little Men* and *Elsie Dinsmore*. Who hid in the basement when the children of their Aunt

Louisa's church friends came storming by for cake and milk after Sunday service.

The two of them still so little when they'd come to live with her. Louisa, their mother's sister, fifteen years older than Maman and nothing like her, though Evan had no real way of knowing this, remembering his mother as a soft haze at the kitchen counter in a house of mist. A quiet voice, glasses. Claire, her name was. She'd spoken English; he and Neil were named for her own father and uncle. Their father, Claude, had been tall, thin, French-speaking; the boys' first language had been French. Evan had been only three when Papa and Maman had left him and five-year-old Neil in Louisa's care, driving off for a weekend holiday in Toronto. Sunday, Monday coming and going. Raised voices on the phone. A blurry scene in a cemetery that only Neil remembers, barely. And then, Louisa, nearly forty by then, single, unencumbered, a registered nurse and a dynamo in her little fundamentalist church, suddenly playing the part of both their parents. Moving them to her house way outside the city in Sainte-Clémence. No more French heard or spoken at home; they were English boys now, going in the blink of an eye from being small boys looking ahead to school, watching any cartoons they wanted on TV, to being Louisa's small boys, officially dedicated to the Lord, with no TV permitted and homeschooling by their aunt's best friend Dorcas Penner to look forward to. Whoever he and Neil had been setting out to be, they were heading in that direction no longer.

His brother had been everyone's darling, an effervescent pixie—until he wasn't. The first changes in him hadn't seemed onerous at all, just an intensification of his unquenchable glee, a high-spiritedness that sometimes went screamingly off the rails, calling stern rebukes from Louisa down upon his head. For Evan, the change had been so gradual, it had just seemed like a heightening of Neil's personal magic. His imagination, always lively, became incandescent; after lights-out, his hot whisper across the abyss between their beds: Neil could *hear* things in vivid colour. He could *taste* sounds! Could Evan do it too? When Louisa sang in church, her voice, Neil reported, was brownish orange and bumpy, and tasted like peanut brittle. Dorcas, their homeschool teacher, had a voice that was green and cool, juicy like honeydew. Lucy Brickwood next door had a voice that tasted like canned peas, but Mrs. Brickwood's was all yellow, and gooey, like lemon pie. Evan had listened, enthralled, assuming that these powers came with the advent of the teen years. He could hardly wait.

Neil went several steps too far the day he swore to Louisa that he had seen God strolling right outside their house, that God was a lady in a sparkly mermaid dress and a mink stole who had smiled at him and said it was okay if he had a chocolate bar even though supper was only an hour away. For this heresy, he was made to copy out eight pages of Bible verses and go without supper, but even the reliably distant and preoccupied Louisa was beginning to sense that her nephew was loitering very near the Checkpoint Charlie of the Land of No Return.

Then, almost overnight, his bright sunflower spirit had blackened, drooping heavy on its stalk. He went miles beyond teenage sullen; he was Charles Manson sullen, his dear, elfin face lengthening, growing spotty, savage. His hair left grease streaks on his pillow. By the time he was fourteen he had adopted contrariness as a hobby, giving monosyllabic answers, if any, to queries put to him by Louisa or Dorcas, squirming in every seat he was confined to, tugging at his shirt collars, raking his hands through his hair. There was no subject he could not turn into heartfelt grievance. Why did the mailman have to work in winter? It wasn't *fair!* Why were the skins of bananas inedible? That was stupid! Who planned *that?* Louisa admonishing with a dangerous frown, "Well, you *know* Who planned it, Neil. And I think you owe Him an apology." Neil didn't care; everywhere he cast his appalled eyes, a boundless sea of crap! Except now he was calling it "shit," and out loud, too.

Evan kept him in his worried, crick-necked prayers, tried everything to cheer him up. Made him homemade cards, drawings of happy woodland creatures canopied with rainbows. Did his chores for him, offered little gifts, Aero bars, bright yellow and blue packs of Chiclets. Relayed stuttered jokes memorized from Dubble Bubble comics. Nothing made a dent.

By the time weary Dorcas threw in the towel, unable to homeschool them any longer, Neil had only his final year to do in a real high school. He quickly became celebrated as the boy who nearly succeeded in organizing a prank whereby all the kids in town would sprawl out dead in the street, waiting for their parents to find them. In the one picture in the yearbook in which he appeared—Mr. Gaiman's drama club, to which he'd never belonged—he hulked at the back, eyes sunken, looking spastic even standing still.

At home, he had thrown off all shackles, refusing to come to church or prayer meetings, picking daily fights with Louisa. Furiously standing his ground, trying so desperately to be heard: "Yeah, but how did Noah get kangaroos and arctic foxes on the ark, huh?" And: "Come on! The sun can't stand still in the sky because it doesn't move in the first place!" And, bracingly: "Where did Cain and Abel's descendants come from unless they got it on with their mother?" Getting his face slapped for his trouble, or having Louisa quote a Bible verse over and over, drowning him out: *And He blinded the eyes of those who would not see and gave them over to eternal darkness! And He blinded the eyes of those who would not see. And He blinded the eyes*—Neil, grinning like a skull at her, even as tears of frustrated rage spurted from his eyes, holding on for dear life against some invisible but colossally powerful undertow.

He shot up eight inches overnight, his walk jolting, elbows out of sync with knees. His jubilant little voice, the silken soprano that had once made grown ladies swoon in the pews, grew dark and coarse. He sat for hours on his bed, hugging his knees, rocking compulsively. Wore the same dour brown sweater every day, even after he'd poked holes in the elbows and managed to detach half the collar from the rest of the garment. His side of the bedroom, once hung with VeggieTales mobiles, was now rank with musk and funk, the very air oily with secretions and filthy secrets, much rhythmic unrest under the blankets after lights-out. On the unfaded square of wallpaper real estate once occupied by the Care Bears, he posted a scrawled notice: YES LOUISA, WON'T WE JUST MISS THE GOOD OLD DAYS WHEN WE ONLY WISHED WE WERE DEAD! He told Evan he'd gotten the quote from Lucy.

He turned with a vengeance to Satan's music, buying cassettes, which he'd learned the hard way to hide from

Louisa—Megadeth, Slayer, Alice Cooper—with the allowance he'd contributed to the mission field in happier times. Music he wasn't allowed to play at home but stuffed into his pockets to listen to over at the Brickwoods' or to take to his greasy new friends' houses after school. Hanging out till past dark with other hooded hellions, lying on their stomachs across swings in the elementary school playground, twisting the chains this way and that, smoking, griping, cursing, seething.

His sheets reeked of furtive sexuality, Louisa whipping them off his bed on Saturday mornings, bundling them under her arm, her face twisted in disgust. Her iciness toward his rebellious, unbelieving spirit was compounded a thousand-fold by this literally unspeakable crime. She made no effort to conceal her distinct preference for Evan, still powder dry, his curly head haloed and shimmering with the brightness of the invisible world as he said grace over supper, calling down blessings upon Louisa's uninspired offering of plywood pork chops and Tater Tots.

Evan was overcome with anguish and unrequited love for his brother, who he *knew* was sorely wounded by Louisa's rejection, no matter how he bluffed and sneered. He longed to somehow make it up to Neil, who needed help now more than ever, and who had nobody but him, dumb little good-boy Evan, plodding along after him, picking up stuff he'd knocked over, feeling like the stupid, blatting tuba bringing up the rear of Neil's storm-trooping, insurrectionary parade. Yes, it was true that Neil had Lucy as a friend and confidante—she had always had such a soft spot for him—but Lucy had no relationship to the Lord the way he, Evan, did, with her nonstop swearing and her cigarettes and her sour opinions. No, Neil had only Evan to lift him up in prayer, aching with sorrow and hope as he begged the Lord to bring his *real* brother, the old Neil, back. He wanted to encourage Neil to hold on, to be strong, but he didn't know how to say it without enraging this rabid stranger whose feelings seemed as raw as a tongue frozen to a lamppost and then yanked away.

After Neil finished high school, his regular disappearances had begun, disappearances that left Louisa strangely unfazed. At first, it was only for a few days. Then weeks. Once, after he'd been gone a solid month, he phoned to let them know he'd joined a "group." Telling Louisa, "We're kind of like monks. We're all celibate." Louisa's suspicious glower had softened somewhat at this news.

"Well, that sounds like a good, sound smack in the devil's face," she'd said, almost convincingly. No fly-by-night cult of heretic monks could be all bad if it involved abstinence.

"Every time you're happy," Neil told her, "the Buddha and I smile."

"That's very nice of you," was Louisa's pert reply. "Are you two sharing a room?"

A couple weeks later there'd been a letter, addressed to Evan, folded into fourths and stuffed into an envelope handcrafted from a brown paper bag. It contained the most joyful words he had heard from his brother in seven long years.

Dear peanut-butter-and-marshmallow-sandwich little brother, I miss your curly-wurly head and your big red ears. Leaving home was heart rendering because of you, and you only. I am undergoing a soul transplant, having the I-ness cut out of me, the proud Self so that I may become a straight, swift arrow in God's bow. Learning to feel the silence within me, catching deep secrets carried by the wind. I am becoming Void. And I ask you, little one, what is demanded of us? Nothing bad! Only what is natural, good and yes-able. Is loving natural? Is caring good? Is you yes-able? Is I? Of course!! With everything I own, which is nothing, and so everything, I love you.

"He's a big boy, the Lord has His eye on him," was what Louisa said, briskly putting the matter up before her prayer group, but only for a couple of days. Still, the prayers must have hit a bullseye, for Neil was back home again a week later, back to his old self, deflated and bitterly resigned to starting a job stocking the shelves at Jean-Coutu.

But not before he'd backed Evan into a corner of their room, poking him repeatedly in the chest with fierce insistence. "If you learn one thing from me, let it be this: You have to die before you die, little brother!"

"I d-d-don't know what you m-m-mean."

"I mean, stop thinking you're so good because Louisa and all her hysterical ninny friends say you are. You're not and they're not either, not even close. Our guru had plenty to say about that. All that thinking you're so special and good? All that thinking the Lord is just crazy about you because you don't break the rules? That's just your ugly, puffed-up ego, your false self needing to be in control. Listen, you can't control shit! Your false self has to die before you can attain enlightenment! You can't find your indestructible centre unless you expose yourself to total annihilation! Over and over and over."

"Uhm . . . what?"

"You have to take the path of the warrior! Lucy gets it, she knows what I mean. You have to let all your dumb ideas about God fall apart and die. Do you understand?"

"Yes," Evan lied.

"Pride is the supreme destroyer of life. Don't let Louisa fool you with all her Bible shit. All that salvation crap is nothing but top premium fire insurance for the afterlife. She's not humble. None of them are. They think they're so godly, but they're proud, because they think they're the only ones on earth who believe the right stuff and because they never think about sex. Lucy told me that."

Evan blushed to the roots of his hair. "Oh."

"Our guru taught us, there's no such thing as good guys and bad guys. He told me all my suffering would stop when I finally realized I'd never be safe by pretending I belonged to the good people. And you neither. *Especially* you neither," he finished, with a really hard poke at Evan's clavicle. Turning away then, walking rapidly to the other end of the room, where he stood with his forehead pressed to the wall for several silent minutes. When he spoke again, it was to the wall.

"It's really hard to stop thinking that way though. I tried. It really hurts. That's why I had to quit the group, my brain started jamming and I couldn't hack it. But I still think it's true."

"You m-m-mean, there's no such thing as God's p-people? You mean . . . it's not us?" Evan barely managed to whisper.

"No God's people, no not-God's people. Jesus, you're slow on the uptake." He'd banged out of the room then and down the stairs, out the side door. Evan watched him through the window as he walked fast, head down, over to the Brickwood house, letting himself in their front door without even ringing the bell.

Lucy must be home, he thought; well, Lucy was always home. Neil would go hang out with her, like he always did when he was finding it hard to hold on. Evan had no idea what they talked about or did, only that Neil always came home cooler, less wound up. Lucy, he thought, must be for Neil what Mr. Gaiman was for him: the one grown-up to whom he could fearlessly open his heart. But he doubted even Mr. Gaiman, smart as he was, had an answer to the awful question Neil had raised: If he, Evan, wasn't one of God's people, then who *was* he? What was he here for?

Was everything he was so sure he knew . . . a *lie*?

Neil had moved out again a few weeks later to some undisclosed location in the city. It was the beginning of eight long years of almost never seeing him at all, his life, his friends enshrouded in mystery. Leaving Evan to finish high school alone, lost, bereft, only beginning to find an unsteady footing and a budding sense of a future, undreamt of till then, under the kind protection of his Speech and Drama teacher. Neil never called, never once found his way out to Sainte-Clémence for a Sunday service or a Wednesday night prayer meeting. He turned up for a few hours on Christmas or Evan's birthday, always shut off, closemouthed, in a big hurry to leave. He'd missed Evan's star turns on the high school stage, but had turned up, quite unexpectedly, to see his performance as Romeo in his first big CEGEP production, squeezing into the crowded dressing room afterward for a quick handshake and a mumbled, "You did good," before ducking out again.

Then, out of the blue Louisa got a postcard—from Osaka!

Came here to change my life, going full Buddhist on you guys, sorry, no teeth-gnashing, please. Truth will be learned at the Source. Sayonara, yours truly, Blackie the Sheep.

No further word for half a year. Louisa and her prayer warriors interceding for his soul in a leisurely fashion.

Then, another postcard, addressed to Evan:

Hello, Brother! Japan Crazy! Now I go Thailand! Live for pennies a day! You come! Thailand is land of wisdom! Yours truly, Neil.

Evan had been closing in on his quarter-century mark, bussing tables for a living, the bud of his so hopefully begun acting career already drooping on the vine. In three years, only one tiny part in a play as a stuttering hotel desk clerk, a part soundly nailed at the audition without even trying. One line in one TV commercial: Honey, did you shrink my sweater again? A couple days on an episode of *Street Legal*: security guard number two, his three lines spoken into an invisible two-way wrist radio hidden in his shirt cuff. A hundred "almost" auditions. His stutter, his lifelong bane, ninety-five percent under control, so long as he remembered to think of what he wanted to say before speaking, and spoke s l o w l y, with deep, calming breaths between sentences.

At twenty-three he too had left home at last, stepping out into the wicked world, exhilarated, terrified. Sharing the third floor of a dingy triplex on Mont-Royal with two other struggling thespians he'd known from CEGEP. Evan was the thespian who, at least once a month, took the bus out to Sainte-Clémence on Sunday mornings to attend church with his aunt. The thespian who never brought girls home, who slept under a thin, too-short blanket on the couch while bedroom bedlam went on behind not always properly closed doors. The thespian who eventually washed all the cracked, mismatched dishes, who thoughtfully lugged Louis-Philippe's and Marc's laundry to the laundromat along with his own. The thespian who went to bed after a half of one beer, when beer was all there was in the fridge.

He was also the thespian who had let two Mormons in because he couldn't bring himself to say no to them, sitting for two hours at the kitchen table spread with their many scrolls and documents. Louis-Philippe, trapped in the bedroom with nothing to do but spark up a series of doobies and listen, had put him on roommate probation: one more dick move like that, and he could kiss these sweet, cheap digs goodbye.

So, yes, then, to the question of whether he'd known the same trepidation Rivka feels about advancing age. Never mind thirty; at twenty-four, with no girlfriend, no backbone, no career success, he had already felt ridiculous, inept, cripplingly shy, used up and destined for the junk pile.

Somehow, from the other side of the globe, Neil's uncanny fraternal antennae had homed in on his little brother's lost and floundering soul. Though Evan had never written a word to him about anything, a second letter arrived, this one on blue tissue airmail stationery, the envelope plastered with gaudy stamps featuring the king of Thailand in five different splendid costume changes.

> *You're no actor, my brother. How does it even work with that stutter of yours? I'm thinking that big splash you made as Romeo was probably your high point. Accept it, you were made, like me, for solitude. Why do you want to make things so hard for yourself? You love the rut, my brother! You love the routine! Your sense of adventure is already stretched to the limit by trying out a new tea, for fuck's sake. Listen to me! I have found all the truth and wisdom needed to live. Get your pussy-ass over here. I have a house, there's work, you can teach English, I do, also I'm in the documentary film game, big irons in the fire, should interest you. This letter will mean—*

It had broken off in mid-page. At the top of a second page, scrawled in a different hand, different ink, were the words: *Elsewhere herein will be discussed*—followed by no discussion. Neil had signed off not on the page but on the back of the envelope, a hastily scribbled, *yours truly, name furnished on request.*

But . . . all the wisdom needed to live?

Could his brother release him at last from the untold sleepless, crick-necked, worry-faced, uplifted-holy-hands nights he'd been enduring ever since Neil had planted those first shrieking doubts nearly ten years ago?

Yes! Because his brother had found *all the wisdom needed to live!*

Tell me, he wanted to shout across continents, oceans—Tell me how to live, Neil! I'm so, so lost!

And I do too have a sense of adventure!

He'd decided right then and there: he'd do it! He'd cross the world to see his brother. He could afford it; he'd just dip into his inheritance for travel money. Their parents' will had left both boys twenty grand each, receivable on their twenty-first birthdays. Neil had blown through most of his already. But Evan had sought the help of one of the elders in church, who had counselled him to invest wisely in U.S. mutual funds, turning his twenty to thirty thousand in no time. Money that was just sitting there twiddling its thumbs.

He missed his brother with a never-ending ache. Not the Sturm und Drang teenaged Neil, but little Neil, free-spirited, openhearted, endlessly inventive. That giddy, beaming kid who woke up every day with a headful of wacky plans for the two of them to share, never anticipating less than golden sunshine, sapphire skies. Always gloriously rumpled, his hair cowlicked, shirt askew, both knees lurid with Mercurochrome. Never fazed by unfavourable attention from surlier children as he pumped along on his bike, treating the good people of Sainte-Clémence to his vibrato-rich, soprano rendition of *I'll Fly Away*.

Oh, how he'd missed *that* Neil.

Well, this romantic-meeting-on-the-mountain idea has certainly been a bang-up success.

It's snowing. It's snowing hard, his head and shoulders shrouded in it, his sneakered feet soaked through and frozen. And still he doesn't budge, the memory of his and Rivka's last big fight, three nights ago, playing on a merciless loop in his head. In her haste to get away from him, she'd left her sweater in his car, a kitten-grey rain cloud of a garment, knit in great gauzy loops, an insubstantial shred of fluff intended only for the enhancement it afforded the tawny shoulder it was always slipping off from. It's been draped with delicate care over the back of his kitchen chair for these last three days, and now lies folded in his lap under three inches of snow as he continues to cool his stubborn heels on "their" bench on the Mount Royal lookout.

How many texts has he sent begging her to meet him? Promising, "I'll bring your sweater!" As if that were a draw; she's so careless about her clothes, has so many, she wouldn't even know she's missing anything.

A two-volt battery's worth. That's how much Rivka loves him now.

He cringes to remember her, three nights ago, bundling her big purse to her chest, throwing open the passenger side door of his car. Spitting, "You give me such a sharp pain in the ass! Really. I can't even deal!" Slam! Stepping lively down Sherbrooke all the way to her block, careless bared arms exposed to the March winds, shiny hair swinging, not thinking once of looking back before turning right and out of sight.

He'd snuffled and blubbered for the entire hour-long drive back to Sainte-Clémence, vowing that he would fix it, he would change, would try harder to be who she wanted him to be. Stiffen his spine, be a man for God's sake! No, for *Christ's* sake! He was no wuss, he could take the famous name in vain, why not? *There! Did you hear that?*

I'm sorry. Don't be mad, Lord.

Such a stupid, stupid fight it had been. About *chicken!* Rivka just back from a week-long film gig in Toronto, her first out-of-town job in four months. She hadn't phoned or texted all week, which boded ill; on earlier work trips she'd FaceTimed him twice a day, bursting with showbiz anecdotes and salacious gossip, never going to sleep without calling to say goodnight, to tell him how much she loved and missed him. But it had been a big film, and she'd been coaching major actors on difficult accents; she'd probably never had a spare minute, so pumped had she been to get the gig after a long fallow period, so anxious to make a great impression. Understanding this, he should have begun drawing her out the moment they sat down in the restaurant: What was Matt Damon like to work with? And Emily whatsername, how was she? Any new work opportunities on the horizon? But from the jump her mood had seemed unaccountably spiky, throwing him off his game and into regression mode.

"We're gonna do the grilled sesame chicken," she'd told the waiter. Ordering for him, as she liked to do, as he'd always let her do. But when his plate came—after a long, miserable spate of silence—it was the wrong thing, it was tuna. Evan loathed tuna, loathed all fish, never mind the warm concerns he entertained for the plight of dolphins. But when the offending dish had been set before him, he'd only blinked and sighed.

"Tell them!" Rivka had leaned across the table, her eyes incendiary, last straws bursting into flame within her.

"Hey, no biggie." An expression he'd gotten from her friends that he wanted to punch himself in the mouth for using.

"Tell them!" Louder this time. "Why are you letting them push you around? You have a right to what you asked for. *Tell them!*" Neighbouring diners were now glancing their way.

Evan, who with every steaming cell of his body did not want to tell them, had no choice but to gesture in a foppy way to the passing waiter. Swallowing the glob of fear in his throat to whisper kindly, "I'm sorry, I know you're really busy, but I think I got the wrong thing." The waiter bunching up his eyebrows, claiming that no mistake had been made, you asked for tuna. Dude.

Evan had backed down immediately. "Sorry. Anyway, it's fine. My bad." Yet another secondhand expression he'd picked up from Rivka's pals that made him feel like some smarmy smoothie on *The Bachelor*.

"Well, if that isn't some sad bullshit right there." Rivka had sat back in her chair, grilled chicken untouched, shark eyes boring into him as he took small, unhappy bites. Extreme anger did her face no favours, transposing her elongated Modigliani features dangerously close to Afghan hound territory.

Five more minutes of arctic silence. Then she'd banged her fist on the table, making the wineglasses hop. Ordered him to march his ass straight to the kitchen and *demand his rights* as a paying customer!

He'd put down his fork, heart bobbing in a sea of nausea. "It's *okay*. I really don't mind." Gagging down another forkful.

"It's not that bad." It was really hard to swallow with her seething at him.

This, he knew full well, had nothing to do with chicken or tuna. This was *cumulative*.

"You're getting fucked over!" She meant by the waiter, of course, but the subtext clearly referenced his brother. He, no, his whole *life*, and hers along with it, was getting well and truly fucked over—thanks to Evan's appalling gutlessness—by Neil.

He'd hung his head, all his circuits jammed, unable to offer a defense, which just made her wilder. "Find! Out! Who's! Responsible! And demand that the problem be fixed! What is *wrong* with you?" She was out of her chair then. "Hey!" Snapping her fingers to get the waiter's attention.

"Leave him alone," Evan had pleaded. "Please. If he made a mistake, I mean, what if his mother died this morning, or, or, come on, Riv, I *hate* harassing people." The 'p' of people inching perilously toward p-p-p, the flashing neon sign of total, irredeemable retrogression.

"Evan, they're sticking it to you! Sack *up*, dude! Because if I have to take care of it—"

She'd had to take care of it. Flipping her glossy burnt umber hair over the shoulder bared by her spider-silk sweater. Clomping through the saloon doors into the kitchen in her mustard Louboutin boots. The doors still going *whomp whomp* behind her, her voice scaling majestic heights, as Evan thought miserably, so much for date night. For ten unbroken minutes, she could be heard getting all kinds of things off her chest, denouncing everything from the doltishness of their waiter to the voracious greed and incompetence of the food service sector of the economy. All talk in the dining room had ceased, forks held in midair, rapt attention and delight marking every face.

They would have escorted anyone else out by one ear. But Rivka was *so* beautiful.

In the end, she got Evan, who could no longer swallow so much as a sprig of parsley, his grilled chicken. She also scored two free drinks, which they poured for her at the bar, all apologies and fawning smiles.

"Oh look, people!" she'd cried, spinning round in mock excitement, holding the two flutes of champagne aloft in her silver-ringed hands, arm bangles jingling. "We're getting *drinks!*" The announcement was met with warm applause. Everyone was on her side. Everyone always was.

She'd taken her seat, downed her glass in one long pull, then drunk his. Sat back. Complained, "I'm hot." Shrugged off her cobweb sweater, under which she wore a pale pink satin camisole. Men, women at other tables eyed her taut, ballerina body. Rivka knew she was being looked at, appraised, love-hated. She took it well.

"Yes, you are. Hot." His mortified stab at a joke.

No smile back. He'd gagged down a few bites of his chicken, which was cold. Perhaps best not to mention that.

Yes, another "date night" in even worse shambles than usual. Bad enough that that's what they'd been reduced to, trying to crank up enthusiasm for increasingly queasy dinners out, promising one another that they needed to "talk," but instead, fanning the sputtering flames of their relationship over largely silent meals in trendy restaurants, trying to force a closeness that had once been so natural. Sticking to safe topics, prefab conversations, always geared to *her* interests, *her* vision of their future. It wasn't enough anymore that he turned up looking "on point," wearing the "statement" jacket she'd gotten for him at Holt's last Christmas. She needed her gal pals around, needed clubs, bars with deafening music, trips to New York to shop and see shows. She'd pulled away from him in tiny increments at first, and then in chunks, whole sliced-off pieces of her suddenly going AWOL. For several months now, the temperature steadily dropping, Rivka never letting him finish a sentence, repeating his words as he was still speaking them, a half step behind, ending with a vehement nod, a "Got it, got it, got it," as if she'd learned all his lines the night before. Fierce resentment obvious in the frigid pinch of her once honey-warm voice, thrumming in the tight cords of her neck. His reticence, his inexperience in worldly matters that had once so charmed her, as if he were a lovely, openhearted fairy child who had just stepped, bewildered, out of a dewy rose, now just stiffened her back, stropped the razor edge to her tongue.

It would do no good to hang his abject head and iterate for the thousandth time his profound reluctance to bother people. Their last barnburner row, when her love for him had had the size and heft of a ball bearing, had been when he'd agreed to play a small part in one episode of a CBC cop drama . . . for *scale!* "It's okay. It's only two days, and they really don't have the budget, and my agent said—" "Your *agent* said? Evan, either the bitch fights for you, or you fire her ass! Seriously, are you high? You're an established actor with a respected body of work behind you. *You don't work for scale!*"

But he'd pushed his chicken plate aside, hung his head anyway. Mumbled softly, "You know I can't take sides in arguments. Everyone always seems to be right when I look at things from their angle." Her scowl blackening. "I just hate seeing p-p-people's faces f-fall. It feels like, like violence." He had a couple of endearing childhood anecdotes on the back burner: the time he'd apologized, in tears, to the rabbit in his colouring book whose jaunty little cap he'd inadvertently ripped by bearing down too hard with the crayon. The time he'd apologized to one of Louisa's cookbooks, when that good woman had sneered at one of the recipes, so hopefully photographed, presented with such pride!

"Stop talking," Rivka had snapped. So he had.

An hour later, he's stumping down the mountain through snowdrifts, a beaten man, the only fool out on the trail on a day like this. Bare trees creak overhead as he lifts the gauzy sweater, wet through and crumpled into a ball in one hand, to his nose, inhaling deeply, fighting back tears. Thinking, of course, of *course* it was his fault. All of it. Everything. Always.

Once upon a time she'd been entirely, unreservedly, devotedly his. Beautiful Rivka, to whom he'd sworn he would cleave for as long as the sun rose and set; Rivka, for whom he would crack open his rib cage with his bare hands to offer her a lifetime pass to his thumping, faithful heart. There'd been no one more dumfounded than he at his having won her. And no one less astonished that he was losing her now.

She'd walked out of a mist into his life, his breath stopped cold when he first saw her emerging from cyber-fog, wavering into focus on Skype. Introducing herself to him and the fellow actor whose laptop he was sharing.

"Hey. I'm Rivka and I'll be your accent coach for the evening." And then starting right in, familiarizing them with the subtleties of the Inverness accent, running through the sound changes, assigning them several pages of exercises based on words from the script: *Oh, he's a gdate bie for the gurrdles, he is! Rrraise a wee ddam, then, fudr Rrrobbie Buddens!*

It was the only big feature film he'd ever done not aimed at the female lonely hearts market. His part was small, but he'd had a couple lively scenes as a transplanted Scot living from hand to mouth in the Nova Scotia of a century ago. They were shooting in Cape Breton, but her face was beamed straight from Toronto where she was working on a major American film at the same time, coaching household-name stars—b-b-but—she'd be coming out to Sydney when she was done to work one-on-one with him and all the rest of the pretend Scotsmen.

Ever since arriving in Cape Breton, he'd been tense, preoccupied, in a constant sweat about Neil alone in the house in Sainte-Clémence. It was no use phoning; his brother would never pick up. Was Nathalie Casgrain from next door checking in every few hours, bringing him his meals, like she'd promised? Had Lucy been by to keep him company, Lucy with her infernal chain of cigarettes? His aching, trembling guilt at his own selfishness, at not being where he so clearly belonged was no longer mitigated by the rush—what on earth had he been thinking?—that daring to accept an away-from-home job for the first time in almost twenty years had given him. Was Neil taking his meds? Well of course, he was; he always did, why would he stop now? But was he lonely, upset? He certainly hadn't seemed bothered in the least when Evan had asked if he minded him leaving for three weeks.

But from the moment Rivka had walked on set, bringing along the previously unseen parts of her, elegantly casual in a down vest and enormous furry boots, gold-streaked hair that grazed her waist, knife-edge regal nose, green Genghis Khan eyes crowded by cheekbones, he had never wanted to go home again. Love and hope—he had forgotten that either thing existed—had cut him off at the knees.

It was—oh, it *had* to be—destiny! Had to be the Lord, finding Evan's torn, coffee-stained folder at the back of a drawer where it had languished for two and a half decades. The Lord, slapping his forehead: Doh! Where's my head? This poor boy is *waaay* overdue for a mate! Evan had to smile, sourly, thinking this; it so smacked of his Aunt Louisa and the old days. But still. It *felt* like destiny. No, better: it felt like the most loving of divine decrees!

Days he was shooting, they'd worked together on set, going over the day's scene. Days when no Scotsmen were required, they'd meet in the extra motel room the production company had rented for Rivka to work in, always at Evan's brown-nosey suggestion that they go over his lines again. He'd been as embarrassed by the bed in the room as a nineteenth century Presbyterian minister, applying himself hyperconsciously to the work at hand, unlike some of the other actors, who weren't doing their exercises, were taking an altogether laissez-faire attitude to Scottishness, perfectly content to do their best Sean Connery or Groundskeeper Willie impressions and be done with it. Rivka had complained with feeling to Evan about this. "If they suck, I'm the one who gets the blame! Sorry, sweetheart. I'm just venting."

Sweetheart? "Vent away!" he'd cried, commiserating with the fullest of hearts.

It had been a bitter, rainy October in Sydney. They'd spent more time in that motel room than they might have under kinder skies. Just talking, when the work was done. When he found out she was a native Montrealer, he was beside himself. She was so young, twenty-eight to his forty-three. But smart! Arguably the best voice coach the world had ever known! And so nice to him! When they went out for drinks with the other Scotsmen, Evan said little, though he was hyperaware that she looked at him differently than she did the others, offering languorous half-smiles, overlong gazes from behind lowered lashes, causing his long-nursed, single glass of beer to tremble visibly in his hand.

Was "opposites attract" an irrefutable law of the physics of love? Her world could not have been more remote from his; she lived amongst movers and shakers, rolling from one big-budget film set to the next, pulling in twelve hundred dollars a day, nimbly sidestepping the louche advances of A-list actors, implying with no more than a lazy smile—he'd seen her do it to the bolder Scotsmen—"I know how much you want me, and I can hardly blame you, but give it up, dude. You're *so* out of your league." There was something almost Jane Austen-ish in her manner, the stern but intelligent virgin, or some proto-feminist version of that which allowed for highly selective promiscuity. Lofty post-postmodern principles, fuelled by cool, unflinching self-esteem. "I do all the choosing around here, my good sir. I, and no other."

And this invincible paragon had chosen *him*, had pointed her elegantly beringed finger of fate at quiet, retiring, damned near invisible Evan Labossière. No, there was no conceivable way, outside of divine intervention, that this could be.

She'd been unaware, of course, that she was choosing a man who had been taught all his young life that the Lord alone decided who was to be hitched to whom in this brief sojourn in the vale of tears. "Until you are ready," boomed that Lord, speaking through Louisa, who channeled him like a medium, "and the godly woman He has reserved for you is ready—you must wait in godly patience." All he had to do was cool his heels and, above all, remain pure; failure to carry out this non-negotiable part of the bargain would, of course, be a cosmic deal-breaker. Best case scenario: if he toed the line, held himself in stern check, the Lord would have the job done by the time he turned twenty. Louisa had been rock-solid on this point.

But the Lord had dropped the ball! Had forgotten all about him!

It wasn't that he still believed—consciously—that this was how life worked. Celibacy had simply become, by the time he'd entered his thirties, a habit. He had read somewhere that it was not unlike sexual debauchery in that both were practiced by people full of deep and troubled yearning. This was highly comforting, giving his quiet, reclusive life an imprimatur of seriousness, and supplying him with a noble excuse that masked the fact that he was staggeringly shy and inept with women. But if he were to be completely honest, by the time he'd reached his forties, the pain and loneliness celibacy had once evinced barely registered anymore.

Until *she* appeared. And all at once, as he heard the first scrapes of the key turning in the lock to his self-imposed cell, his entire being began to fairly scream for a woman. And not just any woman. *This* woman!

Still, he hadn't had the nerve, on the night it had finally happened, to admit to Rivka that she was his first.

Lying beside her on that first giddy night in her Sydney motel room, daft with flushes, a cuckoo joy he hadn't felt since his early theatre days in CEGEP, hugging her klutzily to his long, overheated self, on the awful point of tears, weak from love, and from not having eaten for two weeks, eleven pounds he could hardly spare already gone, earning him a scolding from the wardrobe mistress, who'd had to take in his workpants. Lying dazed while Rivka sat cross-legged and ran through the speech of Birmingham, Newcastle, Manchester, Norfolk, Sussex, Ulster and South Wales, her lipstick kissed off, hair all matted and embroiled, the sheet down around her waist because she was twenty-eight and as relaxed as a kitten about her body. It was the longest stretch he'd seen her go without checking her phone or texting; she knew everyone alive, was always scoping out work opportunities, connecting with her posse.

She'd laughed outright at the shock on his face when her panties had come off, the whole "area" shaven whistle clean.

When had *this* started?

And then just gazing at him, her head resting on her hugged knees. She was in love, she told him, so totally in love with his eyes. "Look at me," she said. "Break my heart with those gorgeous lilac eyes of yours." Enumerating all the things she'd fallen so hard for: his still boyish face, his curly hair, his gentleness, patience, calm maturity, his impossible sweetness. And muteness. He was so spiritual, so pure, so unspoiled! He *so* made her want to be a better person! She truly admired people like him, who were self-possessed, who operated from a hard-won inner strength, who knew how to remain quiet, didn't have to be constantly mouthing off, crowding the spotlight. She didn't see a whole lot of this in her line of work.

She even came out with the "still waters run deep" line, which he had been hearing from his aunt's church friends since he was six.

All of this, particularly that notion of his hard-won inner strength, had given him the heart-sinking sense that he was pulling some pretty thick wool over her eyes. But he'd let it ride. Maybe *her* strength would rub off on him in time and make it true. He certainly hadn't failed to notice that he hardly ever stuttered in her presence.

And never mind her strength; she was the most ravishing creature he'd ever seen. Rivka Lipkin—was it politically incorrect to say she looked stunningly, er, Semitic? What was the protocol here? Luckily for him, perfectly correct protocol could most easily be maintained through perfect muteness.

Her Jewishness gave her grounding in his eyes, elevating and illuminating her, their union a miraculous, living embodiment of the Judeo-Christian tradition. He was hard-pressed to explain to himself why it mattered so profoundly that she be connected to at least some kind of recognizable religious heritage. But it did. Try as he might, he couldn't shake off the old scruples embedded, it seemed, in his DNA. No, Rivka certainly wasn't the right-thinking Christian woman his aunt had sworn the Lord would provide, but somehow, it all boiled down to the fact that if she was Jewish, then the Lord must know her, must have her on *some* kind of provisionally approved list, and thus, it was safe to proceed.

The instant he'd returned from Sydney he'd begun googling Judaism. And borrowing—under strong protest—Neil's Encyclopedia Britannica, Volume Thirteen, *Jerez to Libe*, on the theory that old-school knowledge would be more trustworthy. He took copious notes: *Three categories of commandments in the Torah: The chukim (supra-rational commandments), Eidot (testimonies) and Mishpatim (rational civil laws). Hope in Hebrew: Tikvah. Gevalt, Jews! Don't give up!* All of it inflaming him with a sense of deep spiritual connection he had not experienced since his hyper-churched boyhood, his vaulting romantic hope like a clutchingly sweet memory from the distant future. A memory that looked back on his and Rivka's stupifyingly beautiful life together, the remembering of the world after its redemption by Moshiach.

He'd been astounded to discover there was no damnation of the soul in Judaism. Belief in the coming of Moshiach meant that the world would one day come to realize the purpose for which it had been created. No punishment for anyone! Next year in Jerusalem! The cosmic play needed all the extras, all the walk-ons; there were no small parts, only small etc. Everyone got a curtain call, everyone got applause!

"I learned that *Emet* is the Hebrew word for truth, the reality behind existence," he told her, blushing a little, after they'd been back a week, hanging out in her swank kitchen in NDG, the roomy apartment she wore around herself like an airy mantle, an enchanted space throbbing with her thoughts, her history, the luscious perfume of her being. "The source, the substructure of all energy, if you will," he had continued, and yes, saying "if you will" out loud, but he was nervous, competing for psychic space with her king-size bed, her wide-screen TV, her clothes strewn over the floor, the Arcade Fire playing on her laptop. "*Emet*," he repeated, waiting for her face to brighten. Her smile troubled him a little; it never bloomed full out, always seemed to freeze several crucial degrees short of its apex.

He'd blithered on. "I also know what a *minyan* and a *mitzvoth* are." She was at the stove making omelets, spreading peanut butter on toast, chanting, "P to the Nut to the Butt–E-R!" Not listening very hard to him. "A *minyan* is a quorum of ten men required for a prayer group, and"—knowing her well enough by now to expect some pushback—"it excluded women, but only because they were considered *superior* to men, purer and holier. (Like you, like you!) Women were in charge of the most sacred relationships. (Like ours!) The Talmud says that women's prayers shoot straight to the ear of God with no need for a ritual community."

"Aren't you the bright little scholar."

"And a *mitzvoth* is a good deed."

"And I had shrimp cocktail for lunch. So let's get over ourselves, okay?" But gently she said it, before disappearing into the bathroom, giving him time to leaf through a few of the magazines also strewn about the floor. Trying to memorize the names and faces of people who might be important to her: Gwyneth Paltrow, Naomi Campbell, Lena Dunham. Stavros Niarchos lll. Marc Jacobs. He would never cram it all in.

When she came back, she told him that she could only remember once in her life playing what she called "the Jew card."

"In the third grade, I told this little pig-nosed freckle factory Maureen O'Herlihy that she wasn't allowed to speak to me because she didn't have a bubbe and a zayde. Her face just about cracked apart. I think she thought they were essential body parts. It was *so* satisfying. I could be such a little twat."

He'd gazed at her, blocking his ears to "twat," trying to imagine her long nose not quite so long, her hair in brown, unstreaked braids.

"Daddy and Mummy spoiled me and my sister rotten," she went on, talking through a slug of peanut butter licked right off the knife. "Daddy used to say, 'If you never end up doing anything in life, if you just lie on your couch and veg till you're seventy, it will be more than good enough for me. I couldn't come up with a single complaint.'" She drawled this with that odd lack of affect he'd noticed before in the lavishly praised as they described the quotidian experience of being drenched in that praise.

Her Jewish identity, he began to see, was drawn in simple, Neil Simon terms. She had had a bat mitzvah. She was on familiar terms with kishka, kugel, blintzes. Great uncles and aunts had perished in Bergen-Belsen. Her maternal bubbe and zayde had kept kosher, had had things to say about the importance of community to Jewish identity, the dangers of assimilation. She remembered observant Seders from her lower youth, when all the grandparents had been alive, she and her sister Malka playing the Four Children, asked the Four Questions, two apiece. Evan had made fevered mental note to look up what all of this might mean as soon as he got home.

"We used to chew the scenery to pieces, asking those questions, doing funny accents and stuff, and Daddy would say, 'You two are such *hams!*' Bubbe Rivka would just about pass out at the blasphemy. *Ham*, my darling . . . get it? All this to say, we weren't the most pious family that ever lived."

"Did you know that the matzah stands for the absolute poverty of the person who follows God into the desert armed with nothing but faith and commitment? That leavened bread is symbolic of egotism and arrogance?"

"Oh, probably. I remember me and Malka in the kitchen after, drinking down the glass of wine meant for Elijah. Giggling our heads off. It was only Bubbe Rivka, my father's mother, who took it seriously. My parents kept it up for her sake. The candles, the giant spaz over getting all the leavened bread out of the house, all that stuff. After she died, we were usually in Palm Springs during the Easter break. The old Seder got phased out. Oh! What kind of a face is that?"

"No next year in Jerusalem?" It came out as a whimper.

"Next year in Belize, if the time-share's available," she quipped, poking him in the ribs. "You need to take a pill, dude."

Hearing about her childhood always left him feeling beaten about the head. What was it like to come from all that warmth and wit? To be encouraged to think well of yourself instead of being reminded hourly of how you had been born in sin, separated from God, and that even in your saved condition, the fires of hell would be singeing your ass cheeks if you weren't scrupulously careful every single solitary second of your life. To never *once* wake up to a quiet house, clawed ragged with terror that everyone but you had been raptured. Rivka's grandparents, she'd gone on to tell him, had died, and then her handsome, funny parents had divorced, and her stepmother, Carol, wasn't even Jewish, though she too was handsome and funny. Rivka and Malka had continued to be spoiled, Carol taking them once a week, all through their teens, to a high-end hairdresser in Westmount just to have their long, lustrous hair professionally brushed. Nothing else, just brushed with infinite love for fifteen minutes, the tiny uneven ends snipped off. As a family, they spent a lot of time in hot climes, lounging on golden sands, cavorting in sailboats, wearing very little. Even now, Rivka was in shorts from the first warmish April day till the middle of October.

And who did he have, besides Neil? Louisa. Period. Steel-girded, keen-eyed, imperious, vulnerable only before the Lord, and that just barely. All through his childhood, bustling about in the hall and basement of their church, Sundays, Wednesdays, Saturdays, always hurrying somewhere, lugging stuff, shepherding someone, initiating group huddles. At home, ever on the run, slapping supper on the table as quickly as she could, much high-octane frying and frozen potato puffs. After supper when he and Neil had done their homework and gone quietly to bed, if she were home, she'd still be at the kitchen table paying bills, leafing through her Bible and Concordance, making notes. When she drew night and weekend shifts at the hospital, or had meetings to attend, Lucy from next door would look after them. Still, for someone they saw so rarely, the bird bones of their little lives had been sorely crunched in the iron grip of their aunt's holy hands.

He longed to bare his soul to Rivka about it all, but balked at the gate, grasping in vain for the right words to explain his pious, sheltered childhood. Wanting to be truthful but knowing that anything he said would, under the glare of the noonday secular sun, emerge as brutal caricature. How, for instance, to capture soft-spoken Dorcas, homeschooling him and Neil along with her own kids, every day beginning with all of them chanting in unison: *Whatever is true, whatever is honourable, whatever is just, whatever is pure, whatever is lovely, whatever is gracious, if there is any excellence, if there is anything worthy of praise, think about these things!* Then, on to the day's lessons, arithmetic and history and geography interlaced with hard, indisputable fact: How Satan had secretly planted the fossil remains to blind the eyes of those who would not believe. How slavery was part of God's plan to expose a heathen nation to the Truth. How the young dinosaurs had trotted up to Noah's ark, led by the guiding hand of Providence.

He and Sara and Maribeth, Dorcas's frowning daughters, struggling to concentrate on the day's lessons, while Neil frothed pink as bubble bath, skipping to the cupboard to get their mid-morning crackers, beaming, laughing at everything, funny or not. Dorcas handling four grades at once, for ten interminable years, till she suddenly grew all fluttery, sometimes quietly weeping as they hunched over their workbooks. Finally sitting them down one grey morning and sobbing that she couldn't handle it anymore, it was just too much.

He wanted Rivka to understand Dorcas, not think poorly of her for her backwardness. Perhaps he could just sum her up through her favourite adage, which was, in fact, true: *Whatever you are overflowing with will spill out when you're bumped*. Then just leave it at that. Draw a brief sketch of his boyish joy and pride in their tiny church family, his heartfelt love for the Lord. Draw a discreet curtain over his less joyous teenage years, his sad sack self, slogging door-to-door, as far away from his neighbourhood and people who knew him as he could get, trying to choose houses where it looked like they would speak English. Lurid pamphlets—*Have you claimed the Paid in Full receipt for your sin debt?*—clutched in his damp hands as he rang doorbells, interrupting TV shows or spring-cleaning, irate folk peering through two inches of open door for the half second it took to size up the situation and bang it shut. Or worse, having them listen with chiseled smiles, or respond with a cool, defiant "nope" to the stammered query, "Do you know Jesus Christ as your p-p-personal Saviour?" Handing over one of his torrid pamphlets—*In flaming fire, in wrath and condemnation, He will take vengeance on them that know Him not!*—seized with the horror of having to convince them on the spot, knowing that their very souls hung on his willingness to leap right in and begin the persuading, dragging out the p-p-proofs, p-p-plastering that look of certainty and chosenness over his face. Only to hear, "Yeah, bozo, and how about you sit on it and *rotate!*" from behind vehemently slammed doors.

How could he make Rivka—so cherished, so supported by her own family—understand? Not a day of his youth going by without a lashing, stinging warning about the perils of the World, the Flesh, the Devil. Even by his teens, he'd grown so, *so* tired of always having to say No. No to this, no to that, no to everything lustrous and tempting and fun. The everlasting No beginning to feel like creeping death. Yes, he was supposed to die to the world, the flesh, etc. But why did he always have to be *against* everything? The things he was allowed to be *for* were so few, so dusty, so desert dry.

But now he had a reason to cry Yes at last. Yes to love! Yes to life! Now he could embrace the World, bury himself in the Flesh, free to be a real human *person,* like everyone else! It was high time, he was middle-aged, for pity's sake! He'd been *fifteen* the last time he'd known happiness remotely like this. Yes, it was high time to turn his back for once and for all on being odd, special, sanctified, set apart, still in so many ways the trembling, timorous boy who had lost so many years pretending to be an angel. Now he could be a plain, ordinary man, loved and loving, Rivka all the meaning he could ever possibly need.

Oh, the promises he'd made during their first months together, during that first heady rush of freedom, when she had loved him THIS—arms thrown wide—much! All the changes he was going to make to himself, all the things he was going to fix for her! To make her proud! And not just for her; for him! For the brand spanking new twenty-first century man he was on the dazzling brink of becoming.

For her, he would step boldly out into the world, timid no more. He would get a Twitter account! He would go on Facebook where his beloved had logged three thousand friends and counting! He would blithely toss off phrases like, "Hit me up on Insta!" He would . . . he would learn to dance!

Yes, dance! She'd signed them up for salsa lessons, and he hadn't even flinched. Turned up for that first class trembly but game. Manuel, the wiry little instructor in capri pants had immediately chosen Rivka as his demonstration partner, her slim hips matching his, sway for swivel, the pair of them executing with divine grace the three, learnable-in-two-minutes salsa steps. When she'd resumed her position with Evan, the underarms of his shirt were pungent with stress. He moved like a tree trunk. "Evan, sweetie! It's three steps! Loosen up! There's no firing squad at the end of this!" She shouldn't have been surprised; he had already demonstrated presidential stateliness on the dance floor, stomping like Paul Bunyan to blistering acid techno, longing for death as Rivka turned like a sunflower in the direction of whoever was nearby and *could* dance. Which was everybody on earth except him.

But it didn't matter! Because she needed him, she did, she said so! Tough as she seemed, she had vulnerabilities of her own, not the least of which was the age thing. At twenty-eight, she felt ancient, in a constant sweat of fear that she might not be accomplishing enough, moving up the career ladder fast enough, making a good enough impression. She feared each film gig would be her last. She felt she wasn't listened to at work, was being taken advantage of, wasn't held in the proper regard. Sometimes she snapped, cried a little, inhaled a whole bag of potato chips, moaned, "I'm so fat!" Disappeared into the bathroom for a longish time.

She'd opened up and confessed to him, a few months after they'd gotten together, that all her life she'd been looking for someone to replace her father, someone she could depend on through thick and thin. Who would be absolutely devoted to her, love her unconditionally. She'd said this with tears streaming; then, throwing her arms around his neck, she'd cried, "My angel-eyes! You're so, so, so good! Don't ever leave me, okay? Promise me!"

Undone, he'd chosen that moment to confess that up till their first night together, he'd been a virgin.

Her hairbrush clattering to the floor. "I *thought* you seemed a little . . . out of practice. Or maybe, I don't know, gay? But I never dreamed—" She'd broken off, struck dumb for the first time since he'd known her.

In the spirit of full disclosure, and against his better judgement, he'd kept on talking. Haltingly telling her about Louisa's squeaky marker slashing THE SCARLET SIN in six-inch letters on Dorcas's whiteboard, her voice spiked with nails: It wasn't wrong for a man to be hungry, she said, but it was wrong to steal another man's food. And it was an unspeakably foul sin to defile another's wife, or the girl who would become the wife of another. "Be sure of this! Your sin will find you out! Once your godly innocence is lost, you can never have it back again! You may be forgiven, but you will be forever changed, weakened, once you have soiled the hem of His shining garment in this way." Picking up steam, eyes filling, she'd invoke the stern witness of the Almighty. "Oh, Father God, I just wash these boys with the water of Your precious Word! If you have sinned already in the privacy of your hearts, if you are allowing Satan's filth into your thoughts, you must beg forgiveness now! Let your faith be a spine of steel keeping you upright and righteous!" Peering deeply, fiercely into Neil's face and then his, till they both dropped their eyes, dropped to their knees, lifted trembling holy hands to beseech a mercy they hadn't come even close to forfeiting. Their tears bringing out the little sweetness there was to be found in her, as afterward, she planted a light kiss on Evan's head, or opened a box of Mallomars, urging them both to take as many as they wanted. Saying with a gentle sigh, "It's a heavy responsibility I have for your souls, boys. Sometimes it requires a bold, even a harsh word, but remember, you are children of the King! When He returns, I want Him to find you both serving as pure and proud soldiers in His army of truth and righteousness."

Rivka had stopped him right there with a scream, so aghast was she at the notion of a childhood so steeped in medieval religiosity and pointless guilt.

"Sweetie, your aunt was *psycho!* You poor kids!" And his heart had flooded with the overwhelming conviction that, for all her uninhibited ways, her earthiness, her profanity—no, *because* of them!—Rivka was nearer to holiness and life and truth than Louisa or Dorcas could ever be. She even reminded him a little of Lucy, whose scurrilous tongue had shocked him white as a boy, but whose heart was true as gold to the people she loved. Why should Rivka's integrity count for less than Louisa's? Rivka possessed beauty, pride, fearlessness, honesty, strength! She was brilliant, witty, hardworking to a fault. Stouthearted! Yes, that's what you called a woman like that. She upheld causes with boundless energy: third-wave feminism, the rights of the transgendered, equality, empowerment! She could quote Naomi Klein and Noam Chomsky! And she had opened *him*, unwound his stinking mummy wrappings, thrown wide the windows to the cloistered cell of his mind. For the rest of his days, he wanted to be just like her, to laugh at the things she laughed at, dance the way she did, go off on a tear with her straight into the pumping scarlet heart of the brawling world.

As long as he could be back by nightfall. At home, at his post, with Neil.

She'd railed against his aunt for a few more minutes, before sinking to the floor between his knees, laying her head in his lap and murmuring, "Poor Evan. Poor little boy." And he'd thought, never mind, just let it go. Stop trying to explain. Let Louisa and church and scruples and all the past just *go*. He'd stroked her hair, running his hand along the mermaid that sinewed from her right shoulder down to her elbow—wasn't tattooing supposed to be forbidden to Jews? He was afraid to ask—as they passed a perspiring bottle of Chablis back and forth. Concentrated instead on her jaw-dropping beauty, something ancient about it, like an Old Testament harlot! Pictured the shifting angles of her face, queenly in repose, all mouth when she laughed. Her eyebrows needing an esthetician's attention, her hair bobbing in giant rollers, and still she stopped his heart. The way she strolled around with her phone to her ear, letting cigarette ash fall any old where. Strolling around naked, free, honest, healthy, sacred, his girl, his woman of the world, with—w-w-with—never mind the Mason jar full of condoms—but—with a whole *drawerful* of colourful p-p-plastic apparatuses requiring b-b-batteries.

He had shied away from that drawer as if it were writhing with snakes.

Mumbling, "I don't want to cheapen us," when she'd first yanked it open, suggesting he choose whatever took his fancy. No, no, they should be *one*, one flesh, nothing *but* flesh! Was that backward? Was that stupid? There was something about those plastic toys too near in spirit to the idiotic, faked-up bedroom scenes in his movies, the humiliation of consenting to appear in shiny pajama bottoms, lying in the cold arms of a series of fluff-haired actresses in satin bras, having to shift positions, execute a few decorous grinds under the sheets, the crew standing around gawping.

No, no. Something was missing in all this ease and liberality, something that muttered under its breath like contempt. The Baal Shem Tov's wife wouldn't have a drawer like this, he wanted to say (gently). The Lubavitcher Rebbe would know a sacred thing when he saw it.

"I know who the Lubavitcher Rebbe is," he'd said to her, over the top of her gold-streaked head.

She'd yawned against his thigh. "I know, sweetie, I know. You're such a thug."

He'd known full well that, before the dawn of their glorious wedding day, he would have to bring her before the scrutiny of the now eighty-year-old Louisa. After, of course, a tremendous amount of preparatory song and dance, talking Rivka up as one of "the remnant," which would at least give her a distant shot at salvation in Louisa's eyes and perhaps derail any flinty harangues about being "unequally yoked."

The preparatory song and dance that would have to go into readying Rivka to meet Louisa didn't bear thinking about.

Or to meet Neil.

He'd brought it up so gingerly, that first time. "You'll have to come out to my place to meet my brother. I look after him. He's ill, he doesn't leave the house." He'd half hoped she wouldn't, knowing how awkward it would be for Neil, who might lash out in confusion, yell something shocking, embarrassing them both to death.

But she'd been all sweetness. "Sure. I'd love to meet him, and to see your place. I wish you'd move into town though."

He'd smiled at her. "I know. But it wouldn't work for Neil."

So she'd come. Once. It was evening, and Neil was just up, on his way to the bathroom. Hearing Rivka's voice, he'd stopped dead at the top of the stairs, and as Evan rose from the table to launch into his nervous introduction, his brother had let out a mighty roar, retreating into his room with a slam of the door that shook the house to its foundations.

"Well, well, well," was all she'd had to say about that. For the moment.

He'd never found the courage to open up to her all the way, to pour out, with no shame, his honest feelings for his brother. Never came close to telling her the whole story, from their childhood right up to the Thailand debacle. It was too humbling to remember his inexperienced, so easily intimidated self, upon arrival, turning in dazed circles in the Bangkok airport, stupefied by signage like mirror-image cursive, the kind of rag-and-bone alphabet they might use on Arcturus. Twenty-four years old, knapsack over his shoulders, jostled along by the crowd to the arrivals area where greeters were waving, straining against ropes. And then seeing . . . oh!

Neil. Two and a half heads taller than everyone else, a spiky weed poking up from the pansy bed. Recognizable, but . . . warped.

Fantastically bearded for one thing, scarcely any open face left, and that part barbecued to a turn, and rucked and lined far beyond his twenty-six years. His long, Neil Young hair lying like seaweed flattened every which way against a rock. Dressed in a yellow sarong and a lime-green shirt festooned with hula dancers.

His arm shot up like a periscope. Evan returned the wave, Neil reaching toward him over the ropes, fat beads of white man sweat on his forehead, soggy hula dancers clinging to his armpits.

They walked, holding hands over the ropes to the place where the ropes ended. Clapped one another's backs in manly enthusiasm. Neil pulled away first, shouting over the din, "Let's blow this pop stand," as he set off for the exit at an alarming rate of speed, Evan trotting to keep up.

Outside, slamming heat. Evan shifted his knapsack from one aching shoulder to the other while Neil, already at a taxi stand a long way from the doors, appeared to be in rancorous dispute with a driver. Turning, he cupped his hands to yell, "Motherfucker's trying to rip me off!"

This was startling, and hardly what Evan had expected from someone who had found all the truth and wisdom needed to live. The taxi driver, however, took it in stride, shrugging and climbing into his cab. "You're an asshole!" Neil hollered, giving the car's hood a good pound before wrenching the passenger door open and sliding in himself. With a squeal of tires, the taxi pealed out and spun around, covering, in four seconds, the five hundred metres to where Evan stood. The driver stomped on the brakes, the taxi jolting backward. Neil rolled down his window, his grin a wide breach in the boreal forest that constituted his lower face.

"Going my way?"

Evan tossed his knapsack into the back seat, clambered in after it. Neil, with a viperish smile, laid his prawn-pink arm across the back of the driver's seat. The driver irritably pushed the arm away. With a wink back at Evan, Neil presented the driver with his long, slow, middle finger, putting his arm right back where it had been. Evan studied his lap. Neil turned around again, pleased as punch.

"Why so glum, chum?" He adjusted his arm to make sure it grazed the driver's shoulders. "I swear, I never thought you'd bust out of your funk and show up." His throat sounded rusted-out, scabby.

The driver pulled violently away from the curb while simultaneously lighting a cigarette. He ignored Neil's provocative arm, and after five minutes Neil removed it. They made their manic way from one screaming near smashup to another, weaving through five lanes of traffic on a roadway designed for only two. Evan was continually pitched forward, his face ramming the seatback as the driver veered away at the last possible second from buses, motorcycles, and oncoming herds of bony, flop-eared cows, their flaccid udders dragging over the ground.

It took almost an hour to reach Neil's house in the suburb of Nonthaburi, a place about which Neil had told him nothing other than that it was a suburb. This had called to mind something not presently materializing. The landscape seemed hacked out of a jungle grey with road dust, wilted by car exhaust.

They bumped to the end of a weedy, unpaved lane, stopped in front of a haywire building. A pack of baying dogs appeared out of nowhere, mobbing the cab like paparazzi, jumping back and yelping when the driver flicked his spent cigarette at them. The house looked like an upended shoebox cobbled from plywood and sheets of corrugated metal, its crooked roof tossed on all askew like a lid from some other, bigger box. It was painted, roof and metal included, flamingo pink. Outside the doorless front door stood a miniature pagoda on a little table, far handsomer than the real house, a palace for the Emperor of the Birds. Its imposing front door was flanked by doll-size Corinthian columns; carved tongues of flame coiled from its peaked red roof. The table it sat on was festooned with ropes of beads, yellow paper flowers, bowls of desiccated oranges.

Neil leapt from the cab, pitching a balled-up handful of bills and coins onto the seat. He yanked open the rear door, hoisted Evan's knapsack onto his shoulder like a World War I doughboy marching off to battle. The dogs swarmed his knees, sniffing and whimpering. They had stark marimba ribcages, orange eye incrustations, continental maps of mange. A couple were missing legs. Two others wore ragged sweaters. They were another species entirely from joyful, leaping, Frisbee-fetching Western dogs; these were the very mascots of poverty, long-eyed slinkers, steeped in suffering, cynical and hard. Neil kicked them away. The driver did a screeching three-point and sped off in a hail of gravel that peppered Evan in the back.

"Home sweet home," Neil announced. "Built her myself, can you tell?"

"Really?"

"Yes. Really. I'm Frank Lloyd Wright. Of course I didn't build it, you idiot. I was staying here with some friends till, well, till recently. What're you lookin' at, never seen a spirit house before? Go on, lean in, take a good look. Ancestors live there, but they don't bite."

Evan crouched to study the little table pagoda. "It's beautiful. Did you build this?"

"Hell no. You buy these at big emporiums, like the places where they sell lawn furniture back home." He stood watching as Evan peered inside the tiny, ornate dwelling, before stating flatly, "Ya gotta feed them fuckers regular."

Evan straightened up. "Feed . . . whom, exactly?"

"Whom exactly? Aren't *we* dainty! The ancestors, you nit. Feed the ancestors."

"Whose? Ours? You mean like Dad and Mum?"

"You don't feed 'em, they'll invade your body, shake the living shit out of you. You got a protector in the spirit world?"

"Not . . . that I know of."

"You should tangle with a few demons. Put hair on your chest." He headed for the door, turned back to bark, "Shoes off!"

Evan followed, stopping short in the doorway to gape in three hundred and sixty degrees of slack-jawed astonishment at a space designed and built, possibly in less than a week, by M.C. Escher on killer hallucinogens. Nothing made sense: levels didn't match, staircases ended in midair. Fistfuls of jungle punched through gaps where the outer walls didn't meet. Crackly plastic sheeting covered a floor that rose and plunged like the deck of a ship. Little brown birds whooshed freely from room to room. A bristly six-inch multi-millipede shimmied across the floor inches from Evan's feet.

At least there was electricity: a creaking ceiling fan scraping through a cockeyed orbit over the main room. Piles of water-damaged paperbacks, newspapers, and stacked cardboard boxes bulged damply against the walls, reeking of must and mould. In the precise middle of the room teetered a sofa which might have been mauled by tigers. One barred window gave onto the lane, where the dogs could be heard barking importantly.

"*Hong nam*. Bathroom," Neil announced, whipping aside a ragged curtain to expose fearsome, dripping black pipes, a maze of makeshift rubber tubing, a floor of packed dirt. On top of the cracked mirror lounged a lizard, a miniature crocodile, whom Evan could have sworn gave him a cordial nod.

"That out there," Neil continued, indicating the window, his eyebrows on hyper-alert, "is the *soi*. The lane, the road, *la ruelle*. Where the atrocias are in full bloom and the diagenous florfillae offer as splendid a picture as you'll ever hope to see. So. You hungry? Hold on. Produce department's out back." He grabbed a heavy stick leaning against the wall, went out, crossed the soi, and began poking through underbrush sizzling with insect conversation. The pack of yelping dogs charged up to meet him; he beat them back with his stick.

"Gedoudda here, ya bums!"

Evan stood in the doorway, broiling in jeans and the dress shirt he'd thought was a good idea back in Montreal, watching Neil disappear into a rumpus of poinsettias and banana plants, with Japanese umbrellas poking randomly through their branches to zany decorative effect. He returned minutes later brandishing a bunch of green bananas, tossed them onto his kitchen "counter," a row of lidded barrels that separated the main room from what Evan guessed was the cooking area.

"So anyhow. This guy goes to his friend's house, and his friend says, what you got in that bag? The guy says, beer. So his friend says, if I can guess how many you got, can I have one? Guy says, if you can guess, I'll give you both of 'em. Okay, his friend says. I say . . . seven."

Evan took a careful seat on the mangled sofa, smiling painfully, feeling the chill of a familiar wind, the oncoming icy blast of fraternal diminishment. Simultaneously, in a separate, walled-off section of his brain, he was thinking that he was much the better man than Neil and badly wanted this recognized and conceded.

"Come out and walk with me!" ordered Neil, strapping on a pair of war-torn sandals outside the front door before Evan had finished the second of his underripe bananas. Still famished, logy with jet lag, he trudged obediently after his brother, who strode at a militant pace, kicking open the folds of his sarong, leading the way down the soi back to the bigger road it branched off from. They passed a house on stilts. They passed other people, who, coming toward them, grinned and bowed their heads, their hands forming little temples in front of their faces. A very small boy jumped out from behind a tree wearing nothing but a tee shirt, swinging a complicated orange and pink plastic machine gun at them from left to right and back, making tommy gun noises, his little face fierce. Neil, grinning, finger-shot him back, barking, "Pow pow!"

The brothers continued on, two tall white men with mosquitoes whining around their faces, a giant moth circling Evan's head. They passed a cluster of houses, woodsmoke rising from outdoor cooking fires, women squatting on their haunches stirring things, jostling the flames. The familiar perfume of autumn back home rising to the tops of the tall, tall palms, their fronds arid and ashy. Whole families gathered on crooked porches to stare as they passed, one young man shouting in a frenzy of hospitality, "Come, boys! This night! Join us!" Evan looked to Neil; was this possible? Did he know these people? Neil gave no indication he'd heard, poking intently into the underbrush with his stick. "Snakes," he said briefly when he caught Evan looking. Evan's toes clenched inside his running shoes, even as the indigo breeze cooled his face, his heart, his jets. How mind-bending was it for the Labossière boys, late of Sainte-Clémence, Québec, to be here of all places, and yet, how astounding to discover that, somehow, people were the same everywhere, and no more so than at suppertime.

Neil came to a stop, struck a Michelangelo pose looking over his shoulder at his brother, and smiled woodenly. A fat Buddha moon climbed the sky behind him, a yellow summer moon warmer than the winter sun Evan had left behind. As he followed Neil back the way they had come he felt as if he were pulling it behind them by a string all the way to the screwball shoebox waiting at the end of the soi.

Of course, it's obvious to him *now*: it was right after Rivka's first and only Neil sighting that a "tone"—though rarely at first—had begun to creep into her dealings with him. Barely perceptible, the kind of thing one only hears in retrospect.

In the beginning she'd been so patient with him, keeping her mockery light and affectionate as she explained to him what "packing a bowl" was. What a full Brazilian was. How air miles worked. Continually floored at how a man in his forties, a working actor, could be so spectacularly clueless. She'd regarded his innocence with a kind of hilarious awe, and he too, seeing himself through her eyes, began for the first time to laugh at himself, to lighten up, let go.

She'd taken him clubbing, to shows, to the industry parties he'd always shied away from before. Taught him about wine and weed and what was current in music and on Netflix. Introduced him to all her friends, clinging to his arm, telling everyone what a great actor he was, someone they all needed to be paying close attention to. The only thing she could not do was take him on a trip; he had had to beg off, of course, unwilling, for such a frivolous reason, to leave Neil alone. But she'd understood, she said, and he'd waved her off at the airport with her posse of girlfriends. He knew he'd chosen wisely when he saw the Facebook posts of her and her pals splayed on the beach, as he attempted to insinuate his own image into that wall of hair and thongs. Imagining himself standing there in stupid surfer trunks, all prominent ribs and white, white skin, teeth bared in a nincompoop grin that could not mask the permanent creases of worry in his face, his anxiety over not being home, with Neil upstairs, safely in his care. It was as if that single three-week period he'd dared to spend away from him had used up his meagre, lifetime store of courage, and he would never be able to step away again as long as he and his brother lived.

As it is, even a year and a half in, he and Rivka have only spent a handful of entire nights together, and always at her place; since that first time, he's been terrified to bring her out to Sainte-Clémence. And those nights have always been a disaster, with him nervous, unable to relax, thinking of Neil all alone. She'd been the soul of compassion and understanding at first, as he rose from her bed, pulling on his pants, getting ready to go, but in time she'd grown a little snappish. Asking archly, "You can't get someone else to babysit?" And of course he could have, Lucy wouldn't have batted an eye. But she'd be dropping ash everywhere, a loose butt so easily rolling into the desiccated stacks of old books and newspapers in Neil's room. It was too scary to contemplate. As for Nathalie Casgrain next door, he didn't feel right putting her out. His brother was his responsibility.

"It's because you're afraid of breaking out of your shell," she'd finally told him, with markedly less compassion. "You're afraid of everything that moves, Evan! Boo Radley there is just an excuse."

"Don't call him that, Riv. Please don't be mean."

"Well, somebody has to be. This is total self-sabotage, my dear. Classic terror of success." Her face was all sucked in and sour. "Personally, I think you *need* him to be sick. It's called codependency, my love. Besides, he'd be much better off being looked after by professionals. You're not doing him any favours. This is all about *you!*" Sensing she'd perhaps gone too far, she'd softened a little, suppressing a smile. "And don't start with that tired old 'unconditional love' speech. One word and I'll rip your face off. What about me, don't I deserve unconditional love?"

"Of course, you do. I love both of you more than I can say."

"Uh huh."

But it wasn't just the Neil problem that was exasperating her. She was beginning to chafe about his exclusive work in "brokedick" Harlequin Romance movies, which was actually all she'd seen of his work, apart from the Scotsman film and the commercials and snippets of TV work on his demo reel. When they'd first gotten together, they'd watched a few of his good husband/bad husband movies together, Rivka crying out every five minutes, "Oh, Evan, you're so good! You're *so* much better than this shit! You've got to get yourself out there, go to more auditions, do some *real* films! Where's your hustle, boy?"

She'd tried hard to give his career a boost, generously "onboarding" him to her vast circle of creative pals: actors, makeup people, hairdressers, filmmakers. Willowy dancers too, and models, and poets, and one successful novelist he'd never heard of. Bloggers by the truckload. People with Web shows. Her own career seemingly bubbling away on high heat, her raucous, rascally industry friends always dropping by her place, infringing on their alone time, plopping bottles of wine down onto her kitchen counter, lighting up or laying out lines of a variety of substances. She was always delighted by these invasions, while he sat peeling the labels off beer bottles, constructing little hills of rolled pellets, smiling till his cheeks ached, lost in dense cultural fog: What was twerking? Kimchi? Gluten? TMZ? Self-directed exploration? Why be dairy free, when did that start? What did "being your own start-up" mean? How did you "take ownership of your perspectives"? He listened to the love of his life expound on her goals and ambitions, how stoked she was—though he knew better—to be "rocketing into her thirties." How she wanted to direct one day, to helm productions that reflected the female gaze. How she'd just been talking about this over dinner with one of the major Emmas or Emilys (who could keep them all straight?) How she'd connected with her agent only that morning about the possibility of working with Jen Lawrence and Brad Cooper. Oh, the places she was going!

He worried for her! Because when she got wherever she was going, he knew she'd never be able to stop sweating and straining to protect what she'd gained, would always need to keep climbing higher, to never lose ground. It sounded so onerous that his head drooped to his chest just thinking about it. Her increasingly persistent prodding that he should branch out, go to Toronto, New York, or most heinous of all, LA, made him cringe, visibly. The corporate juggernaut, the powers and principalities of consumerism and success, of relentless self-promotion, of "It's all about ME!" horrified him. Besides, she knew he couldn't just pick up and go anywhere, she *knew!*

But whatever she knew, whatever she knows now, it's clear she no longer cares. She'd made this bracingly plain to him even before the chicken fight, on that horrible night a month ago. Her place once again filled with schmoozers, the party in full swing, when she'd suddenly bumped up against him, leaning in to pinch his cheek as she winked to a gaggle of girls across the room.

"I'm thinking it's high time we beefed up your twinkle, old man. Do some strategic packaging, grow your broke-ass brand before you shrivel into elder-dust. A little Botox, here," poking a finger at the deepening crease between his eyes, "a little Restylane in the cheekies, a little goes a long, long way, Gramps." She was already seeing someone herself for facial peels, light lip plumping. "Nothing invasive, dear heart. A couple skin pops, totally chill. Get you all ridiculous hot and red-carpet ready. Get some new headshots done while we're at it." Then to the girl next to her, behind her hand in a loud whisper heard by everyone: "Whatever you do, don't tell him they get all this plumping stuff from human corpses!" Dropping her hand, her brittle smile at seventy-two percent. "I'm *really* psyched about this. You'll be so gorgeous you'll start slutting around on me." He'd opened his mouth to protest, but she was already answering her phone, advising someone she'd have to re-skedge.

It was more malicious than she'd ever been, especially in front of other people. All of whom had eventually gone home, and there they'd found themselves, alone at the table, Rivka quiet, spent, and Evan bruised, frightened, unsure of what was to come next. Would she yawn, stretch, sashay down the hall to her bedroom? Do one of those teenage belly flops across her bed, sighing into her pillow, "Listen, sweetie, I was up all last night talking to Malka on the phone. You should probably go now." Making him wonder—not for the first time—how a person could talk all night on the phone; what on earth would you *say?*

She'd yawned all right. Leaned over to kiss his cheek but missed. "Please. Don't let me keep you. Rush home now to your favourite person in the world, Nurse Betty. Go on, get out! 'Cause, who am I? Really, who am I?" There were tears in her voice she was refusing to give in to. "After all, I'm not fucked-up, so why should Mister Pure Heart waste his time with me? I don't stink up the place, I'm not a helpless blob, I pull my own weight, so of course you don't get to feel like the Angel of Light and Mercy around me."

He'd stood frozen, shocked by her venom, as she headed for the bathroom, turning to call over her shoulder, cold and flippant, "Call me in the morning. I'm taking you shopping. Don't argue with me." His wardrobe of dark sweaters, plaid shirts and plain, brown shoes drove her wild. "No offense, but you look really depressing. How do you expect to get work when you go to auditions dressed like a dweeb?" He dreaded these periodic buying expeditions, in and out of boutiques on Saint-Denis, getting sprayed with a *bissel* of cologne, coming home with long, pointy shoes, skinny jeans, a floppy gnome hat. She made him model this stuff for her right out in the middle of the store, trying not to laugh at him outright, insisting, "Really. It's the whole package. You look totally dope!" But . . . b-b-but . . . if there was more shopping on the agenda, maybe she wasn't ready to give up on him yet? Wasn't yet ready to dump Mister Angel, who had always brought out the very best in her?

If she ever lost him (she used to say), the bottom would fall out of her soul!

"I'm sorry, Riv," he'd mumbled, head hanging. "Please forgive me. I hate for you to think badly of Neil, but I can't—"

The bathroom door had slammed, hard. "Get out! Before I stab you to death."

He'd pulled on his coat in her silent bedroom. Looked lovingly, achingly, at her rumpled down comforter, her clothes and shoes strewn about the floor, everything reeking of smoke from the party. He thought of Neil's bedroom at home, a hundred times more cluttered, always smelling of Lucy's smoke. Remembered the even worse bedroom Neil had offered him in his Thai house, so long ago.

No more than a tiny alcove next to the terrifying kitchen, closed off like the hong nam with a tattered curtain. A tatami mat on the floor, one of the chewed and shredded sofa cushions serving as a pillow. The thin army blanket Neil threw down smelled as if it had last been washed at Vimy Ridge.

Exhausted as he was, sleep had refused to take, the dream projector continually breaking down, popcorn boxes whizzing through the air, film flapping, hot burns blossoming across the screen.

Neil, who slept in the unattainable magical realm of upstairs, made a sudden appearance just as a promising dream was at last getting off the ground. The curtain rattled and there he stood, out of breath. "Lady goes to the doctor. I hurt everywhere, doc, she says. She points to her knee, her ear, her stomach, her nose, everywhere. The doc says, nothing wrong with you except your finger's broken." Then he was gone. But perhaps it had only been the broken shard of a failed dream.

He'd woken late in the morning. The bathroom looked no better than it had the day before. On a tippy wooden shelf was a plastic prescription bottle from, of all places, a Papineau Street Jean-Coutu. *Restoril. 30 mgs. Take one nightly, at bedtime.* The bottle was full, untouched, coated with hong nam grime.

Entering the kitchen area, he nearly decapitated himself on a shelf jutting from the wall at eye level, a ragged strip of found wood resting on two protruding six-inch nails. A tall stack of cans of "Smiling Fish" brand seafood avalanched to the floor.

"Yikes. Sorry," Evan said by way of shaky greeting. Neil stood at the decrepit, spidery stove, stirring, with a knife, what looked and smelled like a vat of bloodied river water. He bent to pick up a can that had rolled to a stop at his feet. "Hah! Who's smiling, now, fish? You just rolled yourself into my stew." He looked over his shoulder at Evan with a fey, Good Housekeeping smirk. "Secret's in the simmering. It needs a good twelve to fourteen hours." He reached for a jar of violently orange powder from another precariously slanting shelf, but the lid refused to unscrew, even after several grunting, red-faced tries.

"Here, let me," offered Evan. Neil yanked the jar away, smashed it on the floor. He knelt, scooped up a spoonful of powder, oblivious to the broken glass, and dumped it into the stew. He then kicked the pieces of glass away, stomping about on bare, yellow feet among the squalid Thai appliances, all loose wires, pustulating valves and intestinal tubing, reminding Evan of the soi dogs. Flies spiralled over the dish-piled sink, bumping heads, duking it out on the rims of glasses, the tines of forks. A green gecko sprinted across the stove top, just because it could.

"Might toss in a few *jingjoks*," Neil said with a diabolical chortle. "See those little lizards stuck all over the walls? Hey, here's a jing-joke for ya: Two guys are building a roof. One guy throws away every third nail out of the box. What you doing that for, the first guy asks. 'Cause the heads are on the wrong side, says the guy. You idiot, says the first guy. Don't throw 'em away. Use 'em on the other side of the house!"

"Would you like me to wash those dishes up?"

"No. A man and wife hit a skunk on the road but they don't kill it. They want to take him home to try and save its life. They get in the car, and the man says, put him right between your legs to keep him warm. But it smells bad, she says. Okay then, he says. Pinch his nose closed."

The stench of the stew was making Evan's legs buckle. He retreated to the main room, sank down heavily on the couch, which sagged to the floor beneath his weight. The sun slanted cheerfully through the barred window, revealing dust motes in their billions, like underwater murk.

"What's in all the boxes?" he called, after a while.

"My girlfriend's stuff."

"Oh." Evan waited a beat. "Your girlfriend?"

"You heard me. How about you? You got a little honey pining away at home?"

"No."

"Why the hell not?"

"No reason." Was this the kind of visit it was going to be?

A long space of silence, broken only by the ratch of Neil twisting a can under a rusty can opener, "goddammit, goddammit" foaming under his breath. Turning, he banged against another shelf, knocking a decorative plastic parrot to the floor. "Fucking *goddammit!*" he yelled, spit spraying. He hurled the bird, which whizzed over Evan's head, whamming into the wall behind him.

Neil left off his stirring, came to sit beside him, mimicking Evan's slump, his hanging head, his woebegone mouth. Then he sprang to his feet and began pacing, hands behind his back, a troubled ship's captain. "So now you're here, what're we gonna do?"

"Are you working on a film? I thought it'd be fun to hang out and watch, see what you're up to."

"Yeah. Well." A long silence. "We can see some sights." A pause. "There are sights to be seen."

"I was also really interested in your, I guess your, your getting seriously into Buddhism. I know you've been drawn to it for a long time, and I was kind of hoping—"

"Ask me tomorrow. I don't have fuck all to say today."

Hesitantly. "Neil, if you're not feeling well, I, I'm here. Is there something I can do?"

Neil sat, hugged his knees to his chest, his face submerged in red sarong folds. He seemed to Evan to be metastasizing, a black tumour oozing into every catawampus corner of the room. This was the Neil he remembered with such awful, throbbing pain, Neil so embittered by perceived failure, so insanely impatient with himself, with Louisa, with their chokingly narrow life. Neil so lost, turning in hopeless circles. Once, back when they'd still shared a room in Sainte-Clémence, a fit of brooding like this had been the prelude to an outburst of rage so cosmic his brother had hurled himself to the ground and tried to bite the floor.

Now, Neil pried his hands away from his face, sat up, combed his food-flecked beard with his fingers. "Listen. I need to take off. It's not a good day. We'll go sightseeing tomorrow. You mind?"

"Of course not. Is it something you want to talk—"

"No. I'm heading out. There's oranges in the fridge. Keep an eye on my stew. If I'm not back for supper, eat without me." He yanked open a drawer in an old wooden dresser that appeared to be stuffed with cash. Grabbed two fistfuls, crammed them into his shirt pocket.

"You gonna be okay?"

"You gonna be *okaaay*?" Neil minced back at him. He left without another word, disappearing down the soi.

It was already two o'clock. Evan peered into the bubbling stew, dipped a tentative spoon. It tasted like salted nuclear waste. He opened the surprisingly modern, clean-looking fridge, found the bag of oranges, ate the two that weren't covered in green moss. Made a brief, desultory tour of the main room, peering into the cardboard boxes. On top of one damp pile of smelly, unwashed clothes, lay, of all things, his brother's grubby Canadian passport, the picture inside of an unbearded, surprisingly upbeat-looking Neil.

He retrieved his shoes, exited the door space and walked up the soi for nearly a mile and back. Then he lay on the couch, watched birds flit through the room, perching on the beams to chat with the lizards. The house reeked of carbonized food and backed-up sewer. The smell stuck to the back of his tongue. He fell into a blank, unpopulated sleep.

It was dark when he heard Neil mounting the ziggy steps to his room. A door slammed with finality. Evan got up, dizzy with hunger and groped his way through the dark to check the stew. It had boiled down to a black crust, the pot so fiery hot he was amazed it hadn't melted. It took him ten minutes to figure out how to turn off the flame. Being in this insane house was like being inside his brother's head, everything kinked and snarled, inside out and upside down, every step a non sequitur. He returned to his alcove, fell into his foul pillow, slept.

He awoke to sunshine and Neil's rank beard tickling his cheeks as he attempted to ram a sweet rice ball between Evan's lips. "Sticky rice! You like! Eat 'em up!" He dumped a pile of rice globlets wrapped in banana leaves and tied with twine, onto Evan's chest. "You breakfast. We going on bus, go on water! I take you to see Emerald Buddha! You like, I promise you!"

It's now the morning of his ninth day without Rivka. Eight agonizing twenty-four-hour spans since the harrowing Night of the Sesame Chicken.

He's squinting into Neil's better-lit bathroom mirror, guiding the razor around the scrappy edges of his new goatee, another Rivka-sponsored embellishment. Longing to just mow through the stupid thing, but the producers of *A Husband's Plight* have asked him not only to keep it but to try flattening his hair as well, get a kind of Keanu Reeves look going. This unnerves him; isn't Keanu Reeves a teenager, he can't be middle-aged already? But that's the look they want for the character of good husband David Wade, to differentiate him from bad husband Kevin Roberts, who Evan played, clean-shaven and curly-haired, in the film just before this one.

From downstairs, the jangle of the phone.

The *phone!*

Please, please, please, please, please! Let it be her, let it be Rivka, her love for him now probably the size of a millet seed, but still . . . oh *please*, let it be Rivka! Rivka, not mad anymore! Rivka, whispering once again, "There's no one on earth like you, Evan. You're the deepest, most spiritual person I've ever met." Rivka, not yet ready to let him go!

He nearly falls to his death hurtling down the stairs.

"Hello?"

No preamble, no mention of the chicken debacle. Just her lazy drawl, the one she slip-slides into when she's in taunting mode.

"So, I had the famous dream again last night." Eating as she talks, sprawled, he's sure, on her sun-splashed golden hardwood floor in her two-hundred-dollar yoga pants and black crop top, her free hand idly caressing her bare, perfectly smooth, core-strength-is-key stomach. "The one with the goblin baby. Except there was a new twist this time: he gets up on his feet the second he's born and climbs onto my lap all smeared with gloop and starts right in reaming me out. He looked like Gene Hackman. Where are you, at home?"

"Yeah, I'm not on set till one this afternoon." Listen to him, all cool! "We're just shooting one of the kitchen sequences, not even a page."

"Anyhoo." Snorting. "If we produced a child like this, I can just see you trying to tame it. You'd put it on a leash or something. Tell it to use its inside voice. You know you would. Just sayin'," she adds belatedly, when he says nothing.

He can't speak, undone by the mini-movie playing in his head, now stalled on pause. There he is, pushing a stroller on a perfect fluffy-cloud day, bluebirds twittering, background blur of a country house, private rooms for Neil, joy, joy all around. A husband, a father, a *househusband* even, the best there has ever been, because the happy, squealing child in that stroller is no goblin, but the purest sacrament of his godly devotion and love for Rivka Lipkin, and of hers for him.

The film is paused so he can analyze her words at warp speed, desperate for any hint of relenting, of sincerity, of love. "If *we* produced a child," she said, or was it, "If we produced a *child*"—no, it was the *we* she'd leaned on, sneered at. She's only called to stick it to him, the goblin baby one of her recurring dreams, or so she says, lately always making sure to add some variant on, "I think the little monster is meant to be your creepy brother." Now she's batting him lightly with her words, a bored cat with a mouse. "He's all over your clothes, you know. There's such a charming night-of-the-living-dead stink on you after you've been with him. You're turning into a slug, my dear. A scrawny slug, if that's even possible. I know exactly how you're going to age, and these are some scary optics, dude. You'll stay absolutely the same, just get bonier and greyer, greyer and bonier by the day. You'll keep looking good from a distance, but up close, I foresee a kind of Abraham Lincoln thing happening."

Could this be the final kiss-off at last? He knows perfectly well she's set her hopes on him easing into a Karl Lagerfeld dotage: high collars, white ponytail, dyspeptic scowl.

The phone trembles in his sweaty hand.

"Is it really so crazy that I want to m-m-marry you, Riv?" Backsliding into that wretched stutter, damn it, *damn it*, a dead giveaway!

"It's dipshit demented, is what it is. You already have a wife, bucko. Living upstairs from you."

"Please, Riv. P-please don't—"

"Don't even think about it. I will fuck you up, son!"

She hangs up.

It's over. Or, or—maybe—as good as over. Teetering, windmill-armed, on the very brink of the relationship cliff, but still (somehow) salvageable . . .

No, you benighted fool. It is well and truly over.

Upstairs, he hears Neil in the bathroom, the flush cascading through the pipes, the door banging open, his brother's leaden tread back to the confines of his room, back to sleep. Shuffling, heavy-footed, light-years from the Neil of old.

That Neil, too, as over as over can possibly be.

In Thailand, his brother had been aflame with crazed—albeit largely negative—energy. Still, in the beginning, he'd impressed Evan with possessing a kind of wacky stateliness, a man in touch with realms Evan knew nothing of.

It really had felt like the beginnings of an adventure there for a while! Walking down the soi to catch the small, slat-sided truck that served as a bus, which would take them to the ferry dock. Boys hanging off the back, gripping the roof with one brown arm. Everyone staring at the tall white brothers. Evan smiling at a young girl on the opposite bench, startled almost to tears by the uncomplicated warmth of her answering grin.

The ferry was little more than a platform on pontoons chugging across the tea-coloured Chao Phraya River, churning a swath through coconut shells, cigarette butts, sodden cabbage leaves. Neil's tropical ensemble consisted of pale blue pants four inches too short and a shirt abloom with orange hibiscus and yellow canaries, half unbuttoned to reveal a fuzzy, scorched triangle of chest.

The city, when they reached it, was crowded, sooty, clogged with traffic. It smelled of bus exhaust, fried food and burning rubber. Legless beggars tugged at Evan's jeans, wretched dogs trotted past on personal business, their cool eyes briefly meeting his. Neil was already ten paces ahead, hands in his pockets, bouncing along with the cocky swagger of a ten-year-old, stopping occasionally to chuck passing kids under the chin. Evan tried to keep him in his sights, terrified of losing him in the throng. With increasing distance, his brother appeared benevolent, stable, flush with purpose.

At the end of a long block, Neil finally stopped to wait; when Evan jogged up, dripping, his shirt stuck to his back, his brother was peering into a shop window. Smirking, "Check it out," as he jerked his thumb toward a small, clumsily lettered sheet of cardboard taped to the glass. He read it out loud: "Come En! We have massage machine turn in eccentric circle for facial scurfing. Whoo hoo, facial scurfing! That's gotta hoit," Neil shouted, causing people to turn and making Evan erupt into his first genuine Thailand laugh.

The filthy, teeming city enthralled him, and not least its women, who, in contrast, were so exquisite they hurt his eyes. He stopped to watch a line of dancers wearing tall headpieces like little gold Chrysler buildings, listlessly performing for a crowd of tourists, their soft, ivory feet bare on the hot pavement, hands fluttering with limp grace. A girl in the back row yawned broadly, making him laugh again. A motorbike whizzed by, driven by a blond lout, Dirk or Biff, here in this city of ill-repute for the worst of reasons. Perched sidesaddle on the back, her legs folded demurely, was another porcelain-cool girl in a pristine white suit and a smooth chignon. Even the schoolgirls, arm in arm in their middy blouses and modest blue skirts, spotless white socks rolled at the ankle, were dazzling: so clean, so snowy pure, so incongruous in this begrimed place where grit stuck in his windpipe, drifted down onto his head like the ash of Gomorrah.

The Royal Palace, where the Emerald Buddha lived, turned out to be a vast compound of temples, of tinkling chimes and gold and coloured glass, as exotic as a World's Fair on Saturn. Or perhaps the Celestial City celebrated in the Bible, with its foundations—Evan could hear Dorcas's honeydew voice reading the delicious words—of jasper, chalcedony, amethyst, sardonyx. The poor, worn shoes of many lands piled up outside the temple doors.

They moved from one sparkling, pointy-roofed house to another as through a tract of model homes in the Andromeda Galaxy, walking barefoot on cool tiled floors, jostled by packs of tourists, brazen Western women in halter tops and cutoffs, tidy Japanese families in floppy sun hats, everyone having to sound all the gongs and bells, jingle all the chimes for themselves. Still,

Evan sensed an eerie silence behind the clamour. Monks wrapped in saffron sat hunched in the shadows, watching with the Buddha's inward-looking eyes. The young ones with their little round glasses looked like earnest vegan college students on toga party night; the old ones, gaunt, with scabrous feet, were the human counterparts of the roughed-up, feral dogs.

This was how ninety-nine percent of the world lived, he thought. Utterly powerless, light-years from the smug safety enjoyed by the Precious Saved back home, where the Lord had so lovingly placed them—said Louisa—having known from before the beginning of time that *they* were going to turn out to be the kind of people who would accept the Gospel, thus ordering the world in such a way that *they* would be born at a time and place whereby they'd have the chance to hear it and be saved. And as for the rest?

Gedoudda here, ya bums!

Through the doors of another temple then, to where Neil stood pointing up, up, at the Emerald Buddha, a tiny, remote, long-eyed alien with a pointed head, perched high on a baroque golden throne, attended by expressionless golden handmaidens. The saved and righteous Labossière brothers of Sainte-Clémence, Québec stood stiffly, gazing up, hands behind their backs, necks cricked. After a few minutes of this, Neil turned abruptly away, heading for the exit without a word. Evan unstuck his neck and trudged after him.

Outside, an old woman in a brown headscarf stepped into his path, tugging urgently on his sleeve. On the ground behind her were scores of wicker cages full to bursting with tiny hysterical birds. She was shoving one of those cages at his stomach.

"For five *baht*, she'll open the cage and set them free. You make a wish when they come out," said Neil. "Go ahead, do it. You know you want to. My treat."

The giddy birds jostled in the opened cage door, bumping heads, squabbling, before swooshing out, carrying the magic words, *Please. Bring the old Neil back. Help him. Heal him. Please, please!* skyward, even as the woman was already haranguing a new set of tourists, and Neil, his fruit punch outfit just visible through the crowd, was already half a block away, waiting impatiently, slightly bent at the waist like a broken protractor, as if his stomach hurt.

It was getting on to four o'clock; Evan's stomach hurt too, like blazes. He set off, praying Neil wouldn't move again in the interim. Reaching him at last, he panted, "Neil, I need to eat something before I pass out."

"The veil is thinnest when the pointlessness of hanging on is most clear," Neil replied, shifting from one foot to the other, restless as a kid in an appliance store. His shirt was drenched. He ran one nervous hand then the other over his damp, wild hair; his Amish beard dripped. He turned and took off at a run, halting at every intersection, giving Evan just enough time to wheeze into sight before bolting away again, parting the sidewalk hordes, causing an elderly man to stumble and fall to his knees, taking no notice.

Evan caught up at last, nearly weeping with relief to see Neil stopped outside a hole-in-the-wall restaurant. He obediently kicked his running shoes into the pile at the door, but Neil didn't bother, leading the way in rudely shod, stopping to survey the noisy room, his imperial gaze lingering for a brief, condemning moment on each group of diners. He strode to an empty corner table, yanked out a chair with a great clatter, then addressed the room at large. "Hey, gooks! Whose keister do I have to pork to get some service?"

Evan's heart plummeted, taking his appetite with it. "Please don't use that word, Neil. Don't be like this."

Neil dropped into his chair, sat back, arms folded across his flora-and-fauna chest.

"Which word? Gooks or keister? Or pork?" When Evan said nothing, he leaned forward, scraped his hair back with his right hand then his left, foraged violently in his left ear with his little finger, fixed Evan with a steely gaze, and barked, "Memorize this, it could save your life. A *gai* lays *kai*. A hen lays eggs. Okay. So, a merchant can *khai*, which means sell, either *gai* or *kai*. And the Thai word for 'who' is *khrai*. So: Who sells hen's eggs? Repeat after me: *Khrai khai kai gai?*"

Evan smiled weakly. Neil blammed the table with his fist. "I'm not talking to the walls, asshole! Repeat after me! Khrai khai kai gai?"

"Cry kuy kuy guy."

"It's a question, jerkoff!"

"Cry kuy k-k-kuy g-g-guy?"

"Well, that sucked. You're dismissed, my son. Go and speak no more." Neil sat back for a moment before squirming around to shout into the din, "Helloooo? Maiter dee? May I see your wine list?" A girl, no more than thirteen, with a round kewpie face and a tee shirt that read, "Cuddle Me" materialized beside their table.

"Well, hello there, Cuddles. Bring us two of whatever the specialty of the chef happens to be. And pick all the insect life out first, if you would be so kind." The girl smiled uncertainly. "You no speak Engrish? *Heille, ça va mal à la shoppe.* Go get the chef, Cuddlecheeks. Chop chop." The girl stood still, glancing nervously around at the other tables, but no one was paying them any mind.

"Neil, she doesn't understand you." Evan looked at the other tables; everyone seemed to be eating the same plate of noodles with some kind of pink encrustation on top. "I think there's just one thing to eat," he began, even as he noticed a waiter walk by hoisting a platter heaped with what appeared to be fried spiders. He smiled at the girl, pointed to the next table, held up two fingers, adding a tremulous "Please." The girl bowed her head imperceptibly and darted away.

"Awww! Dear little Evan, evwybody's pweshus fwend. Big heart dwipping all over his sleeve."

Evan took a breath. Took another.

"Christ, are all you holy fools such colossal pains in the ass? Was Jesus like you? Big dumb shiny face, clueless as shit, the guy who never got any of the jokes?"

Evan swallowed hard. "I . . . really enjoyed seeing the sights today." His eye roved to a small shrine in the corner of the room featuring a straight-nosed, coldly serene Buddha with yellow flowers on his toes. He didn't appear to think much of anyone there, his flat eyes perceiving them in all their hideous enormity, all their little foibles and excuses blown up to the horrors they really were, like fleas under a microscope.

Neil's eyes followed Evan's, took in the shrine. He let out a quick, bitter hoot.

"We will get Three! Big! Surprises! when we get to heaven!" Evan recognized their aunt's cadences, her laser focus, her ferocious eyebrows. "There'll be folks there we never thought would get there! And some folks we were sure would get there, won't! And, thirdly, we're going to find out that the Lord meant everything He said in His Word and that we'll be judged strictly by the Book! Ha *hah!*"

Evan offered a weak smile. "You've got her down pretty—"

"And I won't give up, shut up, or let up until I've stayed up, stored up, prayed up, paid up and preached up for the cause of my Saviour! When He comes for His own, He won't have any trouble recognizing me! So, little pinchy-face goody-boy, here's what I want you to do. March right up into my Thai girlfriend's face and tell her she's going to burn forever."

"Neil, I could never say a thing like that to anyone."

"Yeah, but you believe it."

"I . . . I don't know. It's something I—"

"Oh! So, you've renounced the faith? Does Louisa know?"

"I haven't renounced it. I'm . . . I'm rev-v-vising. Why are you yelling at m-m-me? You w-w-wanted me to come here."

"I *said*, does Louisa know?"

"I . . . guess so. She's not too hap-p-py with m-m-me these days. She didn't want me to move out."

"I bet not. Mr. Perfect suddenly wants to go on the wicked stage. Repent! Repent, backslidden boy! Get away, Satan! No more, Devil! No more!" He sat back, appraising Evan coolly through slitted eyes.

"Please, Neil, let's not do this. Louisa was a mother to us, she did so much. I mean, who w-w-would've looked after us if—"

"You stammering little fuck. She was no mother. You know who my mother was? My real, spiritual mother?"

"No."

"Lucy, next door. Lucy was the one who saved *my* ass. She told me all that Christer crap was a load of malarkey. Guess you must've been safely out of the room." Neil snorted wetly, removed a bubble of mucus from his upper lip with a grimy forefinger, applied it to his pants. His sorely wronged-child's eyes suddenly met his brother's, two halves of a magnet slamming together. "How is old Lucy these days? We've kind of lost touch."

"She's not that old, Neil. She's only in her forties."

"Jesus. Lucy. That woman was hilarious. She's the only person from back then I could stand to see again. She still living there with her mother?"

"Yeah, she is. They—"

"Lucy thought I was okay, when nobody else did. Lucy thought I was fucking great! She saved my life about eight hundred times." He laughed, a truncated, backward snort. "You remember sneaking over to watch TV at their place? Remember her teaching us to gamble? Aw, Jesus. Lucy. I miss that crazy chick."

Evan smiled. "You'll be happy to know her gambling finally paid off. She won a huge pile of money in the 6/49 last year. She quit working at the library and bought a bunch of cheap properties that she rents out. That's what she and her mother are living off now."

Neil said nothing, his legs bouncing at a galloping clip under the table. He began feverishly patting down his pockets. "Speaking of Lucy, I need a smoke." He swung around in his chair, hollering to the room. "Who's got a smoke? Anybody? Hey! A smoke? Puffy-puffy! Anybody?"

Nobody did. He turned to Evan again, slid his hands all the way across the table and back, seven, eight, nine times. Evan concentrated on his diaphragm, drawing in breath from the depths.

"Neil, you . . . maybe you don't remember, but you were the one who started me thinking about godliness and, and ungodliness, remember? When you came back from that cult you'd been in? You said we had to die before—"

"How about you go fuck yourself, Bible boy!" Neil put two fingers to his mouth and whistled, every face in the restaurant swerving their way. He half rose from his chair to shout gleefully, "As you were, folks, nuthin' to see here!" into the sudden silence. His balled fists quivered on the table as he slumped down again. "Fuck, I thought I could take it, but you make me want to puke, that stupid angelic face of yours. Fucking weakling." He bumped the table hard from underneath with his knees. "My brother is a fucking weakling!"

The girl returned, stopping at the table behind them. Neil tugged hard on the back of her shirt and she spun around, terrified. He held up two fingers, mimed glugging from a bottle. "Beer," he said, waggling two fingers in her face. "Just don't bring the whole horse to the table." An elderly man at the table next to them understood "beer" and conveyed the message to the girl, who sprinted to the back of the restaurant, head ducked to her chest.

"Why don't you speak Thai to p-p-people?"

"You think I can fucking well speak Thai?"

"Well, but . . . you've been working here, so . . . and isn't your girlfriend—"

"Yeah, she's a gook. I already said. Keep up, dumbass."

"Can you please stop saying g-g-gook?"

"Whoa. Somebody's getting pissy. You p-p-pissed, my b-b-bruthah? And tell me, you got a boyfriend back home, maybe? Somethin' you're not telling me?"

Mercifully, the girl reappeared, putting two bottles of Singha beer onto their table as soundlessly as she could. Evan, uncertain as to whether she'd understood they still wanted food, did a quick mime of shoving food into his mouth with chopsticks. She nodded imperceptibly and fled.

"She hates us," Neil smirked. "By the way, excellent mime skills there. Good thing you're the actor, not me."

Evan took a few long swallows of beer. Was the conversation veering out of the danger zone? He wiped his mouth, breathed, began carefully.

"I really loved seeing all the temples today. There's such a, such an aura of peace inside them. I'm . . . I'm so interested to hear about your, um, your spiritual development over here. You've always been so wise, Neil." Would flattery just make him madder? But it wasn't flattery; he meant it!

Neil tilted his bottle to his mouth, drank the whole thing down, burped. Sat coiled as a rattlesnake for a few moments, then lunged halfway across the table. Evan jumped, letting loose a girly shriek. Neil sat back again and gazed calmly at his brother's apprehensive face.

"Okay, let's catch up, Bible boy. What's happened to you since your stuttering loser high school days? What was going on with you back then anyway? Some weird shit if I'm not mistaken."

Evan's heart swelled. Were they really going to talk about *him?* His first stumbling steps out into the world, his budding career, the absolute last thing anyone would ever have expected of shrinking, quaking Evan. That staggering sense of liberty and joy he'd experienced on stage for the first time in high school, his terror overridden, his stutter obliterated, the way it was when he sang. Everyone telling him he was *so* good, his golden future looming, all bets off, because when he crawled into the skin of someone else, all the austerity, all the stringent rules fell away and suddenly—just like Neil said!—there was no right or wrong but only this newborn, rapturously free person, living and breathing inside *his* body. Playing the narrator in *Our Town*, a safe, slow-talking part Mr. Gaiman had chosen just for him. And the year after, the Gentleman Caller in *The Glass Menagerie*. Oh, he'd felt like a real angel up on that stage, his heart bursting, lifting all the hearts of those who beheld him, bestowing courage and hope, helping them along their rugged paths until . . . until the costume came off, and the makeup, and he crash-landed with a thud. The wearying old guilt flooding back in: had that really been true, God-approved joy up there on stage? Or had it been the blackest pride, the wickedest conceit? Wanting so badly to get up there again and again, to make this the work of his life, even as his stomach shrank to a knotted fist at the thought of what Louisa and everyone at church would have to say about it.

Louisa hadn't come to a single one of his shows, not in high school, not in CEGEP. He'd invited Lucy to *The Glass Menagerie*, but she'd turned him down too, told him she couldn't be in crowds, especially in the dark. Mrs. Brickwood had come though, and she'd loved it, she was so proud of him. Of course, the person he'd really wanted to come and be proud of him was Neil, but his brother was in such a perpetual black funk back then that he hadn't dared ask.

He began treading cautiously into the past. "High school was rough. Being in a real school for the first time, all the other kids, well, you remember. But after you left, it got way harder. I was all alone, and I had such a b-b-bad conscience if I liked anything about it, or if I liked some of the kids who weren't, you know, religious. But Mr. Gaiman, the Speech and Drama teacher, remember him? He started helping me with my stutter. I used to go to his place after school and—" He stopped, not yet ready to open all the way, recalling himself fairly screaming, "How am I supposed to live, Mr. Gaiman?" Hopelessly confused, his lifelong beliefs smashed up against a secular backdrop like so many rotten eggs. Science class, history class, everything slanted in a completely new direction. Nobody mentioning the Bible, ever. Swarms of hormonally hopped-up kids in the halls, girls flaunting themselves, boys talking dirty, everybody taking the Lord's name in vain, a reeking swamp of unbelief and sin! And he, in spite of everything he'd ever learned and believed, longing desperately to be a part of it. His face kinked in distress, his stomach bubbling with acid, feeling—it came to him now—exactly the way Neil must have felt at home, every single second of every single day.

"Christ, I remember Gaiman," said Neil with an ugly leer. "Great name. A gift on a plate. Jesus, Evan. Step into my parlour, said the spider to the fly."

"No, no, it wasn't like that, not at all! I mean, he was . . . but he never did anything wrong, ever. I was so messed up and he took me seriously. When I got scared about being on stage, he used to lean in and whisper in my ear, 'Perfect confidence is most often the hallmark of the profoundly ungifted.' Then I'd—"

"Cut to the chase. Any girls in the high school picture?"

"I . . . not really." He fell silent again, remembering his adolescent anguish, wondering if his shyness with girls meant he was under the same curse as his beloved teacher. Dying to ask but choking on the words, the whole subject so tainted with filth. Knowing the Lord's command was that he call his friend sternly to account, tell him that Jesus had paid the penalty for his sin, but only if he would repent. Otherwise . . .

And wondering bleakly now, just as he had then: when did minding your own business, being polite and discreet, cross the frontier into shameful cowardice and egregious dereliction of soul-saving duty? Would Mr. Gaiman burn in hell forever simply because he, Evan, had been too "nice" to speak up and lay God's truth squarely on the line?

"Louisa must have been thrilled to bits by all this."

"Well, I sort of, lied. I told her I was working on my stutter with Mrs. Gimble, a nice, Christian English teacher. There wasn't any Mrs. Gimble. It was the first time I ever lied to her."

"How come you didn't get her and Dorcas and that fruitcake Mr. Toller from the prayer group to lay their voodoo hands on Gay Man and cast out the demons of homosexuality? Force him to *squeeeeze* through that narrow gate and lead him weeping to Jesus."

"I couldn't hurt his feelings, Neil, I just couldn't. He was so kind to me." The two of them, on Mr. Gaiman's velvet couch, sipping lemonade after a hard hour of stutter work. Mr. Gaiman playfully mussing his hair, saying, "You may be confused about a lot of things now, Evan, but you'll be just fine. You have such an innate goodness; it's so pure and inviolable it almost feels like insanity."

And he, gulping, "Oh. That's bad, isn't it?"

"Not even close. It's a rare quality. Hold on to it for dear life."

Neil though, begged to differ. "You as a kid, Evan? Jesus! You were so fucking gullible! I remember you crying about something when we were out with Louisa and she told you she had an ice cream cone in her purse. An actual ice cream cone, just lying in there waiting for you. So, you stopped crying. I don't remember how she explained away the fact that no ice cream appeared. Or no Lord either."

Silence.

"You ever hear about the guy who made chirping sounds to a canary in a cage? The canary hears canary language and gets all excited, tweeting back all these burning questions and listening hard to the answers. But the guy's just whistling notes, he has no idea what he's supposedly telling the canary. Nature doesn't even know we exist, dumbass."

Silence. Neil grabbed Evan's half-finished beer, rubbed the cool bottle across his forehead, guzzled it down. "I fucking hated every minute of my existence in that house and so did you. Tell the truth for once in your pansy-ass life!"

Evan hung his head, defeated. Remembering Neil at thirteen, fourteen, straining to make himself heard, faced with Louisa's God-fearing, all-knowing winner's smile. Remembering him losing control, bawling like an infant, pounding his head with his fists. Louisa, turning abruptly to her angel-boy Evan, ordering him to immediately gird himself with the breastplate of truth—an actual physical ritual they mimed on a daily basis—to strap on his helmet of righteousness. And he, blushing for shame in front of his brother, pulling the invisible strap taut beneath his chin.

He too had wept after these episodes, in private, hunched in a corner of the bathroom, shoulders heaving. *I'll make it up to him! I'm never going to hurt him or let him down. I'll always take care of him.*

"Louisa was wrong about you, Neil," he said now. "You were just being honest. She—"

"Fuck off with your pity, asshole!" Neil lowered his head to the table, began to pound it repeatedly with his forehead. Both empty bottles rolled off the edge and hit the floor. One broke. Neil sprang to his feet, a red welt blossoming above his eyebrows. "Hah! Made ya b-b-blink! M-m-made ya b-b-blink!" He took a wild swing at Evan's head but missed, stumbling forward, falling onto one knee, snarling with rage.

Evan lurched to his feet, avoiding the broken glass, nearly blundering into the waitress heading their way with their two dishes of noodles. He wove through the jumble of tables, bare feet sticking to the floor, picking up all kinds of debris. Outside, he pulled on his shoes, left them untied and flapping, walked blindly halfway down the block, stopped. Gulped back his tears. *Where has he gone, where have I gone, it's all gone, it's all gone, where is the brother I love so much?*

He turned, went back. In the doorway, he nearly plowed into Neil coming out, pounding a furious fist into his palm, his whole being eaten alive by some cancerous thing, tentacles branching off in every direction, a hundred dead-end sois to pointless grey oblivion.

By the end of the week—*twelve* days now since he's laid eyes on Rivka—shooting is ready to wrap on *A Husband's Plight*. The ending, shot over the final two days, is virtually identical to the previous seven movies Evan has done for this production company. His movie ex-wife, a razor-faced blonde named Toni, confronts him with a gun in the abandoned storage facility out on the Old Mill Road, and just before squeezing back her trigger finger, graciously takes the time to lay bare all her evil machinations. "You thought you could cheat me, you and that pathetic little slut of yours, but I knew you'd be too stupid to realize who was *really* in charge all along," blah blah, something to do with an inheritance; Evan is pretty much phoning it in, and is hungry for dinner besides, waiting out eight takes of the long, smirky monologue that conveniently allows time for the little slut in question to sneak up and clobber the ex-wife from behind with a shovel just as a six-member SWAT team materializes out of nowhere, shouting, "Freeze!"

So much for good husband David Wade. If he gets another gig with these people, *he'll* be the one in the next film pointing the gun, carefully explaining his tangled web of lies as the police creep nearer, hearing all.

This, in a nutshell, is his sad career niche, the bloom of his youthful glory long, long off the rose. He's the go-to, early-to-mid-forties, desperately-imperilled-woman-movie man of the hour, ideal for characters who are old and presumably wealthy enough to have acquired a spotless monster home and late model SUV, while still maintaining that imperative dateable look. He's paid dues to get to Husband and Father level, starting out, eight films ago, playing the lesser role of the trustworthy, rumpled, undateable police detective. But he came across, with his tousled, delicately greying curls and killer eyelashes, as too appealingly soft-boiled. It's unclear, however, how much time remains before he's demoted to Investigating Cop number two, last stop before the terminus: Random Face in Party Crowd.

Shooting done, he's in his trailer, thoughtfully hanging up his David Wade outfit for the wardrobe girl when he gets the text from the love of his life telling him she's leaving for Berlin on a major job. For three months. Just like that. No preamble. No regrets. See ya.

Frantic, he calls her immediately, catches her on the run somewhere, she only has two minutes, a thousand things to take care of. Detecting the first snuffles travelling down the line, she snaps, "Evan, stop being a tool!" And hangs up.

In the car on the way back to Sainte-Clémence, after having put in a brief, hangdog appearance at the *Husband's Plight* wrap party, he checks for the eightieth time for another text from her. Nothing. Pulling over to the side of the highway, he types, with one finger and his best text cred: Worst film ever made in the can at last. How RU?

There's no answer.

He drives the rest of the way home in tears. Rolls into the gravel driveway in front of his house, peers up through the windshield. The snow that fell a week and a half ago has melted, the eaves dripping, the April night sky clear and starry with the cruel promise of spring. The light in the attic window is on. Neil's awake.

He opens the front door, immediately tripping over one of the fifteen attachments to the deluxe vacuum cleaner for which he paid top dollar to a door-to-door salesman because he didn't know how to let him down gently. Wades through the scattered mail: Hydro-Québec, an IGA flyer, letters from his foster children, the only kids he'll ever have, he thinks, sour with self-pity. His eleven-year-old girl in Ghana is full of news: *I have never seen snow and snowfall. With one red sweater we come to school. With money you send I purchase rice and festival dress. Please write to me at your possible time.* And from Haiti, a simple: *Mesi pou kado*. He'd sent the grinning boy with the cocky face of a child soldier an elaborate paint set.

Upstairs, feet moving. He opens the fridge to see if Neil's been down to get his nocturnal breakfast. There's less orange juice in the jug than there was in the morning, and half the sliced ham is gone. Neil sleeps through the daylight hours like a vampire, but once in a while, if he can't sleep, he'll venture downstairs during the day when Evan is out, fiddling with things, digging out the vacuum or the rotary egg beater, leaving them lying wherever they are when his interest flags. And leaving notes in belligerent caps, ordering items he needs to have on the double: LADY CHATTERSBY'S LOVER A SMUTTY BOOK SO DON'T GO TO PIECES. ALSO ENCYCLOPEDIA OLDER THE BETTER. Evan had found Lady Chatterley, but Lucy's the one who'd dug up several bereft volumes of the Encyclopedia Britannica in a used bookstore, which Neil's been reading straight through for the last year and a half.

Evan eats the rest of the ham, standing at the fridge, the door open and beeping. Drinks metallic apple juice from the can. He feels like throwing up, but it passes.

He sits down at the table, fishes the week's crumpled sides out of his knapsack, an expensive leather item from Roots that Riv bought him for his forty-fourth birthday. He feels like a risible poseur every time he wears it.

On the back of one page he scribbles a quick grocery list. Orange juice. Ham. Bread. Eggs. Turns the page over. It's the kitchen scene from last Monday.

David and Mollie are toasting one another at the kitchen counter, David with wine, Mollie with a wholesome glass of milk.

DAVID
Here's to you, Babe. The best-looking new law partner at Gresham and Millner. You're gonna knock 'em dead.

> MOLLIE
> You do know how to flatter a girl. *(She smiles; they clink glasses)* I just hope you don't mind being *Mister* Law Partner.
>
> DAVID
> Baby, I'm so proud of you I could . . . bust! *(His eyes drop to her gently swelling stomach.)* Our little one is going to be so proud of his mommy too.
>
> MOLLIE
> *Her* mommy! *(They both laugh. Then their lips meet in a tender kiss.)*

Nausea rises again, and more tears, a bathtub on the verge of overflow. How long has she known about Berlin? And not bothered to mention it!

He sits unmoving in the clock-ticking silence. Checks his phone. Nothing. What now? Don't bother her. Let her be. Try and get some sleep. Upstairs, Neil has settled; once he's in his recliner, the night's reading in his lap, he doesn't move much. Volume Fourteen, *Lighting* to *Maximillian*, will keep him enthralled till sunrise.

He lies down on his bed in the dark, fully dressed. His eyes refuse to close, his heart to cease thumping. He's lost her. She's gone. Accept it.

He's only got Neil now.

I accept it, Lord. Give me . . . just please give me time, okay?

But—with rising panic—for how long would he even have Neil? Was Rivka right? Had he completely bungled his handling of his brother? It was true, he'd never had a clue what he was doing; had he made everything even worse than it had to be? Ever since Thailand, flailing and guessing, trying his best, but Neil never got better, never gave so much as a hint of the person he'd once been. His life, his future, confined to an attic room, all because of Evan's selfish desire to keep him close, to *save* him. To be the angel of rescue, the noble one, the long-suffering hero . . .

He hadn't felt the least bit noble or angelic after that calamitous fight in the Bangkok restaurant. Nor in the two and a half hours it had taken them to make their way back home. Neil saying nothing the whole time, indicating right and left turns with a furious jerk of his head. Only when they were back on the ferry, resting on hard benches across from one another under the falling darkness, did Evan dare a look at Neil's face, instantly recoiling from the nuclear ferocity of it.

He should never have poisoned their time together by talking about the awful past. Except . . . why couldn't Neil remember all the *good* things, the happy things? Two devout, pious boys, loving their little church community and all its special ceremonies: the Sunday Communion service, the morsels of white bread, the tray with the little thimbles of grape juice passed around. The loving smiles, the holy handshakes. The spirited singing, Neil called upon for solos almost every week, ladies fawning over him, mussing his hair, calling blessings down upon his head. His brother so full of boisterous fun back then, spiriting him over to Lucy's house for forbidden TV and the company of the scandalous Mrs. Brickwood, a friendly, chunky lady with short, tidy hair, a quiet heaviness about her that Evan, even at four or five, could detect, and which he attributed to the heinous, unmentionable sin clinging to her, a mysterious something which Louisa knew about but refused to disclose.

And Lucy, shocking him to the bone with the smart-alecky things she got away with saying to her mum, laughing her big, croaky laugh, telling Neil, "Kid, you are the fucking light of my life!" The f-word, right in front of them! Louisa never would have let Lucy babysit them if she'd known. But Louisa hadn't known, though he'd wanted to tell her so many times, if only to set the world right again. He could understand Lucy's clear preference for his brother—how could anyone not love Neil?—but still, it jarred him, turned everything he knew upside down, pricked him with a jealousy he'd never felt before. Wasn't *he* supposed to be the preferred angel-boy?

He'd prayed every night for Neil, begging the Lord not to let Lucy's sacrilegious influence rub off on him. But it had been no use, Neil drifting with every passing year further into darkness, going his own way, turning his back on his church family. Evan, who had no other real friends, was left alone at fourteen, fifteen, to handle the weekly round of Sunday services, the dreaded door-to-door evangelism on Monday evenings, the Wednesday night prayer meetings. Alone, with no brother to sing beside, or to giggle with at old Mr. Toller, alone with Louisa and her flotilla of prayer warriors, every last one of them cut in straight lines with blunt, kiddy scissors.

Those winter Wednesday nights—somehow it always seemed like winter, even in June—were unbearable without Neil, even worse after he'd had his mind blown by Mr. Gaiman. Down in the church basement, fellowshipping, sipping milky tea, Mrs. Lajeunesse working on her list of who'd be coming out for Watch Night to see in the New Year: "Betty's going to try to come out, if her mum's out of hospital. Cora and Flossie said they'd try. How about you, Dorcas? Will you be coming out?" Indeed, Dorcas would. "And won't this be a wonderful opportunity to witness to that man from the hardware store? Do you think you could bring him along? Evan, of course, we know we can count on you," all of them turning to smile at their favourite young man. Oh yes, dear ladies, he'd think behind an impassive face; yes, we'll all be coming out to mark another drab year of walking with the Lord, scurrying through the dark, clutching our coats against the wind and scampering home again, locking our doors behind us double-quick to keep the wolf snout of the world from poking in. Because everywhere outside this holy basement lies nothing but darkness and bondage, the unsaved swarming like maggots on roadkill.

Yes, that's exactly what he'd thought, missing Neil so badly. Stifled, hemmed in by elderly females, giving in willingly to critical, unkind thoughts, less and less quick to beg the Lord's forgiveness. Mrs. Lajeunesse no sooner done than Louisa would start in. "So! How many people have each of us led to the Lord this week? Who wants to share first?" Everyone but Evan and tongue-tied Mr. Toller always had cases on the burner: the gal at the Provigo meat counter, the lady in the bed next to Auntie Beth's in the hospital, the mailman. Out in the world, they steered every conversation toward Jesus like a truck with a blowout on an icy road: Do you know that God loves you and has a wonderful plan for your life? Will you be making your decision for Christ today? If not, never fear. I'll be back!

To Evan, it made Jesus's wonderful nice-guy ways seem so phony, so oily, his representatives slithering around delivering Meals on Wheels, joining craft groups, leading carol sings at Christmas, all with the aim of lassoing "hurting folks" who "happened to come alongside," inviting them to open their hearts, share their pain and be saved. Or else.

Wretched, he'd turned all of it over and over in his mind—the sweet memories and the dread ones—all through the long trek back to Neil's fearsome hovel. He and his brother debarking the ferry, Neil flagging down the little bus just as it was pulling away. Sitting with his head bowed to his knees, hands clasped around it, fingers drumming his skull nonstop. By the time they walked into the dark house at the end of the soi, Evan's legs were crumbling beneath him. He lifted his weary, throbbing head, only to jump back with a yip of terror. A hunched, humanoid shape, blacker than the surrounding darkness, loomed from the centre of the raggedy couch.

Neil went straight to the shape, smacked it lightly. It rose like a column of smoke and followed him into the kitchen. He turned on the overhead bulb to reveal a tiny, wrinkled woman who had to be fifty, dressed in black, the outline of her pelvic bones visible even through three sweaters, her heart almost visibly beating, a little bird hopping in a narrow cage. She wore round sunglasses big as pancakes. She looked like a giant ant.

The ant made a little temple of her hands in front of her forehead, bowed toward Evan. In her tiny ant voice, she asked something in Thai.

"No. We had a shitty time," interjected Neil. He opened the fridge, grabbed a beer, which Evan hadn't remembered seeing before, knocked the cap off on the edge of a nail protruding from the wall. Drank half of it, glmp glmp glmp. Wiped his mouth, said, "Ahhh." Then, with a curt sideways shake of the head, mumbled, "This is Chamnien." Evan took his best shot at a smile.

Chamnien nodded back and turned to make her way up the M.C. Escher staircase. Neil put his beer down and undressed to the last stitch, Evan casting his eyes to the floor with locker-room decorum at the sight of his brother's too-much-sat-upon rump, his skeletal back, his matted, clumpy front. Neil stood for a long moment in a thoughtful stoop and burped before ratcheting himself back into rusty gear, turning in circles as if trying to remember where he'd put something. Then, as if catching her scent, he followed the trail of the ant-woman upstairs.

Evan crashed onto the sofa, asleep before his feet left the floor.

Hours, or seconds later, an upstairs door smashed against a wall, and naked Neil pounded down the rickety stairs in epic fury, Yosemite Sam with steam blasting out his ears, clearly looking for something, peering under furniture, lifting knickknacks, banging them down. A vase on a wobbly shelf was unaware it had mere seconds to live; as Yosemite roared by, it lost heart and teetered. Bellowing, "Fuck off!" Neil punched it to the floor where it shattered and died.

He stomped back upstairs. A moment later, there was a mighty crash like a dresser being tipped over. Then, silence. Just as Evan began to think his brother had spontaneously combusted, he cycloned back down the stairs into the kitchen. Pitched the coffeepot against the wall. Yanked on the overhead light. Sheared a tablecloth—successfully!—out from under a pile of fly-blown dishes and proceeded to thwack the wall with it, shouting, "Fuck! Fuck!" with each thwack. Dropping the tablecloth, he reached up to a crooked shelf crowded with boxes and cans, shoved everything noisily left and right, muscling a path to what turned out to be a box of saltines. He began squeezing the crackers out of the cellophane directly into his mouth, gagging on them, drooling clumps of mashed cracker, large, wet crumbs lodging in his beard.

Evan would have given twenty years of his life for a saltine. He got up, intending to ask for one, and nearly tripped over an elderly spider the size of his fist, haggard and barnacled, making its stately, unmolested way across the floor.

Chamnien was also making her soundless insect way down the stairs and out the door. She'd already scampered as far as the soi when Neil spotted her. He rushed to the door, grabbed a whistle hanging by a lanyard on a nail, blew into it mightily. Chamnien stopped moving, not turning her head, as if unable to proceed without further instructions. Naked Neil went to her, bare feet hopping on the gravel, and shepherded her back inside, an arm around her bitsy waist. He led her to the couch, pressing on her shoulders to make her sit.

"She can't see," he said, not looking at Evan, all rage apparently spent. "Just grey blobs. She keeps thinking she can go off without me, like she doesn't need me." Evan had a sudden sharp mental picture of Neil tugging his ant-woman through the teeming streets, she sightless, he barging maniacally toward somewhere he'd long ago lost the directions to.

Chamnien lay down, turned her back to them. Neil, heading up the stairs, stopped long enough to mutter, "Don't bother her. She's not really there." He continued climbing. He did not return.

The saltine box lay empty and squashed on the kitchen floor. Evan, whose abdomen was so concave with hunger it was nudging his spine, began rooting through the backs of shelves. He found several dusty cans of vegetables—corn niblets, peas, mushrooms, beets—and, praise the Lord, the rusty can opener hanging on a nail. He emptied all four cans into a cracked bowl from the top of the dish mountain in the sink, the beet juice turning everything pink. He ate like a wild man, with his fingers. Returned to his alcove to lie flat and wait.

Neil, his face scrunched and creased, reappeared, still naked, several hours later. Hot light poured in through the barred window, birds and lizards meeting and greeting on the rafters, insect life at full throttle outside. Chamnien rolled over, sunglasses askew, her tiny eyes opening and closing, opening and closing, like a cat in the sun. Neil began to croon in a pleasing Bing Crosby baritone.

"I was strolling through the park one day—"

Chamnien sat up, rubbing her useless eyes.

"—in the merry, merry month of May. Morning, Yoko! I was taken by surprise, by a pair of rogie shies! Evan! My brother! You know everything. What are rogie shies?"

Both brothers' compass arrows quivered in tandem, pointing due north for one second only.

"You got a girlfriend, my bruthah?"

"You already asked me that."

"You think Yoko's not good enough?"

"Of course not! Why would I think that?" He almost said, "I commend you." Was infinitely glad he hadn't.

Neil loped upstairs again. Evan returned to his alcove, went back to sleep. It was the only condition he felt safe in.

When he woke, the room was lit for afternoon. He was so famished he feared he hadn't the strength to sit up. There wasn't a sound in the house; Chamnien was no longer on the couch. He changed out of his sweaty, smelly clothes, again raiding the kitchen, scraping four cans of Smiling Fish onto a plate, though he despised fish, and especially this fish, which was no fish recognized as such on his side of the globe. He went to the sink when he'd finished, gagged up a thin stream of oily yellow matter onto the dishes. He felt better. Thought a brief walk might help even more.

Just two steps out the door stopped him cold. Neil was sitting cross-legged in the dirt next to the spirit house. He had shaved his head, appeared to be fresh off a brain operation. He'd made a few inroads into the beard as well, leaving indentations as if a lawnmower had shoved its way a few hopeless feet into impenetrable thicket. He wore black knee socks through which many toes protruded, and a kind of brown sack that bagged out around his spindly arms. He raised his eyes to Evan, his face lighting up, as if he'd been waiting impatiently all this time for his brother to appear.

"Here's the plan. I'm going to sit here until I attain the necessary degree of goodness. Think I can't keep up with you, goody Bible boy? I can keep up with you, dickhead. Lust finds difficult entry into the controlled mind." He ran a hand irritably between the back of his neck and the edge of his itchy, John the Baptist outfit. "But first, hong nam run! Last stop for forty miles!" He climbed woodenly to his feet, limping into the house like Gabby Hayes.

Evan sank down onto a stray cinder block, at a complete loss. Two or three dogs came nosing around, looked him over, moved on.

Neil returned, sat back down in the same position. Closed his eyes. Swatted at a fly that had lighted on his arm, then cried, "Oops! No kill fly! Buddha say no kill fly!"

Evan went inside. Lay down on his mat. Wanted to cry, wanted to run for his life, wanted four Big Macs and a wastepaper basket full of fries, wanted to be already on the plane home two weeks from now, nineteen hours squashed into a seat in coach infinitely preferable to this lunacy.

He forced himself to wait an hour, then an hour and a half. Went back outside. Neil, now wrapped in a blanket like Cochise, still sat immobile, staring blankly.

"Want nothing," said Cochise, spying Evan out of the corner of his eye. "Make head fly in sky like smoke. Want nothing. I not come back in next life. I free."

"I'm sorry, Neil, but I really hate when you talk like that." Evan's voice sounded petulant in his own ears, full of silly, bleating indignation.

"Yoko's coming to massage me tonight. You want a massage? She has plump little hands, they smell like warm gingerbread. Hot little hands." He sat in stony silence for another five minutes, which was as long as it took for Evan to decide that he was going to cut this sorry visit short. He opened his mouth to say so.

Neil stirred, rose stiffly, stood bent and shaking in front of the spirit house, muttering what sounded like apologies to its occupants, mumbling and trembling until his motor ran down, sputtered, turned itself off. Then he just stood there.

"Neil, come inside, okay? Come lie down."

"Do you think these socks have had it?" Neil asked, lifting one foot, then the other. For a split second, he looked like the loser in every gang there'd ever been, the trusting, hopeful little squirt who just wanted to be one of the fellas, the one always left holding the bag. Then his face imploded. He began to sob noisily, his bony shoulders lurching.

Evan reached for him with watery arms, babbling, "Please, Neil, please come back home with me, let's get you looked after, you can't stay here, not like this." Over and over he said it, trying to drown the racket of his brother's stupefying desolation, Neil roaring over his entreaties, bellowing into his face, blasting him backward.

"Why are you so good and I'm so bad? Why? Why?" He was helpless as an infant, tears coursing down, his nose streaming. Evan grabbed him by the shoulders, trying to hold him square, keep him upright.

"It's not true, Neil! You're the good one, you're the honest one! It's me who's the loser, I'm the b-b-bad one. I did everything wrong, I could never . . . I could never . . ." Hoisting Neil, his arms nearly giving out, fighting the pitiless, inexorable gravity that dragged his brother down, thinking: Never what?

Never what, Evan?

His grip gave out. Neil slumped to the dirt, Evan dropping to his knees beside him. He began to cry himself, his eyes chasing Neil's, desperate to make contact. "In a m-m-million years, I could never have stood up for myself like you did. I don't even know if I b-b-believe anymore, I don't know what I believe . . . oh God, who cares what I believe?" Sitting back hard on his heels. "It doesn't change anything, I can't fix you, I can't make this better. I just . . . I just . . ." Leaning in, he bent his body around his brother's, burying his head in his neck, weeping, Neil jerking beneath him. Recalling Louisa stoutly declaring that faith was like a steel spine, *a steel spine*, Evan! And he'd never had one, ever. Except . . .

Except . . .

Except who cared what Louisa said? Louisa had always been dead wrong about Neil, and dead wrong about him too, so what the hell could she possibly have to say about what faith was or wasn't? Because here he was, his spine and his brother's bent like bows to the ground, and a glimmer of a thought breaking through: THIS is faith, numbnuts! This is where it starts, in *reality*. Faith is just me and Neil and total chaos. Not knowing a damned thing, in control of nothing.

Neil had known it years ago. He'd told him so!

His grip relaxed, his panic subsiding as he spoke what he suddenly knew aloud, softly, to himself, to his brother: "This is what is! Nothing else matters. If there's a God, he's where the suffering is. He's where the losers are. And if he's not, then I don't need him. I always swore I'd stand beside you, Neil, that I'd make everything up to you. That's the only godliness I can stand to be around, anymore.

And you know what? I can do this. I will do this. I'm saying yes. It's as good as done."

Neil was scrabbling onto his knees now, heaving Evan off. Tearing at his own face, raw gashes descending from his eyes to his ravaged beard. Toppling onto his side, rolling in the dirt, howling, "No, no, no!"

"Neil!" Evan threw himself over him, pinning him flat, his mouth pressed to Neil's ear. "We need to get you to a hospital. Help me, Neil! Please! I don't know how to take care of you here, I don't know where to go. Do you want to go home, Neil? I'll take you home. You can trust me, Neil, I'll get you home safe." Neil thrashed his head from side to side to keep Evan's words out, his shrieks vaulting octaves, one long note held until he convulsed. Evan sat on his back, holding his arms down, Neil's wails unabating until, abruptly, as if a plug had been pulled, he ceased to move.

Evan waited, caught his breath, let go with infinite caution, fearing an ambush. But Neil was out cold. In his brown sack in the dirt, sleeping like a baby on his stomach, his butt in the air, face smooshed sideways.

"Neil!" he whispered in his ear. No reply. He lurched painfully to his feet, stepped away. Neil didn't budge. He had to do something, couldn't waste time thinking about what a stupid gamble it might be. He ran into the house, opened the cash drawer, stuffed every last bill—who knew how much they were worth?—into his knapsack. Pulled out a pair of jeans and a shirt, they would fit Neil, he had to get him out of that woeful Fred Flintstone suit. Ran outside again. His brother was still comatose.

He'd seen taxis parked next to a fruit stand on the main road. He took off, sprinting. It was the taxi spitting gravel that made Neil roll over onto his side, blinking.

The driver, at whom Evan had already thrust a wad of cash, obligingly held Neil down while Evan shoved the jeans up his legs, flapped the shirt over his head. Together they dragged him to his feet, limp as a brown cornstalk in November.

"Are we going home?" Neil asked quietly.

"I think it's best." Evan waited for another eruption. None came.

At the very last minute, he remembered the prescription bottle in the bathroom, sleeping pills, better safe than sorry; it was a long, long way back to Montreal. Darting back inside, tucking them into his jeans pocket. Just, please God, don't let them have expired.

And halfway out the door, remembering again: Neil's passport! He ran back, rooted frantically through the boxes till he found it. Pulled out an armful of mouldy clothes as well, but a thousand bugs scuttled out from among the folds, skittering down his arms. The reek was overpowering. No, his brother would have to come home with just the clothes on his back, and nary a speck of the wisdom needed to live.

In the back of the taxi, Neil fell against him like a drunk on a bus, rode with his head on Evan's shoulder, eyes wide and staring. At the airport, he sat by while good boy Evan with his responsible credit card arranged for a series of oddly connecting flights home. By the time they boarded the first plane, he was muttering again, raking his hair backward and forward, standing up repeatedly to glower over the seat back at the other passengers, snarling invective.

Even smooshed a pill into a paper cup of coke, which Neil drank willingly enough. He had to do it four more times, twice waiting in Tokyo, once over the Pacific, and once more boarding the last plane in Chicago, before they finally landed at Dorval.

When Neil was released from the hospital five months later, somewhat becalmed by pharmacology, a bouncing lid on a boiling pot, Evan was waiting with a home for him at the end of Loony Street in Sainte-Clémence.

Neil had found his ponderous way upstairs.

And stayed put. For better or for worse, till this very moment.

Sheila

It's Lucy who called to invite her here, so it strikes Sheila as awfully strange that the woman doesn't ask her a thing about herself: is she married, does she have kids, grandkids? Is her health okay? Possibly it never occurs to her, though it's also possible that Lucy simply assumes Sheila's life has been an unending series of grands jetés from one stellar triumph to the next. By the wry, crumpled look of her, she doesn't seem to be begging for an earful of crap like that.

She seems nervous, though. Shy even, certainly more than she ever was back in the day. Evan had warned her that Lucy was a private person, tricky to handle, suggesting that Sheila not get in touch with her but let Lucy make the first move. Looking at her now, the term "tight-sphinctered" leaps into Sheila's mind, and she has to suppress a smile. But it isn't exactly shyness she's seeing, either; it's something else: a rawhide toughness, a Marlboro Man reticence. Many mystery cards held close to her chest.

Lucy certainly hasn't bothered to dress for the occasion, clearly unconcerned with making an impression in her dun-brown tee shirt that reeks of cigarette smoke, and worn, grey jeans three sizes too large. Sheila, in her blue summer dress, feels as frivolous as a debutante. The two of them are earth and sky, sitting on the *terrasse* of Sainte-Clémence's one French restaurant, drinking chilled wine on this June afternoon. Rustic wooden tables, wicker chairs with fat fuchsia cushions. The whole patio to themselves, a great maple canopied over their heads, sunlight dappling Lucy's face, improving it by a marginal percentage. *I Only Have Eyes for You* drifting from inside the near-empty restaurant.

Look at us, Sheila marvels to herself. How did this happen? When did we turn into *crones?* She's never worried much about her own aging, but seeing Lucy now, so rutted and weathered, she feels, like a hard punch to the stomach, just how much time has gone by since they parted ways.

Lucy's still thin as a teenager though, and sits like a kid too, sprawling sideways, manspreading in her big clodhopper running shoes. Every fifteen minutes or so, she hightails it to the sidewalk for a smoke; it's close enough that she can easily talk from there. From behind, Sheila can see her shoulder blades poking through the thin cotton of her shirt, her neck knotty as a dry twig.

"How do you stay so thin?" Sheila asks brightly, an empty, conventional compliment, but she can't think of a thing else to say.

"Must be my irrepressible zest for life." Lucy's face is turned away as she draws in a deep drag. "I'm quitting soon," she adds defensively, holding up her pack of Rothmans to indicate her meaning, though Sheila hasn't said a word. Lucy flicks her spent smoke into the street and returns to sprawl in her chair. The pack of smokes never leaves her left hand.

Lucy sprawls but Sheila sits bolt upright, the habitual straight-backed posture of the serious musician. Between them, they're gulping down a bottle of pinot grigio much faster than can be good for either of them. The sun is hot, the breeze through the maple leaves lifting Lucy's straight, square-cut grey hair, Sheila's fluffy white, from their foreheads, ruffling the napkins on the table. They both know exactly how they look. Not a damned thing either of them can do about it now.

"I hardly ever drink," contributes Lucy, as Sheila refills their glasses. The wine has reddened Lucy's nose and her puffy eyes release dribbly, allergic tears. A will-o'-the-wisp of memory flits away too quickly for Sheila to catch, a sudden glimpse of Lucy's fifteen-year-old face lurking behind the wreckage. It makes her want to laugh for joy. Then the vision evaporates, a cloud shredding into vapour, and there's old Lucy again, mottled like a paperback dropped in the bath and left to dry out on the radiator for a month. Many long furrows trending downward. A lemon-sucking mouth.

"The social whirl isn't really my thing," Lucy continues awkwardly, and then laughs, an abrupt, plosive jolt, a logjam of mucus plugging up her twiggy system. "Look at me, I can't even drink right. Wine totally wonks up my sinuses." Her voice is raspy, abrading, nothing like it used to be. "You must be thinking old Luce looks like someone who got rode hard and put away wet." She lets go with another damp snort.

"Not at all. You look—"

"Like shite fresh from the microwave? You can say it, I don't care." She turns her yellow Bic lighter end over end on the table. "I do all right. I take care of Lucy. Somebody has to." Her eyes briefly lock with Sheila's before skittering away again.

"I was going to say, you look like you've lived."

"Yeah. Well, there's living. And then there's living. Know what I mean?" Sheila thinks she might but isn't sure; Lucy's face gives nothing away. Trying to read it feels like eighteen tricky bars she's struggling with, an andante passage that drags like the dismal tramp of the army of the dead if she isn't careful.

"So, Lucy. Tell me what've you been up to all these years."

"Just keepin' it real."

"Hah." Sheila smiles, says, "I hear ya, sister." And thinks: Good Lord, I don't talk like this. But the silly remark seems to loosen something in her friend, open her up the smallest bit.

"Evan told me last year sometime that you were teaching at the high school. I just about keeled over. I thought, no way can there be two Sheila O'Mearas who play the violin. Took me this long to get up the courage to call you." She's fiddling with her cigarettes, appears about to spring up for another smoke break.

"I couldn't believe it when he told me he knew *you*. That you were still living here."

"I've known Evan since he was two feet tall. He used to live next door to us. He lives in one of my rental properties now." She's scraping back her chair again, lighter at the ready.

"I know. With his brother. That's how your name came up in the first place. He told me his brother had this amazing friend Lucy, who was always out trying to track down books for him. So I said, 'I knew a Lucy Brickwood once here in Sainte-Clémence who was a real book lover.' And he said, 'That's her, that's the very one!'"

"Evan's a peach," says Lucy, flushing a little, as if the conversation were moving too fast into perilous intimacy.

"He *is* a peach. He always comes to our concerts if we're playing locally. My friend Terri—you probably already know this—Terri, the guidance counsellor at the school? Terri McTavish? No? Well, anyway, she was the one who introduced me to him back when he was trying to get his brother interested in music therapy. Or in maybe just getting out to hear a little music once in a while. I understand his brother isn't well?"

Lucy, up again at her post, is sucking on a smoke for dear life. It's a whole minute or two before she says, over her shoulder, "Neil's been suffering the wrath of God since he was a kid." She takes several more drags, aims her thousand-mile stare out into the street. "He used to be the sweetest little singer you ever heard. But wild horses couldn't drag him out to a concert. And music therapy is the dumbest idea Evan ever had. I told him not to push Neil into that."

"Well, it never came to anything."

"Good." Lucy finishes her smoke, sits back down.

Silence.

"But you, Lucy. I want to know about you."

"My scintillating life story? Try to stay awake. I went to McGill, got a degree in library science. Whoopee. Hold on to your hat. I never used it. I worked for a while as an assistant at the shit library here in Sainte-Clémence and then I quit. Okay, they turfed me out. Have I wowed you yet? What else? I own some property in town, that's what I live off. My mother's dead. My father's dead. I still live in the same house I lived in when we were in high school. I got a little Honda, so I can take road trips, on my own, when the urge strikes me. I'm into online gambling. You might say I'm all fucked-up and nowhere to go. What else you want to know?"

"How about romance?" Sheila asks kindly, and is immediately sorry, fifty years of solitude as clearly etched into Lucy's face as a tattoo done with unsterilized needles.

"Nope. Missed that boat. Never even bought a ticket. If you catch my drift."

She looks so beaten suddenly. It hurts Sheila's heart to look at her; she can feel tears starting. But of course, she's always unstable and overly emotional on performance days.

She tries to change the subject, says lightly, "I guess you know my quartet will be playing at the Église Sainte-Clémence, end of August. I'd be so happy if you came, Lucy."

"Well, fuckin' ay, now that I know *you're* on the bill. Are there still tickets?"

"I would guess many. Many tickets. Probably room for the whole town, extended families, dogs, cats. I'm sure we can squeeze you in."

Silence.

"We kick off the festival tonight, you know, in Saint-Lazare. In a really beautiful old church. Fantastic acoustics. We were in there at seven this morning, rehearsing. It's the first time we've been invited to this festival, which is all original music this year. We're playing eight different towns, like rock stars. They even put us up in Saint-Lazare last night, in the presbytery."

"I went last year, some jazz thing they had."

"Really? Are you a jazz fan?" The thought of old Lucy snapping her fingers to a bebop beat nearly destroys Sheila's composure.

"Not much. I left halfway through."

"Ah."

Now another conversational sandbar, silence for several hour-long minutes. They both pretend deep interest in the maple leaves overhead, a passing plane, a fly strutting along the table edge.

"You're not nervous, are you?" Lucy asks at last.

"I am. Very nervous."

"After all this time, you still get nervous?"

"Nervous unto death. But there's no resolution without dissonance, as we musicians like to say." Hoping Lucy might appreciate gentle, self-deprecating irony, a honed specialty of hers. But Lucy just asks in a squeezed voice, "So, how long have you guys been together?"

"Just over four years. We're based in Senneville, that's where I live now. The second violin, the viola and I are the three, I gulp to say, elder folk of the group. But our very wonderful cellist, Sandrine, is only nineteen. She's just with us for the summer till she goes back to the Conservatoire. She has a marvellous future ahead of her. She's incredibly gifted."

"Wow."

"Our former cellist, Agnès, passed away last Christmas. We used to be *four* doddering elders."

Silence from Lucy.

"It hit us really hard. She was very dear to all of us."

Lucy's eyes are straying, she's not listening.

"I think, on the whole, we work quite well together."

Nothing.

"We've been wanting to perform some original music for a long time now. Scary as that is."

Lucy blinks, gropes for a response. "Wow. So, you write your own stuff?"

"Afraid so."

"Is there no end to your brilliance?"

"Oh, there's an end."

Lucy flicks her lighter on and off, her eyes on the jumping, dying flame. "I used to be so jealous of you."

"There's no need for that, I assure you. Ninety percent of our appearances are at weddings and corporate events. But you can only play the Wedding March and *Pachelbel's Canon* so many times before the thought of your own impending death starts perking you up like nobody's business." The laugh she's hoping for doesn't materialize. "Which might explain one of the four pieces we're doing, if you've seen the programme."

No response, save for the steady click of the lighter.

"So." Clearing her throat. "The piece called *Wake* is a play on words, on the two meanings of the word 'wake,' as in waking from sleep and as in the watch over the dead." Now she *really* isn't listening, her eyes trailing after people on the sidewalk, returning to Sheila a beat too late, her nod perfunctory. Sheila soldiers on.

"And the piece written by Léo, our second violinist, is called *Fugue,* which is also a play on words, both the musical term and the French word for 'to flee, to run away.'" Lucy's drumming her yellow, gnawed-to-the-quick fingers on the table, impatient, distracted. Sheila can feel her throat closing, trying to shut off what must sound to her old friend like pretentious drivel.

But just as she's about to suggest they call it an afternoon, Lucy looks square in her eyes and blurts, "I never get those things from music. Like, the explanations they write in programmes. If they didn't tell me the story behind it, I'd think it was just a whole bunch of random notes. Shows you what an artistic clunk I turned out to be."

"Oh, but lots of people have—"

"So, what happened to all you showstopping O'Mearas, anyway? Where's Hardee these days?" She puts her lighter down, folds her ropey white arms on the table.

"Hardee's in—"

"Did he marry that, whatshername, Valerie?"

"Vi. Yes, he did."

"Get the fuck outta here! For real?"

"For real. And they're still together. They have four kids, they live in Brooklyn. He used to—"

"And your mother?"

"No, Anny's gone."

"From what?" Blunt, graceless, dear old Lucy. Abrupt as a pistol shot.

"Cancer." A twinge under Sheila's left arm. Just the way it started for Anny: a tug, a twinge, a wee hard lump.

"And your dad?"

"Daddy's still with us, in a manner of speaking."

"Yeah, well. They do that, don't they. Refuse to die, even when they're dead."

"No, I meant—"

"You haven't changed much, you know. If anyone had a whizbang future ahead of them it was you."

"So I'm told."

"Anyway, how does this work? Are we supposed to get more wine?"

"I can't, Lucy. I'm onstage in six hours. I have to drive back to Saint-Lazare." At the thought, her stomach plummets without a parachute.

"Okay. Just as well. You can probably tell I'm a crappy social butterfly. Actually, I'm pretty much a full-body, ambulant ulcer, if you must know. It started at McGill. I barely escaped with my life." Sheila's about to ask, "What started?" but Lucy gets up, lights up, walks away, blowing smoke out into the street where it mingles with the wavy, hot exhaust from a passing bus. "Sometimes I drive past your old place," she says to the departing bus.

"Daddy's still there."

"Wow."

"I'm so glad you called me, Lucy. We've probably just missed bumping into one another a hundred times."

"Yeah, well." Lucy squares her shoulders. Addresses the maple branches overhead. "We losers are always curious to find out how our betters turned out, you know. All us poor souls who aren't what you'd call 'normal.' You were the one told me that, remember? Seldom wrong and right again. I botched everything, you'll be pleased to know. Just ask my dad. Oh, wait. He's six feet under. Ask *your* dad then. You're the one with the swell parents."

"Lucy—"

"I'm wondering if I really should come to your show. What if I do something really, really gauche and they're forced to pitch me out? You know, the crank removed from the room to thunderous applause." Her eyes still trained hard on the street, another cigarette stubbed out with her big-shoed foot. "Anyways, I'd better let you go get ready. Should I go in and pay the bill?"

"Let me get it, Lucy. Please." Sheila's broiling suddenly, sweat coursing down her sides as the vision of Lucy's young face suddenly re-emerges from the mist. Crumpling like aluminum foil, watching Sheila run across the grass after she'd stabbed poor Lucy in the heart, cut her to the bone, and mighty pleased about it too. Her last glimpse of that face as it wobbled out of control, lips trembling like a little kid's, trying so hard to pretend she didn't care. Getting to her feet then, opening her arms, as Sheila contrived to shepherd the happy, hugging group of aunts and musical friends away as fast as she could get them to move.

"Lucy, I wish it had . . . I wish it had turned out differently for you."

"Yep. Well, whatever gets you through the night." She's lighting up *again*. "One for the road," she quips. "I promise, I'm quitting. Any minute now."

And with that, she's off down the road and gone.

That wine was a mistake.

In her austere room at the presbytery, Sheila lies curled like a fiddlehead on the bed, eyelids heavy, fingers jumpy with nerves. The ungenerous pillow under her head is musty and grey, redolent of damp cement. The room had seemed oddly familiar last night, especially the close, unaired smell; now it comes to her in a rush what room it reminds her of.

Or rooms; there were several, though in her memory they all merge into *that* one.

This simple, dreary room, so like that other one, visited one of her worst dreams on her last night. The one where she hits someone in the dark with her car. A sickening thud; she gets out, rain pelting, and under the headlights, it's him, his face hamburger beneath her wheels. Recognizable only by his mud-toned clothes.

Wine-addled as she is, sleep will not come. Lucy Brickwood's drooping face hangs as a decorative backdrop to queasy, waking dreams of greasy fingers flubbing notes, a bow that flies out of her hands, decapitating an old gent in the front row. She bunches up the nasty pillow, punches it down, rolls from side to side, her face hot.

Thinking: She remembers what I said to her, fifty years ago. I completely forgot, but that poor, sad girl has carried it with her this whole time.

Left side again. Right side. Flat on her back, coffin style. Her eyes closed. Lucy's young face. Lucy sitting helpless on the wet grass.

She should have apologized. From the bottom of her heart, damn it! Should have taken her old friend by her spindly shoulders, looked deep into her eyes and said: I know you never asked, but here's how it is, Lucy. Here's how it's been for your great, your special, your so *normal* old friend Sheila. This ought to make you feel better. Does normal Sheila have grandkids? Beats me. A daughter, yes, I have one of those. Ten years since I saw her last. She'll be forty-one now. Forty-one! Last time I saw her was years ago, a month after I'd moved to Senneville, six months after I'd picked up my violin again after thirty years. Bet that's the last thing you expected to hear. So, yeah. Some guy dropped her off, said he'd be back in two hours. She was wearing a hoodie, her hair all mashed up and dirty inside. Cold sores on both sides of her mouth. She looked like someone he'd picked up hitchhiking. Maybe he had. He never came back for her. My daughter.

Like it so far? It gets better! Here's my sweet daughter, spilling over with love and good wishes. "Ma, I thought you'd never get off your fat ass. I thought you'd stay in that shit apartment till you were ninety, doing fuck all with your life." Sitting in my new rocking chair, shoving herself back and forth with her Doc Martens, eating pretzels, answering brief questions briefly. Not once looking me in the eye. On the way out, asking to borrow some money. Me, sensing an episode of *Intervention* coming on, handing her twenty dollars. She, smirking, pulling a stuffed-full plastic bag out of her knapsack, thrusting it at me. "I don't need this shit anymore, you take it." And off she goes, trudging away; by the end of the driveway already smaller, by the end of the street smaller still. For all I know she's still walking, crossing distant valleys, trekking through mountains in worn-down boots, getting smaller, smaller, smaller. No bigger than a wee nut by now.

See, Lucy? See how delightfully everything's turned out for me?

That plastic bag was full of unwashed clothes, including this blue dress I'm wearing today. That's all I have left of her. I didn't cry. I just lay down on the couch and went to sleep. Had the dream in which I'm first violin in a major orchestra but no one's remembered to give me the score. The rest of the orchestra plays, but I just sit there, humiliated beyond bearing, and when it comes time for my solo, the entire hall falls silent for the requisite number of bars.

If you think I had it coming, Lucy, you're dead on the money.

She can't sleep, it's hopeless. She gets up, her stomach bilious. Splashes water on her face. Sits in the straight-backed wooden chair against the wall, raises her violin. Quietly plays the thirty opening bars of her piece, which will be heard for the first time in the world tonight. Feeling the now familiar tug under her left arm. Remembering *that* room, where she'd also played as quietly as possible, her back to the wall, ha!

It's twenty minutes long, this thing she's composed. Twenty minutes of random notes, Lucy would say. No. Every note is a drop of her blood.

She should have told Lucy about it, she could have! Opened up about her life, been honest. Lucy might stare blankly over her head during the telling, but one thing Sheila knew: behind that mask of sardonic affliction, Lucy Brickwood would be *listening*.

My daughter's gone, Lucy. She came into my life; she left it. Some things just don't work. *You* know how it is.

But oh, my old friend, if you'd seen me back then, when the whole mess started, you'd have laughed till you split. Remember how you used to try to pass yourself off as Russian? We used to be in stitches, me and Hardee and Marjorie, taking the piss out of you after you'd left, the three of us cramped double, weeping, stuff coming out of our noses. Poor misbegotten Lyudmilova with your dancing bear and your wacky getups, your furious social ineptitude, that fierce, sticklebacked pride of yours. You knew us O'Mearas at the height of our golden time, and I know, I *know* that we hurt you, Lucy. Not just me at the end, all of us. That self-adoring love of ours that had no time or space in it for you. Oh, Lucy, Lucy, I get it now. I am *so* sorry.

It would go a long way to evening the score if you could have seen me, just a few years later, getting my richly deserved comeuppance. You'd bust a gut, hearing about all that abysmal nonsense my sister and I got so tied up in knots over. And who even remembers it now? Historical dreck, a blip in time. Quaint videos on obscure Google outposts, geezers droning, nobody listening.

But this part I *know* you'll understand: it was as if I were under a spell, Lucy. So hell-bent on running away from myself, from expectations, from the impossible possibility that *I,* the adored and shining star, was going to let everybody down. Just like you, I wanted with all my heart to become someone else.

She'd been someone else all right. Clambering onto the rattletrap green bus that would ferry her and her comrades, this militant vanguard of the Canadian proletariat, from Titograd to the Yugoslav-Albanian frontier. Clutching the back of the seat in front of her, turned out like a bargain-basement Ninotchka in a hideous tweed pantsuit, a hand-me-down from Nanna. Ugly, kathunkety, orangey-brown shoes with rubber wedge soles, perfect for militant striding. Her violin case bouncing on her lap.

At the border, soldiers in khaki appeared, rifles slung across their backs. Lean, stern Balkan faces, wood carvings done with a dull penknife. They were handsome, these soldiers, in a peaked, famished sort of way, though none was as meltingly good-looking as Comrade Enver Hoxha, Albania's Great Leader. Enver, who could easily pass for Dirk Bogarde's younger, puffier brother!

All the comrades held their breath, peering out the bus window as the Albanian flag appeared, the two-headed black eagle on a blood-red field. Even hanging limp as underpants on a clothesline, it was whipping the entire delegation's blood into foamy froth.

The bus ground to a halt. Mountains out there, a lake overhung with morning mist. The soldiers raised their right fists to their right temples, palm side facing forward. Astringent smiles were exchanged as one soldier marched alongside the bus, scrutinizing the comrades through the windows, a quick scan for beards, for none may enter here! Listening intently for frivolous whistling, also forbidden. Right-thinking visitors were welcome in the Land of Eagles, but the pigs and swine must wait outside!

"The Party brings us light!" shouted one of their delegation, Comrade Tim, out of his mind with revolutionary zeal. "Heed the call of the Party, comrades! Long live the friendship between the Canadian and the Albanian people!"

They filed off the bus, bumping one another ahead in their eagerness. Vigilant soldiers scanned their legs for any hint of bell-bottoms, which must be stitched up into unflared proletarian trousers before one more errant step into Paradise could be taken. As if superfluous cloth would be found on them! Ahead, the Albanian bus which would replace the Yugoslav bus they rode in on, groaned toward them, grey, dented all over.

The driver descended, lit a smoke, lounged against the side. He was slight of build, not much older than Sheila, twenty-six, twenty-seven. Shiny brown suit jacket over murky green sweater. Saggy, dusty, dark blue pants. He stood by the door, beaming, pumping their hands vigourously between both of his, the cigarette riding his thin lower lip. His briefly glimpsed teeth were caramel-coloured stumps, but his face was sweet, full of unfakeable proletarian honesty, and his brown hair was curly, his eyes deep set and dark. Displaying, when he leapt onto the bus and into his seat, a gazelle-like grace hinting at excellent Marxist-Leninist muscle tone.

The bus had no such tone, nor anything resembling a suspension; it jolted and shuddered, gears screeching at every shift. They were jounced, bounced and slid sideways without mercy on bare metal seats as they watched unkempt, rocky Albania, Beacon to the Wretched of the Earth, jiggle past.

Comrade Elliot could not contain himself; he stood, holding on to the back of his seat with his left hand, and, right fist chopping the air, launched into one of their glorious Canadian revolutionary songs. They all joined in, shout-singing, "Comrade killed a capitalist, a capitalist, a capitalist! Comrade killed a capitalist and now a red day's dawning!"

Surrounded by this forbidding, rockslide landscape, these stark grey mountains, this soil drenched with the blood of martyrs, the song sounded a little . . .

Don't say it, thought Sheila. Don't even think it!

The song sounded like shit.

There. She thought it.

The driver blatted his horn, a rude raspberry as they shimmied past a band of skinny, glowering children clustered by the roadside. Who raised their fists at them! Of course, this didn't mean what it would have at home. They sang on, a song that could go on for a thousand years, Comrade killed TWO capitalists, before petering out, a little flushed. Those ferocious children's faces following them, wheezing, flabby dilettantes that they were beside this proud, fearless, long-suffering people who were Forging a New World from Bare Rock with Their Bare Hands. *Their Bare Hands!*

They'd all put in many fruitless hours back home, spreading the gospel, hammering home the slogans, the talking points, witnessing fervently to neighbours and workmates about brave little Socialist Albania, Saviour of the World, Blazing Red Star, Bright Beacon etc. etc. To which those neighbours and workmates invariably replied, with bright smiles, "Yeah, sure, I know where that is. Just down the Adirondack Northway, after Plattsburgh and Saratoga."

She had asked to room alone so that she could practice playing the revolutionary repertoire—which she needed less than zero time to work on—in the evenings, without disturbing anyone. That's why she was here, after all, to do her humble part to keep revolutionary fervour at a constant boil. But rooming alone would also assure her much-needed downtime from her comrades, with their relentless revolutionary banter and wearying, steely-eyed determination.

Her room was plain, spare, dark. Chubby-cheeked Enver beamed down from the wall, as he did from virtually all walls. A bare overhead bulb, orphanage-style bed, brown Naugahyde armchair, plywood armoire. Everything felt metallic, hollow, as if made of tin painted to look like something better, wood, for instance. The tinny door squeaked, the knob loose in its socket.

But her small window looked out on a large square, traversed even now in the nine p.m. dark by busy workers, the freest and happiest of people, the *klasa punëtore* hard at their tasks! With genuine envy she watched a militant, straight-backed young Albanian woman around her age cross the square with proud purpose, off to night school, or to put in a third shift at the metallurgy plant, unasked! Dedicated heart and mind to ceaseless class struggle, not a stitch of doubt or fear in her.

Watching her, Sheila felt herself fading fast.

Because she didn't have it in her. She knew it. She didn't have the stomach for any of this stuff. She was a fake, in this new life just as she'd been in the old one she'd left behind. A chicken-hearted fake, without the nerve to speak up, to come clean, to walk away.

Turning from the window, sick with self-loathing, her glasses fogged, she stumbled over one big orange shoe, accidentally kicking it under the tinny bed. Down on her knees, reaching for it, she wished she hadn't. There was a scorpion under there, half the size of her hand.

Comrade Liz grew up in a Calgary slum. Comrade Vlad's immigrant parents bent their backs as migrant workers, picking tomatoes under a cruel southern Ontario sun. Comrade Ted spent summers slopping pigs, cleaning out horses' stalls so he could put himself through community college.

It was with prudence therefore that Sheila released as little information as possible about summer master classes at Orford, student chamber ensembles, she and her fellow elites so full of themselves, their futures radioactive with promise. Doing what they loved all day long, their friendships arch and competitive, exploding into romantic supernovas at recital times when stress was highest. Marjorie with her for two summers, Daddy and Anny driving out on weekends to visit, taking them out to eat, sitting in on rehearsals, bringing along whomever they could squeeze into the car: Auntie Maureen, Istvan, Uncle James, Nanna. Hardee and Vi. The full and unfeigned attention of adults lavished upon them at all times; critical attention, yes, but they expected that, welcomed it as a measure of their undeniable worth, their astonishing potential. Nothing less than superlative results ever expected of them, and they hit the mark every time, spirits soaring, feet firm on the ground. Hard work, pressure, and sacrifice were their daily bread.

Colleen did her hair and makeup for her first publicity shots, removing her glasses, plucking her eyebrows while she yelled. Scraping her hair back from her face, making her beautiful, almost as beautiful as she herself was. Posing her against a tree trunk in a long, black dress of Anny's, her beautiful new russet concert violin held against her knee as casually as a shopping bag, Armagnac-warm against the black skirt.

She and Marjorie were so full of burning plans: the Manhattan penthouse they would share, once they'd both claimed with ease their respective first chairs in the Met Orchestra, in the highly unlikely event they were denied world-shattering solo débuts on the concert stage.

Ah, but Colleen was the *delicious* sister. The stunner. An autumn-coloured girl redolent of rusty-warm afternoon light, baskets of Winesap apples, her auburn hair against her grey sweater a thing of knee-weakening beauty. Gorgeous, at the piano under recital lights in a slim, backless dress, the least gifted of the four O'Meara children, but oh, that hair, those dresses, those long, elegant, lightly speckled lily hands! Neither Sheila nor Marjorie, befuzzed and bespectacled, ever begrudged her a thing, nor did Hardee, flushed and lumpy, his hairline, by the time he was twenty, already losing serious ground. Daddy and Anny—here, of course, was where they made their first mistake—perfectly fine with her taking off to Africa at eighteen, her selfless year of giving back. Anny being a lot finer with it than Daddy was, but he surely knew that Colleen would likely never have a real shot at a serious concert career. She alone of the O'Meara brood could afford to put her music away for a while.

Her one African year stretched into two. She came home at last from digging wells, helping to run a women's hygiene clinic, all her new, dear friends left behind. Came home rail thin, her hair and skin parched, to reclaim her place at the heart of her dazzling family.

Except she wouldn't.

At the welcome-home extravaganza they threw for her, she refused to wear the slinky silver dress Anny had bought her, turning up in ragged jeans, an old flannel shirt of Hardee's. Making bitter remarks about the sufferings of the oppressed masses, the cruelty of the greedy rich, the gutlessness of the academic and artistic classes. Dropping insults like burning coals onto the carpet, guests literally taken aback, losing their balance trying to retreat from the verbal onslaught. Women dropping lorgnettes, men losing monocles: that's how backward and ridiculously out of step she made everyone feel.

Back at McGill in the fall, she abandoned her music performance major, then dropped out entirely. Living in an attic on Prince Arthur, holidays at home now just one long squabble with Daddy. Reading aloud strident passages from the *Little Red Book* at the Christmas dinner table, extolling the Cultural Revolution and the Great Leap Forward. Sticking up for Mao and Stalin, for China and its brave little Kemosabe sidekick Albania. And so on and so forth, Sheila shutting herself in her bedroom to sweat over Mozart's Sonata in G major, Marjorie behind closed doors in the kitchen, running scales at a fevered pace.

Colleen went to work, only accepting jobs where she could stand cheek by jowl with the oppressed Canadian working masses. She cleaned hotel rooms, mopped hospital floors, worked the graveyard shift in a bakery. Cut off all her hair, became bloated from her french fry and cheese sandwich diet. Her arches fell.

Meanwhile, single-minded Marjorie was at the Conservatoire, toiling eight hours a day in practice rooms. Hardee, graduated from Juilliard, married with a child on the way, was in NYC, playing with two separate trios, one classical, one jazz, brilliantly launched, shooting for the top, a shining credit to the O'Meara name.

And Sheila? Finished with the Conservatoire, studying with an expensive private teacher. Preparing for competitions, coming in fourth, sixth. The great Genoa Paganini competition come and gone; she hadn't made the grade. Auditioning for embarrassingly lowly jobs, a chance to sub in a small orchestra, filling in for some temporarily sidelined player. Or a chair in some cheesy cruise ship outfit. Always abruptly stopped a quarter of the way through her piece: Thank you. Don't call us.

Then she'd be right back outside again, blinking in the sunlight, knocked senseless by her powerlessness to get one iota better than she was.

She was twenty-two. Her back was beginning to give her problems; standing for long hours was torture. But worse, far worse, was the crippling stage fright that had appeared out of nowhere virtually the moment she'd left the safe confines of the Conservatoire.

Never in her life had she experienced more than mild jitters before performances; now she found herself in such blind panic that she raced through her pieces just to get them over with. Jan, her teacher, quietly advised her to go back to easier works to shore up her confidence, but no, damn it, she was going to bulldoze through this! Refusing to take the tiniest step backward, even when he began making cautious noises about the possibility that she was burnt-out, should consider taking some time off, or (No!) consider another (NO!) career altogether (no, no, no, no, NO!).

She threw herself into learning Ravel's *Tzigane, rapsodie de concert*, which she played as if pursued by Ben-Hur, the notes swimming in frustrated tears. Stopping, starting, stopping, swearing, her back in agony. Refusing to give in, trying something even harder, some Gordian-knotted, opaque French music. Flailing helplessly as the truth slowly began to dawn that not only was her technique, after hundreds of thousands of hours of practice, B+ level and holding, but that something else, something far more crucial was missing.

Except for tears over her shameful ineptitude, music didn't make her weep.

Not for her the wracked, tormented face, the swollen gush of emotion channelled through horsehair and catgut that was the actual purpose behind the whole enterprise. Nothing arose from within her to meet the music her clever hands made. Her iron discipline, her countless practice hours, had developed toughness in her, and pride, steadiness and acceptable competence. But never the one thing that can't be taught: an overflowing heart.

This, at twenty-two, was the first crisis of her charmed life, and Colleen barged straight into it, ferocious, taking no prisoners. Home for the weekend, fresh off an ugly spat with their father, she hunkered on Sheila's bed, her face a thundercloud as she categorically blasted to hell every single one of the contemptible O'Mearas. Their father bore the brunt of her venom: look how irascible, how intolerant he was! After he'd whipped the two of them like a mule team, interpreting their failure to excel as a shameful indignity done to him! To *him!*

This had not once occurred to Sheila, but now that Colleen said it, her face a wrung rag, it began to seem true.

She did a smear job on Anny too, ridiculing the cracked notions that she herself had bought into with such enthusiasm only a few years ago. "All that karma bullshit of hers, how the good draws to it the good, so we know everything isn't random. Sheila, she's like a six-year-old! I told her so, too, I said, 'Class struggle isn't random, Mother. *That's* where your thinking needs to begin and end.' But there's no educating her, she's always going to be a backward element."

Hardee was a preening, self-involved, decadent careerist. Marjorie was a slog, a dull grind, buttressing herself against the coming revolutionary storms with rigid practice routines and crass, self-serving ambition.

"You're the only one with a head on your shoulders. I know you're bright enough to see through all this family-music-dynasty crap. It's time for you to get serious about life, Sheila. The old world is passing away, the new is coming into being! Don't let them hold you back with all their elitist drivel about success and fame. Come join the revolutionary proletariat as we seize the future on behalf of the toiling masses and all of suffering, exploited mankind!"

Sitting there on the end of her bed, bloviating away, still lovely even in her ugly thrift store clothes, her torn army jacket. Her chopped-off hair, her pockets stuffed with leaflets, pamphlets, Lenin's *Imperialism, the Highest Stage of Capitalism* with actual bookmarks in it. Making a *comrade* of her, this Colleen who had always been so sweetly condescending. Declaring them equals, no longer the beautiful one and the plain one, no longer the less talented and the more. The gleefully pitiless debunking of all the O'Meara laws of identity and birthright resonated like a Chinese gong in Sheila's trudging, defeated soul.

Could she really just . . . quit?

Yes! End the pain! Stop flogging herself without mercy for no reward. Never get up on another audition stage for as long as she drew breath. Submerge her being in a greater cause, usher in new worlds—yes, she could handle the jargon just as well as Colleen could! Cheek by jowl, you say? Why the hell not?

Colleen took her to a rally, which she'd expected would be something like union meetings in movies: a passionate speaker, rows of grim workers in folding chairs, caps in their laps. She wasn't prepared for the rowdy shouting and fist-pumping that went on. She joined Colleen and her comrades in the May Day march under a flaming red banner, astonished to discover how much fun it was to yell slogans in the street, hollering about how their blood was boiling over, they'd spill it in a heartbeat, just try them!

She joined Colleen's Marxist-Leninist study group. Communism, on paper, sounded fine to her; it was a system, after all, a complete theory, and she loved systems, doted on theories. And people had clearly put a lot of time and effort into this one.

The other comrades took pains to let her know that if she was going to be one of them, she had to accept the fact that this new life would run her through a class struggle meat grinder, that it would take everything she had, beginning with her most cherished assumptions. For she and Colleen, they explained, did not spring shiny and clean from the toiling classes, but grubbily from the petite bourgeoisie, and so were burdened with all the attendant backward thought processes that had been drummed into them since birth. Privately, Sheila thought Colleen was way worse than she was, a Marxist-Leninist prima donna, her declarations of fealty intensely overdramatized, always managing to call attention to the militant, stalwart, good-looking wonder that was Colleen O'Meara. From the outset, she'd had the pleasant suspicion that the other comrades preferred her serious, plainspoken ways. This went immediately to her competitive head.

But it was when they found out she was a violinist that they really went off the rails.

A fiddler! Would she by any chance be interested in participating in the creation of a Genuine Canadian People's Culture? Would she care to assist in helping to ruthlessly sweep away all decadent, bourgeois, imperialist influences, and build, from the ground up, a new, pure, proletarian Culture of the New Man, based on the people's most deeply felt folk traditions, just as Stalin had done in the USSR?

Okay. Why not?

She was handed a sheaf of typewritten song lyrics, all the o's missing, grisly ditties set to folksy tunes like *Land of the Silver Birch* or *Blow the Man Down*. Verse after verse crammed to bursting, propaganda pamphlets set to music, not a single stanza scanning correctly. Her task: create barnstorming fiddle accompaniments to bring these tunes to revolutionary life!

It didn't take more than half an hour.

But the first time she stood up in an after-hours McGill classroom to play her little down-home riffs, she saw the grey, indoor faces of the small assemblage of comrades in attendance light up like bonfires in the Winter Palace. If only she'd had the same power over auditioners, over competition adjudicators! It felt wondrously liberating not to be nervous, to just stand up there showing off, with no desperate hopes riding on her performance. And best of all, to see Colleen clapping along in the front row, warm in the cheeks, appreciating her to death.

By the time the chance to join the friendship delegation to Albania came up, she'd had three solid years of Marxist-Leninist indoctrination. Had left home, moved to the city, found a cheap apartment on the lightless ground floor of a Saint-Denis triplex, gotten a waitressing job. Was studying the correct books, living authentically, cheek pressed tight to jowl! No more competitions, no more auditions, though she still practiced serious violin in the little spare time she had, alone, bereft of piano accompaniment. Short, yearning, easy pieces: Chopin's Nocturne in C sharp minor, Debussy's *Beau Soir,* Shubert's *Serenade.* Not letting on about this to Colleen or anyone else. And particularly not letting on about the hysterical little bubble of drollery she kept having to suppress whenever the correct-speak and hyperbole and scowling earnestness of the penny-ante, completely fakeroo class struggle they were pretending to wage became too much to bear.

Proof, of course, that she was still an incorrigible elitist, the stench of class enmity all over her cheap, secondhand clothes.

The collective farm cadre leading them in and out of rows of dingy greenhouses wore a man's brown sweater, a knee-length woolen skirt over dungarees, and poppy-red lipstick. To which Sheila could only exclaim—silently—*what the?* As a matter of fact, all the female farm workers' mouths were smeared with any number of carnal shades of red.

How could this be? Canadian Vanguard women would die a thousand deaths before they'd apply a lick of paint to their honest faces. But lipstick aside, with their long, unconditioned hair always parted on the left, the women looked exactly as advertised in the pages of *New Albania,* where they regularly appeared, obdurately shoveling manure, peering into test tubes or assembling TV sets from the fifties.

All the comrades had notepads at the ready, clustering around their Albanian guide, frantic with questions prepared the night before: How was cultural life different in town and countryside? What about measures taken for the eradication of the intelligentsia? What kinds of wholesome fun did the Young Pioneers enjoy? Give examples!

Later, in town, they swooned over new, jerry-built workers' apartment blocks with ENVER emblazoned on the sides in fifteen-foot letters. Studied a roadside display of typewritten index cards in a case behind cracked, smudged glass: powerful messages of socialist "dis-emulation," various enemies of the people being hauled over the coals in words with many unpronounceable consonant clusters, liberally peppered with umlauts. Thrilled to a passing parade of women's militia in olive drab, guns on their backs. Could this get any better?

Their delegation leader, the militant powerhouse Comrade Mary-Lou, claimed she would dig ditches with a fork, no, with her *teeth,* if the class struggle required it of her! What kind of class enemy could hide in the ranks with her around? When they all met in the evening to chew over and digest their revolutionary day, Mary-Lou's breath was ragged with feeling. Her hands shook like a secret drinker's. "We must forge strong links!" she cried, pounding the table. "Strong links between the Canadian and Albanian revolutionary masses!"

Back in her room before bed, Sheila reviewed the day's notes, columns of stats on sugar beet yields per hectare and soybean quotas somersaulting over the page, no framework forming, no burning question answered. Reflecting, not without malice, that lipstick didn't seem to be brightening those farm gals' spirits any. They had callused hands, strong backs, no lack of purpose or goals, but—it occurred to her in an upjet of petit bourgeois peevishness—what choice did they have? They went to work where they were sent, did the job they were ordered to do. They were names on lists, cogs screwed into the humming revolutionary machine. And that machine would keep on chugging till the screw wore out its threads and the cog dropped to the floor, kerthump.

The Party proceeding to issue a glorious call: Cogs! We need more cogs!

This cog business, of course, was elementary, McCarthy-style hatred of Communism. She should be ashamed. She *was* ashamed. And don't think for one minute, she warned herself, that these silent, private notions of yours aren't instantly detectable to the trained Marxist-Leninist eagle eye! These were *dastardly* ideas, eradicable only by the most hammerheaded process of criticism and self-criticism, of fearless, protracted struggle!

And here she was (yawn). Tired to death.

The defection of two of his daughters plunged their father into the blackest grief. What had he ever done but give them love, care, encouragement without limit? Head-butting them down their musical paths, brooking no shortcuts or slackery. Nothing had ever made him happier than to have all his children in the house, in four separate rooms, practicing, while he read the *New York Times* in a lawn chair, the French doors open so he could catch Paganini's Caprice in E flat major drifting from Sheila's bedroom window.

He'd grown up in a musical family himself, playing viola, a little piano. Evenings, after several postprandial cognacs, he'd take out his battered old instrument, Anny curled in a wing chair, wrapped in a shawl, smiling up at him. His four prodigies looking ever so gently down their noses at him, all of them having surpassed him in musical skills by the time they were six. But he always knew what they were working on, what difficulties they were having, when their next competition or recital was, how well or poorly prepared they were.

Looking back, Sheila couldn't help but think: Was it possible he knew something they didn't? Because, what were prodigies like them doing in an ordinary high school? Why hadn't they, at the very least, been packed off at the age of nine to the Royal Conservatory in Toronto? Maybe *then* she'd have been one of the students she later found herself competing against, outmentored and outperformed time and again by maniacs who had been playing Ropartz trios since they were seven.

Of course, they'd had Istvan. Devoted, demanding Istvan, leaping to his feet, crying out, when they finally got something right, "Yes! Yes, there it is!" Or at the piano, playing the orchestral accompaniment to their concerto solos, shouting, "Diaphragm! Please! Make me feel! I feel nothing!" Trying to draw ecstasy out of them, succeeding only with Marjorie.

She didn't know about Hardee and Colleen, but all she had understood music to be was a language of exquisitely precise, mathematical order, its starry heights attainable through a sustained process of control, concentration, repetition. What did she know about loneliness and loss, about despair, about the abysses of anguish and regret where truth and beauty might find a dark, ragged furrow in which to sow their seed? She was concerned with questions of workmanship and technique, shoddy or otherwise; there she would not compromise, would make no excuse, would drill and drill and drill again—never coming within a thousand miles of striking oil.

Did Daddy and Anny know that three of their astonishing children had no business shooting for the stars? Looking back, she saw Anny, moving into her fifties, her mouth beginning to turn downward, her deep emotional needs unmet by her increasingly distant, inexplicably wrathful husband. Letting her hair go grey, shrinking, her little child's spine, soft as a green tendril, beginning to curl forward. Swallowed up by one of her flowered chairs, her ashen, quietly attentive face obscured by shadows as the extended family, her brother James and his entourage, Daddy's old music friends, Nanna and her cronies, came around less and less. Daddy becoming intolerably quarrelsome, prone to black silences, rages, door-slamming disappearances from holiday tables.

Then Nanna died. Istvan died. Unless one of them was home, practicing, the music leaking timidly from under shut doors, the house sat mute.

What shabby stuff, then, were the marvelous O'Mearas made of, that they fell apart so easily? Had it always been ordained, was it long overdue? As teenagers, none of them had rebelled; who had the time? Their resentment was late-onset, Daddy and Hardee squabbling on the phone over Hardee's decision to focus more on jazz, over his not starting his son Jesse off with a Suzuki teacher as soon as he could walk. Hardee and Vi not visiting for a while, and Anny, deprived of grandchildren Jesse and new baby Sean, shutting herself in the bedroom, crying.

But there was so much sweetness to remember, too! Outings *en famille* to the symphony and the ballet, the *Nutcracker* when they were tiny, Sheila and Colleen and Hardee in the front row, standing up so they could lean over the orchestra not twenty feet away. Clapping hysterically, giggling at the male dancers because they could see their bum cracks through their tights. Trips to New York, to the Met, feeling so important, so glamourous, all three girls in their best dresses, white stockings and shoes, studying their programmes, knowing to shout *Brava!* for the soprano. Daddy's presence always so imposing, his luxuriant hair artistically long, always impeccably dressed, with some small eccentricity, a great harp pin on his tie, a red satin vest, Kelly green socks. Anny so beautiful next to him, barely reaching his shoulder, her copper hair let down her back, a floor-length dress of dark velvet or something she'd crocheted herself in a mouthwatering shade of plum or raspberry. The four adored children marching down the aisle to their seats, groomed, composed, chins up, their great worth and inherent goodness beyond question. So pleased to be taken for pampered New York opera children: bright-eyed, informed, and strongly opinionated.

Travelling to the next Albanian town involved a long inland bus drive through bleak mountains. A low cloud ceiling, hairpin turns, a pointless Albanian death never more than a foot away. The bald bus tires, braking on the steep downhill, were smoking; Sheila could smell them.

Their skillful driver, whom their ever-present guide Ramiz had introduced as Sokol, had expressive eyebrows, an elfin grin; more than once she'd caught his brown eyes seeking out hers in the overhead mirror.

Again: *what the . . . ?*

Kindly watch the road, Comrade!

What she was thinking was unthinkable. Should she just put this down to the forging of strong links? It was happening every time she looked up, those eyes, waiting to snag hers. She tried to focus on the passing view. Albania looked okay when the sun was shining, but in grey weather it turned surly, the road lined with pillboxes like giant cement mushrooms, their gun apertures gaping. She counted twenty-five pillboxes, did a swift spot check: yep, brown eyes gunning for hers in the mirror.

Stop it!

The comrades reverently passed around copies of the Albanian newspaper, *Zëri i Popullit,* which they flapped and held up before their faces like commuters on a train, though no one understood a word. Ramiz translated a sentence or two: The class of poor peasants is eager to give even their last grain of maize to the workers, whose vigour and impetus are manifested in the uncompromising struggle of the Party to smash the old and build the new, to guarantee the triumph of the socialist road. Sheila looked out the window. On her side of the bus, a ragtag band of Revolutionary Youth trudged by, straight out of a social realist bas-relief: single file, shovels and picks over their shoulders. The kerchiefed leader at the head of the line gave the flag she carried a militant hoist. For a split second the two-headed eagle looked to Sheila's eyes like a squashed centipede.

Nice, Comrade. Great proletarian spirit there.

But what about their leader? That flag of hers had been drooping pretty sadly until the bus hove into view, she'd seen it!

And again, *again* with the eyes!

Mary-Lou, at the front of the bus, rose, stood jolting in the aisle. "Comrade Sheila! How about you fiddle us into *Fists Aloft*?"

A profound inner sigh. Elitist or not, she *despised* this tinpot, hickory-dickory hayride-to-the-hootenanny music. All the comrades hollering like cats on a fence to the tune of *I's the B'y,* clapping on the offbeat, while she drew out careless scrapes and screeches with the bow that she hadn't made since she was four.

In her room at night, she'd begun playing pieces she'd slaved over years ago. The very act of sitting in a straight-backed chair, drawing something beautiful out of her violin throttled her to the core, tears—where were *they* coming from?—coursing down her face as she played, as well as she could from memory, the quiet first and third movements of Shostakovich's First Violin Concerto in A minor, the last piece of music she could remember performing with something close to joy and abandon. The second movement was her favourite, but it was too loud and frenetic; she had to keep the noise down. She'd spent eight months working on that concerto with Istvan when she was nineteen, miles out of her depth, feeling as if she were running for her life through bolts of lightning, but thrilled to the marrow, refusing to quit. Istvan, half on his feet like Jerry Lee Lewis, banging out the orchestral accompaniment, the whole family there amid the floral riot of their living room, beaming, so proud of her, the fourth and fifth movements absolutely crazed, and she feeling she was almost, almost there, almost bursting the dam holding her in, *almost!*

But playing it *very* quietly now. Stalin hated Shostakovich so Enver did too, although if any of her fellow delegates should overhear, they'd just think she was tuning up, maybe taking the violin apart for cleaning, the way you do a gun.

And she wondered idly, after she'd put her bow down: what was old Enver doing *right now?* How close by was he? It wasn't a big country; he could be right around the corner for all she knew. Was he hunched over his desk in these small hours, cobbling together another chest-thumper of a speech, another jaw-dropping chapter of his voluminous memoirs? Was he in the bathroom, yelling to his dour wife that there was no toilet paper? Did he ever suffer doubts concerning his contribution, his place in world history? Did it ever cross his mind that he might be a *jerk?*

Was he afraid of being found out, waking in the night drenched with terror? Insufficiently soothed by the exceedingly prolonged periods of rhythmic applause from the rows of Sam Giancana lookalikes that followed his every public utterance? Stalin, she'd read somewhere she shouldn't have, needed to be applauded for a minimum of seven minutes. A touchy business for the clappers, because who in hell wanted to be tagged as the first person to stop?

Information like this stuck in her unrepentant mind like a post in cement.

She was counting the days, the hours, till it was time to go home. She didn't *want* there to be a revolution, hoped it never happened, buildings blown up, rivers of blood down Sherbrooke Street, she wouldn't stand for it! The working class and the

Canadian vanguard revolutionary masses, all twenty-eight of them—yes, she said it!—could march their wheezing, blinkered, musically challenged selves straight to perdition.

Sokol grinned outright now when he caught her eye, stubby brown teeth and all. It dawned on her that he might be a little on the slow side.

He ate with them every night, wherever they were being hosted, in identical meeting rooms under the all-seeing gaze of Happy Days Enver. When the plates were cleared, and Mary-Lou elbowed her in the side to start the good times rolling, Sokol always eased back in his chair, lit a hand-rolled smoke, began beating time with one brown hand on the table. Their sea shanties and turkey-in-the-straw rhapsodies were probably crazy exotic to his ears.

They moved to a new place every day. Walked in regimented twos through the sacred grey cobblestone town where Enver was born, a heavy-footed cabal, bundled against the April chill, spiral notebooks open, pens poised, eyes aflame. They dropped in to visit a crumbling elementary school where the children, they were told with a straight face, spent a large bulk of their time doing military exercises and learning to love labour. Said children, in shiny black smocks with white collars, sat with identically folded hands behind splintered old desks, regarding them gravely. The young teacher presented Mary-Lou with a souvenir children's book, *How Much Uncle Enver Loves Us!* The children stood and saluted, little fists raised to foreheads. One boy at the back had an impudent look that settled on Sheila for some reason; she felt exposed, nakedly guilty. What ideological foulness had those pure eyes discerned?

They trailed through a picture gallery, clumping together in solemn reverence before painting after painting of dashing Uncle Enver, who always got the most stylish belted coat, the jauntiest hat, though none of the other stalwarts seemed to mind, filing in lockstep behind him up craggy mountainsides, fairly panting with devotion. There was always one ferocious woman with tree-trunk ankles in the crowd, always one doggedly obstinate old man in a white fez like a jujube. The rest were men of circus strongman brawn and swagger. Where these behemoths could actually be found was a mystery; all the real-life men she had seen tended toward the slight, the underfed, the uninspiring.

Out in the street again, ragged children who for some reason weren't in school followed behind them at a distance, barefoot on the unforgiving cobblestones, though it was hardly barefoot weather. The children had unnerving eyes, wary, watchful under lowering brows. She wanted to shout, "Kids! We are your friends! We've got Uncle Enver's back!" Out from amongst them, an old, old woman, her head swathed in black rags, darted toward their group, toward *her,* clutching at the sleeve of her sweater, one that Anny had made her, rust coloured with an intricate cable pattern, bulky and warm. She let go of the sleeve and proceeded to grab the collar; Sheila didn't know if she was just trying to examine the knit more closely or trying to pull the sweater over her head and make off with it.

Ramiz stepped forward, shooing her off with a brisk bark; for a moment, Sheila was afraid he'd pull out a pistol and blow her away. The woman melted in among the cold-eyed children, no taller than they were. This was entirely untoward and shocking; it was as if they'd opened a door and come upon dear Uncle Enver, pants around his ankles, inflagrante with a comely assembly-line worker. None of the comrades knew how to position their eyes.

In the plywood-panelled lobby of their hotel after dinner, in rows of folding chairs, following an intense tour of a precision tool factory, they kicked back with a little Albanian TV: a small man on a wavy screen, reading the news from a fat sheaf of papers. Ramiz, standing off to their right, stubbed out his smoke in an overflowing pedestal ashtray, sighed, and translated: Preparations are underway for May Day! Today workers picked tomatoes for export at the Eighth of November greenhouse! He seemed fed up, sick of them all, probably counting down the hours just like she was.

Sokol, for once, was not with them. She was heartily ashamed to find herself concentrating on the door, willing him to come in, pump some blood into the proceedings.

The news over, it was time for fun! The "Happy Motives" variety show opened with a funny sketch, called "At the tailor," aimed at criticizing those backward youths—Ramiz was racing to keep up—who went in for reactionary, Western-influenced clothing such as wide trousers, tight shirts. An arrogant fellow declared, "Everyone may choose his own fashion! Keep out of youth's way of dressing!" "You hate our ready-made, stout clothes," riposted the leader of a gang of fiery, right-thinking young militants. "The enemy has shot you and you don't understand!" The players tromped off into the wings, making way for a fresh batch, who milled about nervously, perhaps uncertain of their lines. The sketch began *in media res*, one of them crying out, "Why haven't you fulfilled the plan?" "Why didn't *you* bring the raw material? You're a bureaucrat!" shouted another. Sheila thought she spied Sokol through the street door, but if he was there, he didn't come in.

The actors trooped off, leaving in their wake two entire minutes of empty set, dead air. At long last, a circus performer in a wrinkly-kneed unitard appeared, busily set up his props and proceeded to balance on a plank which was balanced in turn on a large ball. He began juggling three or four little balls, but only a few seconds in, fell off his board, dropping everything. Calmly, on his knees, he retrieved all the balls, including one that had rolled under the back curtain, and began again. They all spontaneously applauded this demonstration of simplicity and lack of conceit, the first time Sheila had clapped sincerely since she'd arrived.

The next night, after a long, sweaty slog through a smeltery, they were promised an evening party. Following a brief talk on steel and chrome production and the breathtaking inauguration of the sixth five-year plan, they would be treated to a performance by a local folk ensemble. They would, of course, repay the favour by dragging out their own deadly hayseed repertoire.

"Tune your fiddle well, comrade," advised Mary-Lou with a turgid wink.

They walked in twos to the party like school kids, past trees just coming into bud, beneath waves of starlings swooping in jellyfish undulations against the darkening sky. What did Uncle Enver feel at twilight, wondered Sheila. Was he in his tinny, plywood office, poring over lists of people caught making jokes at his expense? Was he watching forbidden Italian TV on the sly, chuckling at the reactionary hijinks, discovering himself pleasantly engorged by the wall-to-wall cleavage? Yearning, perhaps, for a pizza?

The party was being held, astonishingly, in a private house, one with a clean, whitewashed exterior and a tiny front yard with trees. Did someone important live here? Could it be . . . the Man himself? Might he suddenly emerge from the kitchen, fist to temple, tie loosened, hair rumpled, grease splashes on his trousers from working—cheek by jowl, what else?—with the cooks?

Sheila let out breath she hadn't known she'd been holding. And she knew why: this room they'd been ushered into, where they sat on low benches running around all four walls, had no plywood, no tin, no Naugahyde. It felt like . . . *home!* No squeaking doors, no cracked tiles on the wall; she recognized it instantly, viscerally, as something she was accustomed to, something she was *owed*. Anny would've adored this room, which was uncouth with colour: a riot of floral cushions, rose motifs in pink, blue and yellow, red and black Turkish-style carpets on the floor, the ceiling gorgeous with intricately carved wood beams. The split-leaf philodendrons—a plant in high favour everywhere, its leaves reminiscent of the two-headed eagle—were full and moist here, not yellow and limp as they usually were, a pot parked beside every squeaking door in the land. Odours of cumin and saffron wafted from a kitchen they couldn't see, Uncle Enver—he had to be!—hard at work in there, sleeves rolled up, forehead perspiring, kneading, stirring, spicing, tasting.

Sokol, at least, was back with them tonight, hunched on a small, separate bench near the door to the kitchen, a soggy smoke between the thumb and forefinger of his permanently begrimed hand.

Uncle did not make an appearance. After twenty minutes, several trays of snacks were passed around by a shy young girl in a plaid pantsuit: some spicy sausages, almond cookies, sticky little baklavas which, being offered no plates, they ate from their palms, smooshing the crumbs surreptitiously into the carpeting, rubbing their honeyed fingers onto the rose cushions.

The five-year plan talk never materialized. The comrades killed time peppering their hosts with questions: "How are raw materials for the food-processing industry ensured? How can the peasantry be stimulated to increase production to exchange with industrial products on a reciprocal basis, thus further strengthening the alliance of the working class with the peasantry?" They were getting good at this. "How is resistance dealt with from the remnants of overthrown classes, merchants, market speculators, and career-seeking elements infected by reactionary propaganda?" Ramiz, working overtime, smoked eight cigarettes in a row, his eyes bloodshot.

From out of the kitchen, a pretty young woman in a modest skirt and white blouse appeared, followed by four men, two young, one middle-aged, the last older than Time, all in white shirts, black vests, white jujube fezzes. The comrades piped down, shifted on their benches. The musicians carried instruments she'd never seen before: rustic, Levantine cousins of lutes and clarinets. They gathered across the room, exchanged a few words in an undertone, perhaps reviewing the playlist. Then they took up their positions.

Silence.

A fat, guttering blat from the clarinet, a billy goat suddenly loose in this room of roses. Then a lone male voice, rough, arid, nasal. A second man responded in kind, and then a third, creating a dissonance so jarring that every segment of her spine shuddered, shifted, readjusted.

She had never in her life dreamed there was music like this, these despairing wails rising, then arcing downward, a crazed neighing like deep-belled sheep plunging down a mountainside. The intervals were as close as lichen on bare rock, as constricting as a too-tight collar, shivering every hair on her neck before the sound flowed away, coursing downhill like fast-moving water. The men howled and then they stopped, going to work with their instruments, a racket like tin cans dragged along broken concrete. One of them whacked the same chord over and over on his two-stringed lute thing, the sound of sure trouble, *bad* trouble massing like thunderheads; then the pinched, inconsolable wails of the terminally powerless, the poorest of the poor, started up again, bearing desolate witness.

There was a fist of tears in her throat, her glasses misted over, her placid soul yanked up by the roots. It was impossible to keep time, the rhythm leaping from 10/8 to 3/8 to 5/8, faster than she could count, the young woman joining in, squealing like a piglet under a rusty knife, her voice rising as the others fell, the music separating in two like a zipper, twisting like a double helix, and always, always, behind the others, as if from some distant valley of eternal misery, the oldest man, toothless, four feet tall, a troll hauled out from under a bridge, sighed on and on and on in an impossibly drawn out, trudging, flat-footed, brokenhearted, one-note drone.

This savage sadness, this sandpaper music that abraded the skin and the soul: what could this possibly have to do with the shining, revolutionary times, this worker's paradise? More to the point, why were these people not immediately rounded up and thrown into prison? Because what were these sounds of abject powerlessness pouring out of them but a swift, hard kick to the New Socialist Man's insufferably upright butt? There *was* no New Man, shrieked this music, nor would there ever be, nor an end to suffering, exploitation and cruelty, failure and death, not here, not anywhere.

Ramiz spoke a few words between numbers, while the old man hacked brown chunks of lung into a drenched grey handkerchief. Informing them that this song expressed the indignant cry of the masses in defiance of the shameful antics of the Gang of Four, that song was a warm salute to the Fifth Party Congress.

Sheila didn't believe a word he said; the whole gang of them was laughing in their faces. They couldn't believe anyone was swallowing this bilge.

Sokol was watching her.

Not grinning now, his face hard, reading her thoughts right through her skull. But there was no time to process this for it was their turn now, time for some thin-blooded, Canadian Vanguard Hee Haw shenanigans. Mary-Lou beamed at her as, profoundly ashamed, she scrabbled to her feet, raised her violin, opening with the most dignified accompaniment she could get away with, the comrades immediately drowning her out with their usual thumping gusto.

After two numbers, the old droning man held up a dark, mangled hand: Halt! He gestured to her, and when she approached, took her expensive, beautiful concert violin gently from her. The Albanians passed it respectfully from hand to hand, stroking the russet finish, plucking the strings, nodding, smiling. They passed it back to her, stood in a huddle, waiting.

"They want you to play," said Ramiz, the "alone" unstated but obvious.

She drew a blank, panicked; what did they want, Chopin? Schubert? *Shostakovich?* Mary-Lou was sitting right at her feet, flushed and very nearly . . . merry! They were all looking up at her, waiting, expecting only the best from Comrade Sheila and her guerilla violin.

She fingered a few chords, calling up some old québécois fiddle riffs they used to play during downtime at Orford. Leaning in, swaying on her bow, easing into *Tout le monde est malheureux, tout le temps*. A pessimistic, anti-communist title, certainly, but the most cheerful of tunes, and it utterly upended the mood of the evening until the Albanians lurched in with the clarinet, the lute, finding their outer-spacey way into the music, turning it inside out till she was up to her neck in quicksand, surrounded by barnyard noise, seven thousand crazed chickens crammed into one coop, a herd of long unmilked cows lowing in mutinous complaint. In the nick of time another musician appeared out of nowhere with an accordion; he too jumped in, and within a few bars, steadied them. They found their paths, dropped back to Planet Earth. The comrades, detecting the restoration of order, began their rhythmic clapping, Ramiz too, and Sokol, clapping and stamping, and as Sheila thought of Daddy and Anny and everyone, the full-bodied happiness she'd once known in their garden-of-joy living room, her heart swelled to bursting and she hardly knew her feet were touching the ground.

Afterward, they walked out into the chilly, ink-black night, headed for their hotel. There was snow in the air; it even *smelled* like home. In the darkness, she could allow her tears to fall freely, some valve within her loosened, her heart still in her throat, her head a mess of sweet homesickness. It was an honest admission of just exactly who she was, a euphoric unshackling from the ridiculous falsity that had led her to this place where she had, unexpectedly, stumbled upon truth.

She sensed rather than saw Sokol edging closer to her as they walked. There were no streetlights, the stars only a few miles overhead, vividly indifferent to glorious five-year plans, to the lofty principles of Marxism-Leninism as embodied in Comrade Enver Hoxha's triumphant speech to the Sixth Party Congress. All these ham-fisted endeavours were no different, really, from her own aborted launch to the stars, and overcome with recklessness, she was a hair away from shouting, "Enver! Party! You're just like me! You know nothing! Ha ha ha ha ha ha ha ha ha!"

She trailed at the back of the group, ogling the diamond-heavy sky, her violin case hugged to her chest. From behind her, a rustle of gabardine. Someone grasped her elbow, pulled her arm back, clamped a rough, hard hand over hers. Sokol's tobacco smell was overpowering. He kept pace with her in the blackness, clutching her hand from behind her back, for a minute, two minutes, four. Tracing with one stubby finger on her palm, a sensation more erotic than she was remotely prepared for, her heart galloping; this was so wrong, so dangerous, her newly vulnerable heart yawning wide, and from one second to the next she'd fallen in love, without seeing him, only smelling him, aware of his fraught breathing, his leathery grip, making her think, fleetingly, of gorillas. The group was so far ahead now, it was safe, she thought, to turn around.

She stopped. Sokol walked right into her. Those bus-mirror eyes an inch from hers, her violin precarious against her chest, and she was so sure he was going to kiss her that she closed her eyes like a dolt, like Sandra Dee, but abruptly, roughly, he spun her around, gave her a little push forward, away from him. Up ahead, Mary-Lou was standing still in the dead centre of the road, looking back. Calling. "Comrade Sheila! Stay with the group!"

A light knock at her door. It's Sandrine, already dressed for the concert in the black, floor-length gowns they've chosen, hers sleeveless with a plunging neckline, Sheila's up to the neck and down to the wrists, to spare concertgoers the onerous experience of her jiggling upper arms. Sandrine's arms are beautiful, lightly muscled, like a Michelangelo angel. Her long side braid is cobalt blue.

She says, "I just came from Jonathan's room. I had to pound the door down to wake him up. Are we going to eat anything before?"

"I'm not, and anyway, what is there?" When she stands, her legs threaten to buckle. Her palms ache something awful. She took a beta-blocker an hour ago, so this is as good as its going to get. At least her trembling legs won't quake detectably, her shoulders won't seize up, her heart will keep its cool under the pummeling meteor shower from her adrenal gland. Her hands won't leave sweat marks on her skirt, a major plus.

She catches sight of herself in the dresser mirror. "Jesus, my hair. Toscanini in a wind tunnel."

"I'll give you some oil to comb through. It'll lie down and smell fabulous."

"In its dreams."

"Sheila, you're beautiful." This with the magnanimous condescension of the young, the gorgeous, the ambitiously jet-fuelled. "How are you feeling?"

Shit-scared, darlin'.

"Not too bad. It's going to be a nice house, I think. Fifty, maybe sixty people. What about Léo, is he awake?"

"I could hear him through the door, warming up. I didn't want to bother him."

"Right. So, my dear. How do you get to Saint-Lazare?"

Sandrine smiles, dutiful. "Practice, practice, practice."

"How much time have we got?"

She takes her phone out of her bag. "It's almost six. So, an hour."

"Okay, I'm going to get my sad self dressed. Then I think I'll just sit here for awhile. How about we meet at the church in half an hour?"

"Okay." Sandrine backs out of the room, winking.

She's slumming with them for the summer, making the most of her chance to have an original work of her own performed. She knows exactly how good she is and exactly how good they are, which is: magnificent, and pretty good for amateurs. Sheila knows most nonmusicians can't tell the difference between good and excellent, but she certainly can.

Oh, if she could go back, if she could be Sandrine! Just starting out, exploding with promise. Sharp, disciplined, insanely confident. No creeping arthritis in her fingers, no heart-stopping memory problems. The end of the road nowhere in sight.

Léo and Jonathan are both older than Sheila, in their seventies now. Gentlemen amateurs, enthusiasts, veterans of many trios and quartets assembled through calls issued online, or in the back pages of trade magazines: "Freelance players, grade five or better, come and have some fun!" Playing weddings, the birthday parties of retiring CEOs. The occasional memorial service. Then just as quickly disbanding.

Their little quartet is no different, this local original music festival their first chance to shelve Pachelbel and *Eine Kleine Nachtmusik*. They are presenting four offerings, one from each of them. None of which will set the world on fire, though they've truly enjoyed learning them, working out the bow strokes, the tempos, the phrasing, exchanging intuitive, nonverbal cues as they meet one another's eyes over music never before heard on the wind of this world. Coming to know one another that much better, a wordless knowing from the inside out rather than the usual way. At least it feels like that to her.

It's barely a stage they'll be on, just the raised area behind the Communion rail. Coming in through the open side door of the church, she sees right away that Réjean, their lone stagehand, has set their four chairs too close together. She's grateful for this; she gets to walk up and spend time repositioning them, respacing the music stands, distracting herself, monitoring her breathing, flexing her fingers to dispel the stiffness. The other three are back in the sacristy, chatting; they're all queasy about the débuts of their pieces but none are as keyed up as she is. She can't sit, can't relax for a second. Wishes to hell she still smoked.

People are already waiting outside, clustered on the front steps on this mild evening, carefree, in shorts and tee shirts, nothing fancy. A few kids are shooting around, squealing. Any minute now Maude will open the main doors, stand across from Danielle to hand out the programmes they designed and printed up themselves, just as they got this little festival gig themselves, because they are nobody special, nor is this festival anything in particular. The programmes are very simple: the quartet's name, L'Air de Senneville, in an ornate font they bickered over for a week. Below it, their names beside postage stamp-sized photos. Inside, the names of their pieces, a few brief words of explanation in French and English.

They will open with Léo's *Fugue,* which she rather likes; it's accessible, reminiscent of Philip Glass but slowed down to Léo's abilities. A piece he's been writing, on and off, for fifteen years. Then Jonathan's *Wake,* which she doesn't like at all, a blatant rip-off of Elgar, but it will probably carry the night as people will think they've heard it someplace before. Then Sandrine's contribution, *And/or Frightening Scenes,* a solo, written over the course of a weekend following a nasty breakup with a boyfriend. It's technically the most challenging, Bartók meets rock cello, and Sheila loves it. Every time they rehearse, Sandrine improvises whole new astonishing swaths; like the proverbial river, she never wades into the same piece twice.

Lastly, there's her offering, *Running Downhill like Water*.

After their first rocky run-through, Sandrine declared she liked it, it sounded extraterrestrial. Léo was mystified by it. Jonathan couldn't stand it. "It's a *festival*, Sheila! Who comes to a festival to hear a twenty-minute dirge?"

"The harmonics are alien to your ears, that's all."

"What are you complaining about?" Sandrine wanted to know. "I'm the one cranking out one endless drone note from start to finish."

Here's what *she* thinks: When your life has run downhill like water till it's just a thin trickle snaking between dry rocks, when all your prospects and hopes have shrunk to the size of a wee little nut, the world can bloody well sit still for the twenty minutes it takes for you to bear witness to it.

Like Léo, she has been working on her piece forever, tinkering, tweaking, playing it a thousand times in the privacy of her kitchen, trying to recapture the original shock to her system, that full-body shudder, to feel once again the heart leaping clean out of her as it had on that long-ago Albanian night. By now she can play the thing in her sleep. Everything she thinks needs saying is in it, but how an audience will take it is anybody's guess.

Her personal guess is: badly. None of her quartet-mates seem overly moved by it one way or another; it's always the piece they rehearse last, time permitting.

It took them a while to make their way back to their hotel, with two socialist dis-emulation displays they had to pass and study first, these lit by faint streetlights. She was at the back of the group, pretending to look over everyone's shoulders, remembering Sokol's hands, the cloudy smoke of his breath, his unwashed hair, the aching music still in her ears. All the way back to the hotel she was so dizzy with distraction that she nearly jumped out of her skin when she saw his rock-hewn Balkan face hovering in a shadowy corner behind a split-leaf philodendron just outside her room.

"Pssst," he actually said, just the way it's written. She froze in the empty hall; he beckoned her closer, and when she looked over her shoulder and then took two tentative steps, he grabbed her hand, yanked her toward him, the now familiar smell of him engulfing her. She was anticipating the coarse bristle of his cheek against hers, but instead, he shoved her backward in the direction of her room, as the thought flashed: How does he know which one it is?

The lock didn't work; it was only a second before they were inside. He was panting and very strong, had her flopped onto the unmade bed before she could think, tugging down her slacks, her underwear, sandpaper hands on her bare thighs. A weight dropping onto her like a heavy sack from a high shelf. She was terrified of noise; the walls were so thin, the springing of the bed would be a dead giveaway. "Wait!" was all she could get out before his hand clamped down over her mouth.

Four, five thrusts, it was over. He sucked in his breath, reared back, sprang to his feet. Fiddled with his ready-made, stout proletarian pants. She sat up, pulled hers back up, the reek of him all over her now, sickening as a dousing with a whole bottle of rancid cologne.

He stood next to the bed looking down at her, and now she *knew* he wasn't all there, his expression befuddled, eyes blundering into one another, perhaps not even aware of what he'd done.

He made a sudden lunge for her, and she scuttled backward, a cry escaping her lips . . . but no, he was prying her hand open, pressing a much-folded piece of paper into her palm, closing her fingers tight around it. He backed away, hands in classic prayer formation, holding her eyes with his, which were now leaking tears. She understood the gesture to mean: Don't tell, I beg of you. I *beg* of you! He pointed to her hand with the paper in it, then pointed at his eyes, said something in Albanian. "Read it?" she asked stupidly, beginning to unfold the paper. He darted forward, grabbed her by one arm, pulled her up to him, kissed her hard on the mouth, his smoky tongue forcing its way in, pulling out fast. Pushed her backward onto the bed, and in a second was out the door and away.

Paralyzed, she felt nothing.

Was she just raped? Or was this love, was this passion, was this how it worked? She, of all people, would be the last one to know.

She unfolded the paper, smoothing it out on the plywood desk. A message written in pencil, presumably by someone other than Sokol, who she was sure knew no English.

> *Pleas, Pleas!!!!! I love youe. My mother she posess varry much segret gold! She want go Germania also I, but no personne depart this land, is not permit. Life varry varry varry bad! Gold for youe also my wif be you!! Beaty girl youe, pley musik like singers berd. Be mary of me if go youe to Germania, send leter how can help mother an me come meet. I love youe. Silent!! Pleas, pleas! SILENT.*

No, no, this simply could not be! Surely he knew, no one could *ever* be silent enough to keep Uncle Enver in the dark! He'd find out . . . no, he probably knew already, had known even before Sokol dreamed up this half-assed plan. Uncle Enver was everywhere, he could shape-shift into a scorpion under the bed, or into some pestilential fiend pouncing light as a cat upon your sleeping chest, red eyes burning through your skull, curling yellow nails, teeth like thorns sinking into your neck. Gorging himself on you like a mosquito, only pulling back in alarm when the rooster crowed, the black room fading to grey . . .

Sheila, stop it!

She sat on the ravaged bed, trying to think. This was insane, it made no sense. She knew Sokol was missing some marbles but to try to pull off something like this? No, no. It was a test, a trap, it had to be. Something they did with suspect visitors, the way they separated true believers from spies and infiltrators. This guy had been playing her since the beginning, and she'd taken the bait!

But his eyes, his panic; could he really be that good an actor? No, no, he was risking everything on her; that was no rape, he *loved* her! It was the only way he knew to win her heart, guarantee her acquiescence, prove his sincere devotion.

But, to put *evidence* into her hand? This was beyond-the-pale stupid. Except . . . except maybe that was just how crafty the ruse, the trap set for her, was!

She could say nothing, pretend it never happened. But if it *was* a setup, then they'd nail her for collaborating, for protecting him.

Okay, so? Who cared? She didn't live here. The second she got home she was going to ditch these people for good. The charade was over.

And if he really was trying to defect, it needed to stop *now*. He didn't know what he was doing. He'd thank her later for turning her back on him.

But Sheila, he raped you! Turn the bastard in!

She was beginning to shake now, to hyperventilate.

Four sharp knocks at the door. She opened it a wary sliver: was he back? What should she tell him? But it was Mary-Lou on the threshold, shouldering her way in.

"What is going on in here, comrade? Why was the bus driver seen coming out of your room?"

"When?" Sheila bleated, trying to buy time, thinking, if she was going to cry rape, it was now or never, Mary-Lou looking over her shoulder to the mussed bed; surely she could smell it, her slacks not even done up, a thin trickle making its way down her leg.

She thrust out her hand with the letter in it.

"He forced his way in here to give this to me." Mary-Lou's face was frigid, as she unfolded the note, read. Looked up.

"Stay here in your room until you're summoned. Do not leave for any reason. You'll be watched." Then she too was out the door and gone.

Watched? Was this an assurance of protection? Or was it a threat?

The night passed. No one came. Whatever the next day's outing was, she was excluded. There was nothing to do but sit and count the hours, the light from the small window dawdling across the floor, the faint noise of honest proletarian activity out in the street a steady basso continuo of stern approbation.

Around four in the afternoon, she worked up the courage to take out her violin. She tried to play quietly, but she was weak with hunger. The window darkened, went black. She was not called for supper. Only at nine-thirty did the tinny knock come, a cold-eyed Comrade Tim summoning her to Mary-Lou's room.

Without a word, Mary-Lou pointed her toward her desk chair. The comrades sat facing her, on the bed, on the floor, like kindergartners. All eyes on her, all eyes hostile.

It transpired that the entire delegation had been privy from the beginning to Sokol's and her flirty eyes meeting.

One by one, they made mordantly insulting speeches about all the foul things they'd observed about her. She never had pertinent, well-thought-out questions at the ready. During group discussions, she never brought up salient, original points, but simply parroted what the others were saying. She'd been overheard in her room playing decadent music. When she played in public, it was with a suspicious kind of enthusiasm that seemed more at home in a bourgeois rock band. When she played in public, it was with an obvious boredom, a discernible lack of revolutionary ardor. When they dined with hosts, she ate more than her share. When they dined with hosts, she didn't make a point of trying food she wasn't familiar with. The vertical buttons of her shirt and the horizontally placed ones on the two breast pockets made a cross formation. A *cross!* One by one they had at her, full of scorn and proud, knowing smiles. How sharp-eyed they'd been! Though she suspected a few of them were making stuff up on the spot just to top the person who went before.

It was what she'd do in their place.

It was long past midnight before they finished. Now it was her turn, her ego a throbbing blood blister, to begin to humbly, brokenly criticize herself. Thinking it was probably best, under the circumstances, to go for broke.

"I'm guilty of petit bourgeois carelessness and selfishness, of undermining the great spirit of the international proletariat with my reckless, reactionary behaviour." No sooner did the words "great spirit" escape her lips than she was petrified someone would pounce, accusing her of adhering to discredited obscurantist

Native American beliefs. "Because of my vile anti-communist behaviour, I attracted the attentions of a disruptive, criminal element and exposed my comrades and the entire Canadian and Albanian working classes and people to grave danger." And so on, throwing in everything she could think of to satisfy them, to make this thing end. But it was another hour before she was bled out, the room choked with smoke, butts stubbed out all over the floor. From under lowered lids, she looked around at her ex-comrades, feeling a stab of genuine remorse: once so friendly, they were now tough, severe, soundly righteous and *true!* Her reprehensible, two-faced phoniness was all over her like Sokol's raunchy stink.

The comrades filed out of the room, blameless heads high. Mary-Lou sat on her bed, reading over the copious notes she'd taken during the proceedings, jotting in addenda here and there. Sheila stood uncertainly in the middle of the room; what could she possibly be writing? She stood and stood, no idea what was supposed to come next.

Mary-Lou looked up after fifteen minutes, blinking, surprised. "Are you still here?"

A glutton for punishment, she couldn't help asking, "What will happen to him?" Hoping the answer would clue her in at last to the true state of affairs.

Mary-Lou shrugged. "The Albanian proletariat is serious," she said with quiet relish. "They don't play games. He and his mother and whoever is helping them will be rounded up and executed."

Oh.

The word thudding at her feet, a steel beam falling from a skyscraper, missing her by a hair.

Executed!

Not for a second had this occurred to her. She'd so convinced herself that she was being tested, and that even if she weren't, Sokol's punishment would surely take his dimness into account: a loss of his job, a fine. An index card-bashing in a socialist dis-emulation display. Robust rehabilitation, hard study; at worst, a few weeks forced labour.

Would there even be a trial? Or just a vast room of igneous-faced Party hacks, right hands raised in a unanimous vote for immediate liquidation, who would then proceed to clap in rhythm for twelve straight minutes: another enemy of the people ferreted out and destroyed, long live Enver Hoxha, long live the Party!

And how would they do it? Hanging? Firing squad? None of her copious notes covered *this* kind of material, nor had anyone had a word to say about the *Sigurimi*, the secret police, or the concentration camps scattered all over this tiny country, things she'd learn about much later. Around the same time that she'd find early pictures of Enver on the Internet, fat as a slug, popping the brass buttons off his uniform, the only overfed shlub in Albania. Putting her in mind of no one so much as Spanky, the ambitious little schemer of the old *Our Gang* comedies.

She came home, a returning soldier, not a visible scratch on her. The reams of notes on crop yields and electrification, the tremendous strides in literacy and the rights of women, all stuffed into a drawer.

She came home hollowed out, arms hanging limp, her beloved violin rudely shoved to the back of her bedroom closet shelf.

Telling herself: A life over is just that, a life over. They'll make more. It means nothing, Sheila, it means nothing. Over and over she told herself this.

She came home to a place where no one had the remotest idea what she'd done, a crime of no importance committed in a parallel universe, an imaginary world just past Saratoga on the Adirondack Northway. A world with no bearing on this one, a dream she'd woken from with a strangled scream, only to see it melt away into the bright, chirping morning.

She fully expected to be hauled before a tribunal of upper echelon comrades, but the call never came. Perhaps they didn't take her seriously enough, or perhaps they thought that by turning in the counterrevolutionary she'd fulfilled her basic mandate and they were quits. At any rate, she was small change, and when she bowed out of her study group, declining to come to any more meetings, they just let her go. Colleen put on a grim face; they'd probably warned her that her sister was an unstable, backward element, but she never asked Sheila any questions, never brought the matter up at all.

Still, by the time she realized she'd carried a wee Albanian nut home with her, there was only Colleen to tell. To lie to, rather, she who had never once in her life lied about anything to anyone in her family.

"A strictly biological encounter," she said breezily, playing the unsentimental materialist she thought her sister would respond to best.

Colleen's jaw hit the floor.

"Who with, for God's sake?" She knew perfectly well Sheila had only had two boyfriends, a self-involved pianist at the Conservatoire, and at Orford, a conceited tenor with floppy hair like their father's. Neither had made an iota of difference to her life, Sheila always insisting with easy grace that she, and Marjorie with her, would remain alone for life and be none the worse for it.

"You don't know him. He's a friend, another student of Jan's. I just ran into him. The day after I got back. By accident." Stop talking, Sheila. Less is more.

"A friend. That you just ran into."

"What do you want me to say? It was an accident."

"Have you told him?"

"Why? I don't want to mess up his life."

"You're getting rid of it, right?"

"I . . . yes, probably." And then what? Pick up her violin, go back to bloodying her head against concrete walls?

"Sheila! What 'probably'? Do it now, as soon as possible! I'll find you a good clinic, okay? I had one two years ago; it's nothing, it's over in a flash, you won't even feel it. Because if Daddy finds out, he'll put out a contract on you."

So easy to wipe away the whole mess. Because it *had* been rape, she thought, on Mondays and Thursdays. The rest of the time all she could see were Sokol's knees crumpling, his stout, ready-made proletarian trousers drenched with blood, the light going out in his poor, naive face. And then she'd cried, choking with wretched sobs, the dam finally breaking, two decades worth of unused tears gushing up all at once.

Her fault, all her fault. If she'd kept her stupid mouth shut no one would ever have known.

She had no stomach for any more killing. She waited another three months. Then she told her mother.

Anny was the one who found an obstetrician. Bought her expensive maternity tops, stretchable pants. Started right in knitting tiny sleepers in gender-neutral greens and yellows. She hated the circumstances but refused to pry. Her second daughter's defection from radicalism along with the prospect of a new grandchild was putting a fresh bounce in her increasingly weary step. If only that daughter would go back to her music, maybe everything could return to how it had once been.

Her father refused to have anything to do with her. If she came to the house, he got up and left, Anny shaking her head, her eyes glassy with tears. "His heart is broken," was all she could get out.

She kept up her waitressing job till the last possible minute, her back in constant agony, which was no less than she deserved. She went into the delivery room alone. Up on her elbows, sweaty, hair matted, bearing down, legs shoved apart like in some pool table assault, awful *gzeeeezes* exiting her nose, and at the final squishing end of a push, out splurted a brand-new person into Earth time from wherever she'd been lurking, slimed with yellow wax, the blue cord still hooked up inside. Dangled by the heels: It's a girl! Fists flailing, strenuous objection to the manhandling, the indignity: What do you bums think you're looking at, take a picture, it'll last longer!

How overjoyed Anny was when Sheila handed her over, a long-lost light rekindled in her gentle face, her tiny granddaughter spit-bubbling against her neck, the bleats and gurgles, the comforting baby-powder smell. She loved seeing Anny's spirits lift. This alone made the enterprise worth her while.

She named her Liri, the Albanian word for "freedom." The name delighted Anny.

"Liri O'Meara. How lovely! It's like the first line to a haiku. So melodic. You could set it to music!"

Yes, she could. But she wouldn't.

Anny joyfully passed on all the baby lore: burping, bathing, diapering, bundling. She wanted to give Sheila baby furniture, a diaper service. No! Liri was her burden to bear alone. Anny thought she knew her, but Anny hadn't a clue what Sheila now knew about herself.

She was a murderer. Not even Anny could love her out of this.

Over Liri's crib, to drive the horror away, she taped a welcome-home poem written by André, her neighbour from two floors up.

> *Sheila a accouché!*
> *Girl is a baby!*
> *And healthfully she is born!*

Gilles and André upstairs were the unlikeliest of stoner couples, Gilles with his berserk Paul Bunyan beard and big, furry *bedaine,* his partner André a delicate waif like some Florentine prince gazing out from a Ghirlandaio painting. André taught piano at home on an ancient, yellow-keyed, purple-painted upright. They shared their apartment with nineteen freely fornicating cats and more unsolicited kittens than there were stars in the sky.

Once a month or so, *les gars* fought like hellcats, André screaming blue murder, Gilles shoving him into walls, yanking out handfuls of hair. On all other days they were peaceful, cooking up vats of *pois chiches à l'ail* and *bouilli de bœuf,* baking peach pies from scratch, and she, the weird *Anglaise* from downstairs, who lived on Kraft Dinner and yogurt she made herself on the radiator, was always invited up to sit on the floor and eat, to drink plonk from chipped coffee cups, while Liri crawled from lap to warm lap and cats leapt over their heads, spat at one another, or dozed inside the warm oven.

She went home only rarely, her father always out of the house. She pretended to be some Alice Munro heroine home from the big city: sardonic, restive, archly out of patience with everything and everybody. Sprawling on the sofa amid floral throws, in the deep, quiet light, perusing expensive art books, raiding the fridge, noodling on the piano while Liri slept in grateful Anny's arms. Accepting with a scowl the generous cheques Anny tucked surreptitiously into her purse or jacket pocket, the only income she had now.

No one ever made the reverse trip, for which she was grateful; Anny would be scandalized by the squalor she lived in, her cramped railroad apartment, the reeking diaper pail in the bathroom, Liri's tiny clothes washed in the kitchen sink and hung on a clothesline that bisected the living room, a dank forest of wet sleeper feet and stained bibs. It was like a cave, the perfect hiding place, where she could jounce Liri up and down the long, dim hall, crooning, "You are mine, mine, all mine!" Imagining everything inside her new little head shiny and rust free, like a brand-new car under the hood, synapses snapping and firing like holiday sparklers. Making up patter songs with lyrics that included "I wuv you." Introducing Liri to herself in the mirror, their two heads touching, bestest pals. Adoring Liri's new-minted baby chortle, her father's flirty brown eyes, her own sleepless, sagging face goofy with love.

Napping together on the couch, Liri sprawled across her stomach, the gentle universe contracting around them: this was all she was good for. Not a fibre of nerve left to her, all the fuses in her head blown, nothing but smoke up there. Not a night but Sokol didn't figure in it somehow, begging on his knees, weeping. Coming for her with a bowie knife. Changing into his own mother, her head wrapped in black rags, a mouthful of gold teeth. Once he transformed, in the blink of an eye, into Enver's tight-bunned wife, who promised to take her to see the Great Man, who all this time had been living in Gilles and André's apartment behind a false wall. Once Sokol, as himself, took her to bed in an Alpine cottage in Germany, duvets piled on duvets, a stag's head on the wall above them. Told her he loved only her.

His teeth were all fixed, his hair oiled and wavy, his English refined. The shatteringly intense love she felt coming off him in wordless waves was unlike anything she'd ever known in her waking life.

Colleen quit. Just like that, pulling up stakes and running off to NYC to stay with Hardee and Vi, Marxism-Leninism rolling off her like fog moving out to sea. At the end of the summer she was back, all mascara and diaphanous dresses, sitting down at the piano, picking up where she'd left off. Her hair long again. In no time at all she'd found an agent, was getting steady work as a studio musician.

She dropped unannounced one day into Sheila's hovel, where Liri, a grubby troll child on her stomach on the floor, was hopping Fisher Price figurines in and out of saucepans full of water, the nipple of a baby bottle full of chocolate milk clenched between her barely budded teeth. Colleen looked around with distaste at the grunge, the mess, the scratched-up Goodwill furniture as if she'd never set foot outside of a well-appointed salon in her life.

"It's so dark in here! Can't you find a brighter place? Do you have any money?"

"I'm going back to work. Any day now."

"Sheila, you really should try and make it up with Daddy. He's just heartsick about you letting your music go." When Sheila said nothing, she condescended to add, "We all make mistakes, sweetie, he understands that."

"Are you here as his emissary?"

"Okay, I'll be honest, I'm Anny's emissary. This is just killing her. She's on antidepressants, Sheila, that's how bad it is. Anny, the most joyful soul in the world! Please, please try to set things right again, if only for her sake. We all miss you so much."

"I'm just wondering about the class struggle. Is it over? Did the good guys win?"

"Shee, I'm sorry I got you into all that. I was searching for something, you know me." She had a look about her, or rather, she had her old look back, the O'Meara look: chin up, eyes aglow, cherries in her cheeks. "I've found a new piano teacher, and he's going to help get me back on track, maybe try a few competitions a year or so from now." She looked as ravishing as she ever had, Sheila standing lumpily next to her in baggy Fortrel pants and a sweater she'd worn in high school, her hair unwashed and snarled, no plans for the afternoon, for the week, for the year. Time moving in with its buckets and bleach, its scouring brush, to obliterate every last trace of the O'Meara left in her.

She held on to Liri for dear life, her scraggle-headed, unkempt, rambunctious child, whom she dressed in boys' outfits bought for three and four dollars out of bins in Hassidic discount stores on Park Avenue. Only leaving her to take the bus to her new job, four to midnight at a souvlaki place in Park Ex, leaving her with Gilles and André, who'd made up a bedroom for her upstairs. Liri thrived up there, a wild child, Mowgli raised by cats. Bilingual at three, sprawling on Gilles and André's living room floor, kittens of every conceivable colour and size scrambling over her, her nose an inch from the dusty, black-and-white TV screen, watching *Barbapapa, Sesame Street, Passe-Partout*. Becoming indignant if Sheila tried to sing along with the tunes she loved, shouting, *"Non! Pas toi! C'est juste moi qui chante!"* Trying to block her mother's mouth with her little starfish hand.

Dreamy, airheaded André would whisper, *"Elle me fait tellement tripper, ta p'tite!"* as they stood watching her draw with her crayons on the wall, swiping kittens out of her way, hollering, *"Non, Minou! T'es pas dans le jeu, toi!"* The bedroom in their apartment was her real one, where André or Gilles tucked her in, *Dark Side of the Moon* playing at earsplitting volume; it was where all the fun happened, where she kept her *Fraisinettes* and her *Shtroumpf* collection and her blocks and crayons. When Sheila came home from work, she carried her, summer and winter, out cold, draped over her shoulder, back down the clanging, spiral staircase to her place, unable to bear the thought of waking up in the apartment without her.

There wasn't a single other thing she had to do but hold down her job, feed Liri and make her smile. Summer mornings in Parc Jeanne-Mance, they splashed in the cement wading pool, Liri in sopping, sagging underpants. Sheila watched her scramble over the rusted playground equipment, pushing her in the boxy little swings, exclaiming in rapture every time she slid down the dented aluminum slide. In the fall, they jumped into piles of leaves on the slope of Mount Royal; in winter, Sheila taught her to skate at Beaver Lake, both of them in secondhand brown boys' skates and Peruvian knitted hats.

She picked up her violin only in dreams. She auditioned for Enver, or tried to, the strings refusing to sound, vibrating dumbly like rubber bands. Or snapping clean in half, sproinging free to deliver a stinging lash to her face. Sometimes she faked it, valiantly string-synching to a hidden record while he reclined in his white fez against his Naugahyde chair back, his face unreadable, sitting and sitting and sitting, waiting for the record to skip and give her away.

She came home only for Christmas now, never for more than a day, Liri on her lap all through dinner, eating off of Sheila's plate with grubby fingers, screaming if her mother tried to put her down. She listened to Hardee's well-mannered offspring plink out their stubby piano pieces, held Liri by her scrappy denim overalls as she banged incoherently on the keys until Vi snapped at her to stop it already. Sheila's violin always left at home, which mystified poor Marjorie; it was as if she'd forgotten to dress, had come home in her unwashed underwear. Her father barked at her to put that damned kid down and sit like a civilized person, but she could not put her down, not for a second, especially not here where Liri was all the violin, all the identity she had left, in her lap, under her chin, beneath her fingers. She would not let her go, would deny her nothing, because she could lose her in an eyeblink: a bathtub drowning, a park abduction! Liri could fall out one of Gilles and André's opened windows in pursuit of a fleeing kitten. She could be blissfully jumping in a pile of leaves swept close to the sidewalk, a motorcycle taking the corner way too fast, skidding sideways . . . No! If

Sheila let go for a second, if she were left for so much as a minute with empty arms, unprotected, she'd have to leap to her feet, screaming, "Leave me alone, Daddy! I killed a man!"

Once only, in her kitchen, her musical-genius hands shriveled from dishwater, she tried taking out her violin to play for Liri. It had been five years since she'd touched it.

Méditation de Thaïs, once so easy; she'd learned it when she was nine.

An hour just to tune the thing, her fingers cramping, stomach in an uproar. A few scraped-out scales, her back hurting already, the long-snubbed instrument laughing in her face. Liri stood in front of her as she played, labouriously, losing her place, stopping, restarting. Liri, jumping up and down, trying to grab the bow from her hands. *"C'est mon tour! Je veux essayer! Donne! DONNE!"* She stopped playing at last, held the violin and bow out of Liri's reach, laid them back to rest in the case. Liri stamped her foot. *"Maman! T'es ben méchante! Pourquoi tu me laisses pas essayer?"*

"It's not a toy," she told her, the first serious "no" she'd ever issued. To which Liri replied with ice-cold dispassion, *"Je te parle plus, moi. Je t'haïs."* Sheila only smiled sadly, thinking, all children tell you they hate you at one time or another. They don't mean it.

Not most of them, anyway.

Upstairs, Gilles and André had the mother of all fights, dishes smashing, cats yowling, furniture kicked over. *Je t'haïs en tabarnak! Moi avec! Touche-moi pas, je t'ai dit, touche-moi PAS! Va-t-en, criss-moi le camp, câlisse!*

André moved out, leaving behind his piano and a raft of fledgling music students ranging from six years old to one codger of seventy-nine. When he called a week later to bid Sheila a tearful goodbye, he begged her to take them over. *"Ça m'fait tellement mal qu'ils soient déçus, Sheila."*

The thought of teaching piano made her bilious with fear. But that one miserable hour on her violin had broken something in her. Her fingers ached to be playing something, anything. She had the splintered upright tuned, reviewed the grade one to six piano curriculum. Her piano skills, rudimentary to begin with, were woefully eroded, but all she really had to do was go upstairs to receive André's old pupils, to just sit and listen. Be encouraging, suggest fingerings, help with phrasing and dynamics. Nag then to practice their scales, tutor them in solfège and basic harmony. Really, just sit still for hours, as they stopped, started, stopped, started, the stiff pedals creaking under their feet.

Her fluency, her love of the language of music, the structure, the mathematics, began to creep back, like reluctant kids at twilight called home by the illuminating of the streetlights. Within a year, she had four full days a week of beginner students, was able to cut her waitressing down to part-time. As three o'clock rolled around, she tuned out her student's halting rendition of *Für Elise*, listening instead for the stamp, stamp, stamp of Liri's feet mounting the iron staircase, home from grade one, dropping coat and bookbag on the floor, tripping over cats, running to the refrigerator for an ice cream bar and a hug from the man she'd come to call Papa Gilles.

Enrolled in French school, she was learning to read at Gilles' kitchen table, sounding out the words in her reader, Gilles correcting her patiently, kicking back with a Molson Export, while Sheila fretted silently that she was taking far too long to catch on, she should have grasped reading in a week, any O'Meara would have. But she said nothing, felt awkward coming between Liri and Gilles, the two solitudes beginning to weigh heavily even though her French was perfectly good by now, all her piano students francophone. She felt in the way, extraneous, listening to Liri giggle at some joke of Gilles' in a way she never giggled at her mother's jokes. Deep inside her, tin cans dragged along broken concrete.

Mère et fille were beginning to separate, like a zipper.

Gilles made Liri supper, and six nights out of seven, she spent the evening upstairs, doing her homework, watching *Lance et compte, Entre chien et loup,* while Sheila stayed downstairs, nodding off to interminable nineteenth-century novels—*Middlemarch, Pride and Prejudice*—featuring upright, indomitable, blameless women. Or lulled by the cheerful jingles and soothing musical stings of *Cheers* and *The Golden Girls*. A kind of agoraphobia set in, a featureless depression as deep as it was wide. Her students wore her out; she couldn't wait for her evening alone to begin, often in bed by eight-thirty. Once in a while she went out to a movie with Chantal, one of her adult students, wanting it to be over the minute they settled into their seats.

It was amazing how fast time passed when a person was doing sweet fuck all.

Her life was running downhill, fast water over rocks. Trouble massed like thunderheads. Liri turned twelve.

The girl had no ear for music, nor the remotest interest. Piano concertos on the radio may as well have been cats strolling across the piano keys. Sheila listened through her closed bedroom door as Liri sang along to Madonna or Cyndi Lauper, her voice pinched and pitchy, and was ashamed of her. The old O'Meara snobbism reared up: was this sorry artistic expression really the best she could do?

She knew the resentment she felt was rooted in fear, guilty fear of the daughter she'd been so good to . . . okay, spoiled, held far too close, been far too needy with. No wonder Liri was pulling away. But did she have to be so dim? So commonplace? Her interests were no interests Sheila had ever had. The girl was hard, tough in a way Sheila simply couldn't comprehend. Did she leave her open diary lying around because she wanted her mother to see it? Or was she as blissfully indifferent as she appeared? Of course, Sheila read it. Stumbled immediately onto the page discussing how she'd been complimented on her blow job skills. Slamming the thing shut in panic, her dear little mouth, this couldn't be! Then, worse panic, trying to find the page the book had been left open at, needing to leave it in the exact position she'd found it, in case Liri had cunningly laid a hair down the middle to find out whether or not her mother snooped.

She'd never given a blow job in her life. Had never even refused a request. Who was this alien child?

The only O'Meara attribute Liri possessed was the one denied Sheila: her beauty. She began to look more and more like Colleen, only her deep-set brown eyes recalling her father. She had Colleen's exuberant hair, more chestnut than auburn, had her straight nose, her coltish body. A slyly blossoming loveliness, the kind that drew slavering men in packs. As a girl, Sheila had never felt less than comely in her family's eyes, but Liri's confidence was something else, carnally charged, men in their thirties and forties turning to stare in the street, her demure eyes cast down, a look of virginal shyness so melodramatically contrived it conveyed precisely the opposite message.

Sheila had never bothered about what she looked like, her bushy hair cut short, her figure a straight waistless drop from shoulders to hips. Folds in her stomach now, wiry little hairs on her chin. She was hopeless with makeup, whereas Liri, who didn't need it, rimmed her eyes in black, slashed broad bands of rose over her cheekbones. Insulted her idly across the breakfast table: "*Maman!* Can't you do something about that rat's nest on your head?"

Rat's nest, she called it. It wasn't her derision that made Sheila's blood rise; it was the commonplace cliché she chose. No O'Meara would ever stoop so low. When they insulted one another, they did it with style, panache!

"How come you never get a boyfriend?" Liri asked her, the clumsy wording of the question making Sheila want to slap her. "So, what, are you a lezzy or something? Or are you just too ugly? You should get a life, you know, you're like a dead body, you should be in the graveyard!" There was no poorly constructed, illiterate abuse she wouldn't heap on her mother, Sheila's passive, trudging, shadow existence a thing of horror to her daughter's explosive sun-blooming self.

There wasn't a trace of her in Liri, unless it was the murderer, the betrayer rising to the surface, the violent, vengeful Sokol of her dreams ghosting over Liri's bewitchingly arrogant features. The meaner she became, the more Sheila backed away into corners, confused, tormented with guilt, ashamed of her, doubly ashamed of herself. She did penance by picking up the scattered dishes, bottles, ashtrays, dirty clothes that blanketed Liri's bedroom floor, humbly gathering up the wet mess of towels she'd stained with peroxide and thrown into the bathtub. Saying nothing, conscious every minute of her own juices long dried to dust, all her nerve, smarts and drive buried with her violin under heaps of dusty bags full of outgrown boots and winter parkas.

The phone rang for Liri at all hours of the night. Tiptoeing down the hall, Sheila put her ear against her bedroom door, afraid to listen in on the extension in case her daughter heard the click. Boys came home with her after school, eyes glazed with lust; Sheila came downstairs unexpectedly one afternoon just in time to see the back end of one of them fly out her bedroom window, as Liri, topless, ducked into the bathroom, locking the door. She was out all the time with friends Sheila never saw, ignoring her timidly suggested curfew, Sheila lying awake night after night, ears pricked like an animal in the woods for the turn of Liri's key in the lock. Sometimes it was four a.m. before the girl got in, knocking into things, stumbling on the stairs. Flushed with relief, Sheila dropped immediately to sleep, ignoring the sounds of retching from behind the bathroom door.

Gilles only smiled, assured her it was nothing, *voyons, avoue,* hadn't she been exactly the same at her age? No, never! And Liri was different with Gilles, showed him a respect she denied her mother; she could sit at his kitchen table and talk like an adult about Québec politics or the music she liked or films, ignoring Sheila, talking over anything she might say, playing him off against her. Unable to glance her mother's way without a face full of *what are you even doing here, loser?*

Sheila came home for Christmas now without her. By the time she turned nine Liri had made it clear that she wanted to spend all her holidays with Papa Gilles because it was way more fun; Jesse and Sean and Bonnie wouldn't play with her, Nanna Anny was stupid, Grandpa O'Meara was mean.

Now only Anny asked after her, out of politeness. She had three purebred O'Meara grandchildren, and a fourth on the way. Hardee and Colleen both had bubbling lives, stories to tell, triumphs to share, expansive plans in the making. Listening to them all, Sheila's face felt like scar tissue: tight and way too shiny.

Only Marjorie, living alone now in Edmonton where she had a chair with the symphony, lent her an open ear. And even she seemed wary, the bond between them slackened, though they loved one another no less. She instinctively played down her musical achievements so as not to hurt Sheila.

Liri, she said, sounded to her like the bad girl from an after-school TV special. "Why are you letting her push you around? That's not the Sheila I remember!"

"Yes, well. She's changed her name now, too. She wants no part of the vowels I chose for her. I've been ordered to call her Lora."

Now she was seeing intellectual deficiency everywhere, Liri barely scraping through high school, setting her career sights on a six-month esthetician course. Gilles helped her find her own apartment at seventeen, and there was a new, live-in boyfriend every year or so: Didier, Félix, Arne. None of this was familiar ground to Sheila. She wanted to wash her hands of the whole sorry debacle, their pairing a miserable accident, as dissonant as abutting microtones. If they'd met as adults, they'd have had nothing to say to one another.

And "Lora O'Meara" just squatted on the page, not suggesting even the most flat-footed of haikus.

When Gilles eventually found a new partner and moved out, Sheila took over their apartment, where there was more space, more light. The whole place was hers now, she had a full slate of piano students, and the cats had been given away to Lora's friends, the place fumigated. A bold step up in the world!

Lora was appalled.

"*Maman! Tu vas-tu rester toute ta vie dans la même ostie d'place? C'est honteux!* Go someplace new, do something, *bouge, câlisse!*"

Sheila began to lose track of her for weeks. Then months. She spent whole mornings steeling herself to call her daughter, only to be informed that her phone number had been disconnected. Gilles didn't know where she was either. "California, maybe," he ventured. "*Elle a toujours voulu vivre à Los Angeles.*"

"Is she in any trouble? Is she still with that Arne guy? Would you know if she's doing drugs? Why would she just disappear?"

Gilles was evasive. "*Ça s'peut. Est ben flyée, ta fille. Pis, elle a beaucoup de peine, t'sais.*" Taking a deep breath, getting ready to unload some home truths. "She tell me one time she want to know who her real papa is, where is he. She say you never tell her his name."

"You have got to be kidding me! She never asked me, not once!"

"To me, yes. She ask me so many time if I know his name. *Elle a pleuré. A pleuré beaucoup.*"

That girl, crying? She didn't believe it for a second. "As far as I could tell, she thought you were her father."

"*Est pas stupide, ta fille.* After she have ten year old, she know for sure it's not me." After a beat, he added, "You never tell me neither."

How could this be, all these secret tears, this unvoiced anguish? Was this why the girl hated her? And what else had she missed, all these years?

"Stan," she snapped. "His name was Stan."

"Stan what?"

"I don't know. I never thought to ask. Just Stan."

A long swath of dead air.

"*Ben, anyway. Elle a quoi, vingt-deux ans maintenant?* She'll come back, those *ado* years are finish, you'll see. After she's gonna find herself, she'll be back."

"She hates me."

"No, no." This without much conviction.

So, she waited. Two, three, six, seven Biblical years in that apartment, flogging those same students, unwilling to move in case Liri-Lora took it into her head to call, to come back. The last drops of her life trickling away, story over, roll credits. The only dream she still had about Sokol was the one where she hit him with her car, in the rain, in the dark.

When Anny began her final round of chemo, Sheila went out to the house to stay with her. It had been only a year from the discovery of the wee nut under her arm till they buried her. Their father was destroyed; Colleen and Sheila had to literally hold him up at her graveside. He was cold and dismissive to all of them as they gathered in the living room afterward, vases and vases of real flowers overpowering the sterile floral prints. There was a quarter inch of dust on the piano. A cookbook on the kitchen counter, right where Anny had left it. Still open to a recipe for samosas.

No one asked Sheila a thing about her daughter, her irrelevance a self-evident O'Meara truth.

She sat with Marjorie on the sofa, hours before her sister had to catch her flight back to Edmonton. Recalling Easter concerts, opera nights, trips to New York, the two of them talking softly, laughing explosively. Finally, sitting in silence, straight-backed, hands in their laps, listening to the music playing low on the radio.

"Shostakovich," murmured Marjorie, closing her eyes. "The A minor violin concerto." They sat, breathing it in, Sheila's fingers beginning to move of their own accord. Marjorie opened her eyes, saw, and smiled. Nudged her gently in the ribs, her eyes shining with tears. Sheila leaned over, fell against her, hugged her for dear life.

"It's time," said Marjorie at last, pulling back to look her sister square in the face. She didn't mean, time to leave for the airport.

"Yes, I'm afraid it is," Sheila replied.

She gave up the apartment, bought a secondhand car, moved out to the very end of the island, to near-rural Senneville. A tiny house, well back from the road, shrouded in trees. Dormer windows painted Delft blue, so small they suggested a dollhouse. The perfect hideaway in which to begin relearning the A minor concerto.

She was beyond awful. But she didn't care anymore. There was no one to judge her; the O'Mearas, like a failed, disbanded circus, were flung to the four winds. Marjorie married, moved to Vancouver, launching a stellar solo career, a series of magnificent

CDs to her credit. Not a week went by without Sheila listening to her play Rachmaninoff's Sonata for Violoncello and Piano, the Andante, the Allegro Mosso shattering her heart afresh every time. Hardee and Vi were still in Brooklyn, both growing quite portly, Hardee a tenured music history professor, Vi working in hospice care. Their portly children turned out to be only moderately musical. Colleen moved to France, married Philippe, a food writer, the two of them running a cooking school. Everybody Skyped on holidays, laughing too much, too loudly.

She was the only one left to look after their father, except for Kristie, his live-in caregiver. He complained bitterly about Kristie's frightful cooking, her afternoon chats on the phone with friends, the Top 40 radio she played in the kitchen while she worked. He complained so much Sheila suspected he was very fond of Kristie.

He was whittled down to ribs and sinew, his once robust gut concave under his limp pajama shirts, his cheeks crosshatched with a tangled thicket of leafless saplings. He fell out of bed at least once a week, Kristie coming in to find him asleep on the floor, sometimes with his thumb in his mouth. A great, sturdy girl, she hoisted him like an oversized teddy bear won at the carnival, as he whimpered piteously about how no O'Meara ever came to help him.

He was hazy on most concepts now. After a major thunderstorm, Sheila phoned, asking, "Did you lose power?" "Yes," he croaked. "I can hardly walk." She couldn't not laugh, and she and Kristie did, no malice in it at all. Other things were less amusing. She tried taking him out once to Place des Arts to hear the symphony; he squirmed in his seat and eventually fell asleep, but awoke suddenly, disoriented and unhinged, staggering to his feet to shout, "Open a window! I'm hot!" Bellowing, "Don't you dare shush me!" when she tried to clap a hand over his mouth. "Nobody shushes me!" Writhing, flailing, as people got up, turned around, ushers pooling in the aisles, ready to lead him out, pulling while Sheila pushed.

But he could sit for long hours listening to Marjorie's CDs, his favourite being Shostakovich's Concerto for Violincello and Orchestra No. 1. Marjorie had once played this very piece in their living room, with Istvan as accompaniment; she'd been brilliant even then.

He knew it was Marjorie who was playing; he talked to her over the music, muttering, "How many times have I been asked to explain, what happened to Sheila? How many times she's hurt her mother!" It no longer pained Sheila to hear this; compunction had been her daily bread for so long now. She kept silent, everything she felt fitting inside her smile.

She made just enough money to get by, her needs embarrassingly modest. Apart from her work with the quartet, she'd begun teaching an introductory course in music appreciation at the new *polyvalente* high school in Sainte-Clémence. She still had time to practice a good four hours a day, but she was starting from so far back she could never hope to regain the ground she'd covered before she was ten. What was once there was there no longer. What *was* there seemed to be just about enough. The quartet she'd founded with one of her new Senneville friends, Agnès, was four years old now, and she hadn't yet humiliated herself past all saving.

In the evenings, sitting at André's beat-up old piano which she'd held on to all this time, she worked on a handful of modest compositions, only one of which she truly cared about. There were pictures tacked up on the wall of several odd musical instruments: the *lahutë*, a one-stringed, egg-shaped, long-necked lute. The *çifteli*, a two-stringed mandolin, one string for the drone, one for the melody. The *zurna*, a kind of oboe. On top of the piano were scattered papers, notes on the structure of traditional Albanian four-part polyphonic music, the roles of the taker, the thrower, the turner, the drone. Notes on pentatonic modal/tonal systems, chromatic scales, polymetric time signatures. Her little piece was dense, major seconds and minor thirds knocking rudely against one another, a gooseflesh dissonance, the music sliding, rolling downhill, flaring and dwindling, voices trailing off, fading away.

Also on top of the piano, she kept a small photograph of elderly Uncle Enver in a five-dollar frame. A wizened wraith at the end, his plump cheeks imploded, his corpulent frame shriven to raw bone inside an enormous, shoulder-padded suit. The longest-running of the Eastern bloc dictators, forty years! As paranoid as a Corleone, many thousands of Albanians nabbed by the Sigurimi, forced to do time in a labour camp, or simply eliminated. But so kind to his children, kissing them nighty-night in their jammies, even putting up a Christmas tree: there was no end to the stuff Google could dredge up. On vacation, dog-paddling in the sea with his glasses on, a loveable kook. Sunbathing on a chaise longue, waving to the wife, smiling for the cameras, ready for his close-up. Then, mute in his wheelchair, in an overcoat, banked with blankets in the sunshine, smiling no more, bewildered, a victim of two strokes and a heart attack. Finally, his funeral cortège, the red-draped coffin, the solemn parade of granite-faced henchmen, arms linked. Public tears, fierce beating of breasts. They declined to carve a death date into his tombstone, claiming such a man could never die. But they went ahead and buried him anyway in the Cemetery of the Martyrs of the Nation.

A few short years later, his statue was toppled just like Saddam's; rocks thrown, police dogs, rioting in the streets. Poor old Uncle was dug up in the middle of the night, carted away to be dumped into an ordinary, crap grave in a no-name people's cemetery. His multitudinous volumes of glorious memoirs pulped and recycled. The travel ban lifted, desperate refugees clinging to the sides of rusted-out ships like bees to a honeycomb. The whole bloated project floundering, dying, going, in the end, nowhere but down.

She looked up at him often as she scribbled on her much-erased staff paper, trying to recreate the feeling that had crawled up her spine that last night of poor Sokol's disastrously ill-placed hopes. Trying, in her own hopeless way, to honour that poor boy's memory.

And now, here it is, finished. Look out, world.

Her knees are like water inside her long skirt. She introduces the quartet, thanks everyone for coming. The faces looking back at her are open, friendly. No one appears to have been dragged here by the hair; they're music lovers, perfectly willing to give L'Air de Senneville a go.

She closes by dedicating this concert to the memory of Agnès Groulx, their dear friend and colleague. Speaking Agnès's name brings unexpected tears to her eyes; there's nothing for it but to take off her clouded glasses and wipe them away in front of everyone.

The quartet stands and bows, instruments in hand. They adjust the music on the stands. Shift about in their chairs. Pause to look at one another. This moment is always the most emotional for her, now as it was nearly half a century ago, when her world-stunning future had been packed like nails and ball bearings into the cluster bomb of, "Look, look, look at *ME!*"

It's the same now, she thinks. Look at me, listen to me. That is, if you would be so kind.

Jonathan clears his throat, then Léo does too. Sandrine smiles at her. They are to begin with Léo's *Fugue*. They raise their instruments; Sandrine, across from her, raises, poises her bow.

A screaming drop from a towering cliff: she's forgotten every note of every piece to be played. The sheet music in front of her is blurred and scrambled, she hasn't the remotest idea how the opening Allegro begins or even what her name is. She's about to lower her violin, her bow, call a halt to everything.

But Jonathan, who opens the piece, is in better control. He begins; there's no running away now. The viola's sixteen opening bars are over in a microsecond; her fingers, her bow enter of their own accord. Léo, out of the corner of her left eye, coming in right on cue, Jonathan falling back, and then Sandrine joining, and it's all right, this one anyway is going to be all right. Her mind, loosening, sits back, kicks off its shoes, starts to spin idle tales: Jonathan is in love with Sandrine, she thinks. Léo is in love with Jonathan. How sweet it all is! The cello grounds them beautifully, there's the familiar resistance of the strings under her bow . . . Don't milk the sixteenths, Léo, work with me here, pull with me, we're almost, almost, almost done . . .

The applause is friendly, not vociferous but encouraging. Then, silence. Time for Jonathan's *Wake*. She takes in a breath, steadying, preparing.

A wrong note out of nowhere, a slash of bow against the cello's strings. Sandrine, inexplicably out of turn, is beginning her piece. Jonathan's eyes meet Sheila's in raw panic, but it's all right, she signals to him, smiling, it's just a mistake in order, let her go. The audience is sitting up a little straighter; the title of Sandrine's piece must have intrigued them, as has lovely Sandrine herself, her blue hair, her strong young arms vibrating over her instrument. Of course, she adds a whole section of zippy improvisational bits, and Jonathan smiles back at Sheila; they're breathing like human beings again. Sandrine's got the audience in the palm of her beautiful hand, throwing her whole body into it. When she's done, someone shouts—incorrectly—"Bravo!"

It's stifling in the church, the ceiling fans turned off because of the whirr. In the silence, there's an uptick in rustling and coughing, much fanning of faces with programmes. Sheila's armpits are sticky damp, sweat threatening to trickle down the sides of her face. They begin Jonathan's piece, far and away the most ineptly composed with its long, arid, meandering patches. She can hear Léo's violin slipping out of tune, can feel them losing the audience, and sixty-four bars in, poor Jonathan's music slides ignominiously from the stand to a heap at his feet. He's immediately lost, lowering his bow in midphrase, his eyes terror-stricken. They play on without him till the end of the Andante, while he sits, red-faced, running his finger between his neck and his shirt collar. How many times have they admonished one another: Don't get caught up in mistakes, don't fret over faults, keep going, put them behind you, move on! Their troubled eyes meet nonetheless, tired dray horses straining to pull a carriage out of the mud. She's afraid this one is a goner.

Perfunctory applause, not at all the wished-for lead-in to her own wee offering.

And now, panic, panic, panic, panic, panic, no, no . . . Breathe, Sheila, breathe!

The twenty-four opening bars are hers alone. Léo and Jonathan enter next, entwined in tight dissension, then Sandrine comes in with the low, one-note drone that lasts the entire length of the piece. Sheila is aware of every cleared throat, every audience fidget; she takes them all personally. They've gotten off to a slow start; the piece is twenty minutes long, legato all the way through, but they're playing at such a funeral pace, they're going to clock in at around twenty-four minutes, far too lugubrious by half. She tries to subtly speed them up. Dire creaking in the pews as some people get up and leave through the back doors, trying to be quiet. The side doors are wide open because of the heat; she's conscious of a bus rumbling by, the shouts of kids on bikes. She's playing mechanically, without any clear feeling, crazed thoughts bumping heads, recalling the fries she had for lunch, Anny in the hospital hours from death, the hilarious havoc this humidity must be wreaking on her hair. A lady in the front row is out cold and snoring. The one thing she doesn't think of once: Sokol's legs buckling before the firing squad.

It ends. A gulf of silence before the applause begins, not tepid exactly, but neither are they crazed with enthusiasm. They may just be happy the whole thing's finished.

It's gone over like most attempts at telling one's deepest truth. Coming out sideways, the far greater part of its blood-pounding resonance lost on the rocky trail from the heart to the voice.

Good! If it hadn't happened like this, how would she recognize it as truth? She poured her heart out to them and they reacted exactly the way people do, the way she herself has reacted to others' truths. To Sokol's. To Lucy's.

In the sacristy, they pack up their instruments. "That wasn't too bad at all," they tell one another, giddy with relief. Jonathan exclaims that he actually enjoyed himself, in spite of his gaffe. "They loved your piece, Léo," he says. "You could hear a pin drop." "Sandrine, you rocked that sucker," says Sheila. "We're not so bad for the walking dead, are we?" Sandrine smiles at them all, excuses herself, dying for a cigarette.

They gather on the front steps of the church, gratefully breathing in the delicious cool of evening, waiting for Jonathan to bring the van around to take them all back to Senneville. They'll do it all again seven more times over the course of the summer, in seven more towns, Sainte-Clémence the very last.

And it'll be what it is every time. Triumph, disappointment—does it really matter? Things come together, things fall apart; who knows that better than she does? Sometimes they even come back together again. Just like that poor little acrobat on Albanian TV: drop all your balls, pick 'em back up. Carry on. Nuthin' to see here.

She feels the tug under her left arm, a little more pronounced than usual.

Oh, but she's going to miss evenings like this!

As soon as she gets home, she'll open all the windows, maybe even go out on the porch, play some Shostakovich, really, just play the living shit out of that thing.

Evan

The summer, the fall, gone. The snow back already and the four o'clock dark, which signals a restless acceleration of directives, demands, and burning needs from Neil, upstairs. Orders scrawled in black Magic Marker, all caps: I WANT A MOUSTACHE CUP DO YOU EVEN KNOW WHAT THAT IS, and NEED YELLOW SHOELACES THE KIND THEY USE IN SKATES BUT CUT THE PLASTIC THINGS OFF THE ENDS, and COMPLEAT WORKS OF SIGMUND FREUD I THINK I'M READY IF YOU MUST KNOW.

Lucy has the free time and the unstinting love for Neil to scour every flea market from here to Ottawa, if it's something her boy wants. Books especially, so in awe is she of the sheer magnitude of reading he gets done. Telling Evan, "I don't have the patience to read anymore, I'm too damn jittery. But my sweetie's gonna use up the world's supply of books any day now, if he isn't careful." Of course, the way she doesn't help is by bounding up to his room, arms full not just of books and the esoteric junk he craves, but also boxes of jelly donuts or giant whacks of fudge, which Neil, who's well over three hundred pounds, isn't supposed to have but cannot resist.

She takes the stairs two at a time, banging on his door for admittance, the two of them up there thick as thieves, gorging, yakking, guffawing. Getting Neil so excited about the stupidest things. A few weeks ago, she'd brought him a chain letter she'd received that had purportedly been around the world nine times. The recipient would receive good luck within four days provided he sent it on. This was no joke! *DO NOT KEEP THIS LETTER*, ordered the letter in the belligerent caps so dear to Neil's heart.

Twenty copies must leave your hands within ninety-six hours! Miguel Gonzalez received $9,463, 000.00! Colin Murphy *threw the letter away. Nine days later, he died! Stella Sutcliffe put it off for too long and was saddled with expensive auto repairs! When she typed the letter as promised, she received a new car! Do NOT ignore this! Do NOT send money. FATE HAS NO PRICE!*

Neil had immediately scribbled twenty longhand copies on the backs of the old scripts Evan gives him for scrap paper. Left them on the kitchen table with an accompanying note: MAIL NOW!!! Banged on the rad the next morning, the imperial summons for a rare private audience in chambers. Barking, "Is it done?"

Evan, sighing. "It's done."

Of course, it wasn't done. Lucy had told him breezily on her way out that the letter was fifteen years old. She put no stock in chain letters, she said. She just loved to see her baby in "a good place." Then she was out the door and gone, and who knew when she'd turn up again?

But four days later, Neil had called him upstairs again, triumphantly displaying an O'Henry bar he'd found wedged between his bookcase and the wall. It could have been there for a decade; what colossal good luck to find it, he with his raging sweet tooth. He'd forgotten all about O'Henry bars! Could Evan get more, like a crate?

Another sigh from Evan, as he slumped back down to the kitchen, his mind not on O'Henry bars, but stalled in the same place it had been spinning its wheels since June. Remembering, over and over and over again, Rivka coming here that one time. Asking her three times to sit down as she flipped her hair, sniffed the air, winced. Murmured, "This is just too quaint to live, Sugarnuts." Looking up then, catching that fatal glimpse of Neil at the top of the stairs, their eyes locking. "Whoa," she'd said, under her breath. And then, "Well, well, well." So kind and discreet, compared to the whiplash malice that had come later: "Do the bolts in his neck need regular adjusting?" And: "If he hits seven hundred pounds, do you think you can get him on a reality show?"

Right there, now, in front of him, was the chair she'd sat in. No one had used it since, though Nathalie Casgrain from next door had come close, last time she popped in. But something had stopped her; moving to sit, she'd immediately sprung up again as if magnetically repelled.

A plain, wooden kitchen chair, now and forever, haunted!

Spring, the whole summer going by, then autumn. He'd sat at this table by the hour, his head in his hands, staring at that chair, his insides gnawed to pulp. Weeping with no provocation, mouthing hopeless prayers: *Who am I, Lord? Who am I without her, what am I good for? Why did you give her to me if I wasn't meant to keep her?* Sometimes, driven to extremes, he checked Rivka's Facebook page, her website, unable to look for more than a few seconds, not wanting to know. Or googled her name, just to see how much laceration he could withstand. It was the only thing he used the computer for at all now, the thing bought to please her, back when she'd wanted him to set up his own website, making him balk like a mule. Always having to rely on Michel next door to jigger it back to life when it froze or sent him cryptic messages: just one more timely reminder of his sadly depleted manliness quotient.

He was an old hand, though, at silence, a master at staying out of trouble in his own room. He had no TV, having learned to live without it at such an early age. Theatre, movies, had lost all charm for him without Rivka by his side, and like Lucy, he was too jumpy to read. He considered taking up knitting to fill the hours. Or possibly, whittling.

Even now, deep into the winter, his first thought upon waking is: I will not call her. A pledge he has kept since the fourteenth of August, when he'd stammered and stumblebummed his way through, "Hey there. Just reachin' out to ya." Trying to sound like her.

"Don't," she'd snapped. Call ended.

He wakes every morning in his creaking wooden house, snow piled to his bedroom windowsill, the lawn billowed with hip-high drifts, the lake beyond a bleak aluminum strip under low clouds.

His agent, Margot, calls with the news that they'd like him to play bad husband and father Marshall Thomas, or was it

Thomas Marshall, in *Stolen Kisses, Stolen Dreams*. No, he will not. Hedging apologetically, "I'm taking the year off." Hoping she won't be angry or disappointed, hoping the production company won't stagger backward in dismay, shut the film down, send everyone home. "It's for health reasons," he lies, partially.

Margot takes it well.

That first week in April he hadn't been able to get out of bed at all. For the rest of the spring and summer, he went out only for groceries, or to pick up Neil's prescriptions. Made some half-hearted stabs at filling Neil's brusque orders: A cat calendar. A crocodile calendar. BECAUSE I LIVE FOR THE SWEET PLEASURE OF CROSSING OFF THE DAYS, read his note. ALSO TRACK PANTS XXL WITH RED STRIPE ONLY. He always came straight back home to resume sitting at the table staring down that chair. Letting the phone ring, Nathalie from next door finally marching over when he didn't pick up, ringing the bell repeatedly, pounding, shouting, "*Est-ce que ça va, vous-autres? Chu inquiète!*" Shuffling to the door in his bathrobe, tears on his cheeks, assuring her everything was fine, he just had a lingering flu.

Louisa always insisted that joy was the central thing in a Christian's life, and sorrow merely peripheral. It was precisely the opposite for unbelievers. Said Louisa.

No, Louisa. No. The ways of God are identical to the workings of corrupt officialdom: empty promises, bluster, henchmen waiting in ambush to break your jaw, drag you down to the river, four going down, only three coming back. The boss never available, always out of town.

It doesn't matter a damn whether he has a job or not. He has savings, he can afford to do nothing for a good long while. Make a career of staring down the abyss, burrowing into the annihilating silence.

Only in October did he take a tiny, grudging step back into life. He began running. A sacred activity: he'd run with Rivka, but only in full sunlight. This time it was pre-dawn, mist shrouding the grey lake. An hour minimum, every day, in all weathers.

Now, in blackest winter, he runs through the town he grew up in, his old neighbourhood only eight blocks away, though it feels so different now, offers such a hazy, unreal sense of his past that it might as well be Siberia. The town hasn't changed much, except it has. It's darker now. Beneath the slate January sky, Sainte-Clémence's wounds are bandaged, swaddled in snow: swastikas graffitied onto the walls of the church, the Couche-Tard robbed twice at gunpoint, kids holed up in basements doing meth, keeling over from fentanyl. The snow muffles it all.

But maybe it's always been this way. How would he have known, his worried little face constantly arched heavenward, or turned resolutely in the direction of the little church on the other side of town where his youth now lay six cold feet under. Those years were long gone, having absconded with his once unblinking faith in a world bright with meaning.

Every morning at half past four—early evening for Neil, his upstairs toilet flushing, water swooshing through the old pipes—Evan dresses in three layers of everything, a black balaclava over his face. He has a piece of brown toast, a glug of orange juice in the kitchen, in the dark. Pulls on his gloves, zips the door key into his jacket pocket. The cold lands him a vicious left hook as he sets out up the middle of the street where the plow has done a perfunctory pass. His shoes are excellent, have cleats for winter running. Three hundred bucks they cost, a Rivka recommendation.

He jogs up to the main road, his back to the lake, panting white cloudlets. *Rivka recommended my shoes* a shard of glass in his gut. Turns left. Minus 30 wind chill, fizzling ice needles rushing full bore at his eyes. Nobody out but him and Orion, the only sound the crunch of snow under his feet, his rhythmic huffing. Down the side streets that lead back to the water, then up again, the plastic Tempos, white or blue or tan, sagging under their freight of snow, the cars inside numb, frozen. There are no streetlights on the side streets, just bare branches clawing upward in mute despair, a few frigid seed pods still dangling. Neil's upstairs window is the only faint yellow square of light for blocks, Neil pickled up there in his cranky solitude. Evan can hear his heart beating from five kilometres away.

After ten minutes, the wool around his lips is festooned with ice chunks. Five more minutes and he won't feel the cold anymore. Twenty more and he'll pass the IGA where Pierre, the manager will be pulling into the parking lot in his Ford Taurus. Spotting Evan, he'll wave a stiff-gloved hand, shouting, *"Bon courage!"*

Forty minutes in, he passes the house at the top of rue Dumas that burned to the ground on Christmas Eve. A wooden frame house much like his own, now a fairy palace with spires, minarets, stalactites of ridged and rippled ice, the water from the fire hoses freezing as it fell, the fantastical sculpture delightfully sugared over with new snow. A single mother, two kids; it's always a single mother, sorrow central, joy peripheral. He knew her to say *bonjour* to, a pretty young woman—they're all young to him now—short blonde hair, olive green parka with fur around the hood; he knows so many people in town by their winter coats. The burn smell is still in the air; the big maple tree in the yard, so spectacular in October, now charred, cancerous. The flattened place in the snow where they'd laid the bodies out like fish on a bed of ice, before throwing a tarpaulin over them. A couple of half-hearted teddy bears, now buried, that will reappear only in April, soaked through, sour smelling.

When he comes home, stamping his snowy shoes on the mat, yanking off his balaclava, there's a new note demanding the complete works of Rudolf Steiner and a new cereal bowl. BLUE ONLY!!! NOT PLASTIC NO DUCK MOTIFS!!! LUCY KNOWS WHAT I MEAN.

Sinking onto a kitchen chair, sweating under his layers, Evan takes weary stock.

The two of them have been here for (counting on his cold-stiffened fingers) sixteen, seven, eight . . . nearly twenty-two years!

Neil, fresh out of the hospital, his face puffy, a gut for the first time in his life. Evan getting his license, buying a used Tercel. The two of them working out the logistics of the lopsided little house on the water at the bottom of Lunenberg Street, Neil claiming the stuffy attic under the sagging eaves; that, and the upstairs bathroom, stippled with mould, its linoleum floor coming unstuck, its dented metal shower stall. Ordering Evan to "Leave it, everything is just the way I want it. You've got your quarters, I've got mine." To Evan went the entire downstairs, the big, old-fashioned kitchen, the living room with its bizarre, vermillion walls, the tiny bedroom at the back looking out onto the lawn sloping down to the water's edge. The better bathroom, the rust-stained claw-foot tub, the peeling wallpaper featuring fox-hunting scenes.

The rent was peanuts. Lucy, out of the several properties she owned, had insisted they take this one. "It's my favourite, it's really special to me. I learned how to play killer poker in this very kitchen." He'd been just back from Thailand, dropping in to see Louisa, and there'd been old Lucy—the same age then as he is now, he realizes with a jolt—out on the porch of the childhood home she'd never left, hulked over in a chair, cigarette going, face in a book. Louisa muttering darkly, "I don't think that girl even works anymore. Just sits on the porch or in the house with the blinds shut, smoking herself to perdition. It's enough to make you ill."

Lucy had hailed him, cutting into his heavily censored description of his trip to Thailand to ask him straight off where Neil was. "Can't even remember the last time he came by. How's he doing?"

"He's, uh, in the psych ward at the Montreal General," he'd had to tell her. Her jaw dropping, her thin, smoke-cured face buckling in unfeigned sorrow.

"It's just temporary. When he gets out, I'm hoping to find a place where we can live together. Somewhere quiet, restful," he'd told her. This had snapped her to immediate attention.

"Look no further, my lad! If you haven't got any objection to moving back to shitty Sainte-Clémence, I got just the place for you kids. Down at the bottom of Lunenberg, real swanky, lakefront property. I absolutely want you guys to have it. I'll cut the rent in half. Shut up. I'm not taking no for an answer."

It was spring when they'd moved in, and warm, Evan spending whole afternoons exploring the little woods across the road. Barely budding trees, cheery, hardworking birds. He walked beside mushy-bottomed streams swollen with spring snowmelt that ran in surprising torrents down the gently sloping land to the water. Invited Neil to come out with him, maybe take a walk through town if he wasn't in the mood for woods, join him for breakfast at the Casse-croûte Odile, or lunch, they could even order the dreaded *mets chinois*, how about that?

Not a chance.

I HAVE MELANCHOLIA AGITATA YOU NIT WE DON'T WALK IN THE WOODS!!!!!!!

His actual diagnosis was severe agitated depression, characterized by bipolar-like swings between episodes of manic, rageful highs and morbid, hopeless lows. His meds, which he took without protest twice a day, stabilized his mood swings, but the paralyzing panic and helplessness he was prey to in any situation not under his absolute control had driven him to decide that he wanted no part of the world anymore.

With carefully monitored medication, he might remain stable for a long time under the right conditions, his doctor had told Evan. In time, with age, the disease might become harder to control, which might require permanent hospitalization. The more he tended to isolate, the worse he'd be likely to do. But for now, he could remain in Evan's care, with the doctor keeping a steady eye out for changes.

During that first year, Neil was still awake during the day, venturing downstairs for meals with Evan, sometimes even slipping out the side door, if he was certain no one was around, his shoes sinking into the muddy yellow lawn. Taking a stiff, uncoordinated walk down to the lake where he'd pitch in a few stray sticks before hurrying back home. Keeping himself reasonably clean, cutting his own hair, shaving when he felt like it, both under Evan's supervision until a year had gone by and he'd proven he could be trusted with scissors, a razor. He could be safely left alone too, allowing Evan to go to auditions, do a few days shooting here and there when he got lucky. Neil seemed calm enough, as long as it was just the two of them, or Lucy on one of her erratic pop-ins. Out of the house, though, not so much; when Evan drove him into the city to see Dr. Courtemanche every second month, he lay flat in the back seat the whole way. In the parking lot of the Montreal General, his head down, muffled like Glenn Gould in a hat and scarf even in summer, he shuffled after Evan, a cartoon of the saddest man who ever lived. Answering the doctor's questions monosyllabically in a tracheotomy voice, metallic and buzzy, the news from the interior always bad. He knew perfectly well he needed to cooperate if he wanted to stay where he was, telling Evan after every single doctor's visit, even though no such plan had been broached, "If you move me, I'll off myself. I don't give a fuck, just watch me."

The attic gradually became his hermitage. He slept away vast tracts of time, beginning to keep nocturnal hours, only leaving his room if Evan were out. He devoted his awake time to wildly eclectic reading, irritably refusing the offer of a TV, a computer. The phone Evan bought him was never turned on, kicked under the radiator, for all he knew. He blew up if Evan tried to cajole him downstairs, shouting, "One hour in my life would pulverize you, so back off!"

Every six months or so, Evan argued himself into the attic, dragging the vacuum behind him, a bucket of soapy water on the landing. Tried to surreptitiously weed out the ever-growing piles of junk, the teetering towers of books, swabbing the floor and the window down as quickly as he could while Neil lurked, balky and cursing, in the bathroom. That was all Evan ever saw of the room; only on choice occasions would Neil open his door a crack, call out for Evan to come up, make a few pithy observations from behind his door. Informing him with a straight face—Evan could never tell whether he was serious or not—that there were bilingual raccoons on the roof, he'd heard them talking. Or, Evan needed to park his car up the street away from the house, because fumes from the gas tank were making it hard for him to keep his balance. Or jokes—How come nobody knew God's real name when it was right there in the prayer: Our Father who art in heaven, Howard be thy name. Evan, sitting on the top step, laughing way more than necessary, desperate for it not to end too soon.

With the years, his acting career had begun to pick up: small TV roles, the odd commercial, work that didn't keep him away from home overnight. Long stretches between jobs, but wasn't that the way it always went? He squirreled away his money, lived thriftily, and didn't mind this reclusive life at all. He could spend entire afternoons sitting out back on the grass, contemplating the water. Or walking in the woods. Or strolling across town to see Louisa whenever he got up the courage. Eating suppers of toaster waffles smothered in corn syrup at her cluttered table, during which she harangued him to come back to church with her, they had a wonderful weekly Bible Study for Singles now. Patting his hand, her face tight with concern. "How is your walk with the Lord these days, Evan? You don't want to backslide, honey. You know I wish you'd chosen a different life, something less worldly, but I never forget to lift you up before the Lord in prayer. Every day I ask that He guide your path and lead you away from Satan's snares, so that you remain pure and unsoiled. Are you choosing only believers as your companions, dear? Still reading your Bible, having your daily quiet time?" Questions he invariably answered with "Fine" or "Yes" or an evasive, "I'm right with the Lord, you don't have to worry."

Her voice dropping then to a thrilling lower register. "That Brickwood girl next door has gone straight to the dogs. I hear she got fired from the library. You do know that she came straight home after university with anxiety problems. I'll just bet! The place is a dump now, I can smell the cigarette smoke from over here. Neither she nor her mother do a lick of yard work anymore. Did you get a look at the lawn? I'm thinking of calling the police, it's a disgrace."

He had to remind her every time that he lived with Neil now, and how ill he was. She always nodded, tight-lipped, no apparent sense of guilt or remorse at all, never once asking for an elaboration. Sitting next to him at the table in her frayed housecoat, her breath none too fresh, gushing over how dear and sweet Evan had been as a boy, as if he'd been her only charge, as if Neil had never existed. Taking him upstairs every time to show him their old bedroom, painted a cloying pink now, with new floral bedspreads, ruffled orange pillow shams, everything tucked in shipshape, and he, in a faint voice, admiring her work, her taste, his mind roiling: *She didn't even ask about him. She never asks about him!* Still so patently her bustling, no-nonsense self, working her francis off—"This old saint is still going strong, praise the Lord!"—organizing a fund drive for the church, doing volunteer work for the Islam Shall Hear Mission, teaching Sunday school. He listened to her only intermittently, choked with anger, excusing himself when he could bear no more, escaping to the front porch to catch his breath.

Sometimes he'd see Lucy, parked in an old Muskoka chair on her porch, overflowing ashtray at her elbow. Looking up, she'd wave brightly in his direction, shouting, "You gotta come over here, your aunt'll raise a holy stink if I smoke on her property. Knock the Hallelujah Jesus clean out of her." Her Rothmans, her lighter, crammed into her front shirt pocket, her voice croaky and clogged, the smoke smell of her making him reel backward.

Lucy, like Louisa, could talk a blue streak once she got started, rehashing the same material every time. "How's Neil doing? How you guys liking the house? I love that place, I couldn't believe it when it went up for sale, it was pure fate. I was gonna move there myself but then I thought, shit, why bother, I'm fine here. People think I'm weird living in the same house my entire life, so what? Mum doesn't mind, and I got my little putt-putt there, so I can take off whenever the two of us get ready to kill each other. And don't even ask how hard I have to work to get up the courage to take these little trips. Long as I can be on my own, though, I'm okay. No crowds, no tourist traps. You know Pauline's not working anymore, eh? Her diabetes is really doing a number on her feet. Anyhow, I'm gonna come down and see you guys soon, okay? You going back inside? You better, before your aunt has to haul out the garlic, ward me off like a vampire, haw!" She leaned in close. "You know it was me cut the heads off all her tulips last spring. With scissors, middle of the night. Haw! Was she pissed!"

She lit a fresh smoke, exhaled a long, grey gust, coughing wetly. "You two kids, I swear, you guys got a raw deal. Your aunt gave up on me years ago, trying to get me to come to her church. Haw! Good luck with that shit! But it's a damned shame about Neil. Breaks my heart. I love that kid like he was my own. When you go back, you tell him for me, anybody gives him trouble, I want to know about it. You just tell him, fuck that shit. Tell him to hold his head up. Fuck it, I'll come over and tell him myself. I got some stuff for him, from my trip to the Maritimes. Hold on, I'll give it to you now." She sprinted, coughing, into the house, the door banging behind her, Evan thinking, great, more junk. He'd only just managed to spirit away a carton of dusty flea market trinkets, a snow globe collection, a torn coonskin cap, an alligator head, forty mouldy old books. But here she came, all skittish cheer, with a cheesy painting of a schooner, a snow globe shaped like a whale, a hideous Christmas sweater featuring frolicking elves of many lands. And eight fat batons of Toblerone. It was impossible not to love her, loving Neil the way she did.

Where had all the time gone? More than two decades, quick as a lightning bolt. Twenty-two years, during which he'd carved out a new identity in Sainte-Clémence, where he was looked upon, to his bashful chagrin, as a local *vedette*. Attracting friendly smiles in the street, backslaps at the Saint-Jean-Baptiste picnic, porky smoke wafting from the hot dog grills, kids tearing across the grass on dirt bikes as he chatted with the local shopkeepers, Eloïse from the Jean-Coutu, Pascale from the bank, Mario from the garage. Sitting down to eat undercooked burgers and coleslaw, bantering with teachers from the new high school, Terry and Solange, who were roughly his age. Hailed, from an adjoining table: *Heille, salut, le movie star!* It was nice, it was comfortable, it was home. He only wished Neil could have a part in it. Or Lucy, who never came out for town events, because "crowds just inflamed her homicidal impulses."

In the early days, attempting to counter Neil's growing isolation, he'd tried to encourage him to come out for local festivities, leaning heavily on the amount of great food that would be available. No luck. Then, a couple years back, he'd hit on the idea of maybe encouraging his brother's early love of music, perhaps finding him a discreet, private teacher who could come out to the house, teach him some easy instrument like guitar, broaden his horizons a little. Maybe even give him singing lessons; could there still be the remnants of a voice inside that jowly neck? It didn't matter what, just so long as it opened him up more to the world. It was Terry who had introduced Evan to Sheila, an older lady who taught an introductory music course at the high school. Sheila had been interested, sure, though she didn't play the guitar; maybe get Neil an electric piano to work on? Evan had liked her instantly, she was easygoing and wryly funny, and he really thought Neil might take to her. But at the suggestion, Neil had stamped his feet and bellowed a NOOOOOOO so long and loud, he'd dropped the idea like a box of spiders.

Still, he thought he'd never been so happy, at least as a grown-up, as on those summer evenings he spent sitting out in lawn chairs in the Casgrain driveway next door, nursing a beer, talking politics with Michel and his peppy wife Nathalie, relaxed and enjoying himself but never forgetting Neil, aloft only fifty metres away, silent, humped up under blankets, completely alone. The Casgrains knew about Neil; Evan had given them an abridged version of the story, and they were polite and unobtrusive, but never forgot to ask after him. Nathalie sometimes gave him a heaped plateful of homemade peanut butter cookies, still warm under aluminum foil, because he'd once mentioned they'd been Neil's favourite as a kid.

The previous spring, the Casgrains had brought Neil even more joy. After years of trying unsuccessfully to conceive, they had adopted a pair of brothers, five and three years old, whom Neil had spotted out his window rolling around on their front lawn. He'd immediately summoned Evan upstairs, demanding to know who they were. When Evan told him, Neil had broken into a smile so huge and dazzling, he almost, *almost* looked like his old, old self.

"They're just like us! Just like us, Evan!" And if he heard them out playing, yelling and chasing one another, he'd open his window and lean out, shouting, "*Heille! Salut,* you guys! *Dis bonjour a mononcle Neil!* You guys have a good day, okay?" Mathieu and Yannick would stop dead in their tracks, look at one another, break into giggles, wave back. A cryptic note appeared in the kitchen one morning: ORDO FRATUM MINORUM MEANS ORDER OF THE LITTLE BROTHERS DON'T FORGET!!! Followed by: GET THOSE BOYS SOME LICORICE OR SMARTIES MY TREAT.

But it's winter again now, outside their door, inside Evan's heart. Even so. If he continues to live frugally, he can last a long time without working. It's high time he stopped pretending to be someone he was never meant to be. Waking up every morning with nothing to do but make sure Neil is fed and gets his meds is pinlight enough in the darkness. For now, he asks no more of life.

Everyone's saying there's never been a winter like this one. It keeps on snowing, socking in basement windows, branches weighed down, snapping off, falling with muffled thunks a foot deep. Over one hundred forty centimetres and it's only February, and now there's more coming, wind howling around the sides of the house, a bus crawling down the rue Principale doing twenty, its tracks instantly covered over.

Today he has nowhere to go but to the bank to withdraw some cash. Pick up some groceries, bags of cookies, multiple loaves of bread and ham and cheese for Neil's sandwiches. Neil hasn't eaten a hot meal in two decades; hot food makes his teeth buzz.

The line at the bank is long; he's only halfway to the head of it when there's a sudden drop in the light, an abrupt cessation of ambient hum. The tellers look at one another in that mix of dismay and elation that accompanies act-of-God work stoppages. The emergency lights flash on after a moment, but they're dim, way too intimate for a bank. The lines disperse; people mill around, peer out the window into the whiteness, speculating, joking. Waiting for life to snap back on, for the lights and computers to resurrect themselves. Waiting five, ten minutes, the tellers out from behind their posts, on their phones, mingling with the crowd. People start to leave, bundling scarves over their mouths.

Evan does the same. Steps out into the snow that lashes, stings his face till he turns down his own street, where it now lashes his left side.

He pushes his front door open, flicks the lights out of force of habit; it's after three and nearly dusk, the kitchen sunk in gloom. No light comes on, the fridge is mute, the clock on the stove stopped at five to three. From the dark fridge he takes the rest of last night's spaghetti and, leaning against the sink, finishes it off. The snow pings against the window, which rattles in its splintery frame.

By five, the darkness is complete. He rummages through drawers for candles, matches; there are none. A flashlight then, yes, here it is, the battery not dead but just about. He looks up weather news on his phone which he's neglected to charge for two weeks; it too hasn't long to live. The blizzard is hammering the province, has only begun, snow predicted in the fifty-centimetre range. Stay off the roads, 900,000 Hydro customers in Montreal and surrounding areas without power already, gale force winds, power lines down all the way from Sherbrooke to Rimouski.

Upstairs, he hears feet shuffling. What's he doing up at this hour? Evan mounts the stairs, flashlight in hand, stands outside Neil's door. "The power's out. Are you okay?" There's no reply, just the creak of the room, like a ship on heavy swells. Or perhaps the rusty-hinged door to Neil's mind swinging open and shut, a derelict barn in a high wind.

"Neil? Are you okay? The power's out. We're having a really bad storm." It's much louder up here, battering the walls, snow probably sifting down through the rotting beams.

"Neil? Can you hear me?" Footsteps. "Neil, open the door, okay?" There's no lock on the door, but Neil has always fiercely insisted that he open and close it himself.

Still no answer, though the footsteps stop. But he does that sometimes, goes all stubborn, even the smallest upset in his routine rendering him rigid, silent, until he's recalibrated, which can take hours. Evan gives the door an experimental shove. Nothing doing; clearly, he's got his bookcase rammed up against it.

"Okay. Hang in there. But you're going to have to unblock the door. I'm going to bring up your meds and something to eat."

The flashlight is so faint, just enough pale shimmer to make out the edges of the steps as he goes back down. He pokes in the fridge, gathers up a plastic container of cold macaroni and cheese, half a baguette, two cans of Coke. Gets a fork from the drawer by the sink. From the cupboard, eight fudge cookies. The day's ration of pills, down to only once a day now, usually left on the counter for Neil to find when he comes down at night. He goes back up the stairs, knocks. "Can you just come and take this?"

Nothing.

"Neil, I can hear you breathing in there." He can't really. He stands for a few minutes, the food in his hand, feeling foolish. "Okay. I'll just leave it here outside the door. I'm going downstairs. Make sure you take your pills. If you need anything, bang the rad."

The pale flashlight beam, the wind, the ice pelting the window: in spite of Neil's cussedness, Evan is enjoying this. Being socked in always brings such a rush of cozy good cheer. As kids, he and Neil spent so much time in their room together, particularly in winter. Two good little boys whose homework was done, forbidden to watch the TV that Louisa only turned on for Billy Graham specials, making their own fun, all the joy that flashlights under blankets could bring. They played a game they called North Pole Igloo, burrowing underneath the white duvet, smacking their lips over invisible whale steaks, exclaiming, "This is delicious! Pass me more blubber, good sir!" Neil always full of insane notions as to plot development, which Evan would try to head off, suggesting practical activities, a detailed inventory of their supply of bullets and arrows, or going out to forage, maybe harpoon another whale. But Neil would be bouncing on his rump, crying, "Hey, those aren't penguins out there. They're crazy clowns, and they're *scoundrels!* They're wrecking everything, smashing up all the igloos! Oh no! Here they come, riding on walruses! They're gonna attack!"

And Evan, breaking out of character, would have to ask in a small voice, "Clowns?" His face creased with worry, because how could there be clowns at the North Pole? But Neil was still bouncing on the bed under the snow roof. "We have to kill them! Lend me some bullets, I'm almost out!" And the game would go on, and it would be better, better than anything he could ever have thought up by himself.

He drops onto the haunted chair, felled at the knees by a sudden tidal wave of homesickness, an unbearable ache of longing for little Neil, happy Neil, bright, ebullient Neil wound up so tight, his spring still unsprung, his purply morning eyes opening huge and joyous, meeting Evan's across the aisle between their beds . . .

Someone is pounding on the front door. He opens it to find Nathalie Casgrain, bundled in Michel's old sheepskin coat, a scarf looped over her head to cover her ears. Stamping her feet on the mat. *"On l'a-tu la tempête rien qu'un peu?!"* She's just checking in, doesn't know how long the power's going to be out; are he and Neil okay, do they need anything, do they want to come over, not that it's any warmer *chez eux*.

"We'll be okay," Evan tells her. Opens the silent fridge to show her they have food.

"Ben, if you need something, don't be shy." Pulling her coat around her again. "I'm here for that!" She opens the door and a blast of snow shoots halfway across the kitchen floor.

"L'hiver prochain," she hollers from the porch, *"je sacre mon camp en République dominicaine jusqu'au printemps, sans joke!"*

The power stays off all night. Evan wakes in the thin, grey, pre-dawn light, wearing two sweaters and his running jacket. From upstairs he hears nothing, shouts Neil's name, gets no answer. Shivering, he bounds up to the landing with another blanket and two more sweaters. Neil's food, his meds, are untouched.

"Neil, open up! I brought you more blankets." Neil does not. Evan tries the door, still blocked. "Neil! Are you awake? Please! Just let me know you're okay in there."

Still nothing. But he could be asleep, and there *are* nights when he doesn't eat anything, when he only comes down for a handful of cookies and his meds in the morning, before turning in for the day.

Downstairs, Evan crawls back into bed, pulls the blankets up to his nose, on red alert for any sound from upstairs. Knees curled to his chest to preserve warmth, he thinks of Rivka: where is she now, how is she faring, her apartment not sunny today, grey, dreary, and who's there with her, dipping into the condom jar . . . no, no, no, don't go down that rutted road! Grey skies reminding him of botching a fist bump with her, way back in wet, dismal Sydney. The shame of the memory at least heats him up.

Upstairs, thumping. Muffled, intermittent howls. Silence. Then louder howls, and howls they are, not cries, not shouts. *Howls*. A baby rabbit swooped upon by an owl; shrill, screaming animal panic.

Evan bolts up the stairs, pounds on the door. "Neil, what's wrong? Open up!" He rattles the handle, shoves the door, which unexpectedly flies open. It's so dark; that has to be what's spooked him.

"Where are you, Neil? Don't be upset, it's just a power failure, we've had them before. Look out the window, you can see it'll be daylight soon. Where are you?" A whimper from the corner. His eyes, adjusting, gradually make out his crumpled brother, his brown track pants and Lucy's awful Christmas sweater which he's had on for months, his feet bare and blue. A blanket over his head. Crazy clowns whooping all around him for all Evan knows. The closer he comes, the tighter Neil stuffs himself into the corner.

He hasn't seen him this way since Bangkok.

"Come on, give me your hands, I'll help you up." Speaking softly, advancing with infinite caution. "That's it, that's the way. You need to come downstairs, you can't stay up here alone, look at you, you're frozen stiff. Come on. Don't be afraid, Neil. It's just me."

Neil shuffles forward in the dark, the blanket still over his head, balking, bleating. There's an overpowering odour of urine. Evan holds his hands fast, takes small steps backward to the door, to the landing, ten minutes to get down the stairs. Sits Neil down on a kitchen chair, not the haunted one, saying, "Sit, sit!" as if disciplining a dog. Bringing him a sedative, his other meds, a glass of water. The house is buffeted, windows whited out. Evan picks up his phone to call Neil's doctor, but it's dead. He could call from Nathalie's place, but he doesn't dare leave Neil alone.

He still has the old North Pole Igloo duvet. He manhandles his brother like a trunk full of cement blocks toward the bedroom, upends his legs, tips him backward into the rumpled bed. Crawls in beside him, pulls the duvet up over both their heads. Lies beside Neil, arms tight around him, his brother bolted to his body, arms noosed around his neck. "Just breathe, Neil. That's all you have to do. I'll take care of you, you're safe." Neil howls into his neck, trembling like a nuclear reactor about to blow.

It takes almost a week for him to settle. Evan doesn't go out, not even to run. He phones Dr. Courtemanche, who advises allowing Neil to wind down on his own, but to keep a close eye on him and call immediately if there are any further big upsets. Asking, "You're sure he's taking his meds?"

"Every day," Evan assures him, his stomach suddenly plunging as he realizes: How does he know? The meds disappear, but have they actually been going into Neil? His heart leaps into his throat as he recalls an odd note Neil had left a while back: LUCY SAID SHE DID IT WITHOUT DRUGS WENT HER WHOLE LIFE JUST ON WILL POWER. I NEED YOU TO GET ME MONOPOLY, NO CARDS BUT I WANT THE LITTLE IRON AND ALSO THE BATTLESHIP!!!!!! AND ALL COMMUNITY CHEST CARDS EVERY SINGLE ONE. The first sentence had been swallowed up by the rest of the message; he hadn't taken it seriously, had forgotten all about it. He resolved on the spot to make sure he sees Neil actually swallow his pills, every single day. No more blind trust.

After two weeks, Neil is calmer, resuming his routine. Evan goes back to running. The mornings lighten, the snowbanks shrink, the balaclava gets stuffed back into his sock drawer.

In late March, Margot calls, asks if he's feeling better; she has a small TV role for him, a high school teacher, two days. Also, does he know any karate, because she may have something else in a month or so.

"I'm going to be out of town, family business," he lies with astonishing smoothness.

April. May. He's done a whole Rivka-less year, and change. Michel Casgrain mows his unruly lawn for him, the whole house engulfed in the unnerving fragrance of cut grass and warm lake mud. Nathalie's out working in her garden, waving, bringing him bunches of daffodils and tulips which he puts in a Ragu pasta sauce jar in the middle of the kitchen table, where they catch the light, seem to glow from within. He remembers how good the bacon is at the *casse-croûte*, drops in for an experimental breakfast. The good bacon reminds him of the excellent raisin bread at the *boulangerie*, bread Neil loves. Also, there are instructions from above tucked into his shirt pocket: GET GUMDROPS, THE BIG ONES SIXTY PACKAGES ALL COLOURS. NO BROWNS.

Gumdrops, tulips. The world is awash in primary colours, the lawn plush with dandelions. The filmy white curtains Nathalie made for him billow softly over his bed, and the perfume of the lilac bush by the front door and the embrace of the sky, the clouds, the sun, lift his heart, nudging him with the near-forgotten wish to loft a few grateful prayers skyward. Along with a question:

So. What is it you want me to do now?

A week after the Saint-Jean picnic, he accepts an invitation to lunch in a house almost identical to his at the bottom of the street on the other side of the little woods. It's the annual teachers' party, the school year ending, a barbecue on the lawn, hamburgers, tequila, vats of sangria, boozy hilarity lasting well into the evening.

Solange is there, and Marty and Terry and Sheila, whom he's especially glad to see, her shimmer of local artistic fame akin to his own hazy movie star glamour, neither of them able to take any of it seriously. He does wonder why, at her age and with her skill, she hasn't had a professional career like her famous sister, but it seems impolite to ask.

She sidles up, a glass of sangria in each hand, and kisses him on both cheeks.

"One guess who I had drinks with before we played Saint-Lazare last weekend. Okay, you're taking too long. Lucy! The beautiful and talented Ms. Brickwood, in the flesh."

"She called you! Finally! Was it weird?"

"No weirder than it ought to be. She said she'll come to our concert when we play here. I really hope she does, and you too. Here, I brought you a tankard of strong drink."

Evan accepts the glass, raises it in a shy toast. "To you and Lucy and your big night. You know I wouldn't miss it for anything."

Sheila's about to say more, but someone is waving, hollering her name from across the yard. "Catch you later," she says, standing on tiptoe to kiss him again.

Left on his own, he drops into a lawn chair. The sangria makes him feel buzzy and goofy. He smiles loopily at everyone, wondering idly if he could be interested in any of the friendly women drinking and laughing on the lawn, matching himself with each one in turn, relieved to discover no particular click of deeper feeling. Everything's fine just the way it is. He feels so happy, in fact, that he lifts his eyes heavenward, a sloshy prayer on his lips: *Lord, am I doing the right thing? Am I living the way you want me to?* And a little more urgently, his empty glass lying across his lap, shoes kicked off, bare feet in the soft grass, the lake shimmering at the end of the lawn: *Please tell me who I'm supposed to be. Will I always be alone now that Rivka's gone? I think I'm over her finally, but . . . I still feel a little . . .*

You won't take Neil away from me too, will you?

People are beginning to leave; it's time he went too. He spies some fat brownies piled on a plate, wraps three in a paper napkin to take home to Neil.

He and Sheila leave together, ambling through the evening village, under the spreading trees, the air soft and balmy. Her car is parked several streets away; she'll be driving back to Senneville, but as they walk, she trips suddenly over a crack in the sidewalk, plunging forward, grabbing his arm in the nick of time. Laughing, "Looks like someone's teetering on the edge of inebriation. I'd better hold off driving for a bit. I'll just nip into the Couche-Tard for a coffee. You want one?"

"Sure," he says. "I'll wait out here." In front of the store, a gang of kids in their early teens are gathered. Four girls, cool sophisticates in shorts, tee shirts and lipstick, sit perched on a wooden railing, flipping their long hair, darting looks at two boys in hoodies huddled next to the store window. They look at the boys, look at one another, pretend to gag, *beurk!* One of them holds a grey kitten against her chest.

Sheila mutters, "Oh, wonderful. The Children of the Corn." She stops. "I know these little buggers, had both of them in one of my classes. Teaching, my friend, is not for the faint of heart."

She approaches the store, addresses the boys calmly. "*Bonsoir, Diego. Bonsoir, Olivier. Ça se passe bien, les vacances?*"

"Miss! You got a date!" exclaims the bigger boy in ostentatious English, eyeing Evan. Both boys snicker, blocking the door to the dep. Diego, the obvious alpha, his voice cracking ominously, makes Evan think of Neil at that age. A little breathlessly, he tries to smile at the boy.

"That's right," says Sheila evenly, edging her way between them. "I'm out on the town, raising all kinds of merry hell."

"Lookin' good, Miss," pipes the smaller one in a little boy's voice. Both kids bend double with laughter.

"Yep, that's the spirit," says Sheila, heading into the store, not looking back.

Evan, smiling shyly now at the girl with the kitten, stands by the window, as Sheila stops for a brief chat with Féti behind the counter. The boys move off, put their heads together, resume watching something on a phone. "Oh, shit!" cries the smaller of the two. "Whoa, man!" They look at one another, turn back to the screen. *"Heille! C'est maladement cool!"* Their voices ride on an edge, a metal plate sent spinning.

The Neil boy, lazy as a lizard, turns in Evan's direction.

"Heille, sir! Check." He holds out his phone with a lethargic, slitted smile. *"Y choppe les têtes pis ça coule partout, le sang."* Against his will, hypnotized, Evan leans over to look. It's an ISIS video of a beheading.

Evan jerks his head back, afraid he'll vomit right there on the path.

"They use the head for play soccer," says the kid with a winsome smile.

"C'est-tu vrai?" asks the smaller boy, in thrall.

"Ben oui," confirms the first, already tapping at his keyboard. He swivels his eyes back to Evan. "Hey, sir. You want look at woman do fuck with horse?"

Evan is helpless, shocked tears beginning to spill over. Sheila, dear, unflappable Sheila is still in there yakking, still without her coffee. She's witnessed none of this, can't possibly help him.

When he can find his voice, he says, softly, to the boys, who stare at him in delighted amazement, "Don't do this. P-p-please. You're m-m-making yourselves sick." It's all he can think of. How could they, how could he, ever return to the blessed time before he'd, before they'd, seen? He stammers, loses his voice, so desperate is he to protect this new-minted Neil just waiting to happen. But he can't protect the boy and he can't protect Neil. He's as weak and craven as that kitten, as wretched as he's ever been, and storms are coming, worse storms, Neil slipping away from him, Dr. Courtemanche increasingly uneasy. He's going to lose his brother, he's going to lose everything, and there's no way he's equal to this; it's as good as over, he's lost, they both are, and there's no help coming from anywhere, ever.

The big boy smirks. *"Toi-même,"* he says, lifting his cocky chin, indolently giving Evan the finger. His breath smells of cigarettes. Inside the frizzling, fluorescent-bright store, Sheila is just winding up her conversation, heading to the back where the hot coffee is.

Evan lurches stiffly away, back to the street under its rustling canopy of trees. A cool breeze wafts from the lake, the brackish green smell of warm summer water. He watches the bigger boy go into the store, push ahead of Sheila waiting at the counter, watches him dicker with Féti, emerging with a supersize blue slushie. He slurps through the straw, smacking his lips. "I need this . . . to cool . . . mah . . . system!" he announces in a gangsta voice, clowning for the girls, who giggle. The one with the kitten passes it to him, and Evan thinks in horror: No, not him! One squeeze and . . . but the kitten scrambles up his shirt to his shoulder, clings to his neck, bats the side of his face. The boy stands stock-still, giggling a little himself. Hope and joy and anguish mingle in the soft air, all of it just beginning for these kids, and all of it, except for anguish, ending for him.

Upstairs, all is quiet. On the counter, there's a note he missed that morning: TYPERITER THE KIND WITH THE BELL TAKE BELL OFF ALSO VERY IMPORTANT I NEED BIG MAGNIFYING GLASS MY EYES ARE KAPOOTSKI.

Evan slumps at the table, feet on the haunted chair, endlessly replaying the encounter with the boys like a tongue worrying an abscessed tooth. Those kids so clearly had his number. So did Rivka; that's why she ran for her life. Who could blame her? If she'd seen him tonight, blubbering, shaking, intimidated by a couple of broken children, whom he should have had the words to help, to fix, to steer toward righteousness . . . but no, not him. He'd just stood there whimpering, a sorry excuse for a man. In the cold light of hindsight, he imagines growling at those boys with a ferocity they could see through but still respect. Keeping his cool, keeping it light. "So, my young friends, looks like I'm gonna have to bonk some sense into your noggins!" Gently knocking their two heads together, which would crack them up, evoke sheepish laughter. And then, asking their names, getting to know them, their families. Leading them out into the world like Mr. Gaiman had led him, with the slackest, kindest of reins. Guiding their thoughts, their hearts, encouraging their talents, steering their young lives to fulfillment, so that they'd grow up to play the French horn or cure cancer or straighten out the Middle East, and he, Evan, twenty years from now, grizzled and stooped, would be sitting in the front row, crying like a baby when they went up to receive their awards and citations. His heart breaking with love.

Then thinking: Really? The French horn? *Noggins*? The two of them were probably packing heat.

Where had that stupid word even come from? *Growing boys like you should keep your noggins focussed on Scripture.* Who was it who said—? Oh. Of course. Mr. Toller. Sidling up to him and Neil—when Neil was still coming—after a Wednesday night prayer meeting. Addressing them awkwardly, trying to be chummy and a strong leader at the same time. Probably not much older back then than Evan is now, though Evan's teenaged self had figured him for at least ninety.

Yes, Mr. Toller. Exactly the kind of person to attract the hilariously malevolent attention of teenage boys. Always alone, coming to prayer meetings with his bright yellow toque riding high on his head above his ears, a fat pompom on top. Never missing a Wednesday night, getting off the bus at the corner in all weathers in his blue windbreaker, old-school rubbers on his shoes. Standing by the church basement door, always the second to arrive, Evan being the first, on Louisa's orders: "You be there at the door to greet the saints, Evan!" The two of them would wait for Louisa to come running, keys jingling on a ring, Evan and Mr. Toller the only males in a foaming fizz of women. And even when Louisa had unlocked the doors, they still had to wait for Deacon Glen Fingus—dubbed Glum Fungus by a sneering Neil—to drive up with ancient Nettie in the front seat of his car, the old lady always in excellent cheer, waving at them as the car turned into the parking lot, her Bible already open on her lap. Evan's heart would sink like a lead weight in quicksand, especially if kids from school were passing by on their way to the mall in their big, falling-down pants, jackets open, shoes unlaced and flapping, pounding each others' shoulders: "Hey! We got fuckin' *haaaaammered* last night, it was fuckin' unbelievable, fuck!" Evan standing there in a white shirt and tie, he and Toller both facing the same direction, like cattle in a high wind. Feeling like a bug pinned to a board, imagining Neil's snickering jibe, "I see by your outfit that you are a loser. I see by your outfit that you're a loser too!"

Nettie got on Evan's nerves. So did Glum Fungus. But he *despised* Mr. Toller. He knew it was wrong, prayed about it constantly, but he just couldn't help himself. Glum Fungus would haul Nettie's wheelchair out of the trunk, unfolding it, then unfolding Nettie, who'd be grunting and squealing, bundled in coats and sweaters and mufflers for the ten-metre trip to the door, smiling round at everyone. A few other ladies there by then, which was Mr. Toller's cue to say, every single time, "Are you ready, gentlemen?" in his Tweety Bird voice. Giving the signal for Glum to lift the footrest of the chair, while he and Evan, facing front like pallbearers, each hoisted a wheel, and then they'd heave-ho down the twelve inside stairs to the stale, dusty basement. Had to do this every time they met and look joyful about it too.

Down in the basement, nothing much. A scarred upright piano shoved into the corner, a moth-eaten brown quilt thrown over it. Tatty sofas and chairs. Fluorescent lights buzzing like a plague of locusts. Louisa and Mrs. Lajeunesse and Madge Nidwick at the refreshment table, fussing over plates of cookies. The kettle thrumming away. Everybody beaming like crazy, so happy to be there, Louisa in her huge, wrinkled tee shirt and the long brown skirt that didn't show dirt, glasses round her neck on a chain, sneaker soles squeaking. She'd give Evan a warm smile as she breezed by with a stack of teacups—dear, cooperative, un-rebellious Evan, cherished nephew and all-round helpmeet, baker of cupcakes, washer of dishes, shoveler of old ladies' driveways, respecter of crosswalks, clean-cut, well-scrubbed, teetotaling, soon to be a tall, stately, manly man, loyal servant of the Lord, light of her already extremely well-lit life.

Neil held a contrary opinion.

"You're the kind of hopeless dork, that if the house caught on fire and everybody stampeded, you'd lag behind, all polite, stepping out of everybody's way, thinking, oh man, this is gonna hurt."

Or, "You're the kind of pussy doofus who starts worrying about his ride home five minutes into the party." Evan would hang his head, only *wishing* he had a party to go to and worry at.

Once the food was seen to, Louisa would clap her hands, summoning the saints. "Gather round, everyone! Let us rejoice!" Hymnbooks out, voices raised in song, black sin rising in Evan's throat, choking him, as Mr. Toller—did he even have a first name—pulled focus as always. The man was so plainly still the pathetic kid he'd once been: staggeringly earnest, red-faced, shoulderless, cursed with childbearing hips, a kid who took no end of grief from his peers, his teachers, girls, stray dogs, bees, from his own splayed, galumphing feet, and who all the while just kept right on singing, eyes rolled heavenward, a tuneless castrato bleat, his mouth forming perfect round O's. Except now he was beyond ancient, getting jostled on the bus, having coffee spilled into his lap by waitresses whose attention was always elsewhere, getting splashed by cars, upended by ice, baffled by the news and anyone under sixty. The tiny manicured lawn in front of his tiny bachelor house always the one dog owners stood sentinel by as their charges unburdened themselves, unerringly the one where passersby tossed their trash. His newspaper landed four days out of five in the thorny rosebush. Some days his own chair turned against him, spontaneously falling on its side, ejecting him just for the outrageous good fun of it. But Mr. Toller kept right on singing, like he just *knew* goodness and mercy were gaining on him with every single passing second.

The sight, the sound of him always turned Evan's soft, quiet heart to flint. He longed to punch him when his bowels bubbled rudely in the silence between hymns. If they met at the sinks in the men's washroom, side by side in the mirror, Evan never failed to take pleasurable note of how moist and spruce cool he looked next to the pillar of lint and cinders beside him, carefully scrubbing his rooster-feet hands. Thinking, against his will, against everything he professed and believed and adhered to, that this intolerable dreariness was his sure destiny, the ultimate and absolute essence of a life lived in the Lord.

That's who those two boys had seen. A Mr. Toller for the new millennium, the saddest, most negligible of men.

Wearily, he turns out the lights, crawls into bed, drops into a fraught sleep.

At half past midnight, he's shocked awake by a mighty pounding on the front door, Lucy's signature knock: shave and a haircut, two bits! Lucy, ever clueless as to social decorum, experiencing a sudden yen for Neil's company.

She's on the doorstep, grinning, a lemon meringue pie in her hands, a plastic bag full of books looped over her arm. Asking, "My baby Neil up yet? Gotta see my boy," as she barges past Evan into the kitchen, heading for the stairs, turning to exclaim, "I'm thinking of driving to the Grand Canyon next week! Whaddya think of that?" She bounds up the stairs, hammers on Neil's door. "Hey! Open up, my bonny lad! It's your long-lost lover!"

Evan waits for the door to creak open, to slam, for the muffling of their two voices. Instead there's only silence.

Lucy knocks harder. "It's me, darlin'. Your Appalachian backwoods, rat-faced gal pal! I brought you a snack, sweetheart. And a big bag of prezzies."

Still nothing. Lucy calls down to Evan, "Is he still asleep?"

"He's usually up by now." Evan takes the stairs, knocks lightly on the door. "Neil? Lucy's here to see you."

From inside, a bark, definitive and final. "NO!"

In twenty-two years, Lucy has never been refused an audience. "Neil," she says, sounding scared, her mouth right up against the door. "I won't stay long, honey. I just wanted to bring you—"

"NO!" Something slams against the door as if thrown hard across the room, making her jump back in alarm. Her face bloodless, she bites her lip, bends gingerly to lay the pie and the bag by the door. She heads downstairs without looking back.

Evan catches her up on the front porch, grabbing her hand before she can make off down the steps. "Lucy, he gets like that, with me too. More lately than usual. It's not personal. He just needs a little time to reboot."

Lucy tries to light a smoke, but her hands are trembling so hard that Evan has to peel her fingers off her lighter and do it for her. She sucks in a drag, leans over the railing, breathes grey out into the night. The whole railing shakes, she's gripping it so hard, a lifetime of grievances crowding her chest, jostling for attention. She chooses one at random off the top of the pile, spitting, "I had another run-in with your aunt today. Bitch . . . sorry, but it's true . . . bitch comes right up to me in the yard, all up in my face. 'What do you do all day in your house? Why don't you clean up your yard?' She thinks I'm one of those hoarders, haw! Keeps coming to the door trying to see in around me. I told her, 'I'm in here gambling all day, on the internet.' Which is actually true, so fuck off, you nosy old hag." She talks at a rapid clip, only stopping for quick drags on her smoke. "She's obsessed with me, especially since Pauline died, like, she let that one get away and now I'm the one who has to pay for it. She's going senile, you know. I try talking to her, she keeps running the same shit by me every two minutes, on a loop. You're gonna have to stash her in a home before too long."

"I know." He too feels a dizzying rush of anger as he imagines seeing Louisa, full of years at eighty, safely delivered into endearing, irresponsible dementia, she who had never given a moment's thought to cleaning up her mess, leaving it all to him, and goddammit, *goddammit*, he hates her for it, *hates* her, hates the whole misguided lot of them, their silly sanctimony, their self-aggrandizement, their clutched-at certainties, complacencies, cover-ups. But he's going to look after her, of course he is. He'll do it, just like bumbling old Toller would, and he'll do it with love, love that will feel like a lie, but a lie that's as close to the truth as a lie can get.

There's a long silence. Lucy pitches her smoke over the railing, lights another one, tossing her head back repeatedly until he realizes she's trying to keep tears from dropping. He reaches out, lays a tentative arm around her shoulder. She shakes him off.

"I'm sorry, I'm sorry, I can't stand people to see me like . . . it's just, I'm so worried about Neil. Jesus goddamn, I know exactly how he feels." She gives the railing a vicious kick. "I get my moods, you know. That's why I take off and you don't see me. I don't want to bring Neil down. Why do you think I had to stop working? I couldn't even hold down a quiet, behind-the-scenes shelf-stacking job. They fired my ass, said I couldn't get along with anyone, said I was abrasive, whatever the fuck that means. Pussies can't take a little gentle abrasion? They had no idea what I was going through. I have to be so careful around people, I can't have them swarming me all the time, I go off the deep end. You get it, don't you? You're a loner too." She was abject, almost pleading. "Why does Neil hate me? What did I do?" A choked sob escapes her; she kicks the railing again.

"It's okay, Lucy. He doesn't hate you, he couldn't. Neil adores you."

"I don't like many people but when I love someone it's for fucking *ever!*"

"I know, Lucy. I know." He wishes he could take her in his arms but knows she won't stand for it. Knowing this makes him feel as if he already has.

She swipes at her eyes, lights yet another smoke, takes several deep drags. "Don't lie to me, Evan. Is Neil getting worse?"

"I don't know." Hedging. "He's not quite as steady as he used to be. Ever since that big snowstorm we had back in February, he seems to get spooked more easily. Lucy,"—he's treading carefully now—"you didn't say anything to him about maybe not needing to take his meds, did you?"

Her face swivels toward him, stricken. "No, I never, I mean, all I said, once . . . a long time ago, only once, I think I told him I'd never taken anything for . . . okay, well, I may have mentioned it a couple weeks ago as well. I can't remember. Oh Evan, is he off his meds? Is it my fault? Oh my God, I'm sorry, I'm so sorry, I never meant—"

"It's okay, Lucy. I don't know if he is or he isn't, but it's not your fault."

She's sobbing now. "Evan, I never, ever meant to hurt him. I'm so fucking stupid. I never know when to stop running my mouth."

"Lucy, it's okay, it's okay."

Defensive, grasping at straws, she ventures, "I noticed he started getting a little wobbly when those kids moved in next door, when was it, last year sometime? He talks about them to me all the time. He's worried sick they'll get hit by a car or kidnapped. He asked me to find out if their mother's mean to them. You know why, right?"

"They remind him of us." Evan fights down a cresting wave of jealousy; there were so many things closemouthed Neil seemed to have discussed at length with Lucy. "Maybe his meds just need adjusting again."

"He does this funny thing with his jaw lately, swinging it back and forth, like he can't stop. Have you noticed that?"

"Yes. I don't know what causes that. I'm afraid I'm going to have to drag him to a dentist before every last tooth falls out." He wants to burst into tears, to shout, "I can't handle this! I can't do it anymore, I can't!"

"You never need a break from all this?" Lucy's calmer now, her tears sucked back. She squints at him through her scrim of smoke. "When I was looking after my mother before she died, I felt like screaming every minute of every day. And that only lasted four months. But . . . listen, don't tell Neil she's gone, okay? I don't want him upset." She hauls in a deep drag. "We never got along that well, but at the end, we made it all up. But you've been at this just about your whole life."

"I'm all right."

"You're fucking more than all right. Sweetie, you're a saint." She sniffs hard. "I believe you'd sign on at a leper colony if you could. For just room and board."

"Some . . . p-p-people have suggested to me that . . . that I *need* Neil to be sick, I need him to be dependent on me, because I'm a weakling. I'm afraid of everything, so I need someone to justify my failure. Some . . . people have suggested this—"

Lucy snorts. "You, a weakling? What fuckwit told you that? I admire the crap out of you." Stubbing out her smoke under her sneakered foot. "A world full of Evans would be a fucking paradise. Only thing is, you need to stand up for yourself, stop taking shit from people. Hold your head up, boy! Haven't I been telling you since you were a rug rat? You've got nothing to be ashamed of."

He blushes, grateful for the darkness, the mere suggestion of standing up for himself triggering his lifelong impulse to immediately crumble into protective repentance.

"Apropos of nothing," Lucy adds, with a crooked grin, "I saw one of your films on TV a couple months ago. You were married to this lawyer, and there was some crazy shit about your ex-wife trying to kill you or something. Oh baby, was it dumb! But you looked cute as hell." She pockets her smokes and her lighter. "Anyway, fun's over. I gotta run. It's supposed to rain buckets tonight, and I just felt a couple drops. Make sure my boy gets his pie and his books, okay? Please tell him not to be mad at me. Please. And about his meds—"

"Don't worry, Lucy. You did nothing wrong." Evan says, reaching out to hug her.

"Hey!" she yelps, backing away. "Stay back. I swear, I will end you!" Letting loose with a choked, "Haw!" as she bolts down the steps, waving without looking back.

It rains hard for the next two days. Lawns are churned to mud, the air breathless with jungle humidity. Warm streams course down the road, and his shoes, when he runs, are soaked to lead weights, his socks balled up inside. After two days of it, he's afraid the roof might give way. He senses unrest upstairs, and by the end of the second day, Neil has stopped eating. Evan, bringing him his pills, finds the door once again barricaded.

"Neil, you need to—"

"No!"

"Please, you've got to open—"

"NO!"

On the third night, the rain amps up even more, hammering the roof and the windows. There's exuberant lightning, aerial bombardments of thunder. The power goes out.

Evan runs upstairs. The door, no longer blocked, is wide open, and so is the window, the racket infernal, rain lashing in sideways. Neil is crouched like a gargoyle on the window ledge, screaming into the furious downpour. "Get the kids in! Get them in! Boys! Come home! Get inside!"

"Neil! No!" Lunging, Evan tackles him from behind, arms locked around his meaty middle, hauling him backward. He falls onto the puddled floor with Neil on top of him, his brother so much larger than he is but weak, flabby, and soon Evan is sitting on him, just as he did in Bangkok, panting, forcing down his flailing arms, his mouth at Neil's ear, promising him that Mathieu and Yannick are safe, that the power will come back on soon, that everything's okay, it's okay, Neil! Understanding all the while that they are fast closing in on a point of no return, that everything's charging downhill, that he has no idea how much time they have left.

He shuts the window, leaves Neil long enough to get him a sedative. Helps him, sluggish and slippery, out of his soaked tracksuit and into a dry one. Navigates him onto his Barcalounger, where they drop to sleep in one another's arms.

In the morning, blazing sun, a scrubbed world bright as sheets hung out to dry. Extricating himself from Neil's torpid grip, getting stiffly to his feet, Evan sees, in the warm light, a sodden note on the floor, requesting a STUFFED CAT I DON'T MEAN A TOY I MEAN REAL CAT ALSO WITH AUTHENTICITY PAPERS, PLEASE LAMINATE ALSO ITCHING POWDER FAMILY SIZE BUT ONLY THE KIND THAT STOPS ITCH. And just behind it, shoved halfway under the rad, a cereal bowl containing at least two weeks' worth of Neil's meds, glommed together into a drenched lump of sludge.

He'd been trying, whenever he could, to watch Neil put them in his mouth. But he'd never checked to make sure the pills actually went down.

He leaves Neil to sleep on, tiptoes downstairs. Throws open all the windows to the steaming morning, his heart, his head in an uproar of guilt and terror. Desperate to relax, he pops half of one of Neil's sedatives, lying like a plank on his bed, comatose, till he's startled awake by a loud knock at the door. Lucy again? But it's not her knock.

No, it's Joe Vaillancourt from the *quincaillerie*, sent over by Lucy to refit some leaky pipes. In no time at all, Joe's head is in the cabinet under the sink, tinkering and clanging. Humming while he hammers, only his blue-jeaned butt visible in the sunny kitchen. Intermittently berating himself for mistakes: *"Heille, innocent! Ça se fait pas d'même!"*

Evan falls back asleep, waking to early afternoon light. Groggy, up on his elbows, he catches a glimpse of six-year-old Mathieu Casgrain out his bedroom window, dawdling up the back lawn, his pant legs and socks soaked, rubber boots gone, snuffling with his head down. Joe's out at his truck; Evan can hear him fiddling in his toolbox as Mathieu plods around the side of the house to the weedy gravel driveway. *"Tu-fait là, mon bonhomme?"* he hears Joe ask, and then, *"Y-est où, là, ton petit frère?"*

From Evan's window a sizeable wedge of the woods on the other side of the road is visible. Something makes him sit up straighter. He sees Joe blur past, disappear into the trees. He stops breathing.

Several minutes later Joe emerges, running, from the woods, a sopping bundle carried like a lamb next to his heart, little Yannick Casgrain's blue jacket drenched through, his small wet head hanging at an odd angle and bouncing.

He lays Yannick down in the muddy yellow grass. Evan, wide awake now, tears outside, sees Mathieu lurking at a safe distance behind Joe's truck, wiping his nose. Sees Joe, on his knees on the lawn, crying, shaking his head. *"Ça s'peut pas, ça s'peut pas, ostie."* Taking out his phone to call 911, his free hand stroking Yannick's bright red cheek, whispering, *"Lâche-pas, bébé, lâche-pas."*

Evan stands frozen at the window, watches Joe put his ear to Yannick's mouth, pinch his nose shut, watches him executing something that might be artificial respiration, a few compressions of his little chest; does he have any idea what he's doing? He sees Nathalie come running, watches as they both bend over the boy, blocking his view. He sees the ambulance pull up, the EMTs huddling, then lifting Yannick onto a stretcher, peeling away with Nathalie inside. He sees Joe taking Mathieu by the hand and leading him home. He sees it all, and he knows if he can't help, he should at least be praying—if this isn't the time for it, then there's never a time.

But he can't. He can't pray, can't think. Can't move. Because all he can feel is the sudden thundering emptiness of the house.

The police find Neil four hours later, three streets away, cowering inside the giant renovation refuse bin in front of the Vachon's house. They haul him out, caked in dust and grime, his hair full of wood chips. He's spectacularly confused. At the police station, he refuses to say a word, only whimpering incoherently to himself, until his brother arrives. Evan holds Neil's hand, promises him an O'Henry bar if he'll be good and tell the police what happened. It takes a good half hour to get Neil to mumble something about finding himself outside because the boys had to watch out for trucks, they shouldn't play in the road. Evan strokes his neck, trying to keep him calm, and Neil relaxes a little, remembers that a man was making a loud noise in the kitchen and he didn't like it. The man wanted to steal the boys. The story tumbles out in fits and starts: from his window, he'd seen Mathieu and Yannick in their front yard, so he'd shouted down, asked them if they wanted to go fishing. They said yes. The man was in the cupboard, banging, and suddenly, Neil was outside, hustling the boys away from danger, crossing the road with them to the woods. They picked up fallen branches to use as fishing poles in the rain-swollen streams that rushed down toward the lake, and he didn't feel scared at all, he was keeping the boys safe. Mathieu and Yannick began poking their fishing poles in the water, looking for sharks. Mud was going over the tops of their boots, and Neil didn't like that. Mathieu shouted at him that the bubbly water made him thirsty, and Neil, reporting this, laughed

softly to himself. "He said, *'Heille, c'est comme du Seven-Up!'*"
And then—Evan could see it as if he'd been there—they wanted
to dive in, jumping up and down on the bank, giggling at the
squelchy sound their boots made, crying, *"C'est super le fonne!"*
And that made Neil scared again. He was standing on a steep
slope, his big, muck-spattered running shoes, bought in 1994,
wedged sideways into the slick mud for purchase. He was afraid
of falling in the water; he missed his room, he wanted to go
home. He saw one of the boys' red boots bobbing in the green
water, and he knew that to be a bad thing; it made him turn
away, but not before he saw Yannick stepping out onto a rotting
log to try and grab it, throwing his little arms out, the other red
boot slipping, that's all it took. But he didn't see any more, struggling as he was to make his way back up the treacherous slope on
his atrophied legs. Did he hear anything, the police asked him,
and after a long silence, he said there might have been a splash.
Or maybe Mathieu laughed. Or shouted, *"Heille, Yannick, c'est
pas drôle!"* But Neil had been terrified by then because he
couldn't remember how to get back home, couldn't remember
what the street, what the house looked like, and he'd scrambled
up the slope and begun running blindly for blocks till he'd found
a safe place to hide.

By the end of the day, he's back in the hospital in Montreal.

And now, how bizarre to be alone in the house. Evan does-
n't know what to do with himself, can't sleep, can't read, sure
as hell can't pray. He goes up to the attic, does a thorough
cleaning, scrubbing the filthy floor, vacuuming the walls, washing the window, airing the place out. Carries out six garbage
bags full of junk, gets Joe to nail plywood up over the cracks in
the ceiling. Swabs down the Barcalounger. Sprays air freshener.
Launders everything Neil owns. Calls Dr. Courtemanche every
day, keeping up with the new drugs they're trying on him,
injectable antipsychotics, Haldol Decanoate, Abilify Maintena,
and the new meds he'll probably be coming home with once
he's stabilized—Zyprexa, Celexa, Evan conscious mainly of
rhymes.

Every day he calls Nathalie for news of Yannick, who is in the hospital in Montreal, already sitting up in bed, giggling with the nurses. Joe had found him washed onto the side of the stream, half on the bank, unconscious, probably from hitting his head on a rock. Concussed, but not drowned. A bullet dodged, but barely, though already, in the punch-drunk euphoria of relief, the drama has sweetened into a silly mishap, a childhood adventure, a wild-ride chapter in the family saga.

The Casgrains, of course, love Evan and understand about Neil. They decline to press charges, as do the police, on the grounds that Evan could not possibly have known that a man who had lived as a recluse for twenty-two years would suddenly take it into his head to leave the house. Neil had had no malicious intent, nor had he caused the accident. Nathalie blames herself more than anyone: she'd been on the phone, she should have been watching them, they knew they weren't allowed to cross the street. *"Mathieu, lui, il le savait bien."*

Four weeks later, Evan is driving a tranquilized Neil—who has completely forgotten the incident—home from the hospital, his brother as groggy and disheveled as if he were the one just fished out of the water's sucking swallow. Flat on the back seat as always. Life, apparently, will plod on.

Evan's at his kitchen table, sitting bold as brass in the haunted chair, reading through the instructions concerning Neil's new meds, vowing to supervise the swallowing of every last one of them, when he feels hot breath on his neck. He springs to his feet with a shrill scream, knocking the chair backward halfway across the room.

"Holy . . . crap, Neil! You scared the pants off me! What are you doing downstairs?"

Neil's gut has gotten so big it folds over the waistband of his track pants, a good eight inches of exposed, beige flab. He's fish-belly pale, inexpertly shaven, his unwashed hair now completely grey and falling over his shoulders. His splotched Christmas sweater, his mangy lumpiness all right out there in the open in the morning glare of the kitchen. So impossibly, so excruciatingly dear.

"I'm delivering this personally," Neil grunts, handing over a tattered old catalogue, folded open, the pages yellowed and encrusted with dried food. It comes with two accompanying notes, the first one reading: TELL LUCY I NEED THIS GET HIM FOR ME!!!

What he needs is a six-foot simulated male bodyguard that can be posed on the couch in front of your picture window, or in the passenger seat of your car, obliging potential burglars, rapists or carjackers to think again, bozo! He's feather-light, has optional button-on legs, and a tote bag for storage and transport. GET LIGHT SKIN BROWN HAIR MODEL ALSO SUN-GLASSES AND BASEBALL CAP AS IN PICTURE DON'T FORGET TO GET LEGS ONLY TWENTY DOLLARS EXTRA, reads the second note.

The fully-inflated fellow wears a leather jacket, holds a rolled-up newspaper in his shiny plastic hands. Evan takes one look, is felled by an attack of laughter so uncontrollable he's afraid his own gut may literally burst.

Neil stands looking at him, expressionless until suddenly he isn't, his lined face cracking into long-unpracticed mirth, a high-pitched whinny spiralling from his throat.

Evan sputters for breath. "Where did you get this?"

"Stuck in a book Lucy got me."

"This is the stupidest thing I've ever seen!"

"Doesn't mean I don't want it."

Evan gazes at the picture, loses it all over again. Hilarity chokes him, fat tears drop onto his shirt, and Neil too, bracing himself on the kitchen table, heaves with donkey laughter, dropping to his knees to hug the one still-righted chair till he and it topple over, just like sad old Mr. Toller's chair right in the middle of *Abide with Me*. Mr. Toller with his girly tenor, his face so open and unguarded, Evan and Neil laughing so hard, not in his presence of course, though it had been rough going not to, but afterward in their room, laughing because of the old man's absolute failure as a grown-up, his execrable fashion sense, his incorrigible looniness, but also out of something deeper, out of genuine joy, as if his silly face were the one they would all have in heaven. Open, innocent, guileless, no apologies required, ever! And this was how they would laugh up there—Up? Who knew? Wherever!—all the misery over and done with at last, grace exploding their incorporeal hearts, shouting one another down in joyous hilarity as they admitted what they'd *really* been thinking all along down there in the trenches.

The blithering happiness Evan had once known with Rivka isn't a patch on the joy he feels now. This is my brother, he realizes, but not with words; his body, his blood thinking it for him: This is Neil! I can't fix him, but we're still here, aren't we? Because of this guy, I'm always shaky, my stomach always hurts. And it always will. This is what's real, and it's okay. This love I have for him, this love in the darkness—I chose this. I knew it twenty-two years ago and I know it now. I'm saying yes to this, to him, to us, saying yes to all of it. I'm exploding with Yes!

And all the tightfisted, tight-lipped Noes I was brought up to worship? They're just the rain below the clouds. Everything above is light and mercy. It always was!

The two of them are on the floor, still heaving and braying helplessly. Neil grabs him around his middle and, finding breath at last, croaks in his ear. "So? Are you gonna get him or not?"

Evan remembers again, with a jolt, just how soon Neil, or he himself, might be required to leave the world. He has a lightning vision, as if from outside time, of that future world without Neil or himself in it. He throws in a flash prayer request that they both might be allowed to leave later rather than sooner. It's a hell of a lot of ground to cover in two seconds.

Doesn't matter. I'm here for him, he's here for me. We're doing it right.

He pulls his head back from the clouds. "Yes, yes, of course. Lucy and I will hunt this sucker down. To the ends of the earth, we'll track him. I promise you, Neil. Nothing in this world is too good for my brother."

On the lawn in front of the church, the beautiful cellist with the gorgeous blue hair is already surrounded by a small crowd of well-wishers. She stands in their midst, taking care to tap her ashes way out to her right, to politely look away when exhaling. People turn to smile at the two old fellows, the second violinist and the violist, natty in their vests and bow ties, greeting them kindly with, *"Bravo, merci."* One of them carries both violin and viola, while the other gallantly lugs the cello. The crowd is beginning to break up, to make off along the sidewalk under the spreading trees with their end-of-summer flecks of orange and brown.

Lucy, ever socially flummoxed, stands off to the side, nervously lighting up, exhaling skyward. Evan extricates himself from a group of teachers and heads toward her, waving, just as Sheila emerges from the church. He stops, smiles, extends his hand. "That was just magnificent. You played beautifully, all of you."

"Thank you, my dear. You're very, very kind."

"I mean it. The pieces were all so different, and each one was special in its own way. All my life I've wished I could play an instrument. There's so much you can say that the p-p-poor rest of us can't." The little trip on the p makes Sheila smile; she takes his hand and pats it.

"It's never easy to say the things that matter. Oh my God, listen to me. How pretentious was that? Honestly, I'm just so glad it's all over."

"That person you dedicated your piece to, I forget the name, Ludmilla? Was she your former cellist?"

"Lyudmilova. No. No, just someone in the audience, at least I hope she was. She did say she'd . . . oh! Yes! There's my girl, trying to hide over there in the bushes." Sheila laughs in delight. "Lucy! You came!"

A middle-aged couple descends the steps behind her, the woman lightly tapping Sheila on the shoulder as they pass. *"Très émouvant. Merci,"* she says. Her husband remains expressionless.

Lucy flicks her smoke far out onto the lawn, pretending not to see Sheila and Evan approach. But Sheila, bounding up, ignores Lucy's instinctive flinch, planting two kisses on her puckered face. Throws her arms around her, draws her into a tight embrace. It's like hugging a telephone pole. She pulls back, takes both Lucy's hands in hers. "I'm so, so glad you made it."

"Yeah, well," mutters Lucy drily, not looking at either of them. She reaches reflexively for her cigarettes, then stops. "I believe I heard my name mentioned," she says, addressing her sneakered feet.

"Yes, I believe you did."

"What the hell brought that on?"

"It was my half-assed way of saying how truly, truly sorry I am that I hurt you, back then. Please forgive me, Lucy. Please."

"Shit, it wasn't *that* bad. I survived."

"Of course you did. You're unbeatable. When I said, 'to the unquenchable spirit of my friend Lyudmilova,' I meant it from the heart, Lucy."

Lucy flushes, snorts, pats her pocket for her smokes and lighter. "Get the fuck outta here," she says, trying not to smile. "That was seven thousand years ago."

"Doesn't matter. My friend Lyudmilova played the balalaika, she had a dancing bear. She finished every book she ever started. My friend Lyudmilova was one in a million. I just wish I'd been able to pull my head out of my own ass long enough to appreciate her."

"Lucy," says Evan with a smile, "This is a whole new side of you. What else have you been keeping from us?"

"You stay out of it, you know what's good for you."

"This lady," Evan tells Sheila, "has been the best, most loyal friend in the world to my brother. He's crazy about her, and so am I."

"I'm shuttin' this shit down," retorts Lucy, as her face begins to ball up like tinfoil. She tries to light a smoke, but fumbles, dropping her lighter in the grass. "Sorry," she says. "Sorry. I should have . . . sorry." She looks up at Evan, pleading, her mouth wobbling. "Is Neil still mad at me?" Then she breaks, sinking onto the lawn, hiding her face in her hands, shoulders jolting. Evan crouches beside her, and she buries her face in his plaid-shirted chest, heaving and spluttering, leaving damp spots and snot trails. The few people around them look, look away discreetly, sneak another look.

Evan pats her back, murmuring, "It's okay. It's okay, Lucy. He's not mad at you. No one is." She carries on for a minute longer, slowly reining herself in, shaking him off, blindly patting the grass to retrieve her lighter. Swiping her nose with the back of a palsied hand.

"It's nothing," she says finally, struggling stiffly to her feet. Then her face crumples all over again. "I just . . . nothing. I just never—" She gives her lank hair a violent shake. "I'm okay," she insists, turning her swollen eyes to Sheila. A wan smile cracks open.

"How about I walk you home?" she croaks, almost inaudibly. Sheila laughs outright, takes Lucy's hands once again in hers. "Then I'll walk you home," she says softly, tears starting, her glasses fogging. They begin to swing their arms like giddy girls.

"Then I'll walk *you* home," says Lucy, furiously resisting a smile, trying to keep her head down, blushing all the way down her neck.

Evan begins backing away. "I've got to be getting home myself. But thank you for a wonderful evening. I wish you guys every success."

"Me too," says Lucy, extricating her hands, edging away, overwhelmed by too much, too fast. She leans toward Sheila for an awkward, forehead-bumping hug. Mumbles, "Don't be a stranger." She backs away again. "I gotta go, before my head blows."

She walks backward for a few steps, biting her lip hard, before she turns and makes off, lighting a smoke as she goes.

Acknowledgments

Profound thanks to the patient readers of early drafts of this book: Arthur Holden, Chloe Gauthier and Tom Maccarone. Your many suggestions were invaluable.

Gratitude without limit to Bethany Gibson for her wise, tactful and endlessly encouraging editorial hand. I could not have done this without you.

I am indebted as well to Arthur Holden for his help in resolving crucial questions of style and taste; to Chloe Gauthier for correcting my eccentric French spelling; to Tom Maccarone for painstaking copy editing; to Emily Kent and Brandi Main for enriching my understanding of the problems faced by budding classical musicians; to Wendy Kent and Amal Abdulkadir for advice on the medical treatment of agitated depressive disorders; to Diane Pitblado for the lowdown on accent coaching; and, finally, to Sphodromantis Kamacuras, just because.